Praise for *Sa*

"*Sarah's Daughter* is first-rat ... and lovingly written, it is a timeless book that readers will savor and long remember."

-Amy Hill Hearth,
author, with Sadie and Bessie Delany,
of The New York Times bestselling oral history,
Having Our Say: The Delany Sisters' First 100 Years.

"Ruth Bass has written a fast-moving story that grabs the reader from the first page. Young adults will recognize themselves in Rose's struggles and her journey toward adulthood."

-Doreen Rappaport,
author of The Secret Seder and *Freedom River.*

"In *Sarah's Daughter*, Ruth Bass skillfully tells the tale of Rose, a 14-year-old in 19th century America coping with the loss of her mother. This poignant story deals with the challenges and uncertainty of the emotional and physical changes in the heroine's life; changes that are sure to resonate with today's young women. Ms. Bass' careful research offers fascinating details of everyday life for young women living in a time that tested not only their strength but their will to survive. This entertaining, educational novel deals with tragedy, but also the promise of early romance and the steadfast support of girlfriends. A timeless treasure, sure to please any young woman who yearns to understand that many generations before her have experienced the same things that she does...and have triumphed!"

-Hannah Storm,
anchor, CBS News The Early Show

Sarah's Daughter

Ruth Bass

G

GADD & COMPANY PUBLISHERS, INC.

The characters and events in this book are fictitious. Any similarity to real persons, living or dead, is coincidental and not intended by the author.

Gadd & Company Publishers, Inc.
An Independent Division of The North River Press Publishing Corporation
292 Main Street
Great Barrington, MA 01230
(413) 528-8895
Visit our website at www.gaddbooks.com

Printed in the United States of America
ISBN: 978-0-9774053-4-3

Gadd & Company Publishers, Inc. is committed to preserving ancient forests and natural resources. We elected to print *Sarah's Daughter* on 50% post consumer recycled paper, processed chlorine free. As a result, for this printing, we have saved:

10 Trees (40' tall and 6-8" diameter)
8,618 Gallons of Wastewater
1,722 Kilowatt Hours of Electricity
957 Pounds of Solid Waste
2,390 Pounds of Greenhouse Gases

Gadd & Company Publishers, Inc. made this paper choice because our printer, Thomson-Shore, Inc., is a member of Green Press Initiative, a nonprofit program dedicated to supporting authors, publishers, and suppliers in their efforts to reduce their use of fiber obtained from endangered forests.

For more information, visit www.greenpressinitiative.org

For Milt, who never stopped believing in this book; and for Rosa, Mabel, Hilda, Elissa, Amy and Michael

About the Author

As a newspaper reporter and columnist, Ruth Bass has been telling the stories of real people for a long time. A descendant of generations of New Englanders, she has also listened all her life to people like the characters in *Sarah's Daughter,* her first venture into fiction.

A resident of the Berkshires in Massachusetts, she has won many awards for writing and editing, and was recently inducted into the New England Press Association's Hall of Fame. She is a graduate of Bates College and of Columbia Graduate School of Journalism, and has been an elected town official. She and her husband, novelist Milton Bass, have three adult children.

She writes a weekly newspaper column on everything from politics to puppies, is author of eight cookbooks, and in her spare time turns to gardening, reading, knitting, photography, travel, tennis and golf.

CONTENTS

Sarah's Daughter

CHAPTER 1
Patchwork

Rose stretched her long legs under the covers, pointing her feet at the ceiling. Between her feet, the thin patchwork quilt became a small mountain range. She moved her toes and the blanket dropped into a valley. The pink blocks wound through the quilt with as many twists and turns as the dirt road through her town. She turned her attention to the height of the quilt mountains. She wondered why her feet were so big. Other girls didn't have size nine shoes. And she was too tall as well.

"Good thing they turned up that much for feet," her father would grumble when she complained of being bigger than most of the other girls and many of the boys. "Otherwise you'd be six foot and an old maid." She wondered, briefly, why her height had anything to do with being married. She could cook pretty well; she could drive a horse and buggy; she could stack a hay wagon as neatly as any grown man.

Maybe it had to do with dancing. She'd noticed how

funny Mr. Hawks always looked at the square dances, trying to promenade ladies in a circle. He was so short he had to reach up to put his arm around most of the women. And she had giggled more than once when swinging ruffled skirts threatened to cover him up.

Most of the time she liked being tall. She could reach up to all the cupboards, and even to the top shelf of her small closet. She didn't have to stretch to scrub blackboards in school. When some of the girls had that chore, they stood on tiptoe, and their dresses hiked up, showing their petticoats. Then, if the teacher wasn't watching, the boys snorted and rolled their eyes.

She wished it were summer so she'd have a better idea of the time. Her room was gray-black now instead of black, so she guessed it must be close to five-thirty. The rooster would be cock-a-doodling in a minute or two, raucous creature that he was. A good word, raucous. Perfect for him, she thought, grinning to think her vocabulary list could go right into the henhouse. She had to get up. She threw off the covers, pulled up her nightdress and squatted briefly on the chamber pot. Finished, she pushed it under the bed to be taken care of later.

Father would be in for breakfast soon, and she had lunch pails to fill. She had set up the table the night before, but it would take a few minutes to get the coffee on and the oatmeal cooked. She had forgotten for a minute—daydreaming about her quilt and pondering her feet—that Mother wasn't down there, rattling around in the kitchen, getting things done.

Father, she knew, would be grouchy. She had heard him come in very late last night, heard him bang into the kitchen table and come up the stairs muttering. He must have been over to the hotel, playing cards and drinking cider, and he'd be holding his head over breakfast, ready to lash out at anyone who crossed him. She resolved to keep her mouth shut, no matter what.

She dressed quickly, putting on underdrawers, camisole, petticoat, cotton print dress and the black size nine shoes. She fumbled for the buttonhook, which had fallen off her dresser onto the floor, and then buttoned her shoes, deftly pushing the little hook into each loop and dropping it over the next button. She stroked the smooth ivory handle before she dropped the hook on her chest of drawers; it was one of her few treasures.

The kitchen was warm, so at least Father had stoked the fire before going to the barn. She set water to boil, and quickly packed bread, cheese and an apple into four lunch pails. The teakettle began to murmur as the water heated. She liked to think the heat woke up the water in the kettle, making it talk. She was just like the kettle, she thought, starting slowly in the morning and then picking up speed. As soon as she heard its first stammerings, she poured some off for coffee, then put the rest in a separate pan and stirred in a couple of handfuls of oats.

"Judas priest, girl, I thought you'd never get up," Father thundered as he slammed through the door, dropped an armload of split ash in the woodbox and quickly sluiced his hands with water from the pump at the sink. Rose opened her mouth, remembered her pledge to herself and snapped it shut so tight that her lips traced only a thin line above her chin. She turned her back so Father wouldn't see the pink color that always betrayed her. Angry, embarrassed, or even pleased, she reddened. "She's pink, she's pink," her classmates would whisper whenever she made a mistake and was spoken to by the teacher.

She wondered if she'd stop turning pink when she became a real grown-up, or would her fair skin always tell the world when her heart was pounding and her knees shaking? Alice's face didn't do that. For a second, she desperately wanted to be Alice. Then she remembered that Alice had acres of carrots to weed after school and on Saturdays. She'd hate that more than being pink, she thought, stirring the oatmeal and turning some into a bowl she'd been warming on the back shelf of the wood stove.

"Pretty thick," her father muttered when she placed the bowl in front of him.

"What would Sarah do now?" she thought, feeling her face get hot once more.

She'd taken to thinking of her mother by her first name in these days since Sarah Hibbard had been buried. It let Rose think about her without the word "Mother," which popped tears out of her eyes and down her cheeks as quickly as her father extracted milk from a cow's teats.

Sarah would pour his coffee and make sure the sugar and cream were close at hand. She'd put a little pitcher of maple syrup on the table as an extra treat for the oatmeal. She'd ask him if he wanted toast. Rose did each thing as she imagined Sarah doing it, and set the little toaster on the stove as if he had nodded an answer to her even-toned question. She cut the bread she'd made the day before, toasted two slices, and fetched a bowl of soft butter from the pantry.

Then she slipped out of the room and ran up the stairs. Moving quickly from one bedroom to another, she emptied the chamber pots into the slop jar and ran downstairs again. She was really trotting now because it was almost time to leave for school. He hadn't said she couldn't go; hadn't said it yet. She emptied the slop jar in the outhouse behind the kitchen and left it there. Then she tossed her mother's shawl around her shoulders and headed for the chicken house. She was sure no one had seen to the cussed hens. As usual they rushed at her, clucking and squawking, when they saw the pail of grain. She filled the feed trays, swished her skirt at the pesky rooster, dumped the watering troughs outdoors and refilled them at the pump, trying not to spill anything on her school clothes.

In under ten minutes she was back in the house, relieved to see that Charles and Abby were finishing breakfast and were dressed for school. Abby had only to walk across the road, but she and Charles had a mile to go on foot.

"Don't forget your sweater," she told Abby, who looked as if she had already been crying. "Don't forget your lunch." She gave her a quick hug, took her father's oatmeal bowl off the table and set it on the floor for the cat, said goodbye to her father, who was still drinking coffee, and then she was gone. After a quick look around the room, Charles loped after her.

"Sorry about your mother," Miss Harty said as Rose walked in. She nodded once, turning away to hide the tears. That dratted pink color had popped up again. If only people would stop talking about being sorry. She knew everyone was sorry. Everyone had liked her mother. But she was dead, she was gone, she was never coming back, and none of them had an idea under the sun about how to get along without her. Why didn't someone talk about that? They weren't even talking about it at the house, never mind with outsiders.

The fear made her stomach turn. Would she have to take her mother's place? So much cooking and scrubbing, cleaning the barn, sewing and knitting, chiding and chasing, yet still finding time to read stories at bedtime or go for a walk in the woods to find the first mayflowers and beautiful pink lady's slippers. She couldn't even think of all the things her mother did in a day, starting every morning with a smile, and ending with tired eyes and a mouth that went straight across her face. She thought of the soft face in the wedding portrait, and the set one that she knew so much better. It had taken only sixteen years to change that face. Was it sixteen? Oh, yes. The date was on the back. October 27, 1871, ten years after the Civil War began. She didn't want to look like that. She didn't want to be her mother.

Rose gritted her teeth, pushed her hair back from her

face and shoved her family into the back of her mind. She took out the little arithmetic book, one of her favorites. She'd never say that to the other girls, though. They would think she was crazy.

"Induction method," the cover read. She had no idea what that meant, but she loved the pages of problems.

"If seven horses eat fifteen bushels of oats in one week, how many bushels would fifteen horses eat in the same time?" Feeling a little contrary, she answered quickly that it might well depend on whose horses you were feeding. But she only said that in her head. On paper, she quickly did the division and multiplication: 32.2 bushels would take care of all the horses.

"A ship's crew of 6 men have provision for 3 months; how many months would it last 1 man?" Would that one sailor kill off the others so he could eat more, she wondered. Shove them overboard or lock them in the hold? She'd read about ships. They didn't seem like good places to live. Too many rats, too many storms, too much dried food. Well, 18 months, of course. She could do that in her head, but she wrote it all down because you had to prove you knew how to solve the problem. The presence of a correct answer without any figuring seemed to make Miss Harty's suspicions stand up like quills on a porcupine.

Her figures were lined up neatly on the paper, precise and accurate. She almost never made mistakes during this part of the day. And she'd discovered long ago that she could make up stories about the problems while the other half of her mind worked out the answers. The idea of fifteen horses was absurd. Not even the livery stable had that many. What colors would they be, she wondered, picturing black, bay, chestnut and roan horses in the narrow lane behind her father's barn. Perhaps a white one, too, or a gray. She bent to the problems again. Maybe if she did well with all these things, Mr. Goodnow would take her on at the store, and she could stock shelves and make change and measure out flour and cornmeal and sugar from the big barrels. That would be so much better than taking over her mother's job.

But she knew it would be no use. No one went somewhere else to work when there was a need at home. The need was named Abby. She was just a child, and Rose would be expected to see to her and turn her hand at whatever else came up.

One of the older boys left the room and came back in a couple of minutes with an armload of split logs. He pushed two into the small fat stove at the front of the room and then stomped toward the back of the room again, his hand flicking out to flip Alice's book shut as he passed. He always has to do something, Rose thought to herself, and then began to drift again. If two logs will heat the room for three hours, how many logs will it take for five days of school, eight to three? Oh, be still, she told herself. You have enough problems without making up new ones. She continued with her work and then noticed that a small folded note had arrived on her desk. She glanced at the teacher, put one hand in her lap with the note and worked it open without moving her shoulder an iota.

"What happened to your mother? I heard my father say the woodpile fell on her. Is he lying?"

It was Emily's neat hand, Emily's abrupt way of asking questions without any lace to cover the ragged edges. She gave a shiver, turned the paper over and placed it carefully on her arithmetic paper. Glancing from her book to the paper, she wrote, "Maybe four cords of wood. He's not lying."

She nudged Emily's back, and Emily reached up to scratch her shoulder. Rose quickly tucked the note between two of Emily's fingers. The pass was successful, to her relief. She didn't need the teacher after her today, and she certainly didn't have time to stay after school. But her luck ran out when Emily read the note and gasped out loud. Rose didn't even look up, but everyone else did. And Miss Harty, who was worried about the solemn look on Rose's face and had been trying to overlook the exchange, fidgeted with her hair for a second and then moved toward the girls, her hand out for the scrap of paper.

"I will see you both at three," she said in a tone that clearly said she was disappointed in them. She put the note on her desk and continued her work with the students at the front of the room.

After school, Rose stood close by Emily, eyes on the worn, oiled floorboards. Her knees felt a little shaky. She didn't know what she'd do if Miss Harty kept them long enough for Father to notice that she wasn't home on time. She wanted to put her hand on the edge of the teacher's desk to steady herself, but she didn't dare. It might make it too easy for Miss Harty to rap her knuckles with the tan ruler that was always on her desk.

As the silence went on for what seemed like more than a minute, Rose began to wish the teacher would at least say something and not just leave them standing there, close to petrified. Then she heard Miss Harty give a long sigh. Rose looked up. The teacher was staring toward the window where dark tree branches traced a black pattern against the November sky. Her eyes were all watery, Rose thought, the way her own were when Father made her put away hay into the top of the barn. Miss Harty turned toward them and gave a small smile.

"You know notes are not allowed in school," she began. Rose nodded and from the corner of her eye could see Emily's braids move slightly. She was nodding, too. Probably couldn't find her tongue. Rose knew hers would not respond if she called on it. She sneaked another look at Emily. Her face was nicely pale. Her own felt as hot as a stovetop in the forenoon.

"I have read this note, so I know Emily was just worried about you and what happened at your house," Miss Harty went on. "But I had to keep you after school because you broke a rule. We are all so sorry about the terrible accident and your loss, Rose."

Rose's hand almost jumped toward the edge of the desk, and she felt her shoulders begin to shake. Then she was trembling all over, and no matter how hard she clenched her teeth, she could not make her body pay attention. Stop, she thought. Hold still, she commanded.

And then she doubled over and realized with horror that the great wailing noises she could hear were her own sobs. She sank to the floor, covering her head with her hands, so tired, so grief-stricken, so embarrassed.

She'd heard them, over and over, at the house and at the cemetery, talking about how Father was holding up well, how Aunt Minnie had held up, how Rose had held up. She was glad to hear the indirect praise, even though she didn't really know what she was holding up. But now, right in front of the teacher and her best friend, she knew what they meant. She wasn't holding up anymore. Everything she'd been hanging onto was spilling out, the way water rushed down the trough when you put all your strength into the pump handle.

Miss Harty was on her knees on the floor, putting one hand on her shoulder, offering her a handkerchief with blue tatted edging with the other. Emily was crouching on her other side, telling her it was all right, that she was so sorry she had made her cry.

"Not your fault," Rose blubbered. "I'm just not holding up."

"What does that mean?" Miss Harty asked.

"At the funeral," she said. "In a book I read, a little girl died and everyone cried and cried and cried. But when Sarah—when my mother—died, no one cried. Father didn't cry. They just kept talking about holding up."

"Some people," Miss Harty began, "think you should never let your grief show in public. Some people never cry about anything. But when something terrible happens to you, when you lose someone you love, it's good to cry. It's the way your mind washes away the grief, the anger, the fear. If no one will let you cry in the kitchen or the parlor, cry in your bedroom. Or take a walk to the cemetery and cry there. Your mother wouldn't mind."

They all eased into sitting positions at the same time. Rose looked at Miss Harty there on the floor and had a sudden urge to laugh. The teacher's skirts were clumped around her like a puffy quilt, and her ankles were showing. Who knew a teacher even had ankles? But then, who knew a teacher could sit on the floor?

"The next question," Miss Harty said firmly, "is whether you want to talk about what happened to your mother or not. Not today. We've had quite enough excitement for today, and you'll need to get home to take care of Abby. I told Charles to see to her."

"Oh, thank you, Ma'am," Rose said, immediately ashamed that she'd forgotten all about Abby once she'd been caught passing a note.

Out of sight, out of mind, she thought. Sarah would never have forgotten Abby. She guessed she had a lot of growing up to do and only a couple of minutes to do it in.

She turned back to the teacher. "I'm all right," she said. "I do feel better now, and I have to go home to feed the chickens, collect the eggs and get supper on. Father will be wanting supper right on time, I expect."

She paused and looked at the teacher. "He doesn't say, really, what he expects. He just doesn't talk anymore."

Miss Harty gave another little sigh, patted Rose's shoulder and gracefully removed herself from the floor. Emily caught her foot on her long skirt as she stood up but quickly regained her balance. They each reached a hand to Rose, who stood up slowly, afraid her head or her stomach might betray her again. But everything was all right. At least her big feet gave her something substantial to stand on in times of need.

"Thank you," Rose said to Miss Harty, feeling her face flush again.

"Wash your face before you go," Miss Harty said. "A little cold water will help you hold up." Again, she allowed a small smile.

"I'll see you tomorrow," she said and turned toward the chalkboard to write the next day's date in her nearly perfect handwriting.

CHAPTER 2
May I?

Rose wasn't taking any books home with her. She wasn't going to have time to read anything anyway, so she had put her texts inside her desk and resolved to forget them until tomorrow. She plunged her hands into the pockets of her coat and followed Emily down the dirt path that led from the school to the road. Emily paused, waiting for her to catch up, and put her arm through Rose's.

"I'm so sorry," she said. "I didn't mean to get you in trouble, and I didn't mean to make you cry. But no one I know ever lost a mother, and no one would talk to me at home, and I didn't know what to do. It was so strange. I began to wonder if it was even true."

"No one at my house is talking either," Rose said glumly, as they started along the road. "And it's all true," she added as an afterthought. She glanced quickly at

Emily, and her toe caught on a stone. She stumbled, and decided she'd better keep her eyes on her feet.

The rain they'd had in September had washed away so much gravel that the road was very stony and rutted. Washboardy. That was what Father called it when the wagon wheels bumped along the small ruts that ran from one side of the road to the other. She thought it was a perfect way to say it. Sarah's washboard had a surface just like that, in miniature, and she'd scrubbed plenty of sheets and work trousers against that rough surface. Her mother always wanted the sheets near-white, and it was hard to get a week's worth of grime out of Father's trousers.

With rain ruts going one way and deep wagon ruts crossing them in the other direction, the road was rough for walking. They separated, each looking for the smoothest place to walk, each of them weaving a little in the search.

"You mustn't tell anyone, Emily," Rose began. "Cross your heart and hope to die."

"I never tell anything you tell me," Emily said.

"Well, I'm scared. I don't want to be my mother."

"Why should you be?"

"Well, Father expected me to make the breakfast this morning and the lunches, and do my regular chores. He growled at me when he came in from milking the cows, even though I had everything ready. If he makes me scrub the floors and bake and help clean the barn and make the cottage cheese and butter and bread and do the sewing and make sure Abby does her schoolwork and washes herself and changes her clothes when she gets home . . . I don't know what I will do," she finished, breathless.

"Get up pretty early in the morning, I'd say," Emily said with a grin.

The tears that had started to blur Rose's concentration on her feet spilled over as she began to laugh.

"Oh, Em," she said, "why couldn't you have been there this weekend when we were all going around the house as if we were Egyptian mummies, unable to talk and not much good at doing anything either? I'll just get up at two in the morning and then maybe Father won't say I can't go to school anymore."

"Not go to school? You have to go to school," Emily said, shocked into realizing that this was more serious than she wanted it to be. "You can't be a teacher if you don't go to school."

Rose fell silent again. She'd been little more than three when she decided teachers were probably the equivalent of God's angels. Her family house was right across from the old school, not far from the general store on the main street. When she was two, she had stood in the parlor window, watching the school children at recess. When she turned three, she was allowed outside by herself, and she would run to the front of the house when she heard the recess bell, morning and afternoon. She watched all the girls come out one door to play on the south side of the building. The boys came out another and played on the north side.

One day she had crossed the road without asking her

mother, and the older girls had invited her to join them in their Rover, Red Rover game. Then she learned to play Giant Steps, and Simon Says. She made mistakes, like forgetting to ask, "May I?" after the leader said, "You may take two hopping steps and one giant step." The little girls made fun of her when she forgot, but the big girls were always nice.

And then one day—she could remember it as if it were this morning—the teacher had come to the door while the girls and boys lined up to go back to the schoolroom. The teacher asked if she would like to come in, and she allowed as how she would, but she'd have to ask her mother.

"You ask her if you can visit us in school tomorrow," Miss Harty had said.

Rose recalled that she had scampered back across the road, barely noticing that a team of horses was coming toward her with a big wagon until the man holding the reins bellowed, "Watch where you're going, little one."

"Mother, Mother," she yelled as she reached the back porch.

"Are you hurt?" her mother's voice asked.

"No, it's just that..."

"Then calm down, and stop making so much noise. The neighbors will think I'm slaughtering a pig on the porch."

"The teacher says I can visit school if you say I can," Rose said, trying not to jump up and down.

"Now, wouldn't that be nice," her mother said. Rose remembered how she had put on her better dress the next day, crossed the road at morning recess and lined up with the girls when the bell rang. The teacher told her to sit on a bench at the front, and she barely moved for the whole hour she was there.

After that, she went almost every day, and before long, she could read the first primer, say her numbers from one to ten and tell time on the big clock at the front of the room. When both hands of the clock were on the 12, she would give a little sigh and go home again.

"Where did you go?" Emily's voice demanded. "You're not listening to me."

Rose pulled her mind back to today. That was twelve years ago, and she still loved that classroom as much as she had the very first time she was there. She often thought how lucky she was that Miss Harty had been promoted right along with them when the town decided to build four classrooms on the hill for the older pupils, leaving only the first three grades in the old, one-room building.

"I don't know what's the matter with me," Rose apologized to her friend. "My head just goes wandering off as if it had unhitched itself."

"You'd better tighten the bridle," Emily said. "You won't look good without a head. Remember that story we read about the horseman without any head? He scared everybody out of their wits."

Rose laughed. Emily always took the sting out of the moment by saying something silly. Imagine her without a head indeed. If her head fell off, would she still have a neck, she wondered, a place to wear the little gold necklace her aunt had given her last year? Stop it, Rose, she said to herself. Your head is falling off again.

"I'm turning off here," Emily said, as they reached the corner of a dirt road. "You'd better watch where you're going, or you'll go right by your house and end up at the railroad depot."

"See you tomorrow," Rose said, walking on and giving a little wave to Emily. "Thank you."

Emily nodded, picked her skirt up a little as she went around a muddy spot and started to run. The two girls still ran as often as they could, but if their mothers or aunts saw them, they were immediately scolded. Girls who were well past thirteen were supposed to start acting like ladies, Mother had said. Used to say, she said almost aloud and her insides turned over again. And now they were fourteen, which probably made it much worse.

A few minutes later, Rose arrived at her own house. It was white, with dark green blinds on the four front windows, two up and two down. Mother had been quite excited about the new paint-mixing service that had been introduced at the general store the year the painting was done.

"You can get any color you want," she said. "It's all on charts, with samples of the colors."

Father had shrugged, but she had told the man at the store that she wanted paint as dark as spruce needles, but not the bluish ones. Mother had wanted blinds on the sides of the house, too, but Father said that was an extravagance. No one had blinds on the back, he said, and they didn't need them on the sides either. Out front was what people saw, he said. Mother had quietly observed that she was usually on the side of the house, but never mind. Rose figured someday she would have a house of her own and put blinds on at least three sides, maybe even the back. After all, if you were in the garden, you were looking at the back. And wasn't it your house, not other people's?

Her feet began to drag as she went up the steps. The black wood stove with its polished oven door handle was sending out a little heat, but nothing was cooking. Usually by this time of day, Mother would have had a pot of soup on for supper, which was never a very big meal. For as long as she could remember, her mother had put dinner on the table for her father at noon, seven days a week, summer and winter.

Rose hung her wrap on a hook just by the kitchen door and poured some hot water from the teakettle over the dishes that Father had used for his noon meal. He must have eaten some of the food the women had brought the day of the funeral, she thought, wondering what he'd done with the lunch pail contents.

She glanced at the wide wood floorboards and decided they were clean enough. She found a baking dish of creamed codfish on the windowsill in the pantry and thought that would do for supper, along with some baking powder biscuits. She certainly knew how to make those.

She dipped flour from the barrel in the pantry, tossed in baking powder from the Rumford box, and set the bowl on the wide pantry shelf, ready for the milk. It would take more wood to make the oven hot enough for biscuits, but when she checked the woodbox, it was empty. With a little shiver, she went down the steps and out to where the old woodshed was tilted to one side, its roof as swaybacked as Grandfather's old mare. A grapevine had made its way up one end of the shed and actually came through a hole in the roof during the summer. She and Charles had hoped grapes would hang down inside the shed. Now, with her eyes almost closed, she fumbled for what was left of the rickety door, which stood open, one of its hinges long gone. She clung to the door, trying to steady herself, but the sight of the woodpile was too much.

All the wood was back in the shed. Her father must have spent a good piece of the day doing that. In her mind's eye, she could see Father and Mr. Chandler flinging those stove-length logs into the yard while they tried to get her mother out. Sweating and cursing, they had worked furiously. She remembered how Sarah's feet appeared first, still wearing the men's boots that she often wore to the barn, then her skirts, then the rest of her. But they were too late. All the weight of that wood had fallen on her when she went to get the wood for the woodbox.

No one could explain how such a thing could have happened. But they all knew Sarah was too fragile to take a bruising like that. Stacked row upon row, the many cords of wood needed to keep them going until spring had begun to slip and then apparently cascaded over the little woman, crushing her. One of the men suggested that she must have been pulling pieces out from the bottom because she was too short to reach the logs on top.

Rose wasn't sure her hands would move toward that pile. She took a deep breath, set her chin, and willed her fingers to work. She laid four pieces of ash along her left arm, then added a second layer and curled her hand up to hold them in place. Back in the kitchen, she rolled the wood down her arm into the woodbox, saving two chunks for the stove. Flicking flakes of wood from her apron, she let out a sigh that made it seem as if she hadn't breathed in five minutes, opened the stove door to add the wood, and stirred the fire a little with the poker.

As she stood in front of the warm stove, the cat—her mother's cat—did a figure eight around her legs, ducking under her skirt in front and emerging behind her. She stooped to scratch his ears, and the cat mewed loudly. She found a few scraps of pot roast in the pantry and dropped them into the dish under the sink. The cat started to eat, and Rose went upstairs to change out of her school clothes.

It wasn't until she was pulling an old dress over her head and doing up the buttons that she suddenly wondered where Abby was. She should have been right here, and Charles, too. How could she possibly have forgotten them? Then she heard them, banging into the kitchen with Abby's high little voice speaking in that funny way she had. Rose always thought of Abby's speech as round. Somehow the words had no corners when they came out of her mouth.

Rose practically ran down the stairs to see what they'd been up to, even though Charles was perfectly capable of seeing to his little sister. To her surprise, they carried a small basket with six eggs in it and said, practically in unison, "We've taken care of the chickens." She was so pleased she almost cried again, but she hugged Abby instead and took the basket.

"Ay-yuh," Rose said. "But you'll have to put this egg back." She held up the pale china egg that her mother kept in one of the nests. "We can't eat this one," she said, tapping it against the side of the sink.

"If it's not a real egg, why is it there?" asked Abby, who had a why for just about everything.

Rose wasn't sure if it was to show the hens where they were supposed to lay their eggs or give them comfort when she went in and took their real eggs away. So she told Abby about both possibilities, wishing she had one herself.

But Abby was rushing on to the rest of her news.

"One of the old biddies grabbed my finger," Abby said, "when I tried to take the egg away, so that one is still in the nest. Maybe you can get it in the morning. But I talked to the other mean one while Charles sneaked his hand under and took her egg. Why do they get mad when we take the eggs away?"

"Because little chicks come from eggs, and the hen's brain tells her she's supposed to keep the eggs warm, not let you have them," Rose explained.

"Those hens have no brains," Charles said. "They have to be the dumbest creatures in the county. They go around pecking at dirt all day."

"Charles says we have to help you because you are in deep water and if you drown, we won't have anyone to cook for us," said Abby, jumping to a new subject again, her eight-year-old face showing her worry about starvation. "So what do we do now?"

"Well first, young lady, you'd better change your clothes into something more suitable for the chicken house and other chores. Then, if you like, I'll show you how to set the table for supper."

Abby ran through the front room to the stairs and pounded up to her parents' room where she had a small low bed under the window. In the kitchen, where the stove was now sending out real warmth, Charles looked at Rose uncertainly.

"Are you all right?" he asked. "When Miss Harty made you stay after school and told me to take care of Abby, I was afraid she was going to punish you and make you do the blackboards."

"She was very nice," Rose said, "even though we broke a rule. And we only stayed a few minutes. Just long enough, it seems, for you and Abby to take care of the chickens."

"We'll do that every day," Charles said. "And pretty soon Abby will be able to do it by herself in the afternoon. She's still afraid the hens are going to peck her hands."

"Well, they are," Rose said, showing a small bruise on

the back of her hand. "That white chicken takes offense whenever you go near her, and she never leaves the nest once she's dropped an egg."

"Perhaps we can eat her," Charles said hopefully.

"That," said Rose, "is an idea with considerable appeal. But I'm not taking over Mother's hen-killing duties. Father will have to do it."

"Maybe he'll let me gut it," Charles said, pleased to see her hand go over her mouth as if she were going to be sick.

"Just for that," she said, "pump yourself a little pail of water and take it to the outhouse. Rinse out the slop jar and take it back upstairs."

"Ugh," said Charles, reaching under the sink for one of the buckets they used to take out dirty dishwater.

CHAPTER 3
"Not bad"

Rose took the box of matches off the shelf and lit the kerosene lamp. She turned the wick up just a little so the flame would be brighter and realized the glass chimney needed washing. It was sooty from the night before, and the black smudges blocked some of the light.

She'd heard her mother talk about trimming the wick, and she wasn't sure exactly what that meant. She should have listened and watched more, she thought. She should have paid attention at home the way she did at school, where she listened to every lesson in the room with one ear and kept the other half of her brain thinking about her own work. Shouldn't there be books to tell people how to do things around the house, especially people who were too young to be doing them in the first place? She needed a primer on cooking, one on housework, one on killing chickens (just in case), and one on doing everything faster.

Abby came back wearing one of her old dresses—one of Rose's old dresses, in fact, put away for several years until it would fit Abby. Ah, she could use a primer on sewing, too. She would have to find time, before Christmas, to make Abby something new to wear. The child must be sick to death of hand-me-downs. And where would they hand it next, anyway? Perhaps it would go in the big barrel at the church and be sent off to some country where people lived in huts made of straw and hunted with spears. She thought Abby's dress would look really funny there.

The two girls, the taller one blonde and the small one quite dark-haired, took out the spoons and knives and forks and laid them around the table. They put napkin rings at each place, and Rose reminded Abby that after the meal, each person's napkin must go back in that person's ring, ready for next time.

"We can't be washing napkins every five minutes," she said, a bit sternly. "No one needs a fresh napkin until Sunday dinner."

"Will I still clear?" Abby wanted to know. That had been one of her chores for almost a year. "I like stacking the plates and taking them to the kitchen."

"We'll need you to go right on doing that," Rose said. "Whatever you did before is still on your list, and I'm going to add things until your head spins."

Abby laughed. "If my head spins, you'll have to knit me."

Abby fetched the little cream pitcher from the pantry windowsill and put it next to the glass sugar bowl they used every day. At Rose's bidding, she went to the cellar to get two pickles from the big crock, and rinsed them off under the pump. Rose said she could use the sharp knife to slice them, and Abby worked very carefully to make slim, even slices. She'd never used a grown-up's knife before.

Rose had put the codfish in the oven and added milk to the flour and baking powder she had measured out earlier. "Rolled or dropped?" she asked Abby, as she greased the pan with a bit of butter.

"Dropped," Abby said. "I like the way they puff up and wrinkle when they're dropped."

So Rose dropped spoonfuls of baking powder biscuit batter on the pan and shoved it into the oven. According to the kitchen clock, it was five-thirty. Father should be coming in quite soon, she reckoned.

She put two tallow candles on the table in the dining room and hoped he wouldn't be late. If he was, the biscuits would either burn or be cold, and he'd fuss about either. But as the evening train whistle blew, Rose heard her father lift the latch on the back door. He almost always arrived as the train was going through, she thought. He had come in without a sound because he had stepped out of his barn boots in the ell.

"Well," he said, "it smells like things are cooking in here. It smells real good, Rose."

"Supper's ready as soon as you are," she answered calmly, but his compliment warmed her. He wasn't going to be out of sorts tonight, she thought.

"Hungry as a horse," he said as he sluiced some water

from the pump over his hands, soaped them up with the cake on the sink shelf and rinsed again.

They all sat at their regular places at the table, Abby next to Rose on one side, Charles at the far end, Father across from the girls. Each of them glanced at the empty place at one end.

"Well," said Father. "Well, well. It's hard to know where to begin. I intend to do my best as your sole surviving parent, but we will all miss your mother terribly. I expect each of you to do your part to keep things going here. I reckon Rose knows pretty much what has to be done, so you other two will have to jump when she points. We will have no time for shirking or shenanigans," he said, looking sternly at Charles and then Abby.

"We will have a moment of silence in your mother's honor now," he added rather abruptly, bowing his head. All three children immediately dropped their heads toward their plates. Rose wondered if a moment of silence meant her mind was supposed to be a blank. She couldn't manage that, and she didn't want to think about her mother. She did wonder what shenanigans were, and thought she'd look it up in the dictionary at school. Then she heard an odd sound from her father's side of the table, almost a sob. When she sneaked a look at him, he had lifted his head. So she dished up the codfish casserole, which Mrs. Packard had sent over the day after Sarah's accident. Charles passed around the hot biscuits. Rose watched as her father broke open a biscuit and buttered it.

"Not bad," he said. "Not bad. And I do like the dropped ones."

Abby looked up at everyone then and gave the first real grin she'd managed since the men had taken Mother away in Mr. Chandler's wagon. And Rose, savoring two compliments within the hour, thought maybe, just maybe, they could manage.

Everyone ate hungrily; it was the first time any of them had enjoyed food in three or four days. In next to no time the codfish and biscuits were gone, and Rose fetched a pumpkin pie that another neighbor had brought in. She cut it neatly into six pieces, knowing that her father would like a piece for breakfast the next day and perhaps at the noon hour as well.

"I'll be going to the street tonight," Father said. "I have to see some people on a bit of business. Charles, you help Rose clean up before you get at your books. And you had all better get to bed in good season. Morning comes early."

He pushed back his chair, made his way through the kitchen to the outhouse and in a few minutes went upstairs. When he came back down, Rose noticed that he had changed his work shirt for a cleaner one and put on regular boots. He pulled on a jacket, nodded to them and was gone.

The children quickly cleared the food and dishes from the table. Rose had water heating on the stove, so Charles washed up while she showed Abby how to crumb the cloth with a table knife.

"You are big enough," she said, "to do this after every

meal. And if you don't have time before school, just remember to do it before you set the table for supper."

She saw Abby nod and realized that the little girl was quite set up by having all these new responsibilities. Well, at least she wouldn't have to clear and wash and put away any more. That was one set of tasks shifted to someone else, and it was nice to see that Charles would help Abby without even being asked. She sighed and wondered when Abby was going to realize that her mother was never coming back; that everything in their world had changed in the crash of a stack of firewood. What would Abby miss most, she wondered, thinking about stories read and told around the kitchen stove in the evening, walks taken in the woods on a spring or fall afternoon, sewing lessons, and—once in a very great while—a small hug or a squeeze of the hand. Some children were kissed, she knew. She'd seen them kissing their mothers goodbye in the morning or hello in the afternoon. But their mother and father didn't do much of that. Almost never, in fact. Her mother had called it "all that sass," although she smiled when she said it.

Maybe she would have liked a hug now and then, Rose thought regretfully. Maybe it was something the daughter should have done instead of wishing the mother would do it. She knew one thing she would miss. She'd miss that hand pushing her damp hair back when she was sick. It wasn't a smooth hand. The skin was rough enough to catch a bit in her hair, but the touch was so gentle. She'd never told her mother how good it felt, but she was quite sure Sarah knew. She hoped so.

Her eyes were getting watery again. She'd better think about the woodbox, tomorrow's lunches, school clothes, whether anything was left for Father's noon meal, whether Charles was doing his homework, or making a new structure with the blocks Uncle Jason had given him for his birthday. She was betting on the blocks. He hardly played with anything else now that he had them, all end pieces from Uncle Jason's woodworking projects, many of them sanded, some cut into arches with the jigsaw. Every day Charles built a new house or barn or bridge or castle in the corner of his back attic room, or even on one of the rafters above his bed.

Suddenly she heard the crash of falling blocks and smiled to herself. Well, she was right. He wasn't doing schoolwork and had just created something that failed. She headed for the stairs, trying to think how her mother would keep Charles on the straight and narrow. She found Charles on the floor of his chilly attic bedroom, with a blanket around his shoulders. The blocks were scattered everywhere, but he was starting to stack them again in an intricate pattern. He had placed two candles on the floor, with glass chimneys reflecting the flame and providing him a fair amount of light.

As Rose crouched next to him, she wondered if he was going to build houses and barns—maybe castles—when he grew up. But all she said was that she thought he had better get to sleep if he was done with his schoolwork. Charles mumbled something she couldn't hear and didn't look up. He went right on arranging blocks.

"Speak up, Charles," she said, in her best imitation of her mother.

"I can't sleep very well," he muttered, just loud enough for her to hear.

"Oh, Charles," she said, "of course you can't. None of us can sleep very well, and when I do fall asleep I have terrible dreams about Mother's accident, and they go on and on and on until I am worn out."

"Really?" he said. "I thought I was the only one. I don't dream about the accident. I just keep dreaming about the wagon taking her away. It rolls over all sorts of roads, up and down hills, winding around and never getting anywhere. I am running behind it, but I can't catch up because whenever I get almost close enough to grab the back, the horses go faster. Then I wake up, as sweaty as if I was really running like that."

"You come downstairs and we'll have some warm milk," Rose said. "Grandmother used to give us warm milk when we couldn't sleep, remember?"

The two went back to the kitchen, where Abby was sitting near the stove, looking at one of her books. Rose put a pan of milk on the stove and told Abby she should bring her nightclothes into the warm kitchen to change, and then have some milk. As the three sipped from coffee cups, Rose decided to tell them some of the things Miss Harty had told her at school that day. So, as best she could, she explained that it was quite all right to cry, and people who didn't want to cry in front of other people could do it in their bedrooms or at the cemetery.

"Or in the outhouse," said Charles, not meaning to be funny, since that was exactly where he had suddenly burst into tears that very morning.

"Or in the outhouse," said Rose as solemnly as she could manage. "And speaking of that, you'd both better take care of your business in the outhouse and get to bed." She felt very old as she partly closed the damper on the stove so the fire would die down a little. She had a little milk left in her cup, so she put it on the floor, and the cat licked it up quickly.

When the two children came back into the kitchen shivering, she considered skipping her own trip to the outhouse but knew that was really foolish. So she went out there, thinking how odd it was that the girls she knew in books apparently didn't have outhouses, nor any need for them. The stories never mentioned anything like that.

Upstairs, as she stretched again under her quilt, she thought the day had seemed more like two or three days. Perhaps, she thought, tomorrow will be shorter. Perhaps there would even be a new dream tonight. She closed her eyes and tried to make her mind a complete blank. Rose had read one time about people counting sheep to go to sleep, but whenever she tried that, her sheep started to run and play. Then a beautiful black and white dog would show up to herd them, and she would start to look for strays while the dog ran through her head. It was hardly a restful experience.

Her mother had given a low chuckle when she explained the problem one morning. Think about a summer sky, her mother said, really blue and completely cloudless. It nearly always worked, Rose had found. But just as she cleared the sky in her head, a thought moved in. She hadn't put fresh water in the pitcher on her father's washstand, and he wouldn't be able to wash quickly when he got up in the morning.

She slid out of bed again, felt her way to the washstand in her parents' bedroom—her father's bedroom—and went downstairs to fill it at the pump in the kitchen. When she came back, her eyes pretty much adjusted to the dark, she took a quick look at Abby, who was sound asleep on her little bed, her teddy bear clutched tightly in one arm. She gave her sister's cheek a light stroke and went back to bed.

She'd never be able to remember everything, she thought. But instead of making any more lists in her head, she thought of a clear sky, a June sky, and in little more than a minute, she was asleep.

CHAPTER 4
Time for the Cat

A week later, Miss Harty stopped Rose as she was leaving the schoolroom and asked her to clean the black-boards before she went home. Rose couldn't hold back a small sigh. She had so much to do. But she couldn't say no to Miss Harty. She didn't seem able to say no to any-one.

While everyone else marched toward the cloakroom, Rose picked up the dusty cloth and started clearing the day's work from the blackboard. As she worked, she thought about all the things everybody wanted. Father wanted breakfast on the table when he came in from the barn. Abby wanted her hair braided every morning. Charles wanted a clean shirt and a different lunch every day.

She already hated washing and ironing clothes. It took so long, heating the water, filling the tub, scrub-bing the clothes, getting the tub emptied and refilled for rinsing, emptying it again. She was hanging the wash on Sarah's rope lines on the back porch, but everything had frozen this week because it was so cold. Charles and Abby went into giggling fits when she stood Father's stiff, icy trousers in front of the stove to dry. At least that was a good thing. Sometimes they still laughed together, she thought, smiling as she wiped away long division examples. Except for Father, who had not laughed since before the funeral.

Moving along the slate, she swept the date away, along with Miss Harty's quote of the day, which told her that: "Life grants nothing to us mortals without hard work." She sighed again, feeling surrounded by hard work and wondering what granting was.

Sarah had three flatirons, so two could be warming on the stove while she used one. She found the slightly frozen articles easier to iron than the things that were all dry. But it had been very late—in fact Father had come in from his evening at the hotel—before she finished enough ironing to take care of today's needs.

He had growled at her about staying up too late, and told her to get on to bed. She had started to say she had to finish one more dress for Abby; that she wanted to get one day ahead. But when he turned toward her and raised his hand, she scuttled off to bed in a hurry, not even taking a lamp or a candle with her. She had undressed in the dark. In a few minutes, she heard his footsteps on the stairs, heard him stumble and mutter. His breath had smelled terrible, she'd thought, and his eyes were so red. She'd overheard her mother talking to Aunt Nell about Father being at something called "the drink," and how it always made him touchy about things. Maybe he'd been at the drink last night, and that was why he'd said all those swearwords at breakfast time.

She stepped back, looked at the board and switched rags. She doused the new one in the water bucket by the school stove. Carefully, leaving no streaks, she washed down the slate. Even though she didn't want to stay after school, she always enjoyed this job. The boards looked so nice when they were clean again. When Miss Harty spoke behind her, Rose jumped. She had been so absorbed with what was churning in her head that she didn't realize the other pupils were all gone.

"What did I do wrong, Miss Harty?" Rose asked anxiously. "I know one of my papers was not neat."

"It's not that at all," Miss Harty said, taking Rose by the arm and leading her to the chair next to her desk. "It's just that I'd like to know how you're getting on. If you don't mind my asking."

"The arithmetic is something I always like," Rose began, "and the writing, too. And the reading—I know I don't always get the new words as quickly as Alice, but I . . . "

"I know you do well here, Rose," Miss Harty said very softly. "I'm just wondering how you're getting on at home with the other two children and so much work to do."

Rose was taken aback. Teachers never asked about home. Fathers and mothers asked about school, but teachers never asked about home. Once or twice a year, the teacher was invited to dinner, but that was a courtesy. Almost everyone in town gave the teacher a meal or two every year. Last year Rose had found out that it wasn't just a matter of being polite. It seemed the town didn't pay the teacher very well, and Miss Harty didn't have a family of her own here. She was a boarder at the Chandlers' when she first came, and now she had the little house near the depot. A meal now and then was a way of giving the teacher a little something extra.

"All right," she said. And then she looked at Miss Harty's face, clear-skinned and so serious. She noticed that the teacher's eyes were brown, and Rose's wandering mind started adding up the number of brown-eyed people she knew. It wasn't many. Oh, dear, she thought, Emily was right. My head needs to be hitched on tighter. I'm thinking about eyes, and she's waiting for more of an answer.

"There's a lot of work to do," she began. And then it all came out as if a nor'easter were whirling through her head, sending everything in sight out of her mouth. In a rush, she told about the washing, the ironing, the early breakfasts, the braids, her father going out every night and coming home in a temper. She said she was in a hurry to fall asleep at night because she had to get up so early, but it wasn't working. The harder she tried to fall asleep, the longer she stared at the ceiling.

"And I don't know how to do everything," she said, "And Mother's cat prowls around and around the kitchen and the pantry, mewing as if he's calling her."

"You're only fourteen, going on fifteen," Miss Harty said. "You can't possibly know how to run a house by yourself. Isn't there anyone to give you a hand?"

"Charles and Abby help a lot," Rose said quickly. "They take care of the chickens by themselves now, and Abby sets the table, and Charles fetches wood. But they can't cook or clean, and Father has the farm work to do, and he can't do all that either without our mother."

It was Miss Harty's turn to give a little sigh. "You'd better run along now," she said. "I've made you late enough, and I'm sure you have to get a good supper on the table. But you need some help with all those chores and those children. I will put my thinking cap on. As for the cat, sit down after supper in a chair with him on your lap and stroke his head for a long time. It will make both of you feel better."

Rose almost ran out the door, pulling her wrap around her as she went. To her surprise, Emily was sitting on the bottom step, looking as if she were frozen in place.

"Em! I'm so glad you're still here," Rose said.

"I would have turned into an iceberg in another five minutes," Emily said.

"You can't be an iceberg," Rose said in her fact-finding tone. "Two-thirds of an iceberg is under water and invisible. You're not invisible."

Relieved at Rose's cheerfulness, which meant that whatever had happened wasn't upsetting, Emily asked, "Can we run for a little way?"

The two took off, hoisting up their long skirts above

their ankles and pounding down the rutted gravel road as if they were eight-year-old boys. A few rods along, they slowed up, pink-cheeked and laughing.

"I was so tired," Rose said. "And now I'm not tired anymore."

"But what did she want?" Emily demanded.

"I think she's worried about me," Rose said, thinking no one except her mother had ever seemed concerned about her before. Well, that really wasn't fair, she thought. Aunt Nell had always treated her as if she were special every time they went there for Sunday dinner or for a family picnic. But Miss Harty had taken her into the school when she was three, and now she was being nice again.

"What's wrong with you?" Emily asked.

"I don't know how to run a house and keep everything in its place and everyone happy," Rose said. "And Father is going to the hotel every night and I think he's at the drink."

"What drink?" Emily said. "What do you mean at the drink? Does that mean the drink is a place, or something he's drinking?"

Rose wanted to pretend she knew all about this drink thing, since Emily didn't. But she didn't either. So she said she had heard her mother mention it and she thought it was something bad.

"Ask your mother, Em," she said. "Then we'll know. I can tell you Miss Harty's face went real solemn when I mentioned 'the drink'. "

"Maybe you should have asked her," Em said. "Sometimes my ma answers questions like that by telling me I'll find out when it's time. Sometimes I think I'm going to be very, very busy when 'it's time.' It's like going through 'stages.' When Jennie fusses or cries or tries to grab my pencils and paper, Ma always says she's 'going through a stage.' I think she's been in a stage ever since she was born."

Rose knew Emily's little sister could be a nuisance, but she was a very pretty child and could be quite charming. "You're just jealous," she said. "You don't like it when Jennie says a new word and everyone gets all excited about it."

"They go into what Pa calls a dither," Emily agreed. "No one is thrilled when I learn a new word—like blossom, bibliography, brougham or burgeon," Emily said, rattling off words from yesterday's vocabulary and spelling list.

The idea of a family going into a dither over broughams and blossoms made both girls giggle. As they neared Emily's turnoff, they began to chant from that day's additions, "colic, contempt, contract, cretin, crimp, cultivate," and laughed so hard that tears ran down their cheeks and Mrs. Munson turned to stare at them as she passed by in her buggy.

"I hope she doesn't tell Ma she saw me behaving in what Ma calls an 'unseemly fashion'," Emily said as she watched Mrs. Munson steer her horse away from some of the worst ruts in the road.

Going on by herself, Rose wondered why she called her parents Mother and Father, and Em called hers Ma and Pa. She'd heard children say Mama and Papa, too. Why did everyone use different words? She didn't like the way Ma and Pa sounded and was pleased that she didn't have to call her parents that. And then it all swept over her again. She'd call Mother whatever she wanted to be called if she could just call her again, she thought. Was that how the cat felt, too?

A surprise stood in the middle of the kitchen floor when Rose walked in. It was an icebox, not quite new by the looks of it, but close to new. Abby was on her hands and knees in front of the square cabinet with the doors open. As Rose came in, Abby lifted the shiny latch on one of the doors, closed it and dropped the latch into place.

"Oh, Rose," she nearly shouted when she saw her older sister. "Now we can get ice and have lemonade."

"And drink milk that's cold but not frozen," added Charles. "We'll get a block of ice every time Mr. Manchester comes by, and we'll have one of those little signs to put in our window. Everyone will know we have an icebox now, not just the milk cooler."

"Where did it come from?" Rose asked.

"We don't know," Charles said. "It was setting right where you see it when we came home."

"Why did you have to stay after school again?" he asked, suddenly remembering that she was late.

"Miss Harty wanted to know how we were getting on," Rose said, shaking her head behind Abby's back so he wouldn't say anything more. "I said you two were taking perfect care of the chickens."

They both jumped up and ran out the kitchen door toward the henhouse. Forgotten the poor chickens already, thought Rose, although she had to admit that an icebox was a fine distraction. Where should it go, she wondered. On the back porch? Next to the sink? Beside the woodbox? Out in the shed? She'd see what Father said when he came in. Right now she had better put a meal together.

She went to the pantry windowsill to get the pot of stew she had made on Sunday. Well, it had chilled nicely there, but it would be so much better to store such things in the icebox from now on. Her mother had wanted one for a long time because she was afraid food would spoil and make them all sick. She had occasionally kept milk and cream and cottage cheese on the ice in the milk room in the cellar. But Father needed most of the space to strain the milk he brought from the barn, and to let the cream rise so he could sell that separately, or give it to Sarah to make butter. He also fussed a little about the family using up the precious ice he kept under sawdust in the icehouse, and about people coming and going in the milk room. Rose remembered her father saying they didn't get sick much anyway, and certainly they could not have every newfangled thing that came down the pike.

It must be that iceboxes weren't newfangled anymore. She guessed she wouldn't ask about that. She had watched Sarah's mouth get so thin that it almost disappeared after Father made the newfangled remark. It was the way Sarah looked when Rose forgot to empty the slop jar before school, or spilled jam on a clean dress. The good days were the ones when Sarah's mouth showed, and the best ones were when she actually laughed out loud. That wasn't often, Rose thought. She must try to remember how that laugh sounded. She didn't want to lose the memory of it.

When Father came in and they all sat down for supper, he gave a little chuckle and asked if they had admired the new furniture in the kitchen, and if anyone had an idea where it should go. They all started talking at once and then all stopped at once. He took a spoonful of hot stew with a slurping sound, swallowed, and then allowed as how he would put the icebox next to the woodbox so it would be near the door.

"The ice blocks are heavy," he said. "You want to get Mr. Manchester to put it right in there if you can. If he sets it down, you'll have the devil of a time picking it up again. And besides, it will make quite a puddle if it isn't seen to right away."

"How big a piece do we order?" Rose asked. "We have to put a card in the window, right?"

"That's it, girl," Father said. "And then we'll see how soon we need a second piece. Mind you—all of you—you don't keep flapping that door open and shut all day. The more it opens, the more cold comes out and heat goes in. That makes the ice melt faster, and ice costs money."

He took two more mouthfuls of stew and said, "Charles, it will be up to you to empty that tray under the icebox. If you don't, the floor will be flooded, and the boards will warp and rot. You see to it morning and afternoon, and take a look at the ice block as well. It will be your job to order ice, and we'll be depending on you.

"As for you, Rose, you decide what goes in the icebox and what can safely stay in the pantry. Your mother was always worried about things with milk and eggs and lard and cream in them. She said we could all get sick if those things spoiled and we ate them anyway. Food poisoning, she called it."

Rose nodded. So her mother was gone, and now he was listening to her. She wondered if he was feeling bad about not getting the icebox when Sarah wanted it. Did he remember when her mother's mouth disappeared?

The children cleared the table together. The icebox was placed against the wall, and Father said he thought the doors should be left open for the night to give the inside a good airing. "It's not new," he said. "But it's in good shape, and it's clean, so it should give us good service for quite a few years."

While Abby and Charles went back to the table with their schoolbooks, Rose washed up the dishes by candlelight in the kitchen. Father lit a tallow candle and went upstairs. Was he going out again? Rose wondered. She didn't have to wonder for long. In a few minutes, he was in the kitchen again, wearing the shirt he'd put on last night. He had combed his beard and his hair, and he was wearing shoes instead of boots.

"I'll be going out now," he said. "You see to things here."

"Yes, Father," she said, hoping she could do that quickly enough to get to bed before he came home again. She noticed that he went to the blue sugar bowl in the pantry and took out some coins before he went out the door. She hoped Em would find out about "the drink." She needed to know if that was why Father was so—what was that word they had had in the first list last week—so aggressive, that was it. She hated it when he was aggressive.

Rose brought a second kerosene lamp into the dining room and then, hearing the cat mewing, went to find him. She cornered him in the pantry, picked him up firmly and joined the other two children at the table. Quickly she went through the list of vocabulary words, smiling at the thought of how silly she and Emily had been that afternoon, and stroking the cat from ears to tail while she talked.

Pretty soon, Tom settled against her body and put his head down. In a few minutes, she heard him purring, the first time she had heard that sweet sound since Sarah had died. Had been killed. Perhaps she had to be more exact about these things so she would accept them.

Tired from her long day, she decided she would read the newspaper and get everyone to bed in good season. The newspaper had just come, and she loved to look at the advertisements for ready-made dresses, and pills and dry goods. Besides, the newspaper always had a few scary stories about people being hit by trains or kicked by horses or injured in a factory. The injured were no doubt well on the mend by the time she heard about them, since the newspaper came by post, but she always pretended all the news was new. And she didn't know any of the people because they all lived miles away in other parts of New England, like Boston and Providence. Some day, Rose thought, she would go to one of those Boston stores and buy new undergarments without anyone she knew watching her. She liked the way they wrote those stories, as if the happenings weren't even real.

But the best part was the serial. This would be the seventh part of a story about pioneers going west in their wagons. In the last part, the little group had encountered a tribe of Indians who turned out to be friendly. Charles and Abby finished their work at the same time and looked up to see her reading the serial, the now contented cat still in her lap, even though she had stopped stroking him.

"Read it to me," Abby pleaded. "Come on, Rose, read it to me."

Rose didn't think it would do any harm, so she quickly told Abby what had happened in the first parts of the story and then read aloud to the two of them.

"Will you keep reading to us every day?" Charles asked. "Mother always read to us whenever she could." It will be one more thing, Rose thought. But at least she was good at reading.

"Of course I will," she said. "If you'll help me with the goodnight things." That was what her mother always called the chores she did at bedtime: setting up the table for breakfast; making sure there was wood for the stove; filling the water pitchers in the bedrooms; tucking the children into their beds.

They nodded, and Abby said, "Ooooh, can I tuck you in?" Rose felt her eyes go all watery again. She really had to hold up better, she thought. But she answered them in a tone that reminded all three of their mother.

"Of course," she said. "And Charles will tuck you in, and then we'll both say goodnight as soon as we hear his bed creak over our heads."

"We'll have to yell," Abby said, mischievously. "Can we yell?"

CHAPTER 5
Sunday Dinner

Two days later, as Rose quickly sliced bread for lunch pails, she heard a horse whinny very close to the house. To her astonishment, she saw Miss Harty's buggy pulling up. The teacher's small brown horse was tossing her head as if to say that this was not a usual stop. But Rose saw that the horse quieted as soon as Miss Harty spoke.

She even makes horses feel better, Rose thought. Perhaps she soothes cats, too, and dogs. Maybe parrots say only nice things when they hear her voice. Rose's imagination was trotting away again, but she didn't stop it. The best test would be to send Miss Harty to the henhouse and see whether that vicious chicken would try to get a chunk of her smooth fingers.

Rose had noticed more than once how soft and pale the teacher's hands were. The skin on the back of Sarah's hands had been brown from the wrists to the ends of her fingers. And her palms were reddened and rough. She'd had a light touch, but sometimes her calloused fingers had caught in Abby's hair when she was doing her braids. But what on earth was Miss Harty doing in their yard at this hour? Perhaps school had been called off. Maybe the building had burned to the ground during the night. Maybe the outhouse had fallen down.

Then she saw Father approach the buggy. Miss Harty was asking him something, and he seemed surprised. But then he nodded and pulled on the brim of his old felt hat. She didn't look angry, Rose thought. In fact, she had that little smile on her face again as she spoke once more to the horse and moved smoothly back into the road and on her way. Rose could hardly wait for Father to come in and tell them what the teacher had wanted. But he didn't come. She waited until Charles and Abby were both fidgeting about being late to school, and then she left with Charles, her mind in what Emily's family called a dither.

She hoped Miss Harty hadn't told Father anything about Rose crying in school and passing notes and failing to hold up. But she couldn't have said anything, Rose thought. You couldn't tell all those things in just a couple of sentences. Settled at her desk, she kept her eyes down so she wouldn't have to greet Miss Harty or even see her eyes. Even so, she could see the hem of her dress next to the desk and knew she was wearing the blue frock that Rose and Emily thought must have come from a city store. It buttoned from the neck to the waist and had a tiny white lace edging on both sides of the buttons and around the high neck. Matching lace circled the skirt a ruler's length above the floor, and trimmed the cloth belt that tied in a bow in the back. When Miss Harty walked, you could just see the toes of her black-buttoned boots. Rose wanted a dress like that some day.

Then she heard her name, spoken in Miss Harty's "why don't you answer me" tone. She put her mind in reverse and could hear several "Roses" being said by the teacher, each a little louder than the one before. She counted four of them before the stern one and figured she'd be doing blackboards again today.

"Yes, Miss Harty," she said as if it were a question.

"Please answer the question, Rose," Miss Harty said.

Rose's mind wouldn't go back far enough to pick up the question. She couldn't do it, even though her head was quite accustomed to running several tracks at once, backward and forward.

"I'm sorry, Miss Harty. I didn't hear the question," she said in a very small voice.

"What do Southerners call the Civil War, and what did the war accomplish?" Miss Harty asked.

"The War Between the States," Rose answered, relieved. "It was the war that freed the slaves," she added, to answer the second part of the question.

"Fine," Miss Harty said. "It is nice to have your mind back in the room."

Rose felt her skin turning pink. She didn't need a mirror to tell her the blotches were starting on her neck and then moving up over her face the way jelly rises in the kettle when it's starting to boil. She felt so hot it made her wonder if she would boil over, with all her body juices spilling out of her mouth and ears and nose.

She didn't suppose anyone ever actually boiled, but her skin seemed that hot. She wanted to hide or flee.

As she turned her head away, she saw Alice watching her from across the room. The dark-haired girl, whose skin never changed color unless they were outdoors in the cold, was trying hard not to laugh. It occurred to Rose that a red face wasn't an evil. She smiled at Alice, gave a great sigh and felt some of the warmth recede. Miss Harty had missed none of this, Rose thought. She was now looking right at Alice, who was still looking at Rose.

"And who, Alice, were five of the leading generals of the Civil War? Their names and which side they were on, please."

Alice stood beside her chair slowly, the way they had been taught. "Sherman, North," she said. "Lee, South. Jackson, South. Grant, North. Longstreet, South, Ma'am."

"Excellent," Miss Harty said. "Do you know any of their Christian names?"

Alice gave the first names of each general, and Miss Harty wrote them on the board. "And can you tell us when the war ended, Alice?" Miss Harty persisted.

"Twenty-two years ago, Ma'am," Alice said, "in 1865. It's the year my parents were married." Rose was so pleased for Alice. She always studied hard, but she had trouble answering questions in the classroom. Rose might blush, but that never stopped her from giving the answers. Alice was what teachers called tongue-tied, an expression that Rose disliked almost as much as she hated slop jars. She knew perfectly well that her friend's tongue was not tied, and it was a foolish expression anyway. How could you ever tie a tongue? What would you tie it to, or with?

The day moved on, and Rose found her attention wandering from her books to the lists of chores she was making in her head, to the question of what Miss Harty had been doing at her house.

They were given a quick recess in the middle of the afternoon session, and everyone hurried to get outside. It was a short break in the day, and sometimes the teacher didn't give it to them. That just made the change more welcome when it came. Ten minutes later, when the bell rang again, they lined up, boys at one door and girls at another, to file inside to their classrooms.

Miss Harty stood at the door as the girls walked in and stopped Rose so briefly that only three girls passed her.

"I will be coming to your house for dinner on Sunday after church," the teacher said, to Rose's surprise. "I expect you and Abby will be setting a nice table for me and your father and Charles."

"Oh, yes, of course, that will be about noontime, won't it, Ma'am? Or a little later? Does Father know, Miss Harty?"

"We discussed it this morning. Now get back to your work, please."

In a daze, Rose walked back to her desk. Almost everyone was seated, and she felt as if her size nine feet were making a great clatter as she walked almost the length of the room to reach her place. She looked first at Emily and then at Alice. Both had their eyebrows raised practically into their hair. She knew they'd wait for her after school today.

Rose couldn't make her feet go down the school steps fast enough. She wanted to shout the news to Alice and Emily, who were both waiting for her, but she was afraid Miss Harty would hear her.

"Miss Harty is coming for Sunday dinner," she blurted out as soon as she was within talking distance. "She came by the house this morning to talk to Father about it. She was in her buggy, and the horse did just what she said. So I have to cook dinner for the teacher—and I don't know what to make," she finished, suddenly realizing that this dinner would end up being her responsibility. She had never seen her father cook anything.

"What will I make?" she asked her friends, in a voice that had a little fear in it. "It has to be special, not cost too much and be pretty easy."

"A tall order," Emily said. "Let's see. You could make boiled potatoes. They're not dear. Or biscuits— they're special the way you make them. Or maybe just your custard pie and forget the rest."

"Em!" Rose almost shrieked. "This is not a joke. We will be putting on a real dinner for the teacher, and we don't even have a tablecloth ironed. I have been so busy that I've just been shaking the cloth out the back door and turning it over every day, hoping no one will spill anything—and that Father won't say anything about the spots."

"Maybe you'd like us to help," Alice said, a little timidly. "We could come on Saturday for a little while—I think Mother would let me—so we could get the cloth ready and go to the store and get what you'll need."

"Oh, that would be perfect," Rose said. "And it will make it fun for me. When I really think about her coming, my stomach does a somersault."

"Didn't you say you had a chicken that was grabbing Abby's fingers all the time?" Emily wanted to know. "Ask your father to chop off its head. That will solve two problems at once. Abby won't get pecked anymore, and you can make chicken and dumplings for dinner without spending too much money at Mr. Tisdale's."

The girls were walking three across with Rose in the middle. She linked arms with the other two and gave a little squeeze. No one in her family ever hugged anyone, but she thought she'd like to hug these two. Alice and Emily were wiping her worries away as if they were just chalk marks in her head.

"I know how to make chicken and dumplings," she said. "You're right. It's really just like making the biscuits. And I can boil up that nasty hen if Father will kill it Saturday and give me time to take the meat off the bones. With our new icebox, I won't have to worry about taking up space in the milk cooler."

"You could make the pie on Saturday, too," Alice said. "As long as you tell Charles not to touch it."

"Abby's worse," Rose said. "She doesn't like pie, but she loves the crust. One day we came down in the morning and all the crust was broken off the top of a strawberry-rhubarb pie that hadn't even been cut yet. At first Mother thought it was a mouse, but then she noticed that Abby had her face almost in her plate."

"What did your mother do?" Em asked, thinking things would go very badly for her at home if she spoiled a pie that way.

"She asked Abby if she thought the mouse had a name," Rose said. "And Abby started to cry and say she was sorry, she hadn't meant to eat all the way around the pie, just take a little piece that had cracked, but it was so good she couldn't stop. And then Mother said she would have to make a crust when she came home from school to replace the ruined one. So that was the day Abby learned how to cut the lard into the flour and roll out the pie crust without it sticking to the board and pinch the edges into a neat row. Mother made her do it over and over until it was pretty good for a seven-year-old. By that time, the crust was as gray as the cat and had to be thrown away. Come to think of it, Abby can help with the pie, even though she can't do the custard part."

"I can't believe your mother didn't just give her a good spanking," Emily said. "I think that's what would have happened to me."

"Well," Rose said, "sometimes she spanked us—or gave us a quick whack with that little wooden paddle she uses—I mean, used to use—to make butter. But Abby was certainly punished. By the time she made a crust that was acceptable, she was probably wishing she'd had a spanking instead."

"I can't believe your mother asked if the mouse had a name," Alice said, thinking how sad it was that Rose had put her mother in the past tense. They had just learned about tenses in school, but she and Emily didn't have to put their mothers in the past tense. She hurried on, hoping to take Rose's mind off her mother's death. "I mean, my mother would have started talking in that tone that makes you want to be in the front room or upstairs. And then she would have asked who ate the crust, and if no one answered, she would have gotten very angry—not asked about a mouse's name."

"But it worked," Rose said. She was certain in her own mind that Sarah hadn't liked spankings. Once she had seen her frown and turn away when Father was paddling Charles for not feeding the horses and for telling a lie about it. She hoped no one would do anything that would make Father bring out his paddle—or his big hand. She knew she wouldn't like it either. She never wanted to see Father give a whipping to Charles or Abby. She must try to keep them out of trouble so it wouldn't happen. She suddenly realized she would have to deal with them herself and not report them to her father.

"Anyway," she said, "I would be so grateful to have you both come Saturday to help me out. I'll make a list of what we need to get and do. One thing I already know—I have to get the front room dusted. No one has been in there since the funeral, and I'm not sure whether everything is back in place or not. Father closed the door, and Charles and I didn't want to open it."

Emily and Alice leaned forward and looked at each

other across Rose's face. The two of them had been talking about how Rose had not talked about the funeral at all. Maybe, Emily thought, the parlor door was still shut, but the door to talking had just opened, at least a crack. The two girls knew that Mr. Chandler had taken Sarah Hibbard's body away from the woodshed after the accident. It was customary, their mothers said, to take the body inside the house, where womenfolk, either relatives or neighbors, would prepare it for burial. But Alice's mother, after the funeral, had told her that no one wanted the children to see their mother the way she was, so they took her to the Chandlers' house. Then, once she was bathed and dressed, and laid in a pine box made by the carpenter who worked behind the store, they brought her home to the front room.

Emily and Alice had shared their thoughts about all of this with each other, but had not talked to Rose. They had not been allowed to go to the funeral because the house was small, and children did not belong at funerals, or so Emily's mother had said. But Emily had heard her mother say that Sarah Hibbard's face looked terribly pale above the lace collar of her Sunday go-to-meeting best. But quite natural, her father had answered, quite natural. The girls wished Rose would tell them about the funeral and her mother's face, but she had said barely a word about it.

Deciding to plunge in, Emily asked, "Did your father put back the table, and the big plant that blossoms for Christmas?"

"I don't know for sure," Rose said, hesitating only a

little. "But he must have. The plant couldn't be outdoors, and I haven't seen it anywhere else in the house."

"Well, if he doesn't mind, we'll get right in there with the feather duster and fix things up," Alice said. "My mother would open a window for a bit, just to clear the air."

"If the air is still as sad as it was that day, then we'd better do that," Rose said. She kept her eyes on her toes, hoping her friends wouldn't notice that she was failing to hold up again.

But she felt a little squeeze on each arm and suddenly knew they didn't care whether she held up or not. She could probably bawl her eyes out right here in the road, and they'd just go on being her friends. She tightened her grip on each of them and looked, a little shyly, at first one and then the other. A smile came from each side, and she tried to give one back, even though her lip refused to stop twitching. To her surprise, she saw that Emily's eyes were watering, too.

"We do want to help you," Emily said. "We can't even imagine what it's like not to have a mother."

"It's not good," Rose said solemnly. "But I was just remembering this morning that when things went wrong, Mother would just say that we had to deal with whatever was put on our plates."

"And you're going to put something delicious on Miss Harty's plate," laughed Emily. "She ought to like dealing with dumplings and custard pie."

"What do you think she'll wear?" asked Alice.

After her two friends turned off at their roads, Rose

went on alone, her feet moving faster and faster and faster until she was almost running. She didn't even know she was hurrying. Her feet were just trying to keep up with her thoughts, which were racing through that day and the next and then Saturday, and finally to Sunday, when Miss Harty would come for dinner.

By the time she reached her own steps, she was so excited that she burst through the door and started talking without even saying hello to Charles and Abby, who were standing by the sink cleaning some of the eggs they had collected in the chicken coop. She didn't even notice that her father was in the dining room doorway.

"Whoa, there, slow down," his voice interrupted. "What's all the fuss about?"

Rose stopped abruptly. "Well," she stammered. "Well, I . . . "

"So, what's this about Miss Harty coming for dinner, Rose?" her father boomed. "Have you and your siblings been up to mischief in school? Why would she want to take Sunday dinner at our table now?"

"Well," Rose began again, thinking that she was beginning to sound like an idiot, "I think she just wants to see how we're getting along here without Mother."

She looked up and saw a strange look cross her father's face. He looked at the floor, gave a little shudder and then looked at her again. At first she thought his eyes were a little watery, but she knew that couldn't be. He'd be holding up.

"We are getting along, aren't we?" he demanded. "We're doing all right?"

"I think so, Father," she said, wondering why his voice had that hoarse sound, as if he had a cold. "I'm doing my best."

"And your best is not bad," he said in a quieter way.

Not bad, she thought. She hated that expression. Why did people say not bad when quite good was what they meant? A beautiful pie was not bad. A sunny day was not bad weather. You put on a new dress and someone said it was not bad. Was it only in New England, or did they say not bad when they ate pie in Minnesota, or danced at the White House? She turned her back on them, taking an extra minute to hang her coat. This was no time for her temper to get out of hand.

As she turned back, she heard her father say, "And what will we give Miss Teacher for dinner? A bowl of oatmeal? A piece of pie?"

In control again, she decided she'd better speak up about her idea. "I thought you might kill the hen that is pecking Abby's fingers when she collects the eggs," she said. "She's not a young one, and she's pretty fat, and she isn't nice."

"Hmmmmm . . ." he answered. "But then we won't have her eggs anymore."

"That's true, Father. But she would be good for chicken and dumplings, and I know how to make that, and since it's our own chicken, the meal wouldn't be too dear."

"Quite right, young lady," he said. "Charles and I will kill that mean hen tomorrow, and I will teach him how to dress it on Saturday morning. Will that give you enough time?"

"Oh, yes," Rose answered. Part of her head set off again, wondering why anyone called the chicken dressed when it was really undressed, all its feathers off and its insides removed. Words were odd, she thought. Out loud she said, "Alice and Emily would like to come Saturday to help me get caught up with the housework and get a tablecloth ironed and do some baking."

She was grateful to see him smile, his teeth very white but his lips barely showing through his generous beard. "I can see that we will be in good hands on Sunday," he said. "And I will say a blessing before we start to eat."

He looked sternly at Charles and Abby. "You two must help your sister. It is a great honor to have the teacher come for dinner. Your mother always spoke very well of Miss Harty. You will keep your Sunday clothes on after church, and put your napkin in your lap and use it to wipe your mouth during the meal. You will help clear the table when everyone is finished eating, but other than that, you will not get up from your chairs. And you will not interrupt while Rose and I and Miss Harty are talking. Now I'm going to the barn to do the milking. I expect supper will be on the table right after the train goes through?"

"Oh, yes sir," Rose said, but he didn't wait for the answer. He was already through the door and on his way to the barn. She wondered what would happen to supper if the train was late or if it crashed and tipped into the river? Would they wait for the whistle, even if it never came? Silly goose, she said to herself. The train is almost never late, and it has never crashed, and almost everyone in this town eats supper right after the train whistle blows. But her rambling head was not finished with this subject. With a small smile, she wondered if you could imitate a train whistle an hour ahead of schedule. Thinking of all the housewives clattering around in dismay, afraid they were way behind, made her laugh out loud.

"What's funny?" Charles said crossly, not yet recovered from the idea of actually killing a chicken.

"Oh, nothing," Rose said. "Thanks for taking care of the chickens."

"And the table is set, too," Abby said. "Did I do it right?"

Rose went with the little girl to inspect her work and saw that forks were on the left side of the plate, knives on the right. The glass spoon holder stood in the center of the table, handy for anyone who needed a spoon, and tumblers were at each place.

"It's perfect," Rose said. Abby gave a huge sigh of relief and announced that she was now going to change her clothes.

"Tomorrow," Rose said gently, "you might do the changing before you go to the henhouse. The doors and walls in there aren't very clean, and there's lots of cobwebs."

Abby nodded and ran to the stairs.

"What was funny?" Charles asked again, this time

in a more normal voice. He had decided that chickens were killed every day, and no one ever talked about it, so it couldn't be too bad. Rose told him about imitating the train whistle and setting off a bustle of activity in every kitchen in town. He grinned. It was a funny idea. He began to think about exactly how a train whistle worked. Perhaps he could ask at the depot one day. Perhaps he could find a way to make such a sound. He did like the idea of all those women in their flowered dresses and aprons running around like chickens with their heads cut off. Oh my, he thought, we are going to cut the old hen's head right off.

On Saturday morning at nine o'clock, Rose heard a rap on the back door. She was adding a good-sized chunk of wood to the stove before putting the potful of chicken on it. She had cut up the bird, filled the pot with water, and added a sliced onion, four cloves, and a dash of salt and pepper. She would bring it to a boil, then move the pot to the side so it would just simmer for two hours or so. Then the chicken would fall off the bones.

"Come in," she called, certain that either Alice or Emily was there. But it was Mr. Manchester, carrying a new block of ice with his black tongs.

"Good morning, Missy," he bellowed. "Here's your ice."

He opened the door where the ice was stored and told her to swish out what was left of the old piece. Then he shoved in the new block and told her she owed five cents for that. Rose went around the corner into the pantry and took down the blue willow sugar bowl. She took out five cents and noticed that the bowl had very little money in it. She was quite sure she had seen several silver dollars there only two or three days back. She frowned, trying to remember if they had used any money. She knew Father had taken something out of the bowl, but it seemed as if a lot was missing.

"Thanks very much," said the iceman, pocketing the five cents. "Once you've had this box for a bit, you'll get into a routine on the ice. Just don't let anybody keep the door open. In the meantime, I'll keep an eye on your window whenever I go by, just to see if the card is up or not."

"Thank you so much," Rose said.

As he went out the door, she saw Emily and Alice coming along the driveway past his horse and wagon. Emily asked if she could pet the horse, and Mr. Manchester gave her a lump of sugar, reminding her that she must hold her hand flat with the sugar in her palm.

"Otherwise, he'll just take a piece out of your pretty little fingers," the iceman said. "Not that he's mean. But his teeth are bigger than your hand."

Emily offered the sugar without mishap and giggled as the horse's soft nose went over her palm. It felt like her mother's best velvet skirt, except for the little hairs that stuck out. Then she and Alice came up the steps and into the kitchen, ready to lend a hand.

"I brought my own apron," Alice said. "My mother said she didn't want to wash even this after-school dress until at least two weeks from now."

"Me, too," said Emily. "Except this is Ma's apron. Mine was dirty."

"Where do we start?" Alice wanted to know. "I have to be home by the noon hour."

Rose pulled out the ironing board and set it on the dining room table. She put a towel over the wooden board and covered that with a smooth sheet. She had three flatirons heating on the wood stove, and she had sprinkled the best white linen tablecloth with water and rolled it smoothly and tightly into a bundle about the size of a rolling pin.

She handed the cloth to Alice and pointed out the irons. "You may need to have Emily hold up the part you've ironed," she said. "Otherwise it will drag on the floor and get dirty and wrinkled all over again." The two girls went to work on the linen cloth, keeping it off the floor, and changing irons whenever the one they were using cooled down. The irons were heavy, and they exchanged places several times. When they were done, Rose suggested they spread the cloth over the sofa so she could put it on the table in the morning. Without thinking, Emily opened the door to the front room and started in. Then she remembered that Rose had said no one had been in there since the funeral. She stopped and stood very still.

"Go ahead," Rose said. "This is the day we have to do this. I'm not feeling very brave about it, so I'm glad you went first." She bit her lip, which seemed to be trembling for no reason at all, and gave Emily a little push into the room. Well, Rose thought, looking around, someone has been here. The chairs were back in the space where the coffin had stood for two days. The candleholders were gone—she wondered if they had been borrowed from the church—and Mother's large Christmas cactus was back on its stand. She hadn't even remembered the plant in all this time, and it must be dry as a bone.

"You'll need to pump a pitcher of water for the cactus, Alice," she said, knowing that the best thing to do was plunge into the work they needed to do. "It must think it's moved back to a desert. I'll get a feather duster and a dust mop, and we'll get the kittens out from under the chairs in no time."

"Kittens?" asked Emily. "I thought your cat was a full-grown boy."

"The cat is a boy," Rose said. "Kittens are what Sarah—that is, Mother—called the dust balls that roll up under the furniture and skitter around the room."

"Did you just call your mother by her first name?" Emily demanded in amazement.

"Well, I've been doing that because then I don't have to say 'Mother' in my head," Rose admitted. "It's just made it easier not to think about her as my mother, but not to forget her either."

Emily shook her head, a little confused. She didn't say words in her head the way Rose did, so she was pretty sure she wouldn't have this problem if her mother died. On the other hand, she wasn't going to tell Rose it was silly. After all, she still had a mother, and Rose didn't. And even if your mother was making lists of chores that would take all day, or yelling at you for doing something the wrong way, she was still someone you needed to have.

In less time than it would take Rose to walk to school, the three girls had run the feather duster over the window ledges and tables and chair rounds, and the shelf that held the black and gold clock, one of Sarah's few treasures. They swept the small rug with a broom and carefully dust mopped the floor around the rug.

"I'll have to reset the clock," Rose said, "but I can't do it until the noon whistle sounds at the factory."

"Not today," Emily said. "It's Saturday. You'll have to do it when the five-thirty train whistle blows."

"Do we have to wash the windows?" Alice wanted to know.

"No," Rose laughed. "This isn't spring cleaning time. It's just Miss Harty coming to dinner."

"Well, it's special when she comes to your house," Alice said, bending down to pick up a black hairpin from the floor. "Is this yours?"

Rose said it wasn't, that it must have fallen out of someone's hair at the funeral; she didn't use pins like that. She had put her hair up the day of the funeral, but her hairpins were pale so they wouldn't show in her light hair.

The girls fetched the tablecloth from the dining room and carefully laid it along the back of the sofa.

"Now what?" Alice asked, ready for the next task. She really didn't like cleaning and ironing, but doing these things with friends at someone else's house was different from doing her mother's bidding at home.

"What about the pie?" Emily asked. "And the chicken?"

"The chicken is stewing," Rose said. "I put it on the back of the stove while you were ironing. I think Charles left his supper down by the barn after he and Father killed the chicken yesterday. He was about the color of that tablecloth when he came in. I don't know what he's up to now. As for the pie, Abby should be pinching the crust right now, so we can crack the eggs and mix up the filling."

Sure enough, Abby was coming out of the pantry, wearing an apron that went all the way to the floor. Her face was a patchwork of skin and flour, but she was holding a pie plate with a nicely crimped crust.

"Gorgeous," said Alice.

"Very pretty," said Emily.

"Some punishments bring great rewards, don't they," teased Rose.

"I want to go outside now," Abby said. "I want to collect the eggs now that the mean old hen has been put in the kettle."

"Run along then," said Rose, taking the pie. "But take off your apron first, and wipe your face. You look like the clown at the county fair."

Rose took down the composition book where her mother had recorded her special receipts. Sarah Hibbard had been known for the smooth perfection of her custard pies, always sought after at church suppers and socials. Rose had made the pie only once, with her mother standing beside her, but she thought she could do it again. And it would be so much better than serving apple, which everyone knew how to make. While Rose stirred sugar, eggs, cinnamon and the other ingredients together, Emily and Alice carefully picked the chicken meat off the bones, keeping the pieces as large as possible. Then they strained the cooking liquid through cheesecloth and set it aside for Rose to make the fricassee sauce. Rose knew fricassee was a French word and hoped Miss Harty wouldn't think she was putting on airs if she told her the name of the sauce. But that was what her mother had always called it.

"What are you going to wear tomorrow?" Alice asked Rose.

"I have only one dress for church," Rose said. "The dark blue wool one with the white lace collar and cuffs. I've already washed and ironed the collar and cuffs and put them back on."

"Are you going to have time for church?" Emily wanted to know. "You have to finish the dinner."

"Oh, yes," Rose said. "I will be up early, and I can have the chicken on the back of the stove in its sauce, and the flour and baking powder mixed for the dumplings. The potatoes will be simmering on the stove, too, and the carrots as well."

"You're going to leave all those things cooking when you go to church?" Alice asked. "My mother is afraid to leave things on the stove."

"It will be fine, as long as I don't put too many sticks

in the fire," Rose said. "Right now I have to think about something for the noon meal here. Are you both going to stay?"

"I'm going home now, if you don't need me any more," Alice said. "Mother has a list of chores for me for the afternoon, and I want to stop at the store on the way. I have two pennies to spend for candy. Or something else, if I'd rather."

"I'm staying," Emily said. "What are we eating?"

"Leftover scalloped potatoes, some cold slices of pot roast, and pickles," Rose said, getting the potatoes out of the icebox. She added a small amount of milk to the baking dish and put it in the oven, opening and closing the door quickly so she wouldn't send a draft of cool air over her custard pie, which she had put in the oven a few minutes ago.

"We have a little applesauce and some cookies for dessert," she added.

"I'll set the table," Emily said, heading for the dining room. "I want to sit next to you."

CHAPTER 6
John Barleycorn

Once the noon meal was over, Rose's father leaned back in his chair and dozed off. He had been up since before dawn, and Rose knew he had been out pretty late the night before because she had not heard him come in. While she and Emily and Abby cleared the table, he began to snore lightly, his head falling forward and then jerking upright before sagging again.

Rose had heated water on the stove for the dishes, and they quickly washed and wiped them. Charles dumped the dishwater outside and asked if he could build with his blocks for a while. Rose told him to go ahead, and sent Abby outside to play. Then she beckoned to Emily to follow her into the front room. Almost soundlessly, she closed the door and turned to her friend.

"Did you find out about 'the drink'?" she asked.

Emily looked down at the carpet, then out the window.

"Yes, I did," she said in a low voice.

"Well?"

"Being 'at the drink' means drinking things like hard cider and whiskey that have alcohol in them and sometimes make people drunk," Emily said. "Ma wanted to know why I was asking, and I told her I heard some boys talking at school about their fathers. She said the men were involved with someone she called John Barleycorn, and he was evil. She said people who were drunk did things they would never do if they were not 'at the drink.' And she said whiskey was expensive."

Rose thought of the sugar bowl and the missing coins. Was that where the money had gone? Was her father spending their money on hard cider and whiskey at the hotel? She knew men drank there. Some of them played cards, too.

"She said people take to the drink when they are unhappy or lonely or don't have anything to do. She said the alcohol makes them laugh, but it sometimes makes them feel really terrible the next day. Sick headaches and even the shakes," Emily finished with a rush. "Your father isn't shaking."

"I knew it was nothing good," Rose said. "Maybe it's just the funeral and all. Maybe he's just enjoying everyone's company at the hotel."

"Is he there every night?"

"Pretty nearly," Rose said. "And sometimes I don't hear him come home, so I know it's very late because I have so much trouble going to sleep."

"How can you not sleep? You must be tired in every bone by the time you finish your schoolwork and all the things my mother does in the evening," said Emily, who had been thinking a great deal about what Rose must be up to, keeping this house and all these people in order. It was certainly not something she wanted to do. She'd been noticing that if her mother sat down, her hands were still busy—mending or knitting or writing letters—and that she only sat down a short time before they went off to bed.

"I keep making lists in my head for the next day," Rose confessed, "because I'm so afraid I'll forget something and then Father will shout at me, or Abby and Charles won't have what they need. I don't know if I want to be a housewife when I grow up. It's much too hard."

"You," said Emily with great confidence, "are going to be a teacher. When you're emptying slop jars and washing sheets and dust mopping under beds, just remember that you are someday going to have a classroom all your own."

"I'd like that," Rose said, but she sounded very doubtful. Even while they were talking, the lists in her head kept growing and growing and growing.

"Shhh!" Rose said to Emily.

"I'm not talking," Emily retorted.

Rose put her finger over Emily's lips and pointed to the door that led to the kitchen. Then they both heard footsteps coming toward the door. As she saw the doorknob start to turn, Rose quickly began to straighten the newly ironed tablecloth on the sofa. Emily caught on immediately, and put out a hand to smooth the other end, just as the door opened.

"What in tarnation are you girls doing in here?" Rose's father said in a voice that made both of them jump.

"We put the fresh tablecloth in here after Alice and Emily ironed it," Rose said. "We didn't want anyone to sit on it. And we dusted and picked up the room, too, because we thought you would want it ready for Miss Harty tomorrow."

"Hmmm," he said, yawning and running his hands through his hair. "I must have dozed off after dinner."

"Yes, Father, you did," Rose answered.

Emily was still tugging at the tablecloth, moving it a little bit this way and that and accomplishing absolutely nothing. She was hoping he'd leave before she had to look up. Rose was handling everything very well, and Emily didn't want to make any mistakes. Mr. Hibbard looked quite fierce, from what she could see out of the corner of her eye.

"We will certainly entertain Miss Harty in the front room before dinner tomorrow, and perhaps afterward, if she doesn't leave immediately. So you were quite right to fix it up, and I suggest you leave the door open. The air in here is very stale."

And with that, Rose's father turned around, fetched his barn jacket from the hook by the kitchen door, and clumped out of the room. Emily felt as if her knees were giving out, so she sat right down on the floor and put her head in her hands.

"I couldn't look at him," she said. "And I couldn't look at you either. I was afraid he would know what I had been telling you about the drink."

"He just woke up," Rose said. "He didn't hear a thing. I was listening for him the whole time we were in here.

I don't want to make him angry, you know, especially with the teacher coming tomorrow. I hope she's going to tell him I have to go to school. He's using up the money, and I'm even more afraid that he's going to send me to the hat factory to do piecework."

"You promise me you'll remember every word that's said tomorrow," Emily said, pulling herself to her feet again and looking more like herself. "You were really perfect just now, you know. You didn't even turn red."

That night, despite her fears of sleeplessness, Rose was sound asleep when her father's heavy steps came up the stairs and woke her. As she came to, she realized he was talking to himself as he stumbled along the hallway. She had been quite worried the night before when he had advised them all to get to bed early, then said good-night and went out the door, again wearing a good shirt and his overcoat. Was he going to be at the drink again? Would he stay out late? What if he was sick with a head-ache or all shaky when Miss Harty came to dinner?

Then she heard Abby cry out, and she almost flew out of her bed and across the hall, her bare feet slap-ping on the floorboards. Her eyes quickly adjusting to the dark, she saw that Abby was sitting straight up in her small bed under the window.

"Kicked her bed by mistake," Father grumbled. "Must have moved it out when you were making it."

"But I didn't," Rose started to say and then woke up enough to stop right there. "C'mon, Abby," she said to the bewildered child. "You can sleep in my bed for the rest of the night."

"Leave her alone," Father said loudly. "Nothing wrong with her. If her confounded bed was in its usual place, she would still be sound asleep."

"She's a little scared, Father," Rose said in as quiet a tone as she could manage. "I'll just take her so you can get to bed in peace and get some rest. I don't mind."

When she bent to pick Abby up, the little girl wrapped her thin arms around Rose's neck as if her life depended on it. Rose made her way back to her own bed and whispered a very short story to Abby, who curled up against her and was asleep again in less time than it took to boil water. Rose sighed, heard her father begin to snore, and wondered if mothers spent half their lives listening for the sounds of other people sleeping. Emily was right. She would be a teacher instead. At least the pupils did not come home with you. She almost laughed then. Maybe the pupils didn't come home with you, but sometimes—if Miss Harty was any example—you went looking for the pupils at their homes.

She was wide-awake now and understood why she'd had no trouble finding Abby in the dark. The moon was quite bright, coming right in the window. She rolled over to look for the tree shadow on the floor, and there it was, black arms curving upward, just the little piece that could fit through the window. She loved the trees in November, when you could see their very bones against the sky, especially at sunset. She supposed they looked like that at dawn, too, but the hill just beyond their house stopped the sun from reaching her first thing in the morning.

Her father's snores grew even louder, a long pig-like noise followed by three little puffs. She wondered how her mother could have slept at all with that racket next to her ear. But he wasn't going out so much when Sarah was alive. Maybe the drink caused snoring, along with headaches and shakes.

She hadn't asked him about the coins in the sugar bowl. Somehow she hadn't dared. She had decided to wait until she had to buy something. Then she would have a reason to ask—and to find out how that money came to be there in the first place.

She didn't have much experience with money, but she was going to need something for the iceman each time he came. And she knew her mother always paid the man who peddled fish from a horse and wagon. He hadn't been around since the funeral, but he'd come along soon. When her mother sent her to the store, Mr. Tisdale or Mr. Goodnow just wrote it down on a card that had their name at the top. She supposed her father went in every now and then and settled up. Or maybe it was her mother. One more thing to put on the list in her head.

The list actually had shape and form, which she knew Emily would think was very odd. Rose visualized all the items on the list on a tablet, each of them in her mother's handwriting. As she considered this, lying there next to Abby, she decided she would never try the drink. She was strange enough already. It was time to count sheep, or think about a blue sky in June. But the lists in her mother's handwriting kept appearing on the blue background. And the hardest one to put out of her mind was the one headed: Teacher's Dinner. She heard the front room clock strike three, but she didn't hear four or five. By that time she was asleep, one arm around Abby's small body and the other curled under her own head.

She came to with a start, afraid she might have overslept. She started to jump out of bed and then remembered that Abby was there. She turned her head to see if she had wakened her, but the little girl didn't stir. She was sleeping on her back, her dark hair spread out over part of Rose's pillow, and her hands outside the quilt.

She looks so sweet, Rose thought, not like a crust eater at all. She wondered how such a person could grow up without a mother. I think I don't know anything, she thought, but Abby really doesn't know anything. She stopped herself. "That is too gloomy a way to start a day," she muttered half aloud. This is the day Miss Harty is coming to dinner. At the very thought, her stomach gave a little twitch, but she felt more excited than nervous.

She slid out of the bed, pulled out the chamber pot and squatted quickly. She put on the knitted booties her mother had made for her with leftover yarn—they had as many colors as Joseph's coat—and hurried downstairs to make breakfast. A kerosene lamp was lit in the kitchen, so she knew her father had already gone to the barn. To her relief, he had also shoved some wood into the big black stove, so the fire was beginning to warm the kitchen and was nearly ready for cooking. She measured oats into a kettle, added water from the pump and put the pan on the stove. She put water and coffee in another saucepan and set that on the stove.

She knew her mother sometimes lifted the lid out of the stovetop and lowered the pans right into the fire so things would cook faster, but she hated cleaning all that black off the pots. So she chose the slow route and easy cleanup, even though she wasn't sure what time Father would be in. It was nearly six o'clock, so it wouldn't be long.

With breakfast started, she sat down in her mother's rocker, close to the stove, and took a look at the Teacher's Dinner list in her head. She was ready, she knew that, but her stomach was acting like a nervous flapjack. What was the matter with her? She knew Miss Harty better than she knew anyone, outside of her own immediate family and Aunt Nell and Uncle Jason—and Emily.

She wished the cat would sit still. But the animal just kept pacing and pacing and pacing, making little mewing cries. As she bent down to pat his head, she heard her father. He'd be bringing the warm milk to the milk room, where he would strain it into clean milk cans. The cans would go in the cooler, which was packed with ice. And he'd bring a quart or so to her so she could let it separate and take the heavy cream off the top. He didn't sell milk on Sundays, so he'd be delivering double amounts tomorrow. So today was the day the family stocked up.

She'd better get a move on, as he was apt to tell her.

He'd think it was pretty peculiar to find her wearing her nightclothes in the kitchen. She picked up the hem of her nightgown and took the stairs two at a time, running as if she and Emily were pelting down a dirt road. In her room, breathing hard, she dressed and then woke Abby with a quick kiss on the forehead.

"We've lots to do after breakfast and before church, so you'd better get up," Rose said.

"What am I doing in here?" Abby demanded, rather cross at being wakened.

"Father scared you when he came in last night, so you came in to sleep with me."

"He scares me almost every night. Why is he out so late? Why does he always give me a smelly kiss and scratch me with all those whiskers? If I'm asleep, my dreams get bad right then. A porcupine or a skunk starts walking toward me, prickly or smelling bad. "What smells so bad?"

"It must be something he eats or drinks at the hotel," Rose said, edging away from the question. "Maybe his stomach isn't just right these days. Anyway, we'll have to figure something out so you don't get your sleep interrupted. You need sweet dreams, not nightmares. A porcupine indeed. Best you not tell him that!"

The idea of calling her father a porcupine made Abby laugh, and she pushed away the covers and hurried to her parents' room to get her everyday clothes.

"Put on underwear and stockings for church, and your old dress over them," Rose called after her. "That will save time later."

Back in the kitchen, Rose took the pot of chicken and its sauce out of the icebox. A layer of yellow fat covered the sauce, and she remembered her mother scooping that off. So she skimmed it away as best she could with a large spoon, and then put the kettle on the shelf above the stove. The chicken was basically cooked, so it wouldn't need to start stewing now.

Rose jumped when Abby's voice came suddenly from behind her. "Do I have time to feed the chickens before I eat?" the little girl wanted to know.

"Sakes, child, make noise with your feet when you come into the kitchen. I need to keep my skin on, or my bones will crumple."

"You sound just like Mother sometimes, Rose," Abby said. "Well? Shall I feed the chickens?"

"Can you do it without Charles?"

"Of course. Especially now that Miss Crosspatch is in the kettle instead of on the nest. The rest of the old biddies are quite nice to me," Abby said. "I hope she doesn't taste mean," she added with a questioning look.

"If they're cooked right, even the toughest old birds taste good. That's what Grandmother always says," Rose answered.

"Do you think it hurt her to get killed?" Abby wanted to know. "Charles said it was awful, with her head chopped off and feathers flying and blood everywhere. He said he didn't ever want to kill a chicken again. But he said Father told him he'd have to do it a lot of times. Did it hurt her?"

"Getting your head chopped off probably hurts for at

least a second or two," Rose said. "But don't worry over it. Think how happy your fingers are going to be."

Abby headed out with a basket in her hand, and Rose smiled. She didn't like to think of the headless hen herself, especially before breakfast for heaven's sake, but it was nice that Abby was no longer afraid of the henhouse. She could probably take over that job entirely, and Charles could pick up the slack somewhere else. And slack was one thing they had plenty of. Hearing her father's heavy steps, Rose gave the oatmeal a quick stir, pushing the slightly crusted edges into the center of the pan. When he paused to take off his boots—one thing Sarah had made plain was that the smell and the mess of the barn did not belong in her kitchen—Rose took down a warm bowl from the upper shelf of the stove and filled it.

He grunted a good morning from the doorway, washed his hands at the pump, and Rose placed the steaming bowl in front of him as he sat down in the dining room. "Well, that's not bad service," he rumbled. Better than just plain "not bad," Rose thought, bringing in a pitcher of milk and a smaller pitcher of maple syrup.

With his shoulders bent and his face not far from the bowl, he spooned the cereal into his mouth. Some of the oats caught in his mustache, some in his thick beard. He appeared not to notice, and she hoped he would comb the flecks out before church and dinner. At least the mustache cup kept the coffee away from the hair. Now that was a vessel invented by someone tired of soggy hair above his lip. The cup had a little band across the top where the drinker's mustache rested. A space for sipping opened at the edge of the cup. Very clever, she thought, even though it was a little hard to get at the coffee stains under that little shelf.

"You going to church this morning?" he asked.

"We all are, Father."

"And dinner will be on time?"

"I think so. I made the fricassee sauce yesterday, and Abby did the piecrust, and the dumplings will go in at the last minute. If it's acceptable to you, sir, I would like to sit near the back and leave during the last hymn, just to have a few extra minutes."

"Why not? Most all the goodness has been given out by that time, and you will just miss the ladies asking you how you are and how we are and how we are getting along without your mother. I expect you have had your fill of that, just as I have."

He looked up then, the spoon halfway to his mouth, and paused.

"It is not the same, and it will never be the same again. But we are getting on aren't we?"

"I think so, Father."

She saw his eyes get all watery before he turned his head to look out the window. She went to the kitchen for her own bowl of oatmeal, wondering if it was going to settle into her stomach properly. When she sat down, her father had begun eating again, his attention on the oatmeal.

"Where's Charles?" he said a minute later.

"Oh, I forgot to see if he was awake, and I haven't seen him." She jumped up, jostling the table enough to make the utensils rattle in the spoon holder, and hurried to the bottom of the attic stairs.

"Charles? Charles? Are you getting up today?"

"I'm coming now," came the muffled answer. "I'm getting dressed for church."

In about five minutes, Charles appeared. He was wearing his best clothes, and Rose almost laughed when she saw how he had tried to get his hair under control. It was always falling over his forehead, and he had slicked it down with water, probably from the basin in his room.

"How nice you look," she said, giving him a smile that helped cover the laugh trying to escape from her mouth.

"When the teacher comes to dinner . . ." Charles began.

"Charles doesn't feed the chickens," Abby finished.

His face fell.

"What's this?" Father said, suddenly paying attention to the children's chatter. "Have the chickens gone without their breakfast?"

"Oh, no," Rose reassured him. "Abby was up so early that she fed and watered the chickens and brought in a few eggs before her breakfast. She's going to do it by herself now that the finger-pecking hen is . . ." She looked at Charles, whose face was getting a little white. "Now that she's no longer there," Rose finished abruptly.

Charles went to the kitchen quickly, saying he was

going to get his own oatmeal. He fussed around the stove for several minutes and returned, bowl in hand, apparently recovered from his brief recall of the chicken's fate. Rose let her breath out slowly. She was beginning to think her mother spent the day jumping from one ice floe to another, just like Eva in Uncle Tom's Cabin. Family living wasn't a matter of life and death, but you just couldn't tell when you were going to be teetering on the edge of something that might crack down the middle. Once again, she wondered how her mother managed to make it seem as if everything was running smoothly. Had Sarah's stomach kept flopping around like a newly caught fish?

"We'd better get these dishes to the kitchen," she said. "And if you two will take care of them, I'll get the clean tablecloth and set up for dinner. Are you going to church with us, Father?"

"Yes, and I'd better get a move on, too."

He picked up his own dishes and took them to the sink where Abby was tying a big apron over Charles' good clothes.

"You do the drying there, Charles," he said. "Abby still has to get dressed for church. She's done chores already today."

"Yes, sir. I'll help with the barn chores later, sir, to make up for not waking up early."

"It's all right, Charles, it's all right. You probably had some extra growing to do last night," Father said, giving him a little pat on the top of his head.

CHAPTER 7
Banishing Barleycorn

Abby poked Rose in the ribs when Emily came into church and moved down the aisle to a pew in the center of the church. The sisters were sitting by themselves in the back row so they could leave early without attracting attention. When Emily noticed that she and her family were sitting right behind Charles and his father, she looked left and right for Rose and then turned around in her seat before her mother could stop her.

She caught Rose's eye, just as her mother's hand turned her shoulder to the front again. Abby gave her sister another poke, and Rose whispered, "I'll be black and blue before this service is over if you don't stop that. God does not like little girls who stick their elbows in their sister's ribs."

Abby almost giggled, and Rose gave her a poke. That made her giggle out loud, and Mrs. Munson peered around the people next to her to see who was misbehaving. Rose nodded and smiled at her. Why was Mrs. Munson so interested in what everyone else was doing? Then the widow sat back, out of sight again.

The minister, a tall, thin man wearing a plain black robe, solemnly took his place up front. The music began, and they all stood up to sing. That was when Rose saw Miss Harty, toward the front on the left-hand side, wearing a black cloak, and a hat with a long black and brown feather curling toward her face. Elegant, thought Rose.

As the service moved forward, she kept looking at that wonderful hat. She couldn't keep her mind on the prayers and scriptures anyway. She had lists rolling through her head, along with pictures of the table and the kitchen and the plates and the dessert. She kept wondering what Sarah would have done differently if she were there when the teacher came to dinner.

Suddenly she focused on the minister. She was quite sure the other track in her mind had heard him say "hard cider," and she knew that cider was part of "the drink." He couldn't have said that, she thought, but she began to listen.

"The hard cider and the whiskey are the undoing of this town's piety," Mr. Lockhead said. "We cannot consider ourselves true Christians, true followers of the word of God, if we have among us those who are drunk and therefore out of touch with their Maker."

He went on and on and on about the evils of drinking, about the tavern and the hotel where these evils were part of daily business, and about the men who wasted their money and destroyed their minds on liquor.

"We must unite on this matter," Mr. Lockhead said, speaking now in a near shout. "We will join with our brethren in Christ, the Baptist parish and the Methodist church, to wipe out this devilish habit in our country town."

And then he announced plans made with the other churches to hold temperance meetings for a week in January in the various churches, and again during the summer in tents on the town green.

"It will be a time for men and women of good will to come together and pledge that liquor will be banished from their homes and from their bodies forever," Mr. Lockhead thundered. "Let us pray."

Rose had her ears on Mr. Lockhead and her eyes on her father and brother's backs. For the whole sermon, her father's head was slightly bent. When the minister said, "Let us pray," he raised his head, and did not bow for the prayer. Was he looking directly at heaven, Rose wondered.

It was time for the closing hymn, and Abby jabbed Rose once more with her elbow. They stood, slipped out of the pew and headed for the door. When the singing started, they pushed the big door open and then closed it softly. Picking up their skirts, the two girls ran along the road toward their house. They knew they had a head start on everyone. The hymn had six verses, and Mr. Lockhead had made it clear in the past that all the words were meaningful. He never let the congregation skip verses. Then he would march down the aisle and pronounce a benediction from the back of the church. And then everyone would stop on the steps to shake his hand and say good morning.

Rose figured the topic of his sermon gave her a couple of extra minutes. People would be commenting on that, much more than they did when he talked about biblical topics like Noah's construction of the ark, or Ruth's love for Naomi, or how God spared Abraham's son at the last minute. She herself liked all those stories, especially if they were just told as stories. The Reverend Lockhead, of course, always had to give the lesson that everyone was supposed to get from the stories. Sarah had said he made the connection between the Bible and their daily lives.

She did hope the river would never flood so high that they'd have to build an ark. Uncle Jason could certainly manage that part, but she didn't want to be on a boat with a pair of skunks, a pair of porcupines and a pair of rats. The deer would be all right, she guessed.

"You are not answering me," Abby's voice said.

"Sorry. I didn't hear you."

"You never hear me," Abby said in a slightly whining tone.

"Just repeat it."

"What are you and Father and Miss Harty going to talk about at the table? Father said Charles and I were to be quiet while you talked. So what are you going to talk about?"

"I have no idea," Rose said, as her stomach lurched for the seventh time that day. "I hope the two of them will take care of all the conversation. You and I will be busy serving Miss Crosspatch and the custard pie."

"I hope she's tender," Abby said.

Halfway through dinner, Rose began to relax. Her father had said grace before anyone started eating, neither Abby nor Charles had spilled anything, the long cooking had taken every shred of meanness out of the chicken, and the dumplings were fluffy. Father had for some reason pulled out Miss Harty's chair and waited for her to sit down when Rose called them to the table, but the teacher thanked him, so it must have been something she expected.

Rose had indicated that the teacher should sit in Abby's place next to Rose, because at the last minute, she realized no one would enjoy dinner with Miss Harty in Sarah's seat. But it didn't seem awkward to ask Abby to sit there, near the kitchen, where she'd be handy to help out. Rose saw her father raise his eyebrows, but he didn't comment. It would have been rather strange, she thought, to crowd everyone in and leave the end of the table empty.

Miss Harty was wearing a green, silky looking dress with a plain white collar and cuffs, and a large cameo pin at the neckline. Father complimented her on the pin and made some remarks about the cold weather. He asked whether she had enough wood at the school to keep warm for the winter and whether the older boys took care of the fire for her. He was very polite, and when Rose brought in the platter with the chicken, he dished it up for each person and then gave himself a generous helping. After that, it was silent on his side of the table. He bent over slightly, his forearms resting on the edge of the table, his head bending to meet each forkful of food, as was his wont.

Miss Harty began to talk almost steadily, making much more conversation than the family usually had at table. She praised the dinner, telling Rose that she certainly would like the recipe for the fricassee. She noticed the print of George Washington on the wall and said she had always liked that Gilbert Stuart portrait. She admired the linen cloth, which looked almost smooth, and Rose told her Emily and Alice had come to help iron it. She asked Abby what she was reading in school, and told Charles he was so tall now that she thought he must be a big help around the farm.

Charles looked at his father, who had told him not to talk at this meal, and looked back at the teacher, who had just asked a question. He had no idea whether to answer, or to obey his parent. That's when Rose saw Father's head come up.

"Are you writing a report on us?" he asked in the steely tone that always made the children wish they could hide in the pantry.

"Why, whatever do you mean?" Miss Harty said in her most pleasant tone.

"You keep talking about everything in this house and on this table. You have never asked to come to dinner before, so I figure you came to see if we were eating proper and keeping clean and taking care of each other."

"I am very fond of Rose, Mr. Hibbard," the teacher answered in a voice so gentle that Rose could hardly hear her. "I know that she—all of you—have suffered a great loss, a sudden, shocking loss. I would like to be a friend, especially to Rose. Girls need an older woman to talk to, just as Charles would need a man if something happened to you. I'm sorry if I have talked too much, but I often eat alone, so it is a great pleasure for me to be with a family like this."

Father's body relaxed toward his plate again. He took a sizable mouthful of chicken and dumplings, and before he finished chewing, he said, "Forgive me, if that sounded rude. We are a little tired of questions here. I do not mean to be standoffish, but we are doing the best we can without a grown woman in the house. I know you mean well, but talking about our troubles does not produce any new answers. Rose knows as well as anyone that we cannot go on this way into the spring season, with calves and baby chicks and then the haying. She will be able to stay in school through the winter I expect, but after that, we will need her here at home."

A scrap of dumpling stopped halfway down Rose's throat. She coughed; then coughed again. Her face grew red, not from embarrassment this time, but because she was having trouble breathing. School? No school? This was the moment she had been dreading ever since the funeral, but she hadn't expected it today, hadn't even thought about it today.

Miss Harty stood quickly and gave her a hard thump in the middle of her back. The dumpling went down, the coughing stopped, and her face started to return to its normal color. Suddenly she was mortified. She had caused a scene at the table with her choking. She felt the pink coming back into her cheeks.

"Rose is such a good student, Mr. Hibbard," Miss Harty began. She hesitated.

"I know that just as well as you do, Miss Harty," Father said. "But she also has new responsibilities here."

"Perhaps there's some other way," the teacher said, an anxious frown creating two creases between her eyebrows.

"I see no other way," Father said, in a voice that Charles and Rose knew well. This, Rose thought to herself, is when Sarah's mouth used to disappear. She wondered how her own mouth looked at that moment. She had put her hands in her lap, holding them together as tightly as she could, to prevent her whole body from shaking.

Her dreams had just flown out the window as if they were birds who had found the cage door open. She would never be a teacher. She would never even be a clerk in Mr. Goodnow's dry goods store. She wouldn't even work in the hat factory. She would just cook and clean and buy the ice and feed the cat and iron and wash, and wash and iron. She would get up in the morning smiling, and go to bed grim and tired.

I don't want to be my mother, she thought, and instantly wondered how she could think such a horrid thing. Her mother had been wonderful. She missed her so. And now, it came to her in a rush, she missed her for another giant reason. She missed her because it was Sarah who had stood between her and a future she would hate.

She felt tears sting her eyes and blinked rapidly to make them go away. She could not cry now. She had to hold up. She had spent days planning this dinner, and it was not over.

"I'll get the pie," she said, pushing her chair back and standing up, hoping her legs would behave.

"I'll clear," Charles said, giving Abby a look.

"I will help," the little girl said. She moved toward her father's place to take his plate, and said in a small voice, "Father, how can Rose become a teacher if she doesn't go to school?"

"We will discuss this later," Father said. He turned to Miss Harty, who was looking down at her plate and was as still as a statue, and said, "Will you have tea with your pie, Miss Harty?"

She pulled on the bright white cuffs of her dress for an instant and then looked up.

"Yes, thank you, Mr. Hibbard. I take it with a little milk if you have it."

Rose went quickly to the pantry and closed the door. A great shuddering sob shook her body. The sound was so loud that she thought everyone in the dining room must have heard it. Her grandmother would say she sounded like a sick calf, Rose thought, trying to choke down the second sob, which was fighting toward the surface.

She picked up the pie and took it to the kitchen.

"Abby," she said, "maybe you'd like to take this in since you did such a good job on the crust. You could set it in front of Miss Harty and ask her to cut it."

"Rose," Abby said, taking the pie. "What about you being a teacher? Father didn't answer me." The little girl looked so upset that Rose almost burst into tears, but she swallowed hard and repeated what her father had said.

"We'll talk about it later. Right now we have company, you know."

Abby slowly turned toward the dining room and walked very carefully with the beautiful custard pie.

"I made the crust," she said, putting the pie in front of Miss Harty. "Rose wants you to cut it. I'll get the pie server."

The pie server was silver, and it was one of the few things among the dishes and spoons and glassware that appealed to Abby. It was pointed and had holes cut in it in a flowery pattern, and the handle had flowers on it, and the initial S.

"Mother said this is called 'pierced'," Abby said, pointing to the pattern. "And the 'S' is for Sherman, which was her maiden name. That's why we have grandparents whose last name is Sherman. They live in Vermont now."

Miss Harty looked at Abby gratefully. She admired the pie server, and now that her attention had been distracted from the alarming news she had just heard from Rose's father, she took a good look at the pie.

"Why, this pie is exquisite," she exclaimed.

"Rose made the filling," Abby said. "But I really did do the crust. I used to eat crusts, just nibble around the top of the pie when no one was looking. Mother was very angry when I did that one day because she thought it ruined the pie. So I had to make crusts until they were perfect. I think I made a hundred."

"Abby!" Charles said, coming back to clear more of the dinner fixings. "You never made a hundred. That would take years."

"Well, I made a lot," the little girl said stubbornly.

"And you learned to do it perfectly," Miss Harty said, almost able to smile again.

Rose, who was still having trouble controlling her need to wail and scream and perhaps even pound on the table, heard all this in spite of herself. And like Miss Harty, she almost smiled through her tears. Abby was babbling like a brook, filling up the silence that had followed her father's pronouncement. Did the little girl know what she was doing? Rose had a feeling—because she knew how much Abby loved her—that her little sister knew exactly what she was doing; at least at her eight-year-old level.

Miss Harty made a careful, clean cut across the pie. She turned it, and with what seemed like great concentration, divided it carefully. Charles watched, fascinated. She was doing it in fractions, just the way his teacher put diagrams on the board to teach them fourths and sixths and eighths. He hoped she wouldn't carve the pie into little sixteenths.

"I will need plates, please," Miss Harty said in a steady voice.

Charles brought plates from the cupboard in the corner of the room, and put them down in a stack next to Miss Harty's place. Neatly, she extracted the first piece and slid it onto a plate.

"The first piece is sometimes so hard to get out," she said, "but this is a beautiful pie." She handed the plate to Rose's father with a smile. Mr. Hibbard's beard wobbled a bit as he gave her a small smile back.

"Thank you," he said. "I hope . . ."

She looked at him the way she looked at the big boys when they slammed their books around or made too much noise with their feet.

"I hope it tastes as good as it looks," he said weakly. Rose returned to the table, placing mugs of tea at Miss Harty's place and at her father's. She sat down, eyes on her place, hands in her lap.

"Pass this one to Rose, Charles," Miss Harty said. In a few minutes, they were all eating the pie.

"Not bad," said Father. "Not bad at all."

CHAPTER 8
Kick the Cat

Rose had put a pan of water on the stove right after she ladled the chicken onto her mother's best platter, so when it was time to do the dishes, hot water was available. Now, with the partly eaten pie still on the table and her father gone to the barn, she picked up the pan of hot water and carefully poured half of it into the chicken kettle, which she had already rinsed with cold water from the pump.

She took the platter from the top shelf of the stove and began to swish away the small scraps of biscuit and the little globules—now there was a word she really liked—of sauce. As her dishcloth moved over the platter, she felt her shoulders start to relax. She must be careful of this particular dish. It was precious to all of them. It was useful, too, she thought, not just a pretty thing. It was turned up at the edges so the sauce could not run off. She wished she could remember where it had come from. It had belonged to either Sarah's mother or mother-in-law.

As she scrubbed, she wondered how many chickens had been served on those delicate green flowers. The platter was still perfectly smooth to the touch and hadn't a nick or crack, but it was covered with a tracery of fine lines that seemed to be below the surface. She could not think what her mother had called those lines that looked like cracks but were not. She rubbed a cake of soap rapidly between her hands and rinsed them in the pot to get more suds. Abby was at her elbow, her apron on and a clean dishtowel in her hand, ready to dry the dishes. She's being so good, she'll make me cry all over again, Rose thought.

"I'll carry them away," Charles announced, coming up just behind Abby. "I don't think there's room out here for the rest of the dirty dishes, so I left them on the table."

"Fine," Rose said, snuffling a little as she bent over the sink. "But you'd better rinse these things before Abby dries them, or we'll have soap for dinner next Sunday." Crazed, she suddenly remembered. When all those little lines appeared on china, the glaze was crazed. That was the word Sarah had used.

She was crazed, too, and getting more so by the minute, the more she thought about what Father had said at the table. Did that mean she had cracks just below the surface? Did it mean she looked the same on the outside? Would she and the platter shatter into a thousand pieces when they became too crazed? A terrible shudder ran along her shoulders and down her back, then split into two and turned both her legs into rubber. It was gone in an instant, and Rose had not made a single sound. But she knew both Abby and Charles had seen it. They were staring at her. Both their mouths were opening as if they were going to speak, but they didn't say anything. She must have looked like a tree in a windstorm, all atremble.

Just then, Miss Harty pushed open the kitchen door. She had asked about the outhouse and had gone to use it. Rose frowned a little. She'd been gone a long time. From the corner of her eye, however, Rose could see that the teacher looked all right. She was a little red around the eyes, probably from the smell in the outhouse, but she didn't look sick. Rose wondered what a family would do if they fed the teacher dinner and she came down with a stomach sickness right afterward.

"I'd better be going along," Miss Harty said. She paused a minute, looking at the way the three had organized the dishwashing. Charles was taking a dipper of steaming water from the stove to the sink to rinse soapy dishes, and Abby was handling the hot plates carefully.

"I would have thought you'd have running water here," she said. "You're just off the main street, and most everyone along here has water piped into the house. It doesn't require a pump, you know, because it's a gravity-fed system."

Grateful not to talk about school, Rose finally looked up from the sink. "I'm pretty sure we could have it," she said. "I heard Mother and Aunt Nell talking about the water and how much easier it would be. Aunt Nell has faucets now, and she has a water tank connected to her stove so she can have running hot water, too. But we don't get newfangled things here."

The teacher looked puzzled, but she didn't ask what that meant. Instead she said, "It would make housework and cooking and everything much easier for all of you. Perhaps you could ask your father . . ." She stopped abruptly and reached for her cloak. She put it on, then reached an arm toward Rose and pulled her close. Enveloped by the soft black wrap and surprised by the gesture, Rose nearly crumpled against the teacher.

But she knew she must hold up. She straightened and said, "Perhaps I will. We are very glad you could come today, Miss Harty."

The teacher rarely missed signals, whether they were from whistling trains or purring cats. She knew she must let Rose go, so she did. Then she thanked them all with great formality, and asked Charles if he would show her where her horse might be. "Your father put her in the barn, I think," she said.

Charles pulled on a coat and went out the door with the teacher. Rose sank into the rocking chair in front of the stove, put her hands over her face and her head on her knees. She began to rock, and as she rocked, she sobbed with such grief that Abby almost ran from the room. Instead, she tiptoed over to Rose, who was crying too hard to hear footsteps anyway, and laid her face against her sister's hair. After a minute, Rose reached out and put her arm around the little girl, who burst into tears herself.

They must have cried for five or ten minutes, pausing to wipe each other's faces with the edges of their aprons, and then starting all over again. It seemed impossible to squelch these sobs, which kept coming, one after the other, like puffs of smoke from a chugging locomotive. Rose knew she wasn't doing the right thing by Abby. Here she was, blatting like a cow, and she had made an eight-year-old cry, too. She sat up, pulled Abby onto her lap and said, "We have to stop this right now. We are going to run out of tears, and then our eyeballs will dry up like red kidney beans and fall out on the floor."

Abby took a long look at Rose's eyes before she answered. "Yours look very wet," she said, "so I don't think they're going to fall out right now. How are mine?"

Rose solemnly inspected the upturned face.

"You will be all right this time," she said.

Abby started to grin. "That was supposed to be amusing, wasn't it?" she asked. "I just wasn't ready to laugh. But now I feel better. I must have had too much water in there in the first place."

That made Rose smile. Perhaps, she thought to herself, this was a good thing, this outburst. Perhaps Abby really did have too much stored up inside, and her own wailing had given the little girl a chance to let it out. Silver linings, she thought. Sarah always talked about silver linings. Well, even Sarah would have to say that only a small part of this cloud carried any bit of silver lining. But Abby's waterfall was a small good thing.

The big gray cat came out from behind the stove, stuck his tail up in the air where it curved as if it had been shaped into an "S," and walked past Rose, rubbing hard against her skirt. He turned and went back again, pushing against her. He turned and did it a third time, then made a loud mewing sound that was close to a whine. Rose scooped him up, and the two girls were stroking the cat and taking comfort in each other when they heard feet running through the ell toward the kitchen door. Two seconds later, Charles burst through the door as if he had been pushed, slammed it behind him and sat down on the woodbox, panting.

"Who's chasing you?" Rose asked, frowning a little. "Are you all right?"

"Oh, I'm just fine," Charles said. "But I came to tell you that Father and the teacher had a big row after I took her horse out of the barn. She and I were hitching up the horse to her buggy when Father came around the corner of the barn and saw us. We finished with the harness, and she climbed into the buggy and pulled a blanket over her knees. She was about to go . . ."

"Charles," Rose said sternly. "Are you going to tell us about the row?"

"Well, yes. But I wanted you to hear everything."

"All right. Go on."

Charles took a deep breath. "Father's face was all red, and he yelled at her to wait, so she pulled in on the reins. He saw me and told me to skedaddle, so I came to the house. But I could hear their voices pretty loud, so I went all the way around and hid by the woodshed where I could hear everything."

"What were they talking about?" Rose asked, almost as breathless as her brother.

"You."

"Are you going to tell us?"

Pleased with the attention he was getting, Charles opened his mouth to speak just as they heard heavy boots coming toward the kitchen door. Rose jumped up so quickly that Abby nearly fell down as she was catapulted from her lap. They both went to the sink and started doing dishes again. Charles picked up a dishtowel and began to wipe some of the rinsed flatware, now quite cold. When their father opened the door, he saw a busy trio, cleaning up the remains of Sunday dinner. His face was still red, angry red. His feet hit the floor with hard thumps, and he had not left his barn boots in the ell.

"Not done with those dishes yet?" he growled. "Take you three a month of Sundays to get a simple job finished."

He started for the stairs just as the cat came out from under the rocking chair. The animal stretched his front legs, yawned, and then gave another of those whining cries that had become part of the household sound since Sarah's death. Rose and Charles were facing the sink, trying to keep their faces as blank as possible, but Abby had just turned to get another stack of dirty dishes, so she saw the booted foot shoot out; saw her father kick the cat; saw the cat fly across the room and hit the frame of the front room door.

The cat let out a piercing yowl, and as Rose and Charles whirled to see what was going on, they heard Abby shriek, "Father, you hurt Mother's cat."

"Goldurned animal isn't worth the fur on its back," Father said, as he went on to the hall and up the stairs.

The cat scooted through the open door of the front room and disappeared behind the Morris chair before any of the children could move even an eyelid. Then Abby ran to the front room and fell on her hands and knees, reaching out her hand and calling, "Kitty, here Kitty, it's all right, it's all right," in her softest cat-talking voice. Rose felt the sobs coming up from the depths of her stomach again, but she knew she must comfort Abby and make sure Charles was all right.

"Rose," Charles said in a shaky voice, "he's angry about the teacher, Rose. We'd better finish up here and get outside for a while so I can tell you. I have to tell you now."

Charles' words were barely getting into her ears and her brain, but she backtracked, the way she did when she was caught daydreaming in class, and replayed what he had said.

"All right," she said, choking back the third or fourth sob. "Abby, you come back here and help us finish quickly. The cat needs a few minutes to himself, and then we'll get him and take a Sunday afternoon walk to the river."

Charles started to say, "In this weather?" but instead let out a long breath and started drying dishes so fast that Rose figured they'd lose half of them. But he didn't drop a one, and within five or six minutes, the children had finished putting things away. They heard footsteps in the upstairs hall, so they grabbed their wraps from the pegs by the woodbox, and headed for the door. Rose called the cat, but he would not come, and she decided the animal would be safe enough behind the chair. She pulled the front room door shut and followed Abby and Charles.

The children ran to the road in front of their house, made a quick turn and then another. It had taken less than two minutes, Rose thought, for them to get out of sight. They crossed the main road and took the path next to the old schoolhouse, heading for the river. The water was high when they reached the big willow tree, where they had spent hours at all times of the year. Rose looked at the November sky, the bare branches of the willow and the torrent of water rushing over the rocks. It seemed such a long time ago that she and her mother had walked down here, gathered fall asters and stopped in the shade of the big tree to get out of a too warm September sun.

"Only mad dogs and Englishmen go out in the noonday sun," Sarah used to say. Rose never knew exactly what that meant, except that it didn't sound as if Englishmen were very smart. She sighed, remembering, and both children turned to look at her.

"Are you all right?" Abby demanded, her face pinched

with worry. "Will you just go to school anyway and stay up all night to do the housework?"

"Miss Harty wants to help," Charles said. "She says you are ex . . .exceptional, I think it was."

"That's a good thing," Rose told him, feeling a little surge of pleasure that made the stone in her stomach a bit lighter. "What else did she say?"

"Well," Charles said, "Father told her he wasn't going to stand for no interference with the bringing up of his children. He said she was hired to teach at the school and that's all. Then he really started to yell, and he told her she should mind her own business when she was outside the school, that she was being pretty uppity for a teacher."

"Did Miss Harty say anything?" Rose asked.

"She kept saying, 'Mr. Hibbard, Mr. Hibbard,' in a quiet voice, but he didn't really hear her. Finally, she raised her voice, and she said, 'You must let me talk for a minute, sir.' The 'sir' was kind of loud. That's when Father stopped yelling, and she said you were 'exceptional' in every way in school, and that she was not trying to tell him what to do, but she hoped there would be some way for you to stay in school and become a teacher."

Rose could hardly breathe at this point, and Abby was sitting so still that she looked like a small statue.

"Father said you had no business thinking about working out somewhere when the family needed you at home, and that teachers just ended up being old maids anyway, and he expected you would marry a fine young man and have children of your own someday."

"What's an old maid, Rose?" Abby interrupted.

"A woman who never gets married," Rose said. "Go on, Charles."

"Miss Harty didn't like that. She said you had a lot to give to the world, and she wanted you to get a chance to give it, and you could get married later on if you met someone you liked. Father said he wasn't thinking about the world, he was thinking about his household and his children. He said his wife was gone, and the family was on hard times, and you would have to give up things because that was what women did.

"Miss Harty's voice was softer after that, and I couldn't hear everything she said, but it was something about him getting water and someone to take care of the washing. That made him really angry, and he started yelling again. He told her womenfolk were all the same, wanting every newfangled thing that came along, and that you could get along with what you had. He said money didn't grow on trees."

"Even I know that," Abby said.

Charles gave her a look that told her she had better keep quiet. "Then Miss Harty said, 'Oh, newfangled, eh? I see.' I didn't see at all," Charles said, his eyebrows pulled together, "and apparently Father didn't either because he said, 'What's that supposed to mean, Miss?' And Miss Harty didn't say anything. Then I heard a slapping noise. I think he gave her horse a whack because the wheels of her buggy started to roll, and he said, 'I think you should git now. I've had enough of this.' Miss Harty said she would be talking to him again soon, and he said, 'Not if I can help it,' and she left."

Charles looked at Rose, who was starting to cry again. He reached out one hand and put it on her arm, and she put her other hand over it. She tried to smile at him, but she couldn't. Abby was crying again, too, and Charles looked as if he wished boys were allowed to do that.

"What are we going to do?" Abby asked.

"We are going to stop adding all this salty water to the river," Rose said, "or it will overflow its banks. We're going to pull ourselves together and go back to the house where we all have chores to do. If Father says I have to leave school, then I will have to leave. You both know that. But we can certainly put our thinking caps on and see if we can find any way to make things better. You must keep in mind that when we lost our mother, he lost his wife. Maybe when he is not feeling so sad about that, he will change his mind about school."

"You're very brave, Rose," Charles said.

"You are both brave, too, Charles," Rose said, thinking how true that was, and wondering at the same time if Father had listened to the Rev. Lockhead and whether he would go to the church temperance meetings.

"Not me," Charles said in a rare moment of total honesty. "I can't even watch a chicken die without getting sick."

"That is not the same thing," Rose said firmly. "And now we'd better get up or we will catch our death from sitting on this cold, damp rock for so long." She gave Charles' hand a small pat and stood, pulling Abby to her feet as well.

Each holding one of Abby's hands, Rose and Charles started walking back toward the main street and their house. As they came to the edge of the road, they heard their father's voice coming from the back porch in a bellow.

"Rose! Charles! Abigail! Answer me. Answer me now!"

CHAPTER 9
Nodding Off

Two weeks went by, and no one mentioned Miss Harty or the Sunday dinner. Rose worked harder and harder at home, trying to keep everything in order without any fuss, hoping Father would change his mind about school. She went to bed late, sometimes so tired she couldn't fall asleep even when she tried to think about a blue and cloudless summer sky. She was up early, often finding the kitchen dark and the fire nearly out because Father had not yet gone to the barn.

She found she couldn't fall asleep until she heard him come up the stairs, and some nights the clock struck ten or eleven times before he came home. She wondered if he had trouble falling asleep, and thus, trouble getting up again in the morning. In school, where she had to sit still, she had quite a different problem. She couldn't stay awake. She tried hard to hold her head up, but it kept bobbing. She remembered the day Emily had told her she needed to hitch her head on tighter because it was always floating off. This was different. This was like having your neck break. Slowly her chin would sink toward her chest and then she would snap upward, looking quickly to see if anyone had noticed, and trying at the same time to pick up the thread of what Miss Harty was saying or doing.

Did that happen to Father when he was milking the cows? She had a picture in her mind of the way he placed the little three-legged stool beside the cow, balanced the shiny milk pail between his knees, and leaned in to draw out the milk with quick, strong strokes. His head was nearly touching the cow's flank. Did he sometimes just fall asleep there? The pail would fall, she was sure. She had dropped a pencil one day when she was dozing, and when it hit the floor it sounded very loud inside her head.

Once in a while she was almost certain Miss Harty had been watching her, but the teacher's eyes seemed to be on some spot over Rose's head, so she couldn't be sure. Besides, she knew she'd have to stay after school if the teacher actually caught her sleeping. Miss Harty didn't have much patience with those who didn't pay attention. Sometimes Rose's eyelids closed without warning, but her head didn't fall over. She would hear children reciting their lessons—it sounded far away—while she had what she supposed was a catnap. She had noticed many times that when the cat stretched out during the daytime, his eyes were closed, but he wasn't really asleep. He opened them in tiny slits at the slightest sound or movement, so Rose thought he was pretending. At night, sprawled out in front of the warm kitchen stove, he slept as if he were dead.

She wished she could sleep like that at night. Sometimes lately, she'd even wished she were dead. When that thought crept into her mind, she always shoved it aside right away, knowing she had no room for such ideas. Things were bad enough with her there in the house. She knew they would be worse if she were gone. Still, they said in church that Sarah had gone to heaven, and perhaps if Rose were dead too, she could join her there. Would her mother be angry that Rose always called her Sarah in her mind these days? Would she understand that the very word "mother" put that cold stone into her stomach once again and pushed all that water into her eyes?

Rose vaguely knew that she was napping, so she tugged at her mind and her eyelids, but she couldn't pull herself back into the classroom. Her mind was hearing a spelling lesson, and tending to its own thoughts as well. She guessed she wasn't quite like the cat. He would have been able to open his eyes, and hers felt as if they had been sealed with the paste she and her grandmother had made last Christmas. Pretty soon she'd be mixing up flour and water to make that paste again, helping Charles and Abby cut strips of red and green paper to make chains for the Christmas tree. She didn't think Grandma Sherman would be here, not so soon after coming for the funeral. They'd make popcorn and thread it for the tree. Maybe Father would let them have one of the special candles from the store to go on the top of the tree. The pupils' voices faded as her dream about Christmas became brighter and clearer.

Then Rose's head sank slowly, all the way to the top of her desk. Her tired brain had won out. She was sound asleep. Miss Harty saw the head drop and noticed that Newton Barnes, who sat behind Rose, was about to give her a little nudge. Miss Harty waved her hand at him and put her finger to her lips.

"Shhh," she said. "Let her rest for a bit."

The whole class turned to look at Rose and then back at Miss Harty. Some giggled, others looked amazed that the teacher wasn't marching down the aisle to give Rose a sharp tap on the shoulder.

"Teacher's pet," muttered one of the older boys at the back of the room.

"Bite your tongue," Newton whispered back.

"Shhh," Miss Harty said again, putting her finger to her lips with one hand, and lightly tapping her pointer on the blackboard, where work was written out for the older students to copy.

"Go on with your handwriting lesson, please," she added softly.

Thirty minutes went by, and one of the older boys raised his hand to go to the outhouse. Miss Harty nodded to him, and he quickly pushed back his chair, scraping the legs on the floor. At the sound, Rose's head came up from her desk so quickly that Newton jumped. Across the room, Alice had been watching Rose from the corner of her eye, and when her friend's head popped up, she said, "Oh, dear," right out loud, and then clapped her hand over her mouth.

Rose looked around, feeling a little dazed. It took her only the wink of an eye to remember where she was, but it seemed like forever. She felt the familiar rush of color to her face and wondered what to do. She must have fallen asleep right on her desk, and everyone in the room must know. Oh, drat her face. It felt so hot, and she was . . . what was that word in last week's vocabulary? Mortified. That must be it. She remembered that the mort part meant dead, like mortuary and mortician. The connection must be that when you were mortified enough, you just wished you were dead. There was that wish again. She pushed her thoughts aside, took a deep breath and looked toward the front of the room. Miss Harty was just standing there, looking at her. She didn't look angry. She was just looking. Rose glanced around her. Everyone else was looking at her, too.

"Perhaps you'd like to go to the pump and splash some cold water on your face, Rose," Miss Harty suggested gently. "The rest of you may just continue with your work, please."

Rose stumbled to her feet and left the room to wash her face. When she came back, not a single person looked up. The schoolroom was silent except for the crackle of the fire in the wood stove. Miss Harty glanced at Rose and then continued to walk around the room, looking at everyone's penmanship. When Rose sat down, Miss Harty said, "We are all copying the work on the blackboard, Rose. Please do each line three times in your best hand."

Rose took her pen from the desk, along with a piece of copy paper, dipped the point into the inkwell, and began to write a row of capital Ps, carefully making each letter as much like Miss Harty's as possible. The water had cooled her face a little, and she could feel her normal color returning.

An hour later, the bell rang and school was over for the day. Rose took one book from her desk to take home and started for the cloakroom, hoping she could escape before anyone said anything to her about her dreadful behavior. But she could not get by Emily.

"I couldn't even see you," Emily whispered. "But I knew you must have fallen asleep because Alice gave me a signal. I couldn't turn around and look, but your breathing sounded as if you might be in the Land of Nod."

"And now I'm going to be in Coventry," Rose muttered, seeing Miss Harty coming toward them.

"I'd like you to take this home with you," Miss Harty said, holding out a small book. "Perhaps you can find time to read one of these each day."

"Thank you, Ma'am," Rose said politely. The other part of her mind was almost screaming, "Time, time, time! I barely have time to button my shoes, or my shift for that matter."

She waited a minute, thinking something more must be coming, but the teacher just smiled at her and waved her on. Rose moved quickly toward the cloakroom, took down her wrap and started for the door. Then she heard Alice calling her name. She would have to stop. Alice and Emily were so dear. You couldn't walk away from your friends, even if they were about to tease or say something mean. She hoped they wouldn't be too hard on her. She wasn't a teacher's pet, she really wasn't.

"You must be so tired," Alice said as she came up behind her. "I could never do all the things you do and stay awake in school, especially when it's right after the noon recess and I've eaten, and the fire in the stove is really warm. It's all I can do to make my eyes stay open." Rose looked at her gratefully. Alice wasn't going to tease. They really were wonderful friends. She didn't tell Alice all the things that went on in her head, not the way she told Emily. But she liked Alice so much, and she didn't know how she would have gotten through these past weeks without her and Emily. Should she tell her that? Would it embarrass both of them? She had no time to decide because Emily ran up to them so fast just then that she had trouble stopping beside them.

"You're not behaving in a ladylike fashion," Rose said in her most disapproving voice.

Emily's laugh started high and went down the scale until it disappeared in a silence. "And I was afraid you were going to be all fretful about not staying awake in history and penmanship," Emily said. "Were you really asleep, or were you just testing Miss Hearty Harty?"

"Don't make fun of that lady, Missy," Rose said, still in her schoolmarm voice. "She's a saint. She saved me from blackboard washing, floor scrubbing, and possibly a thrashing this afternoon when I took to my bed in her schoolroom."

"So you can go home to sink washing, floor scrubbing and possibly a thrashing for not working hard enough or fast enough," Emily snapped back, a little alarmed at the way Rose was making light of her near disaster in school.

"No thrashing," Rose said. "I think I must have outgrown that stage. I haven't been thrashed in months—never was much anyway. And I washed the sink this morning. If I could just think of something simple to make for supper, I could get Abby's school clothes ready this afternoon and have time after we eat to do a little schoolwork. And then go to bed early enough so I don't turn into a daily disgrace at school."

"We'd better go with you and help for an hour," Alice said. "You really have to get caught up right now or Hearty Harty is going to have your head on a silver salver."

"What on earth does that mean?" Emily wanted to know. "Head on a silver salver, I mean. I'd be glad to help for an hour. My mother was going into town on the train this afternoon so she won't be home anyway."

"It's what my Mama always calls 'an expression,'" Alice said. "I don't know where it comes from, but it means your head has been chopped off and placed on a silver platter, and is ready to bring to the king. Not for him to eat. Just proof that his orders to remove your head have been carried out."

"That's very distasteful," Emily said.

"Worse than chicken killing," Rose said.

Emily and Alice looked at each other. They looked at Rose. Then all three started to giggle.

"What made you think of that?" Emily choked out.

"Charles," Rose said. She was giggling so hard now that her words came in little spurts, punctuated with gasps. "He compares everything . . . to killing chickens, ever since . . . he had to help kill that mean old biddy . . . who kept pecking Abby."

"Well," said Emily, trying to stop laughing, "it's quite true that having your head on a platter is much worse than killing a chicken. When shall we tell Charles?"

Off they went again, laughing so hard that tears ran down their faces, and so absorbed that they didn't notice Newton Barnes coming up behind them until he spoke.

"Rose?" Newton said, trying to interrupt. "Rose?"

She turned, surprised to see this boy right next to them.

"Yes?"

"I just wanted to say that I wanted to let you know that I'll keep a better eye out from now on so you won't fall asleep like that. Just don't jump out of your skin if I give you a little nudge in the back," Newton said, looking down at the three with a small smile.

"Oh, thank you very much, Newton. But I shall try not to do that again. Thank you very much," Rose said, feeling her face getting red. Newton was three years older than she was, and one of the most presentable boys in the schoolroom. She couldn't quite believe he was talking to them, talking to her, in fact; talking about helping her out.

He went right on standing there, and she suddenly knew what it was to be tongue-tied. She glanced at Emily, who immediately said, "And who will be in charge of nudges during the months after you leave school early to work on the farm? What if you don't even come back in the fall?"

Newton laughed out loud then, saying quickly, "Oh, I'll be back in the fall with the other older boys. But it's true. Come spring, a young man's fancy turns to planting seeds. But the short year is the reason I'm in your class now, ready to nudge."

"Thank you," Rose said again, recovering her voice, but wishing she didn't sound as repetitious as a clock at the noon hour.

"You are quite welcome," he said. "I will see you all tomorrow." And he was gone, loping down the road after his friends.

Alice and Emily started prancing like a pair of horses just turned out to pasture in spring. Rose fully expected them to fall on the ground and roll over. As soon as they figured Newton was well out of earshot, they grabbed her and shrieked.

"Can you believe that?" Alice said to Emily. "Can you believe Newton Barnes wants to help Rose out?"

"Wants to keep her awake," yelped Emily, starting to dance about again. "Doesn't want her sleeping in front of him! Wants to look at her long braids and her big blue eyes when they are open, not shut! Be happy to trade places with you, Rose, and take a little snooze there at the magic desk."

"What on earth has taken the two of you," Rose demanded. "Stop it, stop it, stop it."

"Only that he's the best-looking boy in the whole school," Alice said. "That's all. And he wants to take care of you. And he told that awful Granger boy to bite his tongue, looking as if he'd like to pull it out."

"I think he's sweet on you," Emily said, suddenly speaking seriously. "That's what I think."

"Oh, stop it," Rose said. "He's just being nice."

"Ay-yuh," said Alice. "Very, very nice."

Rose felt a warm feeling in her stomach where she more often felt the chilling weight of a cold stone. It was nice to have someone like Newton be nice. But she didn't know about the business of someone biting his own tongue. So she asked her friends.

"Oh," Emily said immediately, "you were asleep, and Miss Harty told everyone to let you rest, and one of the Granger boys said, 'teacher's pet,' right out loud, and that's when Newton told him to bite his tongue."

"I hope he didn't," Rose said, thinking how much it hurts when you accidentally bite right into a bit of tongue or cheek. The pain could last a week from one of those things, especially if it swelled up enough to get in the way and made you do it all over again.

"Serve him right if he did," Alice said. "He's mean. I saw him taking the wings off a fly on the first day of school this year. And then he laughed when the poor thing bobbled around on his desk."

"Mother always said," Rose began. Emily and Alice stood still and looked at her. Rose realized she hadn't talked about her mother for days, except inside her head, or when she was muttering in the kitchen before the sun came up.

"Mother always said," she began again, "that people who aren't nice to animals aren't nice at all. She included everything, from finger-pecking chickens to honey bees. I remember one time when the fish peddler came, and he had his dog on the wagon with him, and the dog started to bark, and he gave him a swat, and Mother went right back in the house, even though she really wanted some oysters. He came up to the door and knocked, and she opened the door and in her church-talking voice said, 'I couldn't eat a fish I bought from a man who hits his dog for no reason a-tall.' The peddler looked as if a fishbone had just stuck in his throat, and Charles and I barely got ourselves into the pantry before we started laughing.

"We heard Mother close the door, and then she came looking for us, to find out why we laughed. Charles said it was just the way the man looked, as if he were choking. I said how nice it was she took the part of the poor dog, but how did we know he wouldn't hit it again? And she said he wouldn't that day at least, and maybe next time he'd have second thoughts. Mother was big on second thoughts. And then, then she gave us each a hug and told us . . ."

Rose's face suddenly looked as if she had swallowed a fishbone. Emily took one of her hands, and Alice took the other.

"And then what?" Emily asked softly but insistently. "Don't get stuck on the hug, Rose. Don't get stuck now."

"She told us," Rose said, her voice quivering a little, "never to trust anyone who was mean to an animal, large or small. And she said we could be sure that people who were kind to animals had good hearts."

"My mother says we are animals, too," Alice said. "So does that mean we can't trust anyone who is unkind to people?"

"It sounds as if it must be true," Emily said. "But if we don't get along home here, someone is going to be very unkind to us. And it wouldn't be fitting for us to stop trusting our mothers."

"You weren't going home anyway," Rose said in her practical tone. "You were coming along to help me out for an hour—although it's more like three quarters of an hour now."

"So let's run," said Alice. And they pelted down the road.

CHAPTER 10
Hot and Cold

As they came around the last bend in the road, still panting from their unladylike gallop, the three girls saw two heads moving along the front yard at ground level. Rose shut her eyes and opened them again. How could two hats and two heads be on a level space without any bodies? Then she saw earth fly up and realized it was two men with shovels, digging up the front yard. Emily remarked that one of the heads—she must have seen the same funny picture, Rose thought—looked like Mr. Hibbard's. When they were a little closer, the girls could see that Mr. Chandler's was the other one.

"They're digging a ditch," Rose said. "But why?"

As the three girls neared, both men stepped out of the ditch, dropped their spades, took up their pickaxes and attacked the ground between the ditch and the house. There's frost in the ground, Rose thought. For some reason they are breaking up frozen ground. Then she remembered her father saying there wasn't much frost in the ground yet. She had been looking out at grass all white with frost, but he had said that was only on the surface. The wagon wheels were still making ruts in the ground down by the barn, he had said. That was just this very morning at breakfast time.

Mr. Hibbard suddenly noticed them and straightened.

"Father," Rose blurted out, "whatever are you doing?"

"Milking the cow," he said, and bent to the digging again.

"Going to have water in that house yet," he said, looking right at her. "Bit of a chore to get through the frost, but it's only down an inch or two here on the sunny side of the house, so we'll pretty much have the job licked by milking time. Tomorrow Mr. Chandler will help me with the pipe, and we'll get it covered right over before it can freeze. Weather looks right."

"Water?" Rose said, her voice squeaking. "Water in the house? With faucets?"

"Darned right," Father said. "Can't have you wearing yourself all out with pumping and boiling and hauling. High time we joined the neighbors."

"That will be wonderful," Rose said, barely able to breathe. "It will be just wonderful, sir." She felt Emily and Alice elbowing her. She hoped they wouldn't say a word. As they started toward the house, she glanced over her shoulder and thought Father had smiled, just for a second, at Mr. Chandler. He had, she told herself. His teeth had made a small white line in the midst of his shaggy dark beard.

"Thank you, Father," Rose said. Running water, she thought. What would Sarah think of that? She knew her mother had wanted water pipes, just like Aunt Nell and most of the other houses near them had. Would they get hot water, too? Naw, she thought. Water is newfangled enough. Hot water would be out of the question. She pushed open the kitchen door and held it for Emily and Alice. As soon as the door closed, the three of them joined hands and started jumping around the kitchen in a circle.

"Ring around a rosy," chanted Emily, laughing. Rose knew they were all thinking what a strange day this was. First, Miss Harty hadn't punished Rose for falling asleep, then the best-looking boy in the school had promised to take care of her, and now the Hibbards were going to have water.

"Stop, stop," Rose said suddenly. "Father will either hear us or see the curtains waving around, and he'll be asking why all the unseemly behavior."

"Let's get to work on whatever it is you have to do, then," said Emily. "Shall we pump pails of water as a kind of farewell?"

"Don't be foolish," Alice said. "I think we'd better pump a pan of water, fire up the stove and get going on all those dishes in the sink. You may have hot water in this kitchen one day soon, Miss Rose, but you ain't got it today. And what about the chickens? And the ironing?"

Rose looked at her gratefully. Alice was a great one for making lists and checking off things that had to be done. She used old envelopes and all sorts of scrap paper for her lists, while Rose just kept them all in her head.

"Charles and Abby do the chickens," she said. "If you two wouldn't mind getting a little firewood, I would be pleased with that." Emily and Alice exchanged a glance as Rose turned toward the almost empty woodbox and picked up two sticks for the stove. They knew she hated going to the woodpile, and while it didn't make them very happy, they went to do it for her.

Rose put three flatirons on the stove and set up the ironing board. Alice was quite right. She and Abby both needed fresh clothes for school, and Charles might be almost out of shirts, too. Oh, if they would iron, it would be such a blessing. When the two girls stepped back into the kitchen, they each had an armload of wood, and they stood side by side, letting the stove-length logs run into the woodbox with a great clatter. They brushed their hands to get rid of the scraps of bark and said they were ready for work.

Rose had dampened some shirtwaists and shirts in the morning, rolled them tight and put them in the icebox, so they were ready for ironing. Alice spit on her finger and touched one of the irons with a lightning movement. She heard a small sizzle and knew the iron was ready, so she went to work. Emily, broom in hand, went upstairs with Rose to sweep the bedrooms and straighten up.

"I can do this," Emily said. "You get on down there to that stack of dirty dishes. In no time, you'll have to put supper on the table, and your father is going to be hungry enough to eat a horse."

Rose watched her start sweeping out little dust balls from under Father's bed and departed, thinking that her friends were going to get her caught up on her work and in a few days—she really couldn't quite get it into her head yet—in a few days she would have running water in the house.

She stopped so suddenly on the second stair from the bottom that she teetered back and forth to keep from falling. Did this mean, she wondered, that they'd have a toilet, too? Would slop jars be no more? Would she not have to sit on that splintery wooden hole when it was cold enough to get frostbite or when the sun beat down on the tin roof and made the privy into a small oven with a terrible smell? Well, she supposed people might want chamber pots and water pitchers upstairs, just so they wouldn't have to go downstairs in the dark, but maybe the privy would be gone. Burned or buried, she wondered. Have to be buried. If you burned a smell like that the neighbors would be fit to be tied.

"Alice," she said, as she reached the kitchen, "did you hear my father say something about not pumping and boiling any more?"

"Certainly did," Alice said. "So, using that logic Miss

Harty is always talking about, I am thinking he is going to connect water pipes to the back of your stove, and you are going to have faucets both hot and cold right in that sink over there."

Alice's arm was moving quickly back and forth on the ironing board as she talked. She had Abby's shirt-waist already hanging from the arm of the rocking chair and was working on one of Charles' shirts. She didn't look up when she talked, just kept ironing. Rose saw how nice and smooth the fabric was around the buttons and on the cuffs of Charles' shirt. She knew she never ironed anything that well, so she hoped Charles wouldn't expect all his things to look that perfect from now on. She'd noticed that he was taking a little more time in front of the glass these days, combing a straight part in his hair and adjusting his clothes before he went off to school.

"I hardly know what to think," Rose said. "Miss Harty said we should have running water, but Father was so angry with her that day—the day she came to dinner—I reckoned anything she suggested would be the first thing he would not do."

"Mama says you never know with men," Alice said, nodding her head up and down. She put her iron back on the stove and took a new, hot one. "She says the men always make jokes about women changing their minds, but it's really the men who do. She says the worst thing is when they can't make up their minds a-tall. And she says that's a good deal of the time, too," Alice said with a final touchup on one of Charles' sleeves.

Sometimes she talks as if she's a hundred, Rose thought. Out loud she giggled a little and said she guessed this time Miss Harty had made up Father's mind for him, whether he liked it or not.

"Better not say that very loud," Alice said. "And you'd better start supper. Emily and I have to be going as soon as I finish ironing your dress."

Rose went to the icebox and took out milk and butter. She fetched a box of salt cod from the pantry, slid back the wooden top and emptied the fish into a bowl, pulling the chunks apart with two forks. She set a small pan on the stove and melted some butter. Then she stirred in a little flour and added two teacups of milk. Someday soon, she thought, I'm going to buy one of those tin cups with the measure up the side. Teacups are not all the same size. She stirred until the mixture was smooth and then put the pan on the back of the stove where it would stay warm but not really cook.

She greased a pan and took down another mixing bowl from the pantry shelf. She quickly mixed a batch of biscuits and dropped them on the pan. Then she pulled the white sauce back over the heat and stood there, stirring steadily.

"You really do know how to cook, don't you," Alice commented.

"Ha! And you really know how to iron," Rose answered.

Just then Abby came running into the kitchen, carrying a basket of eggs and bubbling over with the news about water pipes.

"Father says we will have water day after tomorrow," Abby said. "And I asked him if we would have hot and cold, and he said we would have only cold the first day but if all went well we would have hot by the weekend. And then, Rose, can I have a tubful of water of my very own for my bath?"

"Take a breath," Rose said, laughing. "We'll have to see how much hot water we have, but we'll let you take your bath first when the new hot water is in. You won't care if someone else uses it after you, will you?"

"Well, Charles says he wants water of his own, too," Abby said.

"What a long time it's going to take all of you to get clean," Alice said with a giggle. "Filling and emptying tubs from supper hour until the clock strikes twelve on Saturday night. Won't any of you be ready in time for the square dance next week if you can't share a tub."

"Square dance?" said Abby, her face as bright as a newly opened black-eyed Susan. "Oh, Rose, can we go, can we go, please?"

Then a cloud passed over Abby's face, and she looked at the floor.

"I guess we're still in mourning, aren't we? So it wouldn't be nice for us to go."

"Yes, Abby," Rose said. "But it's been quite awhile, so I think we could ask Father. At least you and Charles should be able to go."

"And you, too, Miss Rose, even if we have to come over here again to work like hired girls getting your work done," Alice said. "You can't stay home. My mother says you could turn into a prune before you are eighteen if you keep going the way you are."

The words were barely out when Alice clapped her hand over her mouth.

"I'm sorry, Rose, I'm sorry. I shouldn't have told you that. My mother is always telling me that words spill out of my mouth before they have gone through my brain. You're not a prune, you know you're not a prune."

"What's a prune?" Abby wanted to know.

"A dried plum that has a great many wrinkles," Rose said. She turned toward the glass and examined her smooth face. While she looked the dreaded pink color started to come up her neck, but she kept staring at her reflection.

"I just don't see any prune wrinkles here," she said solemnly to Alice. "So it doesn't matter that you have spoken before you thought, leaped before you looked, let your tongue rule your manners . . ."

Rose broke off quickly and ran into the pantry, slamming the door behind her as Alice started to chase her, hot iron in hand. Abby was looking from one to the other in alarm until she realized that Alice was laughing and that she could hear Rose laughing and panting behind the door. Alice tried to turn the knob, but Rose was holding firm.

"All right," she said. "All right. I am putting the iron back on the stove. I am apologizing for talking too much, and I want you to go to the dance with us." She paused for a second and then smiled wickedly. "Maybe Newton will be there," she said, as the pantry door opened just a crack. At that, Rose slammed it shut again. She could feel her face getting very red now and wondered if it was going to do that the next time he spoke to her. If he spoke to her. She hoped he would.

At the supper table, Charles asked whether having water meant having hot water.

"I reckon," Father said.

"And a toilet, Father? Will we have a toilet?" Abby asked.

"Ay-yuh," Father answered, his head bent over the creamed codfish. "But not if I don't get to eat my meal in peace."

The two youngsters rolled their eyes at each other. Rose shook her head at them, frowning, and supper was finished with no further conversation. The two younger children cleared up as usual, folding the napkins and putting them back in their rings, then taking the crumbs off the table with a knife. They washed and dried the dishes and returned the large spoons to the glass holder on the table. They put out plates and bowls, and Rose added her father's mug and her own cup and saucer for coffee, so everything was ready for tomorrow's breakfast. As they were finishing, Rose heard Father coming down the stairs.

He'll be going out again, she thought. She had counted the money in the sugar bowl late that afternoon so she would know how much he took the next time he went to the hotel in the evening. Three dollars and twenty-seven cents was the amount. She had written it on a slip of paper and tucked it in the pocket of her apron, just so her mind wouldn't play tricks on her and forget.

"Would anyone like to play euchre?" Father asked as he came into the kitchen. "Or do you all have schoolwork to do?"

"Abby can stay up another half hour, and Charles an hour," Rose said. They both did their schoolwork this afternoon."

"Well, then?"

Charles and Abby ran to the dining room and quickly shifted the breakfast settings to one end of the table. Rose opened a drawer in the dry sink and took out the cards. She and Charles had played this game many times with their mother, who was very good at card games, but Rose wasn't sure Abby knew about right bowers and left bowers, or even euchre itself. Perhaps she and Abby could play together until the eight-year-old understood the rules.

She checked the deck and could see that the thirty-two cards needed for euchre were still separate from the rest of the deck. She dealt five to Charles, five to her father and five to herself and Abby, and they began to play. Except for what needed to be said to play the game, they were silent until Father said, "Your mother and I used to play this game, two-handed, when I was courting her. Her mother would sit in the rocker by the kitchen door and watch us, making sure we didn't get into mischief."

Charles wriggled in his chair, finding it hard to imagine his father playing games with a young lady while his grandmother kept an eye on them. What mischief could anyone make at a dining room table anyway? Rose saw Abby's mouth start to open, and figured a question was coming.

"Father, did you beat her? Or did she win all the time? She almost always beat Rose and Charles."

"Oh, she won all right, almost every game. Once in a while I think she gave me a game, just so I wouldn't throw the cards on the table and get on home. My mother, your Grandmother Jane, didn't really approve of card playing, so we didn't learn as children. You probably don't remember her very well, except maybe for Rose."

"But we've looked at her picture, Father," Charles said. "And she looks stricter than any teacher I ever saw."

"And how many teachers have you actually seen, young man?" Father wanted to know.

"Well, three, I guess, sir," Charles said.

Father chuckled a little—Rose couldn't remember the last time she'd heard that sound—and went on. "Your grandmother told your Aunt Nell that if she sewed on Sunday—the Lord's Day, she called it—she would be taking out every stitch with her nose when she reached heaven."

Rose touched her nose thoughtfully. She had trouble taking out stitches with the sharp point of the scissors, or with a needle. Her nose was pretty big, but it wasn't sharp enough for that task. She guessed she wouldn't sew on Sundays; it was probably just one of those grandmother things to say, but she saw no point in chancing that kind of thing.

"Your turn, Rose," Charles said impatiently.

She played a card, whispered why to Abby; and tried to keep her mind on the game. But her head felt as crowded as the schoolhouse on town meeting day. The worry about noses and stitches had pushed its way into a place where toilets and slop jars and being a teacher and that handsome Newton had already taken up most of the space.

"Rose," Abby said, jabbing her in the ribs with her elbow. "It's our turn again, and I don't know what to do!"

Rose played a card quickly, scooped up the trick, played another and scooped up that one as well. Concentrating as hard as she could, she counted up what had already been put on the table and quickly finished the game.

Abby clapped her hands in delight.

"We won, we won, we won," she said. "Do you want to play again?"

"I aim to figure up the piping we'll be needing inside the house, Abigail," Father said. "So one game is enough for me. One loss is enough, too."

He stood up, pulled his rule out of his back pocket and started to unfold it as he headed for the kitchen stove, where he spent a considerable amount of time on his hands and knees, measuring and making little sketches on a tablet and then measuring some more. Rose added a couple of small sticks to the fire so it would be warm until bedtime, and then stood near where her father was working. The rule was one of her favorite tools, and when she was younger, she loved playing with a broken one Uncle Jason had given her. She would flip the pieces back and forth, folding and unfolding, and then try making letters and triangles and squares. She'd lost the rule one day and it seemed no one she knew had broken one since.

She shuffled her feet a bit, but her father didn't look up. She cleared her throat.

"Speak up, child, if you have something to say," he said abruptly.

"We were wondering, Father, if we might all go to the square dance next week, or if we are still in mourning and cannot go or . . ." Her voice trailed off.

"I wonder what your mother would have to say about that," Father said, still not looking up.

"I don't know, sir," Rose said. "So I didn't know what to tell Abby."

He eased back from his hands and knees. Sitting on his legs, he looked at her.

"We are in mourning, near as I can figure out, for a year. That's the New England tradition. But respect for the dead means thinking about what the dead would think if the dead could think. It appears to me that your mother would want no part of people staying home and carrying on about her. She would want us to just plain carry on, which is what we've been up to. So you tell Abby we will all go to the square dance, and we will dance if we're a mind to."

Rose thought this was one of the longest statements she had ever heard her father make. She was so accustomed to his muttering "ah-yuh" or "no" that she had to send her mind back to the beginning to make sure she had it all.

"Thank you, Father," she said solemnly. And before he could change his mind, she headed for the stairs to tell Abby and Charles, who were waiting for her to give a final tuck to their sheets and blankets. She found Charles constructing yet another building with his blocks, so she gave him the news and a lecture at the same time. She could hear Abby in the next room, scrambling for her bed so she wouldn't get scolded, and she wondered how her mother always kept a straight face when these things happened. Sarah must have known when they weren't doing what they were supposed to do, but she rarely said anything. It wasn't because she didn't care, Rose thought, so it must have been that she didn't think it was important enough to mention.

Father must be right, she decided. Sarah would want us to have a good time at the square dance. It doesn't mean we've forgotten her. It just means we have to go on. And if all the work gets done, we will fill the bathtub without pumping. Her eyes filled with tears then. Why couldn't he have dug the ditch and brought the water in for Sarah? Why now?

CHAPTER 11
Silly Goose

Rose carefully placed her feet on the treadle of her mother's sewing machine, one a little ahead of the other, dropped the needle into place and started stitching the bright, plaid fabric. She had found the cloth in a nearly empty bolt at Mr. Goodnow's store, and he'd sold it to her for fifteen cents because it wasn't enough for a lady's skirt. But it would be just right for Abby, who was going square dancing for the very first time.

The treadle rocked, the needle moved up and down, and Rose's fingers guided the fabric along. In an hour, she had the skirt stitched together, with a gathered waist and a deep ruffle on the bottom. She had searched through her mother's blanket chest and found a thin band of lace that was just long enough for the ruffle.

Rose wondered why it was always called a blanket chest when not a single blanket lived there. She added that on, looked at her handiwork with some surprise and decided Abby would like it.

It was a good thing, she thought, that Grandma Emma had insisted she learn to run a sewing machine. She had liked it from the very beginning; liked the rhythm of the treadle, liked the wheel and the way the needle went down into that little hole and somehow caught the lower thread to make a stitch. It was a bit of a mystery, but it worked if you made your feet behave.

"Not so fast," her grandmother would say when Rose tried to speed through a project. "It's tortoise and hare; slow and steady wins the race." Rose put the skirt aside and picked up one of Abby's petticoats. She had taken the good parts of an old sheet to make a double three-inch ruffle so the new skirt would stick out and give Abby ruffles like everyone else's when someone swung her at the dance. While she sewed, the square dance calls started running through her mind, and she had to slow them down to match the motion of her feet. Do-si-do your partner, allemande left and gra-a-and right and left . . . Would Newton be at the dance, and would he talk to her? She sighed, thinking that if he even looked at her across a square, her face would get all red, and he'd think she was a silly goose.

Her mind darted on as her fingers worked the fabric. Her neck was nearly long enough to be goose-like. But she didn't remember ever seeing a goose act silly. They swam, and they honked, and they flew south in those beautiful Vs, and when Aunt Nell had a roast goose for Christmas, she saved the feathers to stuff a pillow. But people were always saying you shouldn't be a silly goose. How could such good eating and such soft pillows be silly?

There was that time she remembered people telling about, the time when her grandmother had gone out to do a little weeding in her flowerbed after supper. It seemed the gander was on shore, just standing there, and she had bent over with her back to the pond and was pulling on a tall pigweed, when the gander took a notion to fly right at her.

"Bowled her right over," Grandfather would say, hooting with laughter. "Sent her sprawling into the four o'clocks."

Grandmother never liked that story, Rose knew. Whenever it was told, which was several times a year, Grandmother would leave the room on some errand or other and not come back until the laughing was over, her face a bit stern but never red. But Rose knew hers was going to just burn up, and then she'd be embarrassed and send more red up there to keep the fire going. Well, maybe he wouldn't look at her. Keeping her awake in school and talking to her at a square dance were certainly not the same thing. Besides, she wasn't going to have a new skirt. She'd just be there in one he'd sat behind dozens of days. Maybe he'd never noticed what she wore to school. Maybe boys didn't notice.

When she finished the ruffles, she had good parts of the worn sheet left over, so she went to her chest of drawers and pulled out one of her petticoats. At least she could have extra ruffles so her skirt would stick out and whirl around properly. Rose suddenly felt better. She cut two long strips, gathered them and added them to her petticoat. She'd be plain Jane on top and fancy underneath, and some of the time at a square dance, what was underneath showed.

She pushed back her chair, dropped the sewing machine into the cabinet and closed the top. She'd have to get a move on or supper and baths would not get finished in time for them to get to the dance early. And Father had clearly said at the noon hour that they would be at Town Hall when the dance began. As she ran downstairs with the new skirt over her arm, she felt a little shiver of excitement. She was so glad to be going, so pleased that it wasn't an insult to Sarah. And on top of everything else, they'd be taking their baths with the new hot water.

In the kitchen, she put a flatiron on the stove. She'd at least have to press the seams of the new skirt. Then she went out to the ell and fetched the bathtub. She'd bathe now, and let Abby use her bath water while she ironed. Where was that little girl anyway, she wondered. There was so much to do. Then she looked in the dining room and saw that Abby had already set the table for supper, which would be a small, cold meal that was as good as ready. And as she lowered herself into the tub, hoping to get in and out before anyone came, Abby opened the kitchen door and came in with a basket of eggs.

"Shut it, shut it, shut it," Rose yelled. "I will have drops of ice on my back in another twenty seconds." Abby grinned and slammed the door. Then she saw the skirt and ran over to give her soapy sister a big hug.

"It's beautiful," Abby said. "Where is yours?"

"I'm not wearing a new skirt this time, Abby," Rose said. "But I put extra ruffles on my petticoat."

"You did mine first and you ran out of time, didn't you," the little girl said, planting her feet wide apart and putting her hands on her waist with her elbows sticking out.

"You look like a garden scarecrow," Rose said, laughing. "I didn't need a new skirt, and you did. And I did run out of time, and I'm going to run out of more time if you don't run out of here while I get dried off and dressed."

"I'm taking a bath, too," Abby said.

"Right after me," Rose said.

By the time Charles and Father came in from the barn, the two girls were bathed and dressed, Abby's skirt was pressed, and the light supper was on the table. Father noticed the tub in the middle of the kitchen and said he'd just add a little hot water after he ate and get off at least a few layers of dirt before the dance. Rose thought he should scrub all the way down to skin rather than stop with a few layers, but she didn't say anything. She was still so surprised about running water and square dancing that she had been keeping her mouth shut all week long. She hadn't forgotten that Father would be taking her out of school come spring, but she had put it on one of the back shelves of her mind.

Father ate without saying anything about the food. He didn't say anything at all, in fact, until he started his piece of pumpkin pie. Rose had hoped he would mention the pie, but he just ate it quickly. She had never made pumpkin before, and she had mashed and mashed and mashed the pumpkin to get the pulp smooth. Even then, she had to push it all through a sieve to get out the stringy parts. She hated it when someone left those strings in a pumpkin pie. They made your throat feel funny. He looked up just once to tell Charles to skedaddle into the kitchen and get his bath immediately.

"You won't want to soak in my dirt," he said. "You can have your pie when you're ready for the dance. And I want you to get the horse out and hitch her up to the buggy, soon as you're ready. You able to do that?"

Charles looked as if he would pop open like the dried outside of a cherry tomato.

"Yes, sir, yes, I can do that," he said. He moved toward the kitchen, pulling off his clothes as he went. Rose added some water to the tub and fetched a dry towel for him.

"I'll scrub the back of your neck," she said, secretly worried that he might not do it. "And then I'll have pie."

The moon was just coming up when Father headed the buggy for home. Quicker than you could say Jehosaphat, Abby's eyes closed and her head tipped onto Rose's shoulder. The girls were riding behind Charles and Father, and they were tucked under the buffalo robe, snug as they could be. As the buggy rocked along, Abby's head slid further and further down until it was resting on Rose's lap.

Rose didn't feel even a little bit sleepy. She pulled the blanket over Abby and tucked one side under her leg so it would stay in place, but she didn't feel cold. In fact, she didn't know when she had felt so warm. It wasn't just that her face had been the color of a fully ripe tomato since the beginning of the square dance. It was also that the square dance had been more fun than she could possibly have imagined. She had even stopped caring that her face turned red more regularly than the clock struck in their front room. After the weeks of mourning and missing her mother and doing all the housework, she had danced and danced and danced, and it was like being set free, even if it was only for an evening.

Cinderella must have felt just like this, she thought, thinking how funny it would be if the buggy turned into a pumpkin before they could get home and Charles had to take the harnesses off a large white mouse instead of the docile Dolly. She reminded herself that she wasn't much like Cinderella tonight. The fairy tale heroine had a fancy ball gown, and she had only found time to add a little lace to her petticoat. Still, her day had been something like Cinderella's, scrubbing people instead of the hearth, and sewing for Abby, not wicked stepsisters.

But even Cinderella could not have had a better time. Sharing a glass of cider near the refreshment table halfway through the evening, Rose and Alice had giggled over the fact that Emily's skirts had practically smothered Mr. Hawks when Emily was his corner lady and the caller commanded each man to swing his corner.

"He does insist on trying to get everyone's feet off the floor," Alice said. "He swings so hard, and he's so short."

Rose smiled to herself as the buggy rolled along. She had never liked Mr. Hawks, but tonight he hadn't bothered her at all, even when he squeezed her too tight. She was too tall for him to get her feet off the floor, and for once, she was pleased to be that tall. But the best part of the whole night, she thought, with a pleasant warmth stealing up her neck and down into her chest, the best part was when they did a grand right and left and she ended up with Newton as a partner. That one dance was so perfect, and she was glad it was one of the squares she could do blindfolded.

What on earth did that mean, she asked herself, looking up at the three-quarter moon that was providing a good deal of light on the road ahead. Blindfolded. The only thing that was folded as far as she knew was the cloth they put over your eyes when you were playing Pin the Tail on the Donkey. Then, true enough, you were blind. The one or two times they had played the game at school, she was quite sure the Granger boy wasn't, though. He had fumbled around with the tail and headed for the donkey all right, but then he seemed to move from side to side in a way different from everyone else. After a time, he'd plant the tail right on the donkey's rear end. Everyone else had placed tails on the nose, the ears, the hoof, even one of the eyes. She didn't like Peter Granger that day, and she had never liked him since. She just knew he had been peeking out from under the blindfold and had carefully placed the tail right where it was supposed to be.

Anyway, Newton had looked at her several times during the evening and had been in the same set with her at least twice. Not at least, she thought. Twice. Twice exactly. Emily would say she shouldn't think about it, that the only way to not blush and not stumble and not look like a complete fool was to concentrate on the dance steps and look only at the person who was your mate of the moment. But Emily wasn't interested in dancing with anyone in particular, and Rose knew all night long exactly which square Newton was in and who else was in it.

She couldn't believe, even now, that she had been paying such attention to the location of a boy who sat behind her in school. But when he appeared in her square to replace someone who had decided to sit out for a while, she had the feeling he could see the pulse pounding in her wrist and could hear her happy thoughts.

The pink rose, of course, over her chin and right up past her nose, and then she decided not to worry about it. She couldn't fix it. It was as much a part of her as big feet and blue eyes. So she concentrated on the dance instead, managing the first tricky steps ordered by the caller. As partners switched around the square, she soon found herself standing next to Newton with his arm carefully around her waist and his other hand holding hers across his body. It had been hard to breathe normally, and she had started to worry that she wouldn't do the dance right. Then habit took over and told her feet what to do, and they did it, moving as quickly as if they were size sixes.

"What a good dancer you are," he had said, looking down at her from his six foot height. "You must have been doing these routines for years."

"I was Abby's age when I came to my first square dance," she had told him. "She's eight," she added, in case he didn't know.

But he had answered, "I know," and she couldn't figure out how.

What she did know was that she felt no heavier than a pillow full of feathers when he swung her around. And while she hated the rocky feeling in her stomach, she also liked it. She wondered if she was getting crazed again. She'd always thought girls looked so silly when they were looking at boys in that funny way, and now, suddenly, she understood what was going on. Maybe there was more to boy-girl things and getting married than just getting the breakfast and scrubbing the barn-dirty trousers.

Rose realized they were almost home when the horse entered the covered bridge and the sound of its hoofs turned from soft to sharp as they hit the board floor. Abby stirred, and Rose stroked her head while she dreamily watched for the windows on the south side of the bridge. In each one, she had a quick glimpse of the moonlit white water of the river spinning over the rocks. And then they were through, back into the chilly wind, with the horse's hoofs making a quiet sluff, sluff, sluff sound on the dirt road.

Rose knew sluff wasn't a word, but she liked making up words that fitted the sound or the smell of what was going on. She'd heard Grandmother Emma do that very thing when they were sewing together. "Gather smoothly," she'd say. "You don't want it all putched up." Now there was a good word, perfect for a seam that wouldn't lie flat, perfect for a cake that fell in the oven, or a drawer that looked as if someone had stirred it with an eggbeater. Putched. Rose whispered it aloud, liking the feel on her cold lips. Dolly took a right turn, and she shifted her brain to the nighttime list of duties: check the fire; set the table for breakfast; empty the bath water; make sure Abby and Charles had clean, ironed clothes for church and that Father had a clean shirt; tuck the children into bed and get herself there as well. She hoped Father wasn't going to the hotel tonight.

Maybe he would be worn out from the square dance, although she didn't actually remember seeing him dance at all. Most of the time he had stood near the door, talking to some men she didn't know very well. Once, she noticed him at a table, having a glass of cider and a piece of cake while he talked to a woman in a white, ruffled blouse and a very full skirt made of a green, shiny material that seemed to change color when she moved.

She sighed. The dancing had been wonderful, but it was only a few hours in a year of her life. She hoped Newton would talk to her in school. Maybe she would fall asleep again, and he would be kind enough to wake her up without Miss Harty knowing. Miss Harty was at the dance, too. Rose saw her doing the Virginia reel and showing some of the smallest children how to do a grand right and left in a big circle. Miss Harty joined a square toward the end of the evening, and Rose noticed that her dress, dark blue with small white flowers and a very full skirt, had sailed out around her when she swung. Rose hoped her father had said hello to the teacher and treated her politely. She didn't want Miss Harty to stop liking her. That would be too much, just plain too much.

"All right, everybody out," Father said, as he stopped the buggy by the side door. "Charles, you come along with me and help unharness the horse and put her in for the night. You, Abby, get along to bed. It's late for a child like you to be out."

"Yes, sir," Charles said.

"Yes, Father," Abby said, rubbing her eyes and wondering if she had done something wrong.

"It's all right, Abby," Rose said softly as she lifted her down from the buggy. "You fell asleep and now we're home. Let's get you to bed."

With another little sigh, Rose went in to take care of the list that was now at the front of her brain. The evening was losing its warmth as quickly as fresh milk put into the cooler.

CHAPTER 12
After Christmas

Three weeks later, Rose put Abby to work taking down the red and green paper chains. They took the stringed popcorn off the Christmas tree and draped it over the lilac bush outside the door, hoping the winter birds would find it. Then they pushed the Christmas tree out of the house and onto the front lawn. Charles said he would drag it to the woodshed. When it was dried out, the tree could be used for kindling in the fire, as long as they didn't use too much at a time, Rose told him.

"Why is that?" Charles wanted to know.

"Because it's hemlock, and it will crackle and snap in the fire. It has a lot of sap," Rose said.

"I like that noise," Charles said.

"Maybe so," Rose answered. "But that means it can send up sparks every time you open the stove, and you don't want hot coals flying around the room. They could start a fire."

"How do you know all these things?" Charles demanded, a little upset that he, a boy who could unharness a horse, did not know as much as his sister.

"You listen, you learn," Rose said, sticking her nose in the air.

"I hate you when you talk like that," Charles said. "You sound just like a grownup."

"Actually," Rose said, giving in a little, "Sarah . . . I mean, Mother . . . stopped me from putting a whole bunch of hemlock into the stove one day. She said it would crackle us right out of the room and put too much soot in the stovepipe and the chimney. So that's how I know."

"Did you just say 'Sarah'?" Charles said. "Sarah?"

Rose felt the color coming into her face. "Well, yes," she said, making a quick decision. "I think of Mother as Sarah in my head because I have to think about her a lot. It's mostly when I am figuring out what to do. What would Sarah do with this or that, how did she do this or that . . ." Rose paused. "When would she swat Charles . . ."

Charles shrieked. "You aren't going to swat me, are you?"

"Don't hit him, Rose," Abby cried out. "Please don't hit him."

Rose laughed. "No. I'm just trying to explain that if I thought of her as Mother all the time, then I would certain sure be down in the dumps almost every hour of the day. If my brain uses her first name, it is much easier."

"I am going to try that," Charles said, looking very solemn. "Rose?"

"Yes?"

"Am I too old to cry?"

"Of course not. Not if you have a good reason, like getting your hand cut off in the saw, or if Dolly steps on your foot and breaks four of your toes . . ."

She stopped and looked at Charles' face. He was so serious. She had better stop riding him.

"Or if you really miss your mother," she finished in a quiet voice.

"That's it," Charles said. "That's why I'm going to try thinking of her as Sarah from now on. You don't think she'd mind?"

"I think not," Rose said firmly. "I think not at all. And she won't mind if you cry, either, but it would be better to do it at home than at school."

"I cry at the cemetery," Charles said, looking up at her. "Abby and I go there after school sometimes. We both cry," he confessed, glancing at his little sister to see if she was going to change her mind about the swatting. But she was already on her way out of the room with an armload of Christmas chains. "And it's so cold there now, and there's no gravestone and no flowers."

Rose put her arm around her brother's shoulders, thinking of how many times she had cried into her pillow. Some nights it was so soggy she had to turn it over before she could get to sleep.

"I cry, too," she said. "And in the spring, we'll put up a gravestone, and you can take flowers every day if you want to. But it's getting better, isn't it? The crying, I mean."

"Yes, Rose. But is it wrong to cry less as the days go by? Does that mean we don't care about her anymore?"

"Heavens, no. She will be part of you for all of your life. Before Christmas Aunt Nell said it was time for us to start remembering all the happy times we had with our mother and to stop thinking about the accident. That's why we decorated the house just the way we always do. And you hung your stocking for Santa Claus . . ."

Charles interrupted. "And there was a beautiful orange in the toe, just the way there always was. I know, Rose, that Santa isn't real, you know. I am not a child anymore."

"The Santa spirit is real, Charles. That's what Sarah told me when I was eight. I woke up with a stomach-ache, came downstairs and found her pushing an orange into my stocking."

"Thanks, Rose," Charles said.

As he walked away, Rose felt as if the weight of several flatirons had just been lifted off her head. When I was eight, she thought, the same age that Abby is now. And now I'm nearly fifteen, and it's 1888. If I live to be as old as Grandmother Emma, I'll have kept house for somebody for seventy years.

I do hate him, she thought. I hate that he didn't get her running water. I hate the icebox. I hate the way he stacked the wood. She felt her face redden as her anger grew. Sarah had often told her that her temper would get the best of her some day. Was this what she meant? Well, she had reason to be angry. Her hands were red from hanging wet clothes on the back porch, her eyes had big circles under them because she didn't get enough sleep, and her back felt so tired.

Then she thought about Charles again and hoped she had told him all the right things. Poor boy. It wasn't just killing chickens that made him feel sick. Like everyone else, he missed Sarah. She certainly did. It had been pretty bad some of the time Christmas Eve and Christmas Day, but she could see Father was making an effort to talk and to keep everyone busy. And after they had their stockings and small presents and dinner, he had taken them for a sleigh ride to see Aunt Nell, who had hugged everyone and given them more presents.

But it seemed as if the problems never ended. She had been so relieved to get through Christmas without bursting into tears and so pleased that Abby and Charles enjoyed their stockings. And then Father had started going out to the hotel at night again. When she went to the sugar bowl two days after Christmas to get a little money to buy clothespins, she had found only a dollar there, in coins.

She took a dime anyway and went to the store to see if Mr. Goodnow had the new clip clothespins. The monthly newspaper said you just pinched them open and then they clipped onto the garment and the clothesline. She was tired of the old pins, which were so worn that they often split when you hung out something thick, like Father's trousers.

Mr. Goodnow had laughed when she asked about the pins.

"Quite the little housewife you are, Rose," he had said cheerfully, giving her seven cents worth of pins. She knew he meant well, but his words gave her that sinking feeling in her stomach again. She didn't want to be a good little housewife, at least not yet. She was annoyed enough to decide she'd get penny candy with the leftover pennies instead of returning them to the sugar bowl. So she spent another five minutes picking out six pieces of candy, including the peppermint sticks that Abby and Charles liked.

She loved looking at the many kinds of candy, the horehound drops she hated, and the red-hot cinnamon pieces that made your tongue burn. She was stooped down by the candy case when she heard the door click open—she knew Mr. Goodnow never left his candy out because he figured children would help themselves—so the two women who came in didn't see her. She couldn't see them either, but she heard their voices and knew it was Mrs. Munson and someone she didn't know.

"I just don't see how those children can manage with him out carousing half the night and teetering home to sleep a few hours and then start his chores again," Mrs. Munson said.

"Miss Harty says the oldest one is managing everything very well," the stranger answered. "But she's just a child, and someone ought to tell him a thing or two about raising young ones."

They're talking about us, Rose thought. They're talking about me. She stood up and heard Mr. Goodnow making shush-shush noises from behind the counter. She walked over, feeling as if her ankles were made of jelly, put three pennies in front of him and asked for the peppermint sticks. To her amazement, her voice actually came out of her mouth, sounding the same as always. He hurried to the candy case and she watched as he put eight in the bag instead of six. He handed it to her with a smile, and she turned to leave.

Mrs. Munson looked away just as Rose turned around, but Rose's temper had surfaced again.

"Good morning, Mrs. Munson," she said. "Isn't it a fine day?"

Why, she thought, her face is getting as red as mine. She tossed her head back, shaking her braids, and walked to the door with her two little bags; clothespins for the "little housewife," and candy for the two who were still allowed to be children, at least some of the time.

As she walked away, she was glad she had worn her long coat. It would just be too much if, somehow, the back of her dress was soiled, and Mrs. Munson saw. Two mornings before, she had found a bloodstain on her sheet, halfway down the bed so she knew it wasn't a nosebleed. She knew what it was, the thing called menstruation. "Men-strew-ay-shun," she said to herself. It was a tough word and another foolish one. Why should something that only women have start with the word "men"?

Emily said her mother called it "the monthlies" because it happened just about once a month. Alice's mother called it a "period." Rose only vaguely remembered her mother saying something about menstruation one day when Rose found her washing some stained ragged cloths in a basin in the sink. She recalled that Sarah had told her women had this bleeding on a regular basis, and that it had to do with bearing children. Anyway, Emily had been full of information when her "monthlies" had started in late November.

"You have to wear a thick padding of cloth so it won't leak all over your clothes or your bed," Emily had said in some disgust. "And your stomach gets all cramped up sometimes, and you can't say anything about it because then someone will know you have it. It seems to be a big secret."

"And you have to wash them out, don't you, Emily?" Rose had asked.

"Ay-yuh. That's one of the worst parts. Finding a place to dry them is another problem. You can't just hang things like that on the back porch," Emily said.

Remembering that conversation, Rose had ripped up an old flannel nightgown of Sarah's, and folded pieces into thick strips that she could pin inside her underwear. She checked several times before going to school that day, but still she stood up to recite with a terrible fear that a red or brown stain would be spread all over the back of her dress.

The first person to see that stain would be Newton, of course. He was still sitting behind her, and ever since the square dance she had been aware of his every move. She heard his work boots shuffle on the floor. Once she had been quite sure he stretched his leg out far enough to touch her shoe on purpose, and then she chided herself for being ridiculous, a silly goose again. She heard the scratch of his pen, she knew when he opened or shut a book. The good thing was that all this listening was keeping her awake.

But so far everything had been all right. She had washed out the used rags and hung them on her windowsill overnight, then hid them in the closet for the day. She wondered what it all had to do with childbearing, but she hadn't asked Emily yet. She also wondered how often this was going to happen to her, and did she need to just wear wads of rags all the time so she wouldn't be taken by surprise? Why didn't anyone talk about these things? Well, not just anyone. But someone. It was like dead people. No one talked about them, either.

Rose sighed. She would really like to spend a whole afternoon talking about her mother. She wondered if Aunt Nell or Uncle Jason could do that. She wondered where she would get an afternoon. She guessed she'd settle for an hour. She resolved to find an excuse to go to Aunt Nell's soon. Growing up had seemed quite simple when Sarah was alive. In those days, she just wished she were older. Now she would like nothing better than to be three again, skipping across the road to be a guest at the old one-room schoolhouse.

It was three days before Rose actually went to see Aunt Nell. It was a Saturday, and at breakfast, carrying coffee and oatmeal to her father, she announced that she needed help with some mending, so she was going to Aunt Nell's as soon as Abby and Charles had eaten.

"Better take along three or four eggs," Father said. We can spare a few, I reckon."

"Oh, yes, sir," Rose said. "We have quite a few in the icebox. I was even thinking about making a floating island pudding, except I'm not quite sure how."

"Nell can certainly advise you on that," Father said. "Now run along and let a man eat his breakfast in peace."

Rose went to the kitchen quickly. She knew it was not a good idea to talk with him much when his eyes were as red as raspberries. But she had to let him know when she was leaving the house and the other two children. At least he hadn't yelled at her. Sometimes when he was out really late, he raised his voice over almost nothing. Those times made Rose wish she could shrink until she was too small to see.

What she needed, she thought, was some of the stuff the wonderland Alice had taken. Sometimes, Rose thought, it would even be nice to disappear down the rabbit's hole. Certainly the fearsome Red Queen would be no more scary than her father the morning after he had been at the drink. She hadn't found much time for reading in the past few months, but she had finished that one book, and it had sent her imagination flying. She had looked at the big tree outside the back door in a whole different way after that, wishing Sarah's cat could sit up there and vanish except for his smile. As long as he came back later, of course.

When Abby and Charles finished their Saturday chores, Rose told them she was going out for a bit. She found four pairs of her father's stockings with holes in the heels, and a dress that was a little too tight for Abby, packed them in a basket, nestled the eggs into the fabric and set off for Aunt Nell's. She was pretty sure her aunt would be home because Saturday was her baking day. In fact, she thought, I am Red Riding Hood in reverse. I have a basket, and I'm going to my aunt's and she will give me goodies. She wondered suddenly if she should be taking something nice to Aunt Nell. Well, perhaps she'd think the five brown eggs were nice. Rose's feet made a sharp crunch, crunch, crunch in the frozen snow on the road. At least, she said to herself, a wolf will not be jumping out of the woods at me. That made her smile. Emily would say her head had come unhitched again.

In a few minutes, she knocked at Aunt Nell's back door, lifted the latch and opened the door, calling "Halloo, halloo," as she stepped inside the little room that led to the kitchen. Here she could sit on the bench and take off her boots. She knew her aunt wouldn't want her wet coat in the kitchen, so she took that off, too, and hung it on a hook, alongside the various farm jackets and sweaters. Aunt Nell was very particular about people tracking mud and water over her kitchen floor, and she never allowed barn clothes beyond this little room.

"I won't have my house smelling like a herd of cows lived in it," she would say, looking at Uncle Jason over her spectacles.

"I only have three cows," he'd always answer. "I'm not a farmer. I'm a carpenter."

"Three or three hundred, the smell's the same," she'd say in a sharp voice. But she always smiled when she said it, so everyone knew it was just one of those jokes married folks seemed to repeat all the time. Like Grandfather and Grandmother and the goose, Rose thought. Only that was a much funnier story than having your kitchen smell like a cow.

Anyway, Aunt Nell's kitchen usually smelled like coffee and something baked. It was a delicious kitchen, Rose thought, wondering how her aunt found time to scrub the wood floorboards and do the washing and make the meals, and still seem to be forever baking. She didn't have but the one child, of course. That must make a difference.

Rose moved into the kitchen, ready to call out another greeting and found herself face to face with Aunt Nell, who was on her way to answer the door.

"Now you are a sight for sore eyes, child," Aunt Nell said, reaching out her arms to give Rose a big hug.

Rose felt her stomach flop and her eyes start to water. Was she going to fall apart again, she wondered. What was the matter with her? She couldn't hold up worth a tinker's dam. Was that swearing, she wondered, her mind rattling on even as tears started to run down her cheeks. She hugged Aunt Nell and thought if they just stood there long enough, she could get things under control. But she felt a little foolish with the basket draped over Aunt Nell's shoulder. "The eggs," she said suddenly, and pulled away, setting the basket carefully on the floor.

"Now, now," Aunt Nell said. "I expect you haven't had much for hugs at your house, what with all the work to be done and your father not much on hugging anyway, at least not hugging his children. You come in and set right down and tell me the news from your house, and show me what's in that basket. Eggs, I should be glad to see. How is Abby doing? She had the most beautiful skirt at the square dance. And is Charles giving you trouble, or is he trying to grow up and help out a bit?"

Rose started to laugh, found her handkerchief and mopped up her face. Aunt Nell talked out loud almost the way Rose's own brain ran around from one subject to another. She tried to backtrack and figure out what all the questions were so she could answer them.

"Not much news except that I started my menstruation and wasn't sure what to do, and the basket has mending that I can't figure out. And five eggs, too. They're not very big because the pullets just started laying, but they're fresh. I made Abby's skirt from a small length of fabric that I bought at Mr. Goodnow's, and Charles does so many chores every day that his hands are all calluses. Did I leave anything out? Oh, Father never hugs anyone that I know of. I don't believe I ever saw him hug Sarah."

Aunt Nell's eyebrows went up at the use of her sister's

given name, but she didn't say anything, and Rose was concentrating so hard on the answers to all the questions that she didn't notice what she had said.

"Oh, my dear child, he did love her, you know. Your mother, I mean. I remember when they were courting, he was as sappy as a tapped maple in springtime. Your Uncle Jason wouldn't let him near a saw or splitter that year for fear he'd forget what he was doing and cut off his hand or his leg. Guess some hugging must have gone on when you weren't about."

Rose felt teary and warm all at the same time. He had loved her. He didn't talk about her because he couldn't. She knew how that was. It was all she could do sometimes to answer Abby and Charles' questions about Sarah.

"Is Father afraid he won't hold up?" Rose asked, sniffling a little as the tears tried to exit through her nose.

"Hold up?" Aunt Nell said, frowning. "What do you mean?"

"Oh, everyone the day of the funeral—and the day of Uncle Cal's funeral last year—kept talking about people holding up. Miss Harty said that meant they didn't cry, but she didn't seem to put much stock in anyone's ability to 'hold up.' She said you should cry if you felt like it, especially when someone you loved was gone."

"I expect your father is trying very hard to 'hold up,' Rose. He would think that was important. He's a man, in the first place and probably thinks they don't cry or even shudder a little, and in the second place, he's a

Hibbard. They never were much for letting on how they felt about anything."

Rose sighed and wished she'd come here a little sooner.

"I should have been up there to your house long since," Aunt Nell said. "I was so wound up in mourning the death of my sister that I did not let your troubles inside my mind. And then, you must be old enough to know how most folks hereabouts put up fences around their lives, don't want anyone interfering. Your father might think I was being helpful if I showed up every other day with food and chatter, but more than likely he'd tell me to get home and mind my own business. Still, I'm sorry, Rose, I should have been thinking more about you and less about him. Now you set there in the rocking chair—pull it a little closer to the stove—and unpack that basket, and we will have ourselves a mending and talking time."

Rose sat and fished out the smallish brown eggs one at a time. Aunt Nell put them in a little bowl and placed it in her icebox, as far from the ice section as she could get it.

"Don't want those little darlings to freeze," she said. "You came just in time. Jason killed the last two chickens at Christmas and says he won't have another chicken on the place. Says they smell bad, they're not friendly, and they eat dirt. All that may be, but as far as I'm concerned, a nice fresh egg makes up for most of it."

Rose laughed and pulled out the four socks that had

holes in the heels, and Abby's dress. She gloomily held up a sock she had tried to darn, and said she had gotten out her mother's little wooden ball with the handle and put it inside the sock, but it still came out all wrong.

"It's putched," she said, hoping Aunt Nell knew what that meant.

"Indeed, it is," her aunt answered. "Let's start with one you haven't tampered with."

So she took a ball of darning cotton from her sewing basket, threaded a needle and showed her how to hold the darning tool and weave back and forth across the hole. "Don't pull that thread tight," she cautioned. "The idea is to fill in the hole with a little patch of fabric made of thread."

The two quickly made Father's socks wearable again, and turned to the dress, which was a greater problem. But Aunt Nell brought out a wide piece of plain fabric, separated the skirt from the top, and inserted a band of the plain color to make a wider waistband. Then Rose loosened the gathers in the skirt a bit and pinned it together again.

She was surprised when her aunt then cut about three inches of fabric off the bottom of the dress. She was about to say that it was already too short when Aunt Nell measured a length of the same plain fabric and set it in between the two pieces of skirt.

"Now when she wears this, the two stripes will look as if they belong there, not as if we were trying to make a dress last longer," Aunt Nell said. "If we just put in one or t'other, everyone would know it was a stretch fix."

"That's very clever," Rose said. "I would never have thought to do that."

"But you will next time," Aunt Nell said.

While Rose sewed the pieces together by hand, Aunt Nell started to talk about Sarah. It was the real reason Rose had come, and while her eyes stayed on her needle and thread, her ears concentrated on what her aunt was telling her.

"She was my younger sister, you know, and she always was headstrong. Knew what she wanted and went after it. She set her cap for your father almost as soon as she saw him driving past with a team of horses and a load of logs. I remember her looking out the window and saying, 'What a handsome man that is with the logging wagon.' Soon after, somehow, she found out that he was hauling the logs here from just over the state line, getting up before sunrise so he could get back home soon after dark, coming up once or sometimes twice a week. He was pretty shy, but she got acquainted with him right quickly, and pretty soon she invited him down to one of the square dances.

"I don't know where he stayed that night. He hadn't the money for the hotel, so he probably slept at the stable with his horses. He loved that team, and he had a nice buggy, in addition to the wagon. She liked riding in that buggy. Pretty soon he was coming into town every Sunday about noon, stopping at our house for dinner and taking Sarah for a buggy ride.

"We all knew his goose was cooked. Probably before he knew. Anyway, your Uncle Jason told Sarah her young man was mooning around like a sick calf and didn't know enough anymore to drive those horses safely back up the mountain to his folks' house.

" 'You'd better marry him before he gets killed,' Jason told her. She was intending just that, so she took his comment very seriously, and about six months after she met Silas, they were married. You came along a year or so later, and Sarah was a happy, happy woman, even more so when Silas talked Jason into moving down here, too. We were always close, and it did both of us good to at least be near neighbors."

"But she didn't look happy to me at the end of the day," Rose interrupted.

"Tired, probably. But not unhappy, child. She picked out your father, and she loved him. And he loved her. If things are too silent at your house—if he's not helping all of you with your grief—it's because he can't begin to accept that she's gone."

Aunt Nell patted Rose on the knee. "It's not easy for any of us," she said softly, her eyes suddenly wet.

"No," Rose said. "Not for any of us."

"And perhaps I shouldn't say this to you, but there's talk around town that your father's been at the drink pretty heavy—drowning his sorrows, they call that—so you might as well hear it from me, or sure as anything you'll hear one of those gossips at the store when they think you're out of earshot."

"I knew that, Aunt Nell," Rose said. "And I did hear the gossips, just the other day at Mr. Goodnow's. They didn't see me. It was Mrs. Munson and another woman.

Father takes money from the sugar bowl, and he's out almost every night, and he has red eyes, and Emily said that was from the drink. And he kicked Mother's cat one day after he'd been out particularly late. I was wondering if the reverend's meetings would be something he'd take to."

Aunt Nell's friendly face seemed to freeze slightly. The lines that usually moved up and down around her eyes and mouth were still for just a few seconds. Then she uncrossed her feet, leaned forward in her chair and put both hands on Rose's knees.

"You get yourself on down here anytime things aren't going right up there, Rose. You are a levelheaded girl, but you are just a girl, and if you need help, Jason and I are here to help you. Don't you forget that."

"Thank you, Ma'am," Rose said, feeling a couple of the knots in her stomach come loose. "Sometimes I worry about Abby and Charles. They are grieving. They even go to the cemetery by themselves, and Charles told me the other day that they sit there in the cold and cry."

"That's not bad for them," Aunt Nell said. "They have you to lean on, and I'm sure they're doing plenty of that. The people I worry about are you—because you have too much on your shoulders—and your father—because men don't do well on their own. Maybe I should keep my nose out of these things, but you are better off hearing it from me than from a stranger or a neighbor. Sooner or later, Rose, probably sooner, he's going to be looking for another woman to take Sarah's place, and you won't like it a-tall."

"Oh my goodness," Rose said, shocked at the very idea. "Someone to take Sarah's place?"

This time she heard herself say Sarah, and she quickly explained to Aunt Nell how she'd gotten into this habit. She was relieved to see that her aunt only nodded and didn't seem perturbed.

"Well, the good thing about that," Rose added quickly, "would be that I could stay in school."

"And who said you were leaving?" Aunt Nell said, a little shocked herself.

"Father."

"Why?"

"Because when spring comes, there will be too much work, and I will have to take on Sarah's share of the farm chores, in addition to the house and the cooking."

Aunt Nell tapped her foot four times, staring at it as if it weren't attached to her at all. "I shall have to go see your father," she said. "Sarah always said you were a smart one and that she wanted you to have your chance to teach school. Said that's what you had talked about since the age of eight. I shall have to talk to him."

"Miss Harty already did," Rose said. "And it just made him very angry. Angry with us, too, and the cat."

"Don't you bother your head about what I might do," Aunt Nell said. "I won't make him angry at you. But I will try to help out. Did he hire a girl to help you with the washing?"

"No, but we have running water and an icebox."

"Things Sarah should have had," Aunt Nell muttered almost to herself.

"That's what I thought," Rose said. "I was glad to get the icebox and even happier about the water, but they both made me cry again."

"I think," Aunt Nell said, "that you'd better be getting on home to your chores, and I think you had better set aside enough time next Saturday for a trip into Ripton for some shopping and lunch at the restaurant, and maybe even some ice cream. Not Abby and Charles. Just you."

"Oh, oh, oh," Rose said, instantly so excited that she for once could think of nothing else to say.

"We'll go," Aunt Nell said firmly. "I have a little something in my sugar bowl, and we can take the train."

CHAPTER 13
A Little Wobbly

It was late afternoon before Rose headed back to her house. Now she really was Red Riding Hood. Aunt Nell had packed the mended socks and the dress into Rose's basket, then added a small tin of filled cookies and a loaf of bread, still warm from the oven. One of the best things was the small ham she had fetched from a hook in the coldest part of her attic. They hadn't eaten ham in some time, and Rose's mouth watered as she thought about sticking in a dozen cloves and then spreading some of Sarah's strawberry-rhubarb jam over the whole thing. An hour or so of baking while they were at church, and Sunday dinner would be really special. At the last minute, Aunt Nell had taken a little jar of what she always called Dutch cheese from her icebox and added that to the basket.

Rose knew the whole family would be happy to get the curdy cheese her aunt had made. She had tried to make it, but hers didn't come out right, and she ended up using it in a pudding. And that pudding wasn't just right either. Father and Charles had eaten it without a word, but Abby had made a terrible face and pushed it around with her spoon for ten minutes before she finally swallowed it all.

Every few steps, Rose skipped a little and realized each time that she felt better than she had in months. Aunt Nell had a way of making you think things were going to come out all right. Rose was pretty sure Father would make her leave school in the spring, but she was putting that problem in the attic of her brain, slammed inside one of those dusty trunks where Sarah put things she didn't want but couldn't get rid of. She needed another worry right now about as badly as she needed a straw hat.

When Rose opened the door at her house, she called out a greeting, but no one answered. She put down the basket and went through the downstairs, finding no one. Then she heard faint sounds from above and found Charles on the floor of his attic room with a tablet of paper on his lap, and an elaborate structure of blocks in front of him.

"I'm drawing it," he said without looking up. "I decided I wanted to be able to make one just like this again, so I'm drawing it."

He'll turn out to be an architect, Rose thought, going around behind him to look over his shoulder. "Oooh, that's quite nice, Charles," she said.

"He's a horrid person, and I hate him," Abby's voice said from the door.

"Abby? Charles? Can't I leave the house on a Saturday afternoon without you two forgetting to behave yourselves?"

"Well," Charles said, still not looking up, "she wanted to help me build and when I said she couldn't, she tried to knock my building down."

"So he hit me," Abby said.

"Hit her, Charles?" Rose asked sharply.

"Oh, I gave her a little tap on the arm, just before she hit my building," he said.

Rose took Abby's hands, pushed up her sleeves and looked at both arms. She saw no sign of a bruise or even a red mark.

"Abby?" she said.

"He didn't hit me very hard, but he scared me," Abby said, starting to cry.

"Making people afraid is a very bad thing, Charles, and I don't want you to forget that—ever," Rose said in her best imitation of a parental tone.

"I'm sorry, Rose," Charles said.

"Apologize to your sister. She's the one you hit or tapped, or touched in some way that upset her."

"I am sorry, Abby."

"And I won't do it again," Rose prompted.

"And I won't do it again."

"As for you, Abby, you are not to touch Charles' block buildings unless you have permission. They are quite special, and they are not yours."

"Yes, Rose," Abby said.

"So wipe your eyes and go wash your face," Rose

said, thinking that this was a side of teaching that she wouldn't like very much. But at least she was getting her way with them this time, so maybe she'd be able to manage a whole classroom. Or at least a classroom that didn't have anyone like the Granger boys in it. And she didn't even have to worry about Grangers, not while Newton was there. The now familiar warm feeling gave a little dance around her stomach. At first that odd sensation had upset her, but now she decided she quite liked it. It was a happy thing, not the sort of stomach wiggle that came right before you lost your dinner all over the floor. Vomit, Sarah called that kind of mess. It was a good word. It sounded sudden and nasty, and vomit was just that. But this flip-flop in her stomach didn't mean vomit at all. It was just a nice feeling that came when she thought about the square dance and Newton. Oops, there it went again.

She giggled, and Charles looked up, surprised.

"Aren't you still mad at us?" he asked.

"No, no, no," Rose said. "I have been to Aunt Nell's, and I've brought home goodies, and I mended the socks, and we talked about Sarah for a long time. Aunt Nell is upset that she hasn't visited us more, but I told her we were doing all right. We are, aren't we, Charles?"

Charles placed a triangular block on top of two thin ones that looked like the columns at the church in Stony Brook. He added the three blocks to his drawing, while Rose waited. How precise he is, she thought. Those lines are almost as if he had used a rule.

"We are doing all right, Rose," Charles said. "We

really are. We wouldn't be if we didn't have you . . ." He looked up and grinned. "But we do have you, like it or not."

He looked back at his building. "Abby and I," he went on in a voice soft enough so Abby wouldn't hear if she were still in the next room, "are really afraid of Father. He scares us. He kicked the cat, and he doesn't smell good, and sometimes he wobbles when he walks."

"When did you see him wobble, Charles?"

Charles scratched his head and looked as if he'd been caught taking a cookie. "Well, I heard him come home late one night, and I looked over the railing, and he went down the hall going from one side to the other. It looked as if the wall was pushing him back to the middle, and then he'd just keep right on going over to the other wall. I thought it was a good thing the hall had walls on both sides."

Rose had no idea how to respond to this confession, so she didn't say anything at all for a minute or two.

"I think," she said finally, "that you need another triangle over there," and she pointed to the far side of the building. "And I think that Father will be all right, too, if we just help him along by doing what he says and getting our work done quickly and well."

"Ummmm," was all Charles said.

"You'd better come to the kitchen and see the things Aunt Nell made for us," Rose said. "And it's time to feed the chickens."

Rose nearly pranced through the next week. She hummed as she did the housework, she felt wide-awake in school, and she did a lot of talking. Miss Harty could not help but notice the change, and at the end of the day on Wednesday, she stopped Rose when everyone started for the cloakroom.

"How is everything going, Rose?" she asked, hoping Rose's father had given up the idea of taking her out of school.

But it was something much simpler.

"Aunt Nell is taking me to Ripton on Saturday," Rose said, her eyes dancing. "She is taking just me, and we are going shopping, and we will eat our noon meal at the hotel or a boarding house. We are going on the train, right through the big tunnel."

"Oh, that will be a wonderful trip," Miss Harty said, barely able to hide her disappointment that it was not more earthshaking news than a day away from the village. "You run along now and get some fresh air."

Rose thanked her, ran to the cloakroom to get her wrap, and joined Emily and Alice at the bottom of the stairs outside. They both knew about the Saturday outing and wished they had been invited to go along. They told Rose how jealous they were and then told each other that they could not be really jealous, not when they had mothers and Rose didn't.

"We have a plan," Emily said, as soon as Rose came down the steps. "We are both coming, if you'll let us, to your house on Friday afternoon to help with the Saturday work so you won't have to get up at three o'clock in the morning. Surely a lot of things can be done Friday? We did lots of things before Miss Harty came to Sunday dinner." Emily stopped short, thinking how that dinner had changed Rose, how sad she had been afterward because her father wanted her to give up school. But Emily didn't have to worry. Rose apparently wasn't connecting the last work bee and the disastrous dinner.

"We are fearful," Alice chimed in, "that you will fall asleep on the train, going and coming, and will be drowsy through your meal at the restaurant and won't be able to tell us anything when you get back."

"Oh, how wonderful," Rose said. "I could not figure out how all the Saturday things were going to happen without my being there. And if the Saturday work doesn't get done, I have to sneak it in on Sunday when the neighbors aren't looking or it all spills into the next week. And then Father might take me out of school for the winter, too."

Alice and Emily looked at each other, dismayed by the very idea that their friend would become a housekeeper from dawn to dark. But Rose was in no mood to think about anything that far in the future. She had already planned what she would wear on Saturday, had hunted up Sarah's black umbrella in case it rained, even though she knew it was more likely to snow, and had asked Father if she might take fifty cents from the sugar bowl. To her surprise, he had told her to take a dollar, and promised that he would put some more money in the bowl at the end of the week. She knew her friends wanted to go with her, so she would get each one some kind of treat in Ripton, especially now that they were going to help with her work.

The wind started to come up as the three friends turned toward home, and they walked quickly, heads down, in an effort to keep warm. In spring and fall, the walk to and from school was their chance to catch up on everything that had happened, and they usually chattered without stopping. Today was not talking weather, but Rose put her arms through Emily's and Alice's, pulling them close to her, and they walked in step, heads down, moving like one person instead of three.

"You make some lists, now," Alice shouted as she turned off. "If you have a hired girl, you have to keep her busy!"

"She has the lists in her head," Emily said. "They spin around in there all the time, arranged alphabetically."

All three laughed, and Alice waved as Emily and Rose pulled scarves over their faces and bent into the wind again.

CHAPTER 14
Cussed Cow

Rose woke Saturday while it was still dark. As she pushed back her quilt and swung her feet onto the cold floor, she heard the front room clock striking six. She had actually slept all night—too long, in fact. Father would be coming in for breakfast in just a few minutes. She put a robe over her nightdress, put on her slippers and almost ran downstairs, even though the hallway was as black as tarpaper. When you live in a house a long time, she thought, you could go blind and still do everything. You know where all the doors and steps and stairs are; you even know where the splinters are in the floorboards and how many steps it is from the woodbox to the stove. But she stretched out her arm in front of her face as she turned toward the kitchen. She didn't want to run smack up against a door that was closed, or a chair that had been moved.

In the kitchen, the fire was going in the stove, which meant Father had poked it up before he went out. She added wood, put coffee in a saucepan with water and filled another for the oatmeal. She put the maple syrup on the table, along with the butter dish, and went to the pantry to slice bread for toast. With luck, it would be ten more minutes before Father would come banging into the milk room downstairs, and she would be just about ready.

It was more than ten minutes, as it turned out, and she decided that was a sign that the day would turn out well all around. When she heard him in the milk room, she stirred the oats into the pan and pulled it slightly off the fire to cook gently. At the last minute, she fetched one of the Christmas oranges from the icebox, peeled it and put half the sections on a small plate at his place.

Rose loved the Christmas oranges. They fit perfectly into the toe of each stocking and provided enough weight to make each one hang properly. They didn't have any fancy Christmas stockings at their house, so they always hung Father's socks because they were the biggest. She had heard that Mrs. Munson knitted up some special ones in green and red yarn and only used them at Christmastime, but she didn't know anyone else who did that. The other thing about the oranges was that they were the first of the season. They came from Florida, the state that put the little tail on the bottom right side of the United States map. And they were very dear, so very few people could buy them after Christmas. But Sarah had always saved enough money to get oranges for every stocking, and Father had said Rose could look in her mother's handkerchief drawer for the money. Sure enough, it was there—he hadn't touched that.

She heard Father's footsteps coming through the ell, sounding peculiar. Clomp, clomp, clomp, he usually went. Today it was more like clomp, scuff, clomp, scuff. She went to the kitchen door and opened it. He was limping toward her, favoring his left leg, and his face was screwed into a terrible look.

"What happened?" she cried, reaching for his arm.

"The brown cow took a notion to kick me," he said. "Right in the knee. She sent the milk pail flying and me sprawling. I expect I've bruised my hip pretty good, too."

Her stomach somersaulted. He's going to make me stay home, she thought. I'm going to be a nurse today instead of having a good time. I hate cows. I hate milk. I hate him. I hate . . .

Her father broke into her thoughts by putting his hand on Rose's arm, and she helped him into the kitchen where he sat down in the rocking chair.

"What can I do?" she asked, turning her face away so he wouldn't see her tears.

"If you could chip off some ice from the block in the icebox and roll it into a towel, I guess a cold pack would be as good as anything," he said. "Don't think she managed to break anything. But she did waste a couple of quarts of good milk."

Rose had a little trouble chopping any ice off the

block because she could barely see, but she eventually managed and rolled it in a tea towel for him. He slapped it right onto his knee over the pants and said if she fetched him a stool or a chair, he'd get that leg up in the air a little. Rose quickly responded, lifting the leg onto a chair. How could she be thinking about her trip to town when he was in such pain, she scolded herself. She gently pulled his boot off and then slipped a cushion under his leg.

"Well, now," he said, "that's not bad, not bad a-tall. I washed up in the milk room, so if you found a little table and moved my breakfast over here, I could eat that while you get dressed for your trip to town. Nell will be along pretty early, you know."

"I can't go if you're hurt, Father," Rose said.

"Certainly can. You standing there wishing you were on a train is not going to take any of the pain out of my knee. Might add to it, if you looked gloomy enough. Besides, Charles and Abby can fetch whatever I need, and by milking time tonight, I'll probably be quite all right."

Rose looked doubtful, but when he said, "Get a move on," she scurried for the stairs.

Once she and Aunt Nell boarded the train, Rose forgot about her father's injured leg. The day seemed like a dream, but she knew it was all real, a day without any work and with the kind of enjoyment she hadn't felt in a long time. First they went to stores, four of them, including the butter and cheese shop. They bought fabric for a new square dance skirt for Rose, a half yard of shiny blue ribbon for Emily's hair and a half yard of green for Alice, a pair of suspenders for Charles and a small silver locket for Abby. Rose used sugar bowl money for Emily and Alice's presents after Aunt Nell insisted on buying the things for her brother and sister, and the blue and green plaid cloth for the new skirt.

Rose wasn't sure what her father would like, but Aunt Nell led the way to the tobacconists' shop, where they bought him a small packet of tobacco for his pipe.

"He doesn't smoke it very often," Rose said, not sure it was the best present.

"I'm certain he smokes a pipe in the evening, Rose," Aunt Nell answered. "He wouldn't smoke a pipe in the barn, you know, because a spark could easily fall in the hay. But he takes a pipe at the hotel."

When he's at the drink, Rose had thought, wondering exactly what those women in the store meant by "carousing." She would have asked Miss Harty, but she was pretty sure it wasn't nice, and Mrs. Munson had made it sound worse than being at the drink. To Rose's surprise, they ate their noon meal at the drug store, where Mr. Hawks boasted that his counter and stools were the latest thing in the big cities, that everyone who was anyone in New York and Boston would get a quick bite at a counter like this. He was proudest of all of the tall glass container filled with long paper tubes.

"Drinking straws," he said to Rose, but in such a kindly, enthusiastic way that she didn't feel at all like a country bumpkin. "You set it in your tumbler of cider there, and then suck on it."

She slipped the straw into the drinking glass and sucked, watching the bronze liquid move up the straw. A taste of cider came into her mouth, so she pulled her breath in even harder, and then spluttered as she choked on more cider than her throat could handle. But when she glanced quickly at the giant mirror on the wall behind Mr. Hawks, no one seemed to be looking her way, so she took another small sip through the drinking straw and the cider slid down her throat nicely.

At first she found it a little embarrassing to look up from her bowl of stew and see her own face staring back at her from the mirror opposite. But she could see what a good thing it was. Not only could she tell who was looking at her, but Mr. Hawks could still see everyone behind him when he had to turn his back to wash plates or dish up an order. She noticed that whenever a new customer sat down, he bustled right over with the small card that listed the specials of the day. She thought Mrs. Hawks must have written out the card—the handwriting was as pretty as the letters in the Palmer book at school. She had seen Mr. Hawks dance, and now she watched him scurrying about in his shop and thought he was the kind of person who would dash through his letters with more enthusiasm than precision.

Aunt Nell ordered the chicken pie, but Rose had decided on the stew because they were always eating chicken at home, and she had never made a real stew herself. She thought it was a little heavy, perhaps because of the fat on the meat. She could probably get the same rich flavor if she trimmed the beef more and cooked up the scraps for the cat. The carrots were brown from the thick gravy, and the potatoes were very soft. She tasted small pieces of onion and figured the long cooking had reduced the onions to scrap pieces. A stew probably must simmer on the back of the stove for the better part of a day—maybe even a night. Oh, dear, she thought. Am I becoming a housewife?

Then they walked all around the dry goods store once more. They looked in the windows at the butcher's shop and stopped to watch the cobbler making shoes. They looked at the fire wagon standing inside the open door of the firehouse. Rose noticed that the horses tied next to the firehouse were all harnessed. It wouldn't take long for the volunteers to get that wagon out of the station and on the road, she thought. In her village, she was pretty sure the volunteer firemen brought horses from home when the alarm sounded. A house there could probably burn to the ground while they were still hitching up.

Their last stop was at a house near the end of the main street, where Aunt Nell knocked at the door and waited until a woman answered.

"Why, aren't you a sight for sore eyes!" the woman had exclaimed, opening the door wide. She was a short lady, shorter than Rose, and she looked quite round; rather like Tweedledee, Rose thought, immediately wishing that picture had not pushed into her mind.

"May I introduce my niece, Rose Hibbard?" Aunt Nell had answered, stepping up to give the woman a quick hug and a peck on the cheek.

"Delighted, I'm sure," the woman said.

"This is my good friend, Mrs. Tucker," Aunt Nell told Rose. "We are going to visit with her for a bit and have a look at her beautiful hats."

Rose had never met anyone who made hats. As they stepped into a small room next to the parlor, she could not believe what she saw. A long table was covered with boxes of buttons, ribbons, feathers and bright jewels; and scattered among the boxes were several carved wooden heads in different sizes. The shiny heads had necks, but no eyes, noses or mouths. Several piles of plain hats were stacked on a side table, where another wooden head was wearing a black felt hat with a beautiful pheasant feather stuck in the black grosgrain ribbon that was used for a band.

"Would you like to try on a hat?" Mrs. Tucker asked.

Rose said, "No, Ma'am," right away because she knew she couldn't buy a hat. She didn't even need a hat. But Mrs. Tucker wasn't looking to sell anything. She just thought Rose would enjoy the hats. So she made a place for her to sit down, put a hand mirror on the table and gave her several hats to try.

"Have a nice time," she said. "You are welcome to put ribbons on any of these that you fancy."

Then, turning to Aunt Nell, she invited her to have a cup of tea and hear the latest gossip. The two women went into the parlor and left Rose to her own devices. It was a wonderful hour. She wound a red ribbon around one gray hat. These must be go-to-church hats, she thought—they certainly wouldn't keep a body's head warm—and then added a second narrower ribbon in black. She crossed the ribbons over on the back, pinned them in place with the ends dangling and tucked a tiny black and white feather—was it from a woodpecker?—into the ribbons on the side. She tried on the hat and picked up the hand mirror. Do you have to kill a woodpecker to get a black and white feather, she wondered, and then looked in the mirror. Why, she didn't look like Rose a-tall, she thought. Who was this person in the hat? She began to giggle and wished Emily and Alice could see. It was more fun to laugh with your friends than by yourself. But she would tell them about this part of the day. About the whole day actually.

This, she said to herself, looking in the mirror again, is the kind of hat a teacher could wear to church, the kind she would wear when she was a teacher. If she ever was, she thought, remembering the housewife stew again.

Just then Aunt Nell came through the door with Mrs. Tucker.

"Sakes alive, child, if you don't look ten years older in that hat," Aunt Nell said.

"And very pretty, too," Mrs. Tucker added, "if you don't mind my saying so."

"It won't go to this one's head," Aunt Nell said. "She has her feet on the ground and a few too many things to keep them there."

Rose felt her face flush and wished they would stop talking as if she weren't in the room. Why did grown-ups do that? Children should be seen and not heard, they often said, but not being heard didn't mean you couldn't hear. And where would her feet possibly go if they weren't on the ground? It must be another one of those things Miss Harty called "expressions."

"We must be on our way," Aunt Nell said. "You need to get home to check on your father, and I will have to scrabble some supper together in a hurry for Mr. Harris. He'll not be pleased if there's no sign of me when he comes in."

Father, Rose thought. There he is with a banged-up knee and all that pain, and I haven't given him a thought since we boarded the train. Except for getting the tobacco. But even then she had not considered how he might be getting on without her. She carefully removed the hat and started to take off the feather and ribbons.

"You may leave those right on there, young lady," Mrs. Tucker said. "I think I'll try to sell it just like that. Perhaps you will be a hatmaker yourself one day."

"She's going to be a teacher," Aunt Nell said with a touch of pride in her voice. "Now say goodbye, and we will head home."

The bottom dropped out of Rose's stomach for a second. Did Aunt Nell think she could still be a teacher? Then she saw Mrs. Tucker looking at her with that expression grown-ups have when they are waiting for you to say the right thing.

"I had a lovely time," Rose said. "Thank you for letting me play with the hats and ribbons."

"You are most welcome, dear child," Mrs. Tucker said. "I hope you will come again soon and bring your aunt. We do not get enough time for visiting these days. And," she rushed on, "I am sorry about your loss and hope you are managing."

"Thank you," Rose said, looking down at the floor so the ladies wouldn't see her eyes filling up. When was she going to get over this crying? She wanted to remember her mother forever, but she wanted to do it without snuffling like a five-year-old with a head cold.

CHAPTER 15
Dirt in Layers

"I hope Father is all right," Rose said, frowning as she sat down next to Aunt Nell on the train. She put her parcels on the floor between her feet, and sat very straight, twisting the top button on her coat with her right hand.

"Don't fret yourself," Aunt Nell said. "He probably took it real easy today and will be all straightened out by the time you get home. I intend to go with you and see to it myself. But you can't heal his leg with worrying."

"But the ice would have melted in a short time, and he wasn't putting his weight on that leg a-tall, Aunt Nell," Rose said, her forehead tightening even more. Aunt Nell gave her a little pat on the knee and pointed out that they were going past a herd of cows that were heading for the barn.

"It's milking time," Aunt Nell said. "And either your

father or Charles, or both of them, are at the barn at this very moment, doing the milking."

"Well," Rose said, "I don't know if he could walk there. And I hope the cow doesn't just haul off and kick him again."

"You really are a worrier, aren't you?" Aunt Nell asked, a hint of concern creeping into her voice. "At your age, you should just be thinking about whether you have your sums right, and whether you can hem a skirt so the stitches barely show even on the wrong side, and whether you can read the Evening Star when it comes, and if you're going to get your bath first on Saturday night."

"I worry about all those things, too," Rose said, but she had started to smile. "And I always get my bath first because the rest of them can't seem to make up their minds to get at it. Besides, with the new system, we don't all take our baths in the same water. I did hate," she added, "taking mine after Father. He has layers of dirt, you know."

Nell thought she would not ask right now exactly what that meant, but she knew a working man wasn't very clean by Saturday night, so she could hardly blame Rose for managing to be first. At least, she thought, we've gotten off the subject of the bum leg, but I shall have to see to it, or he'll wear the child out waiting on him. He never was good about being laid up. She gave a little sigh, thinking of the time when that rambunctious calf had slammed into Silas Hibbard and he'd got one of his fingers broken. You'd have thought it was his neck, the way he carried on, moaning about the pain as if he were having a baby. Sarah had to milk the cows until the splint came off and even then Silas had fussed that he couldn't carry two pails at a time. She hoped his ears had been turned on when the Rev. Lockhead was preaching about the hard cider and the whiskey being bad for the whole town. She wondered if she should ask him about going to the temperance meetings. Probably take her head off, she guessed.

"Here's the tunnel," Rose exclaimed in delight, and Nell pushed her thoughts aside to look. "Someday I'm going to take a train all the way to California."

"I hope you do," Nell said. "Perhaps I'll go with you."

As the train moved through the mountain, they were silent, the girl thinking dreamily about seeing the Mississippi River and the prairie and the ocean and cowboys and huge mountains; and her aunt wondering if there would ever be a time when either of them would be allowed to be that far from home. Even if they had the money to buy a ticket.

By the time they reached their stop near the hotel, Rose was so excited about getting home and giving out her presents and showing everyone the things Aunt Nell had bought for her that she had put Father's leg in the back of her mind again. She gathered up her parcels and started along the street toward her house with Aunt Nell.

"Hello, hello," she called as she opened the kitchen door. "Anybody home?"

The kitchen was empty, but she saw that Father had moved to the dining room table, and that he had company. She started toward him, but stopped when she heard a gasp behind her. Turning, she saw Aunt Nell's face darken, and Rose quickly put down her packages and took her aunt's arm.

"Are you all right?" she said. "Did I walk too fast? Are your things too heavy?"

"I'm just fine," Nell said, brushing past her. "Good afternoon, Silas. I came to see how your leg is doing and whether you might need some nursing or some help from Jason. I see you have taken care of the nursing need in your own way."

In a voice that sounded almost impolite—and Rose had trouble remembering when Aunt Nell had ever sounded even a little bit rude—she heard her aunt say, "And good afternoon to you, too, Miss Jenny."

"Been gone so long, I thought you'd run off for good," Father said. "This is a friend of mind, Miss Graves, come in to give me a hand. Charles fetched her for me, and she's been keeping the ice packs going, so this leg is about as numb as a dead beech. Still hurts some, though."

"I'd best take a look, Silas, even though you have had all this care already," Aunt Nell said.

Her words sound like she's clipping them with scissors, Rose thought. What's going on? Aunt Nell never talks like this, and now Father's face is getting red.

"First, I'll just clear up some of these dishes," Nell said, taking two half-full tumblers off the table.

Father started to protest and then stopped, glancing

at Rose. Nell was already on her way to the kitchen sink where she poured the contents of the tumblers down the drain.

"By thunder," Father said, starting to get up and then wincing with pain. "I won't have you coming in here and wasting good cider that way. A man has a right to quench his thirst."

"Your thirst and that of your friend," Nell began, her eyes as dark as the centers of black-eyed Susans. She half turned to Rose and said in a softer voice, "I don't suppose you could find a couple of warm eggs at this time of day so I could use them for supper?"

"Why, there might be," Rose said. "I'll go have a look."

Pulling her coat back on, she headed for the door, but as she closed it behind her, she hesitated and stopped to listen.

"I can't believe you brought this woman into my sister's house," Nell was saying, her words still sounding as if each one had been cut with a knife. "I can't believe it. Bad enough that you are the talk of the town without bringing your . . ."

"By thunder," Rose heard her father roar. And she ran down the hallway and out to the henhouse, not wanting to hear another word. Eavesdropping, she remembered Sarah saying, is as bad as reading someone else's letters. You may well hear, Sarah had said more than once, something you didn't want to know. Rose knew she wanted no more. Aunt Nell didn't like this Miss Graves, and she was in some kind of a fury about Father. And now he would be in a fury. She yanked open the door to the henhouse and moved in so quickly that the hens fluttered away from their feeding tray and then fluttered again when Rose sneezed as her feet scuffed up dust from the litter. The chickens scurried toward the back corner of the henhouse, and Rose felt bad that she had frightened them. But she caught sight of an egg when one of the nesting hens fluffed out her feathers a bit, so she retrieved it quickly, talking to the rest of the flock while she continued her search, but couldn't find a second one. That meant Abby had already collected them. Why, she wondered, would Aunt Nell want warm eggs?

She was on her way back to the house when it dawned on her. Aunt Nell just wanted her out of the way because trouble was brewing there in the dining room. Well, she was old enough to hear whatever those three people were saying, she thought, even though she had run away from eavesdropping. She could not imagine what had made Aunt Nell so angry. Some nice woman was there—someone Rose had never heard of before—taking care of Father while they were in town, and Aunt Nell was all worried and upset about it. She walked through the ell, not tiptoeing but not stomping along, either, hoping she'd catch enough conversation to figure out what was going on.

She pushed open the door just as Father shouted, "You can take yourself out of here now, Nell, and your nosy nose as well."

Rose hit the door with the palm of her hand so it slammed in against the wall with a whack. Silence greeted her, and she felt suddenly very shy about approaching the dining room door. But just as she started to move forward, Aunt Nell came out, her face redder than Rose's had ever been. She hardly looked at Rose, walked right past the parcels she had left sitting on the woodbox, and started toward the door.

"I have a warm egg for you, Aunt Nell, just one," Rose said timidly. "Shall I wrap it up in something so it will carry home without breaking? And stay warm?"

"Oh, child, I nearly forgot. Yes, yes, wrap it in an old cloth or something, and I'll tuck it in my pocket. Thank you, thank you."

"Is everything all right?"

"Fine, Rose, fine," Nell said. She lowered her voice and added, "But if ever it's not, you are to just get yourself down to your Uncle Jason and me, you hear?"

And then she opened the door and was gone, before Rose could even thank her for the wonderful day. Already, she thought, it seemed so far away. It was hard to understand why good things melted like ice cream in July when people started yelling at each other, and nothing ever melted bad things. They just stayed on, coming in bad dreams in the night and echoing in your head for days. The sight of the wagon and the creaking of its wheels as the men took her mother away were as vivid in her mind as if they had just happened, but she could hardly remember what Newton Barnes looked like when he was square dancing. Why was that?

"Rose?" Her father's voice seemed a trifle loud still, even though Aunt Nell was gone.

"Rose, where are you?"

"Right here, Father, coming right now."

She went to the dining room door and saw that Miss Graves was sitting in Sarah's chair at the foot of the table. She wondered if Miss Graves knew where she was sitting. She didn't remember her ever being in their house before, so probably she didn't.

"Miss Jenny will be staying for a bite of supper, Rose, so I expect you'll be getting that together pretty soon now. I wasn't able to take much for the noon meal, but my appetite is on the mend now, even if the leg hasn't improved much."

"Is Charles upstairs, Father? And where is Abby?"

"Oh, they went off somewhere to see a friend. I told them to skedaddle after Miss Jenny came in."

"But, Father, it's already dark, and they should be here by now," Rose said, feeling a frown gathering between her eyes.

"There will be no need for fussing, Rose," her father said, his voice starting to rise. "They know their way home."

"Perhaps I should give her a hand in the kitchen," Miss Jenny said.

Rose had already started for the icebox when she heard her father answer, "Hah! She knows a lot more about kitchens than you do, Miss Jenny. Your worth is not measured in that room of a house."

"Hush yourself," she heard Miss Jenny say. And then their voices became so low that she couldn't hear any more.

In the kitchen, Rose's fingers trembled as she pulled two bowls of leftovers out of the icebox and set them on the shelf at the back of the stove. Company for supper, she thought, without any warning or anything. And the tablecloth hadn't been turned over, and she didn't even know this woman. But she fetched a spider from the pantry and put a dab of sweet butter in it. Then she added the contents of the smaller bowl, the few pieces of chicken left over from dinner. She sliced up the boiled potatoes from the second bowl and spread them on top of the chicken. Then she added a couple of spoonfuls of water and covered the spider. Odd name for a fry pan, she thought, her mind trekking off into the land of words even in her nervousness. A pan doesn't scoot around, can't spin a thing, doesn't lay eggs or hang by a thread. Where on earth did that name come from? She would ask Miss Harty. She set the pan on the hottest part of the stove.

She pulled the teakettle, which was barely humming, onto a hotter place, too, and then added two sticks to the fire, noticing that the woodbox had not been filled that day. She decided not to make any hot biscuits. They still had half a loaf of bread, and she thought it would do. Dessert would have to be some of the plums Sarah had preserved last year.

She let out a deep breath as she realized that she could manage this, and was about to start worrying about Charles and Abby again when she heard faint footsteps in the ell. She saw the doorknob turn soundlessly and then the two children's faces appeared.

"Where have you been?" Rose demanded.

"We had to leave, Rose," Charles said, almost stammering. He looked around her into the dining room and saw that Miss Graves was still there. Speaking more softly, he said, "She didn't want us to stay. She almost said so, and then Father gave us three pennies to go to the store for candy . . ."

"And I got a peppermint stick," Abby said.

"Let me finish," Charles said crossly. "And he said we could just get lost for a while after that. So we came back to feed the chickens and pick up the eggs, but we didn't come in. We left the eggs in the ell."

"But where did you go? It's pretty cold to be out all afternoon."

"We played in the hayloft for a while, and then we went to Emily's house, and her mother said we could stay if we wanted to. I told her Father had sent me to the hotel to find Miss Graves and that you had gone to town with Aunt Nell—she already knew that—and her face went all funny, so I didn't tell her Father said to get lost."

"We had fun today, Rose," Abby said. "Did you?"

"Oh, yes," Rose said, thinking that her trip to town already seemed something that had happened last year. "I'll tell you about it later. Right now, you'd better set the table so we can eat supper."

"Is she staying?" Charles asked.

"Father said so," Rose said.

Rose's feet felt as heavy as a new block of ice as she clung to the stair rail and almost hauled herself toward the second floor. She didn't know when she had felt this tired. She had the feeling that if she stopped for even a second, she would not be able to get moving again. She held the small kerosene lamp in her left hand and realized the light was dancing about as if a breeze were blowing. How could that be, she wondered, with the chimney protecting the flame and all? Then she realized that her hand was shaking as if she had the palsy.

Uncle Jeremiah Hibbard's hands both shook like that, she remembered. The last time they'd had a family get-together—before the funeral, that is— everyone had been talking about how he could no longer milk a cow, had trouble pouring milk from a pail into a can, and wasn't much good at feeding himself with any sense of neatness. She recalled the aunts shaking their heads and saying he couldn't be cured, that it might get even worse, since he was no chicken anymore. Palsy, the aunts said. She had thought it a strange word at the time, so she had asked Miss Harty. A muscular problem, the teacher said, something that usually only happens to very old people. Usually. But she had fed herself with no spilling at suppertime, so she guessed her problem was that she was all nerved up over being there at the table with Miss Graves sitting in Sarah's place and talk-talk-talking as if she were an invited guest for Sunday dinner.

And Father had actually lifted his head up and looked at her while she talked instead of having his chin almost in his plate. And he had laughed at almost everything she said, even though he had told her the pain in his leg was "turrible." It was hard cider Aunt Nell had poured down the sink, Rose thought, her mind tumbling about from one subject to another. She could tell by the smell that it wasn't sweet cider. So if Reverend Lockhead was right when he had thundered on and on about hard cider and whiskey, then Father was out of touch with his Maker and destroying his mind. Was that why he seemed so happy? If you didn't have a mind, you would have nothing to worry with, now would you?

Rose reached the top of the stairs, heard another laugh from below and decided she couldn't figure out Miss Graves, Aunt Nell's rudeness, hard cider, or the minister tonight. It was only eight o'clock, but she was going to bed. Tomorrow she would show Charles and Abby the things she had brought them from town. And she would give Father his tobacco. Perhaps it would have a savory smell—she liked the way the sweet tobaccos added spice to the air. She hoped he would like it.

Reaching her bedroom on the back of the house, Rose set down the kerosene lamp and held her hand out in front of her, fingers spread wide. There now. It wasn't jumping around like leaves on an aspen anymore. She guessed she was curable, even if Uncle Jeremiah wasn't. Funny that the aunts had said he was no chicken anymore. Didn't they know chickens were girls, and boys would have to be roosters?

She undressed, put on her nightgown and went to the window to see if it was cloudy or starry, and heard the clop-clop-clop of a horse's feet coming. She barely made out a buggy that came around the house and stopped by the milk room. This was a strange time of night for company to just drop in, even on a Saturday, but she couldn't make out who it was because the moon hadn't come up yet. She opened the window a crack and heard one person's heavy footsteps and a knock on the kitchen door.

"Hello, in there," came Uncle Jason's deep voice. "Anybody home?"

"Come ahead in," she heard Father say.

"How's the leg, Silas?" she heard Uncle Jason say rather loudly. "Nell was in such a hurry to get home that she forgot her parcels, so I've come to collect them. Oh, hello Miss Graves, fancy meeting you here. Taking on the nursing duties, I see."

"Doing what I can," Miss Graves answered in a very low voice.

Rose crept into her parents' room and put her ear on the register in the floor. Warmth was coming up through the grate, which was over the kitchen, and the voices traveled nicely as well.

"Well, I expect you could use a ride home as long as I'm here," Uncle Jason boomed. "Get your wrap while I gather up Nell's things—oh, ho, no wonder she didn't fetch her own belongings. Quite a few bundles for one person to tote a half mile or more."

"I don't know as Miss Jenny needs any escorting, Jason," Father started to say. "But it would sure be helpful if you could give us a hand getting me up the stairs. I don't expect to have a problem coming down, but I'm not quite certain how this leg is going to behave tonight."

"I'll take you up there right now," Jason said. "Sorry not to stay chatting, but I haven't had my supper yet, so I'm in a bit of a hurry. I can manage this, Miss Graves, you just get your things together."

Rose tiptoed back to her room quickly and slipped into bed, shivering as her nightgown crept up and her bare legs hit the cold sheets. If she hadn't been so tired, she would have warmed a soapstone and put it in the foot of her bed. Sarah always did that for each of them, every night in the winter. Sometimes Rose hadn't even noticed her feet hitting the warm spot when she went to bed. She heard her father fussing about the pain in his knee as he and Uncle Jason slowly came up the stairs.

"I'll come by in the morning and see to the chores," she heard her uncle say.

"Charles and Rose can do that if I am laid up another day," her father said in a gruff tone.

"They might manage tomorrow, I reckon," Uncle Jason answered. "But they'll be off to school on Monday."

As the two men went past her door, she could tell that her father was favoring one leg, so she figured he must be leaning heavily on her uncle.

"Rose will be giving that up pretty soon anyway," she heard him say, and her stomach did a do-si-do that was becoming all too familiar to her.

She heard Uncle Jason clear his throat and then he said, "Well, let's not hurry her. She's a girl who needs her schooling."

Her father growled an answer that she could not

hear, and she realized they had reached his bedroom, where Abby was already asleep. A few minutes later she heard Uncle Jason's footsteps go quickly along the hall and down the stairs.

She slipped out of bed and went back to the window, hoping she wouldn't step on the floorboard that squawked like an old biddy. She pushed the window a little higher and turned her ear to the opening just in time to hear Uncle Jason say to Miss Graves, "It's very nice of you to help out like this, but the family can take care of things for the next few days, now that Rose and Nell aren't gallivanting off to town."

"I'm pleased to be of assistance," Rose heard Miss Graves say in a voice that sounded as starched as Father's church shirt collars. "I will come by tomorrow to see how things are."

And then they were gone, clop-clop-clopping back to the road and taking Aunt Nell's purchases with them.

Rose moved toward the lamp but didn't put it out. She was wide-awake now, so she reached under her pillow for the little book Miss Harty had given her. She opened it in the middle and began to read. These tiny tales were really quite odd, and she wondered why Miss Harty had given them to her. But never mind. Here was one called "Hard Work," and she could certainly relate to that. As she started, she began to smile. The story read, "Hard work for a poor old body to pump the water all by herself; but she must have a cup of tea, and every one is out, so there is no help for it."

Maybe she was trying to make me feel grateful for

the things I don't have to do, Rose thought, and then read, "Very tired she will be after the exertion, and I daresay will take a nap while the kettle boils; she will then be ready for her tea." And no old bodies to see to, Rose said to herself, putting the little book away and turning down the wick until the lamp went out. Just one middle-aged one with a bad knee. And within a minute, she was asleep.

CHAPTER 16
Hard Work

"You stayed home, but you have homework anyway," Charles teased as he came through the kitchen door. "And you'll have to do it. Miss Harty-har-har said for me to bring the work to school tomorrow if you still couldn't make it."

"Don't call her that," Rose scolded, taking the books from his hands. "She's one of the best friends we have, and she's a fine teacher, too."

"Harty-har-har, Harty-har-har," Charles chanted and then dove for the door as Rose jumped toward him with the books raised over her head. "I'm going to feed the chickens now, like the good boy I am."

"Just a minute, good boy," Rose said, going after him. "Where's Abby?"

"Oh, I forgot. She's going to Ida's house until the first

train whistle. Then she'll come home for supper. I told her I would collect the eggs for her. Her teacher waited for me and said to tell you. She said you probably had enough things on your mind."

Rose turned back to the kitchen and muttered, "That's true enough."

Miss Graves had come by during the noon hour to sit in the dining room with Father. Rose had stayed in the kitchen, making bread and doing a little of the ironing that had started to pile up again. About an hour ago, Miss Graves had left, saying Father had nodded off, which was perhaps the best thing for him. Rose had said, "Yes, Ma'am," and thanked her for coming, just the way she would the minister or the iceman. And once the door closed, she sat down in the rocker near the stove to read the newspaper, and dozed off herself.

She guessed she'd better check on him, now that Charles had woken her. She went to the dining room and saw that her father was stretching his arms out in front of him.

"What in tarnation was all that racket?" he demanded, with a yawn that took the edge off his words.

"Oh, it was just Charles, Father, coming in from school and giving me my homework assignments. He's gone to feed the chickens and collect the eggs. I am sorry if he woke you."

"I wasn't sleeping, girl. Men don't sleep in the daytime. I was just resting my eyes a bit. Pain in the leg always makes the eyes dry, you know." Rose didn't know, but she figured it wasn't a good time for talk. She tidied up the tablecloth, used a table knife to sweep a few crumbs into her hand and then noticed two soiled tumblers on the table. She picked them up and went back to the kitchen.

"You might fetch me a tumbler of water," her father said.

Rose filled a clean glass at the new kitchen faucet, wondering again why anyone would be against newfangled things. She set the glass in front of him.

"You go ahead with that homework," he said, taking a long drink. Little beads of water ran from the lip of the tumbler onto his beard and stayed there, like dew on the grass. "You won't be doing it much longer, but there's still snow on the ground, so it won't do any harm for you to keep up another few weeks."

"I can manage school and the housework, Father," Rose began, feeling suddenly very timid.

"And the garden and the preserving and the haying, too, I reckon," he said, frowning at her. "No sir, young lady, you'll not be killing yourself just to read a few more books and do a few more sums. And I'll not hear any more about it." He thumped his fist on the table, making the spoons rattle in their glass holder.

"Consider it settled," he said.

Rose turned quickly so he wouldn't see the tears in her eyes. She decided to get some onions from the root cellar. If she had onions to peel, she could just weep away and no one would pay her any mind. On her way, she remembered the two dirty glasses and went to wash them out. A pale brown ring circled the bottom of each, and she felt a little twist in her stomach, which seemed to misbehave more every day lately. She sniffed one glass. She didn't know what Miss Graves had brought her father, but it wasn't root beer or sarsaparilla—or even hard cider. It had a strong smell that tickled her nose. Was this "the drink"? She sighed, her tears forgotten already, and washed both glasses.

The onions can wait, she decided, and had just settled into a chair to begin the reading assignment from Miss Harty when she heard her father's chair scrape in the dining room. With several loud grunts, he had gotten to his feet and was hobbling toward the kitchen. She pushed her books under the rocking chair and went to help.

"You'd better get me to the barn," he said gruffly. "Just steady me on the steps a bit, and I'll manage the rest. Charles says he's been taking care of things down there, and Jason did the milking, but I need to get going again. And then I am going over to the hotel."

Rose knew better than to protest, so she went ahead of him on the back steps so he could put a hand on her shoulder. He leaned so hard she thought she might sink into the wood, but she stayed upright. At the barn, she helped him up the steps and heard him shouting at Charles almost as soon as he went through the door.

"How many times have I told you not to stand so close to that cow's hindquarters? Where's the clean straw for the horse stall? When did you last clean behind these critters?"

"I am working at it, sir," came Charles' voice, low but

steady. "I have another hour of light, and I will get it all finished."

Rose left it to them. She walked back to the house feeling more alone than ever. Aunt Nell was a mile away, Miss Harty might as well live on the moon, she had not seen Newton Barnes or Emily or Alice for four days, and even the Rev. Lockhead had only come by once since the funeral. She stopped at the woodshed, remembering that Sarah had never wasted a trip; had rarely taken a third step if two would do. She reached for a stick of wood, and the pile shifted a bit. She jumped back, remembering once again that Sarah was dead. Dead, dead, dead. It was time for her to face that fact at every moment of her day, and Father was planning on her doing just that. Pretty soon she would never see anyone except Father and Charles and Abby.

She reached the kitchen, starting to sob, but stopped when she heard a tap on the door.

"Well, child, it's a great pleasure, but I didn't expect to see you here," Aunt Nell said, as Rose opened the kitchen door and let her in. "How is school?"

"I haven't been to school since our day in town," Rose said. "Father has needed me here to help him get around and to do some of the chores."

"And Charles? Is Charles going to school?"

"Yes, Ma'am, but he is home by now."

"Well, I never," Aunt Nell said, shaking her head so hard that the little curls on her forehead bounced. "A young lady stays home to shovel manure in the barn while a boy goes off to do his sums and fashion Os and

Ps and Rs in a penmanship book. Your father's mind must be situated in his kneecap."

Rose thought her ears must have stopped working. Aunt Nell's voice was as sour as lemonade before you beat in the sugar; as hard as a Gravenstein in May. She had never heard any lady talk in such a tone, not even a teacher who was cross enough to give one of the older boys a whack with her pointer.

"Why, Aunt Nell . . ." she started, but her aunt was on her way through the kitchen to the dining room, then to the parlor and then to the bottom of the stairs.

"Aunt Nell, wherever are you going?" Rose asked, hurrying after her.

"Jason tells me Abby is still sleeping in your parents' room, so I came to see about that," Aunt Nell answered, speaking a little more like herself. "I thought I would speak with your father, but he apparently is not at home, or at least not in the house."

"He went over to the hotel shortly after we finished the chores," Rose said, hoping that news wouldn't bring the lemon voice back. But her hope died quickly.

"The hotel? He's at the hotel at this hour? I do believe that cow kicked him in the head as well as the knee, and he has not taken notice of it yet."

As she talked, Aunt Nell swept along the hall into the larger of the two bedrooms and was standing there, her hands on her hips, staring at Abby's trundle bed, when Rose caught up with her.

"Now, Rose," she said, "the question is whether you want this little bed in your room, or whether you would rather be less crowded and just share your bed with your sister. It is entirely up to you. I am sure Abby will accept your decision."

"Oh, we can share, Ma'am," Rose said. "She has slept with me before, and she doesn't take up much room. Besides, we are both quiet sleepers, I think. It's Charles who flails about in his bed like a fish out of water."

"When did she sleep with you?" Aunt Nell asked, turning to look at Rose with surprise.

"Oh, a few times," Rose said hesitantly, suddenly thinking this might well be another sour topic.

"When?"

"Well, Aunt Nell, Father sometimes makes quite a bit of noise when he comes upstairs to bed, and he woke her up several times, and she was frightened, so I just took her into my room."

"Is that when he's been out for the evening, or whenever he comes up to bed?"

Rose looked down at the floorboards, wondering if she had to answer.

Aunt Nell put her hand on Rose's arm with a touch so gentle that it almost wasn't there.

"You need to tell me now, Rose."

"It's when he's been at the drink," Rose burst out. "When he takes the money from the sugar bowl and goes to the hotel and comes home very late and has red eyes and a bad temper in the morning."

"Oh, my dear child," Aunt Nell said, putting her arms around Rose. "You could have told me all that just a little sooner, now couldn't you?"

"Yes . . . no . . . I don't know, Ma'am."

"Well, what we are going to do now is strip the sheets off this bed and take the bed apart and put the whole thing up in the attic where I assume Charles has not taken up every inch of the space."

"No, but the dried beans are up there and quite a few other things, Ma'am," Rose said, wondering how she was going to explain all this to Father, who seemed to be more crotchety every day, even though she did think his leg was much better.

"We will manage," Aunt Nell said, quickly removing the coverlet and the quilt and the sheets. Rose took the bedding and started folding it up. Then the two of them took the bed apart and carried the mattress up the attic stairs. When they came back for the rest of the bed, Aunt Nell said perhaps it would be more practical to just put all the pieces right under the big bed.

"Plenty of room there," she said, dusting her hands with satisfaction and looking around at the rest of the room.

"Now, where are her clothes?"

In a few minutes they had moved Abby's clothing to Rose's room, and rearranged a few things to make space for her.

"Now we shall have a cup of tea, Rose, and then I will go tell your father what I've been up to over here. No reason you should have to tell him. It wasn't your idea."

Relief ran over Rose like a soft breeze, and she almost ran down the stairs, where she pulled the teakettle toward the front of the stove. She took the small metal ball from the pantry shelf, spooned in tea leaves and took down Sarah's lusterware teapot and two cups. If they were going to have tea, she knew Sarah would want it served properly.

When the water began to talk, Rose rinsed the teapot with warm water so it wouldn't be cold, and hooked the tea ball chain over the side. As soon as the water bubbled, she filled the pot.

"Do you take milk?" she asked.

Aunt Nell started to laugh. "Child, you are the limit. You have had a dreadful week here, your father is not an easy man to see to even if he's himself—and right now he is far from himself, grieving as he is—you have too many things to do for a person who is just fourteen years old, and you are now making tea for me as if I were the queen."

"The queen won't be coming here," Rose said, starting to laugh herself. "The only way we can have tea like royalty is to drink it ourselves. Sarah always said it was one of the niceties."

"Quite right. And I will take a little milk, but not the top milk. I don't care for all that cream in my tea." So Rose fetched the lusterware pitcher and sugar bowl, and they took all the fixings to the dining room where they could wait for the tea to steep.

"Now, child, we need to do some talking. I have some questions to ask you, and you are to just answer them. The first question is whether your father has ever hit Abby when he wakes her up and she cries in the night."

"No, Ma'am," Rose answered, quite taken aback.

"Did you always go right in there to get her?"

"Yes, Ma'am."

"You can call me Aunt Nell, please, not Ma'am. I am not the storekeeper's clerk."

Rose started to smile a little, her mind immediately picturing Aunt Nell at Mr. Goodnow's store, measuring out flour or cornmeal and being nice to that dreadful Mrs. Munson and her friends. The lemon voice would appear, she was certain.

"Why are you smiling, child? We are taking up very serious business here."

"I'm sorry, Ma . . . Aunt Nell. I sometimes have funny thoughts running beside my serious ones. It's sort of like trains going in opposite directions. They don't hit each other because they have separate tracks."

"Mercy on us, it's a complex place that brain of yours. Not much doubt that you would be a treasure in front of a classroom, and that's what we must keep in mind here. But in the meantime, I want to know if you think Abby is safe here. Your Uncle Jason was quite put out when he found out where she was sleeping."

"Oh, I think she's safe enough," Rose said, not quite knowing what Aunt Nell meant. "Father almost never even talks to her. He leaves her to me, and she is a very good girl, Aunt Nell."

"I'm sure she is," Aunt Nell said, her forefinger finding the tiny mole on her neck and worrying it a bit. "I'm sure she is. But little girls don't share rooms with their brothers or their fathers, Rose. It isn't right. So now she's moved, and . . ." She poked at the mole again. " . . . and I'll go tell Silas."

The two sipped their tea as if they were at a church social, and for a few minutes the only sound was Aunt Nell's foot lightly tapping under the table. Rose looked over the top of her cup as she drank and saw that her aunt was watching her.

"I have not been paying enough attention to you, Rose, and I apologize for that. It's not easy to keep a house and a family, and it's entirely too much for a fourteen-year-old girl, even one with railroad tracks in her head. Now you listen to me . . . and look at me, Rose. It's not your teacup that's doing the talking."

Rose looked at her aunt and realized she had never heard her talk like this before, except the other night when she had emptied Father's glass of hard cider down the sink drain.

"Abby is going to sleep in your room. You are going to attend school, and you are going to become a teacher. Your father will have to hire some help to run this house because a house, without a grown woman in it cannot work properly for very long. Women can manage men's work for quite a time when it's necessary, but I have never met the man who could walk in his wife's shoes for even twenty-four hours without slipping and sliding about."

"Father's planning to have . . ." Rose stopped. She knew something she had overheard, and Sarah had told them again and again that if they eavesdropped and heard something terrible or something wonderful, they had to forget it. Eavesdropping was one of the evils, she said. Whatever you heard eavesdropping, you did not hear. For a second, Sarah's voice seemed to be right there in the room again, and then it faded. Rose felt the flush coming up her neck, so she put her head down a little and tried to sip tea. But she was thinking about her face turning red, and she made a slurping noise.

"Father's planning what?" Aunt Nell demanded. "You had better tell me before I go to the hotel and make a fool of myself talking to him."

"I overheard something, but Sarah always said. . ."

"What your mother would say now is that you must tell me," Aunt Nell said, suddenly speaking very softly and reaching her hand across the table. "Trust me, Rose. You have no better friends than your Uncle Jason and me."

"He said he needed a woman in the house. He told Miss Graves that when they were talking in the dining room last night."

"She was here again?"

"She's here almost every evening," Rose said, and felt Aunt Nell's fingers tighten on hers.

"And what did you hear them saying?"

"Only that he knew everyone would say he should still be in mourning, but that he needed a woman in his . . . in his . . ." Rose cleared her throat and hoped Aunt Nell would go on talking. But her aunt just sat there, waiting.

"In his kitchen and in his bed," Rose finished in a rush.

"Lord have mercy on us all," Aunt Nell said in a voice that was barely louder than a whisper. "That it should come to this."

Then she sat up straight. She took Rose's hand in both of hers, and Rose felt warmed by her aunt's touch. "Well, it's not your concern, my child, not your concern," she said briskly, in that tone grown-ups use when they've decided children don't need to know any more.

"I think it is," Rose said calmly. She freed her hand, stood, picked up the lusterware teapot and her own cup and saucer and turned toward the kitchen.

"I fear you are quite right," she heard Aunt Nell mutter behind her, as she left the house.

Rose was in the kitchen when she heard a sharp knock at the door. It must be Aunt Nell, she thought, coming back from the hotel. She gave a little shiver as she crossed the kitchen to the door and lifted the latch.

"How do, Miss Rose, how do," said a cheery voice. Rose's face flamed. Newton Barnes was standing there, right on her doorstep, grinning in his friendly way.

"How do, yourself," Rose answered, smiling back. It was hard, she had discovered, not to answer Newton's smiles. "Why are you here just as school is out?"

"What I carry here in this sack must be delivered forthwith said the great Miss Harty," Newton answered. "Forsooth—that's Shakespeare, you know—a boy must be on his way long before the ringing of the afternoon bell."

Rose started to laugh, then quickly remembered her manners.

"Come in," she said. "Please come in."

He stepped inside the kitchen door and looked quickly around.

"Is your father here? We heard he was not able to get around, that a cow had kicked him in the knee and hurt him rather badly."

"It's better," Rose said. "He hobbled off to the hotel this afternoon to see if the leg would hold up. It's only across the road and down a hair. But if you ask me, which he did not, the leg isn't quite ready for walking on rough, snowy ground without anyone to lean on."

But Newton's smile had faded, and he was shifting from one foot to another.

"I must turn tail and run," he said. "I can't even stand in your kitchen if you are unchaperoned."

"Unchaperoned? In the kitchen?" Rose let out a yelp of laughter like the ones she usually shared only with Emily and Alice. "This is not a dance."

"My mother has told me thirty times if she's told me once: 'You cannot be in a room or a house alone with an unattached woman.' I'm sure she would count you among those persons."

His smile returned, and he suggested, "So put on your wrap and come stand outside with me where any passersby can plainly see us."

Rose sighed, thinking how ridiculous it all was. She was alone with the iceman almost every week, and sometimes the fish peddler stepped inside the door as well. But she took the sack of schoolbooks and papers from

Newton, pulled her shawl off the hook, and stepped outside with him.

"When are you coming back to school?" he demanded. "I have come to realize that I miss you."

Just as Rose started to blush again, he added, "Without you there, Miss Harty can see every move I make, every breath I take. I have done more work in the past two weeks than in all previous school days because I have no privacy."

Rose laughed again. She wondered how she could be feeling so happy when Aunt Nell was down the road telling her father how things were going to be, which meant that when he came home, he'd be madder than a wet hen. Even as she tried to concentrate on Newton, her meandering mind pondered the idea that she had never seen a wet hen. They just didn't get wet as far as she knew, no more than cats. They didn't bathe in a puddle like some other birds. Sarah had told her they were cleaning themselves when they hunkered down in the chicken house litter and flapped their wings to make the dust fly. Maybe that was why it made them mad if they did fall in a puddle, she decided.

"Where did you go?" Newton said. "You seem to have wandered off, the way you sometimes do in school."

"I'm sorry. I just was thinking about when Father would be coming back."

"I will be on my way before that happens," Newton said. "I do not want him to think I was at your house when no one was home but you and me."

He reached out suddenly and grabbed her hand with both of his. His fingers were chapped and rough, but warm, and Rose felt another shiver, this one quite pleasant, run through her whole body.

"Come back to school soon," he said. "I want to hide behind your back and, once in a while, speak to your face." He dropped her hand, turned and loped off toward the road, moving quickly out of sight.

Rose stood there, looking at her hand. It didn't look any different. A sizable hand for a girl, Father had remarked more than once. A little red around the knuckles from housework and forgetting to wear mittens. Not a pretty hand, she had often thought. But now she quite admired it.

It didn't look different, but it felt different, as surely as if she had exchanged it for a new one. Could someone's touch do that? Well, now she knew for certain that he liked her. His face had betrayed him, as hers so often had. She grinned, thinking how red he had become when he told her he wanted to hide behind her back again.

She turned back toward the house, feeling warm all over despite the cold, and wishing she could talk to Alice and Emily. It would be so much easier if they could use smoke signals, she thought.

CHAPTER 17
Chaperones

Three days later, Rose woke when it was still dark. She lay still for several minutes, trying to see the outlines of furniture in her room. She wiped what Aunt Nell called sleepies from the corners of her eyes, digging her fingers in to get every last bit of the annoying crustiness, and sat up slowly so she wouldn't wake Abby. This, she remembered suddenly, was the day she was going back to school, and she hoped her father had it in mind and wouldn't raise a fuss about it. After all, it wasn't spring yet, and his leg was doing quite nicely. And she needed to take her place in the classroom so Newton Barnes could hide behind her again. That thought sent a little tingle down her back and made her smile, even though it was much too early for smiling.

She slid out of the covers, squatted quickly on the chamber pot, then wrapped a heavy shawl around her shoulders and tiptoed off to the kitchen. To her surprise, she could hear snores coming from her father's room, and she wondered why he wasn't at the barn already. He had been going, unassisted, for two days now. She hesitated and decided not to call out to him. If she woke him, it would cause a commotion. If she didn't, she knew that might be a commotion of another sort.

"Damned if you do, damned if you don't," she muttered to herself, astonished at how quickly the farmers' expression had tumbled from her lips. Well, no one had heard her, so no harm done. Besides, it was true; she couldn't win, no matter what she did. She had breakfast under way in no time, and was on her way to the stairs to get dressed and wake the children when her father came into the kitchen, shrugging his suspenders over his shoulders as he walked. His hair was disheveled—Rose liked that word because it sounded like a mess—and his eyes were red. He yawned, grunted in her direction and went out to the barn.

By the time he came back, Charles and Abby had nearly finished breakfast and Rose was washing up her own dishes. All three were dressed for school, although Charles would be going to the barn to feed the chickens and give them fresh water.

"You are going today, Rose?" Abby said questioningly. Out of the corner of her eye, Rose saw her father turn toward her, then back to Abby.

"Unlikely, child, unlikely," Father said, not waiting for Rose to answer.

"Yes, I am," Rose said quietly.

"By whose authority?" he asked, his voice starting to rise.

"I believe it would be the town's," Rose answered, keeping her voice as low and even as she could. "We are required to go to school until we reach a certain age."

"Not if you are needed at home," Father said. "I have told you and told you, we cannot manage here without your full attention on this household and its needs."

"I believe everything is taken care of for today, Father," Rose said. "If we have a day when I am truly needed here, as I was while you had difficulty walking, then I will be here, assuredly." I sound just like the minister, she thought. I sound as if I am reading from a book.

He sat down at his place abruptly and began to spoon hot oatmeal into his mouth, dipping the spoon into a little bowl of fresh milk in the way that he liked best. He paused to pour a stream of maple syrup in a circle on the oatmeal and went on eating in silence, scooping up a bit of the special sweetness with each mouthful. Charles looked at Abby, asked to be excused, and left the table to take care of the chickens. Abby seemed to be tied to her chair as tightly as the small cushions that covered the cane seats, so Rose told her she was excused. She had to give Abby's arm a little tug to get her going. A short time later, without looking into the dining room again, the three set off together, with Charles on one side of Rose and Abby on the other, each so glad about her return that they forgot their usual way of acting as if they didn't know her.

"He's going to be an old grouch about school, Rose," Charles said in his most grownup voice. "He keeps talking to himself when he's doing the milking, saying that girls don't need to know numbers, that they're just fine if they can read receipts and the medical book, and that they can practice penmanship by writing the news of the day to relatives."

"Aunt Nell thinks I should go to school and you should stay home, Charles," Rose answered, waiting for him to explode.

"I am not rising to that bait," Charles said in a calm voice. "I am not an ignorant fish."

"Or a smart one," Rose agreed, and they both started to laugh.

The trio stopped at the roadside because Abby needed to turn off to her school. But the little girl wasn't quite finished. "You are going to be a teacher, Rose?" she asked, her voice as solemn as when she was saying her prayers.

"I hope so, Abby, I hope so," Rose said, giving her hand a little squeeze. Apparently satisfied, Abby ran toward her friends outside the girls' entrance. But deep down inside, where all those tingles and queasies and floppy-fish feelings lived, Rose wondered. So far, Father had not said a word about Abby moving to Rose's room. He had come back from the hotel for supper and had left almost immediately afterward, telling them to do whatever Rose needed and get to their beds early. She noticed that he took some coins from the sugar bowl on his way through the kitchen.

At their own schoolyard, Emily and Alice picked up their skirts and ran toward Charles and Rose with such delight that Rose stopped frowning over her thoughts and smiled back. It was good to be here, where she could see her friends and read her books. No dishes, no scrubbing, no unpredictable father. Charles moved away. The girls linked arms with Rose and chattered so fast that she could not decipher any of their news.

"Stop, stop," she said, laughing. "I have an ear on each side of my head, but there's just one brain in the middle to figure out what those ears are hearing. So I can't manage two conversations at once."

"You hear more than one thing at a time if Miss Harty is talking and someone behind you is whispering," Emily said.

"Sometimes you hear seven whispers at once," Alice added. "I never knew anyone who could hear so many things at once and still have a thought on its own track in her head."

The bell rang, and the three went up the steps into the school, left their wraps in the cloakroom and took their places in Miss Harty's room. The teacher looked up as they came in, greeted Emily and Alice and smiled at Rose.

"I am very glad to see you today, Rose," she said.

"I brought back the work you sent me, Miss Harty," Rose said, handing a sheaf of papers to the teacher. "I hope I'm not too far behind, Ma'am."

"If you did all the work I sent you, you will be right with your own group, Rose," the teacher answered. "Please take your usual seat."

Rose went past the front desks to the center of the

room where she usually sat. She had noticed when she first came into the room that Newton Barnes was already in the seat behind hers, and she kept her eyes on the floor as she walked, studying her feet as if they were in danger of being tripped up by rocks and tree roots. She sat down without looking at him, but she could feel her face getting red anyway.

"I am very glad to see you today, Rose," came a high whisper from Newton, as he mimicked the teacher's cadence perfectly.

"I am very glad to see you today, Rose," came another voice, trying to imitate the first two but with no kindness.

"That will be quite enough, Mr. Granger," Miss Harty said, hearing the second whisper but not the first. "We are all pleased to see Rose, but we will make no further fuss over her return."

The forenoon went quickly, and Rose was surprised by how easy the work seemed and how much she liked doing it. When the bell rang for the noon recess, she took her lunch pail from the cloakroom and joined Alice and Emily. The trio went outside where they could sit on a low wall in the sun with the warm clapboards of the school behind them. It was their place, and most of the time, no one joined them there.

"So," Emily began almost immediately, "Newton Barnes delivered your schoolwork to you, did he not?"

"Yes," Rose said, hoping that was the only question anyone would ask about that day.

But she was not surprised when Alice chimed in.

"What did he say? What did you say? Did your face get all red?"

"He said we couldn't be in the kitchen unchaperoned," Rose said, laughing at the memory of Newton Barnes shifting from one foot to the other and quoting his mother's admonitions.

"Unchaperoned?" Emily almost shouted. "What does that mean?"

"It's a rule, Emily, just a rule at his house," Rose answered a bit crossly. "It had nothing to do with doing anything. Or saying anything. His mother brought him up to not be in a house or room with a lady unless another person was present. That's what he said."

"And she's quite right. His mother, I mean," Alice said. "My mother said the same thing, but she was talking about gentlemen. And she said sometimes they seem like gentlemen and they are not. But she did not explain that part to me. Do you think they just jump on you as if you were a cow or something? Or steal your money?" At that moment, Emily and Rose each had a mouthful of bread and cheese, and they nearly choked trying to laugh and swallow at the same time.

"I think," Emily said, "they try to steal a kiss first. I don't think they look at ladies the way a bull looks at a cow."

"But you have no way of knowing," Rose said, beginning to think she should have stayed in the kitchen with Newton to find out what the hazards were.

"Well," said Emily, her eyes seeming to have an extra light in them, "perhaps you will find out for us. Perhaps you can stay home another day, and he will come to the house, and you can just invite him in, unchaperoned."

Suddenly Rose remembered how Newton had taken her hand, and she did not want to talk about this anymore. She could feel her face redden, and before she could turn away from her friends, Emily saw it.

"Or maybe you do know something, and you're just not telling," Emily said in a whispery voice. "Maybe . . ." and then she stopped. She saw Rose's mouth close into a very thin line, and she knew it was time to talk about something else.

"We have," she said quickly, "twice as many words in our vocabulary lists now as we had before. Did Miss Harty send those to you?"

"What is the matter with you," Alice demanded. "We are talking about Rose and Newton, and suddenly you start on vocabulary lists as if they were interesting or important. Neither, I say."

"We," Emily said in a haughty tone, "are moving on to another subject. Choose one if you please. Miss Rose is all finished with the Newt—, the chaperone topic."

Rose laughed then, laughed until tears started to run down her cheeks. She had missed these two, had not even known how much. She grabbed Emily's left hand with her right, and Alice's right with her left, and squeezed their fingers so hard that they protested.

"I will not be able to write Ps and Qs this afternoon," shrieked Alice. "You have broken my finger."

Rose acted as if she had not spoken.

"I cannot leave school," she said. "Unless you both

promise to visit me in my kitchen every day. Unchaperoned," she added, and started laughing again.

Rose went to school the next day and the one after that. She stayed up late with her schoolwork and crawled out of bed before the rooster crowed, long before the sky had begun to lighten. On the fourth afternoon, while Miss Harty talked about President Jefferson, she felt her eyelids thicken and knew she was on the edge of falling asleep. She rubbed them with her reddened knuckles; she pinched her legs through her dress; she squeezed her hands into fists until her fingernails dug into her palms.

For a quarter hour or so, it worked. But the older boys had built up the fire in the wood stove during the noon recess. The room was warm, and Miss Harty's voice talked steadily. Rose's eyes closed, and she dozed. For a minute or two, she continued to hear the sounds of the classroom, as Miss Harty called on one pupil after another to recite. Then it all drifted away and her head sank toward her desk. She woke with a near jump when she felt something sharp on her back.

"Rose?" Miss Harty said. "Rose? Whatever is the matter?"

"Nothing, Ma'am. Although I seem to have something in my eye."

"You may take a dipper of water outside and see if whatever it is can be removed," Miss Harty said, looking over the rims of her glasses at Rose.

Rose did as she was told and splashed the cold water all over her face once she was outside the door. She came back, wide-awake, her skin flushed from the slapping she had given herself. Miss Harty looked at her, raising her eyebrows.

"I believe it is gone," Rose said very primly. "Thank you, Miss Harty." She put the dipper next to the pail of drinking water and went back to her seat without looking at Newton, who was toying with the pen he had stuck in her back to wake her up.

When the final bell rang that afternoon, Rose hurried toward the cloakroom, keeping her eyes on the floor, hoping Miss Harty would not stop her or keep her. But Miss Harty was standing by the front door of the school, seeing each child off, and when Rose came along, she pulled her aside.

"Wait here, please," she said in a pleasant voice.

When Newton came by, he said good afternoon to the teacher in a solemn voice, then raised his eyebrows at Rose, who nearly giggled, even though half her brain was filled with foreboding. Once the last pupil had left, Miss Harty turned to her.

"You are worn out, Rose," she said. "You have dark circles under your eyes and you can barely keep your eyes open once we are past the noon hour."

Tears washed across Rose's eyes, making the teacher a blur of blue dress and pale face. She tried to will the unwelcome tears to stay in place, but she knew if she squeezed her lids shut, the overflow would be immediate. Why did she always end up crying when Miss Harty spoke to her?

"I'm s-s-sorry," she stammered. "I stayed up too late last night."

"And the night before and probably the night before that," Miss Harty said. "And were up too early this morning, I reckon."

"I'm s-s-sorry," she said again, feeling as dumb as a chicken. They were the dumbest, she thought, pecking in dirt for something to eat when it was just sand and sawdust, and droppings they had put there themselves. Really dumb. She wrenched her mind back to Miss Harty, realizing that her chicken thoughts had made the tears go back where they belonged.

"I must come to school," Rose said. "I must, Ma'am."

"Yes, you must," Miss Harty said. "But I am making a plan that I hope will help you manage school and your house. After today, you will come at nine o'clock instead of eight, and you will leave at two. It will not be an easy day, but you are an excellent student, and I think you will be able to keep up."

"Will that meet the requirements for school attendance, Miss Harty?"

"Indeed," the teacher said, turning her head quickly to peer out the window. "And I shall expect your eyes to be open while you are here, which means you will go to bed earlier and get up a bit later. After this week, you will take one afternoon each week at home, to help you catch up with your housework and other chores. Now run along."

"Yes, Miss Harty," Rose said.

She hurried out the door, sighing when she saw that Emily and Alice were not waiting at the bottom of the stairs. And then she realized why they had gone on without her. Newton Barnes was leaning on the railing, looking up at her with a strange expression on his face.

"Is everything all right?" he asked as she came toward him. "Is she angry because you fell asleep again?"

"Oh, no," Rose said. "She's been very good to me, you know."

"And why shouldn't she be?" he said. "A star student like you with all those neat arithmetic papers and never a mistake anywhere."

She wondered if he was teasing nicely or making fun of her. She didn't feel strong enough to take either, as a matter of fact, so she looked at her feet moving forward, one after the other, and said nothing. Her busy mind was counting the steps they had taken—it was a good thing, perhaps, to have feet long enough so they stuck out from under your skirts—and she noticed that he took the same number she did. Did it mean he had short legs, or was he being nice about that, too?

"I have a new school day for now," she said suddenly.

"Whatever do you mean?" She explained the arrangement, and he let out a howl about having an empty seat in front of him.

"You must not yelp like that," Rose said. "You sound like the hounds under a treed raccoon."

"Next thing you know, some old man will be shooting out his front window," Newton said. "Think I'll howl again, just to see if I can bring on fireworks. In the meanwhile, give me those books. I look pretty bad here, walking with a young lady and treating her as if she were a pack mule."

"So I'm a mule, and you are a hound dog," Rose said, starting to laugh. "What a pair."

"Pair sounds nice to me," Newton said, pressing his fingers against hers as he took the books away. She felt the flush creeping over her chin and shooting up into her cheeks while her stomach dropped two inches and her knees wobbled. What was it about this boy that made her arms and legs and insides misbehave so? And should she respond to that "pair" comment? And how? She decided this was one of those times when silence was golden, and she sank into it.

He was quiet, too, and they hurried along toward her house without talking any more. At her door, he handed her the books.

"Probably empty in there," he said, grinning in his usual way. "Can't carry the books in there."

"I'll manage," Rose said, turning the doorknob. "But does Abby count as a chaperone?"

"I doubt it," Newton said. "And I will not ask my mother that question."

He paused and then took his turn at inspecting feet. Then, barely looking at her, he touched her shoulder gently and said, "But I will ask if you are going to the square dance on Saturday night."

"I think we will," Rose said, hardly able to breathe.

"Then I want every single square," Newton said. "Promise?"

"Oh, yes," she said, quickly pushing open the door and going in. "Oh, yes."

Rose almost ran up the stairs to her room. This time, she thought, I must have a new square dancing skirt. She closed the door to her room and fairly danced across the room to her bed. She reached under the pillow and pulled out the book Miss Harty had given her, *A Splendid Time.*

These were the smallest stories Rose had ever seen, just eight lines to a page, with a drawing at the top. She treasured the little book and ever since that night when Uncle Jason had put Father to bed, she had tried to read one of the stories every day. She had gone back to the beginning and tried not to look ahead. It was like eating ice cream at the fair, she thought. You never wanted to get to the last spoonful because then it was all gone.

She had finished all the stories, so she opened the book at random again, first looking at the cover once more. She loved the cover. It showed a lady in a large hat and long gown, with gloves to her elbows, standing beside a creek with a kneeling man who was dressed like a prince. She could see herself in that dress, but it made her laugh to think of Newton Barnes in slippers and hose and a ruffled shirt like the man in the picture.

The little stories were not nearly as romantic as the cover. Many of them, like the one about Tommy coming home with his arm in a sling, were about people's troubles. But Rose liked them all and decided she had learned a great deal about what people do and what they should do.

The book opened to "Morning Prayer," and she sighed a little, thinking that she never said any morning prayers, unless she were allowed to count things like, "Please, God, don't let him come in from the barn until the oatmeal is cooked."

But she read on: "Obedient to her good mother's teaching, Flora kneels down as soon as she is dressed in the morning, and thanks God for keeping her safely through the night; praying that He will take care of her during the day, and for the Savior's sake bless her and make her a good girl, by giving her a new heart."

She looked at the drawing of Flora—all neatly dressed, her hair perfection—on her knees before a little table. Flora didn't look as if she had a new heart. She just looked very, very good. She did not ever get angry, Rose was certain. But did her new heart do somersaults the way Rose's did? Perhaps without even knowing it, she had a new heart herself.

Well, at the very least, obedient to her good mother's teaching, she could sew very nicely, and she would have a new skirt for that dance. She tucked the little book back under her pillow, changed into an old dress and went downstairs to stoke the fire, set flatirons on the stove, get out the clothes that needed ironing, and put the soup kettle on the back of the stove.

She ironed for a few minutes and then heard Charles

and Abby running through the back ell toward the kitchen door.

"Saw you, saw you," Charles shouted as he came through the door.

"Saw me what?" Rose asked in her most adult manner.

"Saw you with Barnes," Charles said, dancing around the kitchen, picking up Rose's books. "May I carry your books, Miss Rose?"

He dropped the books, took off his coat and swirled it around before spreading it on the floor.

"May I lay my coat across this puddle? May I . . ."

"Oh, be still, Charles," Rose said, trying not to laugh. "We did not even see a puddle. It's too cold."

She saw the look on Charles' face change into disappointment and knew he was trying to get her goat. Goat? Now where did that come from? She knew why it was in her head; Uncle Jason had used the expression. But she didn't have a goat, and he didn't have one either. And no one would want to say anything that would make you give them your goat anyway. Heavens to Betsy, words were confusing. Who was Betsy? Rose reined in her brain. That was going too far, she thought, a goat leading to Betsy, and both of them a mystery.

"We have to ask Father at supper whether we can all go to the square dance," Rose said.

Charles didn't answer.

"Barnes," Rose said, her eyes dancing, "asked me if I could go."

"Oh, Rose!" Abby almost shouted, running across

the room to throw her arms around Rose's skirt. "Is he going to come calling on you?"

"Oh, Rose!" mimicked Charles, hoping to regain some of the ground he had lost. But then he looked at Rose's happy face and added in a more thoughtful way, "I reckon he will let us. He had a nice evening, too, the last time we went."

"And you can have a new skirt for this one," Abby added. "Can you? Do you have time? Is there any fabric?"

"I think I will be able to come up with something," Rose said, "especially if you can wear your skirt again."

"Oh, I can, I can," Abby said.

And a good thing, thought Rose. Probably she will have to wear it until it is too small for her, and then we'll let it out. Fabric was costly, and she just did not have any money to spend. She could not figure out where the coins in the sugar bowl went, or for that matter, where new ones came from—because some days she discovered more money in the bowl in the evening than had been there in the morning. So far, she had not found the courage to ask Father.

"I think, Miss Rose," Charles began in what he thought was his all-grown-up manner, "I think I recollect that you purchased a bolt or two of yard goods on your last journey to the city."

He gave a little bow, and Rose shrieked with delight as she remembered the cloth she and Aunt Nell had bought in Ripton. Abby began to hop up and down as if she were jumping rope. Following his lead, Rose picked up her skirt a bit, dipped her knees in a small curtsey and said, "Quite right you are, my lord, correct in every way, my lord. A priceless length of square dance material awaits me in the upper regions."

"Upper what?" Abby demanded, as the older two collapsed in a fit of laughter. "Upper what, Rose? Upper what?"

"It just means upstairs," Rose said, putting her arm around her sister's shoulders. "So much has happened since that trip to town that I had quite forgotten. But I shall certainly have a new skirt now, if I have to stay up all night sewing it."

"Ay-yuh," said Charles. "And if he says we can go, then you will get a chance to wear it."

CHAPTER 18
A Time to Sew

The next day, Miss Harty called Rose to her desk at the start of the noon recess. It can't be anything bad, Rose told herself. I am keeping up, I have not fallen asleep, I haven't passed any notes to anyone. And I reckon she likes me. But she still walked to the desk feeling a little uncertain.

"You are happy today, Rose," Miss Harty said, as soon as everyone had gone to the cloakroom to get their lunch pails.

"Yes, Ma'am," Rose answered, thinking this was an odd reason to keep someone in.

"I don't mean to pry," Miss Harty went on, "but you have come to mean a good deal to me, and I wondered if you had received good news about staying in school."

"No one has said anything about that, Miss Harty," Rose answered. "The only good news today is that we are all allowed to go to the square dance at Town Hall on Saturday night, and we didn't know if Father would let us go, so I am very pleased about that. Ma'am."

"You did go last time, I believe," Miss Harty said.

"Oh, yes, but this time . . ." Rose's voice trailed off. She felt her face starting to flush and wished she could just pull a pillowslip over her head whenever she had to talk to anyone. That would probably make her voice sound funny, she thought.

"Yes?" Miss Harty prompted.

"This time I will have a new skirt if I can find time to make it, because we bought fabric the day I went to Ripton with Aunt Nell and I had forgotten all about it, but Charles remembered, and the cloth is perfect for a square dance skirt," Rose said in a rush, this time completely forgetting to say Ma'am or Miss Harty.

"Perhaps tomorrow you should leave right after the noon hour, Rose, and make yourself some sewing time while the light is good. It's very hard to sew at night by lamplight, don't you think?"

"Oh, that would be very fine," Rose answered. "If you think my work is not going to suffer, Miss Harty."

"Your work is better than ever, Rose, and I think you already know that, don't you?"

"Yes, Ma'am, oh, I did hope so, Ma'am, but it's not my place to say that."

"You go along now, and tomorrow you will be dismissed at one o'clock."

"Thank you, Miss Harty," Rose said as solemnly as she could. And then she went quickly out the door and down the steps where she found Newton Barnes leaning against the big sugar maple that stood in front of the school.

"Have you given Miss Harty-har-har offense?" he wanted to know as she came near.

"A lady is never offensive," Rose answered with a giggle. "Nor does she ever giggle," she added quickly.

To Rose's surprise, Newton began to laugh.

"Most days," he said, "you are so solemn that I forget you are younger than I. And now you are letting your sense of humor out of whatever chest of drawers it's been hiding in."

"Gentlemen," Rose said, in the teasing voice—a voice that sounded quite unfamiliar to her own ear, "gentlemen don't speculate about what's in a lady's chest of drawers."

Newton bent double, and at first Rose thought he had been taken with a bellyache. But his chuckle reached her as he started to straighten and then went right over again.

"Wouldn't think of it, Miss Rose. Wouldn't think of it," he gasped when he was able to choke out the words. "May I see you to your door?"

"Today, yes," Rose said. "Tomorrow, no."

"And what misbehaving is going to punish me tomorrow but not today?"

"Tomorrow I go home from school soon after the noon hour. That's what Miss Harty—and you ought to keep a respectful tongue in your head about her—wanted to see me about."

"And that will let you get caught up on all your chores so you might be at the square dance on Saturday?"

"Mostly time for sewing my new skirt," Rose said and

then turned red, wishing she had not announced that she would have a new skirt.

"I look forward to it," Newton said, his face solemn now, and his blue eyes looking straight at her. He reached for her books and took them over her mild protest, and they walked slowly toward her house.

The next afternoon, facing the window in her father's bedroom, Rose placed her feet carefully on the treadle, right toe down, left toe up. She gave the wheel a little spin and began to move her feet, pushing with first one and then the other. The needle began to move up and down, and she held the fabric evenly, watching the little stitches emerge behind the needle.

This wouldn't be the time, she thought, for my mind to go careening off on an expedition. Too many things to think about. The treadle rhythm, the needle, the fabric, the stitches. When she was first learning to use the machine, Grandma Emma had told her about a woman who had put the needle right through her finger because she looked up while she was stitching. Rose gave a little shiver, just thinking about that story and how the woman had to make the treadle go one more time so the needle . . . u-u-u-g-h . . . would come out again. She loved sewing with Grandma Emma, and wished she could have talked to her for more than a minute when she and Grandpa Will had come for the funeral. But her grandmother had been so upset and had shocked everyone when she interrupted the Rev. Lockhead by saying, "Mothers should not have to bury their daughters." And then they had gone right back to Vermont because they had to do the milking and the other chores.

She concentrated on finishing a seam and creased it open at the waistline with her thumbnail. She took another piece of fabric and quickly ran a second seam, again creasing it open at the top. Then she added the fourth piece. This, she knew, was a gored skirt. Why ever did they call it "gored," she thought, her brain rambling despite her first efforts. Mr. Leonard had been gored a couple of years ago, and he wasn't a skirt.

She giggled for a second but caught herself, realizing that being gored in the barnyard by a bull was not an entertainment. Putting her mind back on the skirt, Rose worked without thinking about anything else for almost two hours. She was nearly finished, except for the hemming, when she heard Charles and Abby come into the house from school. Her special afternoon had flown by, and it would soon be time to put supper on the table.

"Rose, Rose, where are you?" Abby's shrill voice demanded.

"Up here, coming down," Rose answered, clattering down the stairs as fast as she could.

"You did not forget that I would leave early today, did you?" she asked as she came into the kitchen.

"No," said Abby, peeling off her mittens and putting them on the ledge at the end of the stove. "But what have you been doing all afternoon? I was hoping you baked filled cookies for us."

"As a matter of fact, Miss Abby, I was making my square dance skirt, and it's almost done," Rose said. "I had no time to think of your sweet tooth or your belly."

Charles laughed but quickly said, "You'll have to think about our bellies pretty soon because it's going to be time for supper, and we are already as hungry as a Chinaman without rice."

"Where on earth did you get that expression?" Rose demanded. "It doesn't sound nice."

"We learned about China in school today, and they have silkworms, they eat rice, and they tie up the ladies' feet so they will be small," Charles answered. "And some of them have come to Brewster to work in the glove factory there, and they don't speak English."

"Then how do they ask for things at the store?" Abby wanted to know.

"They point," Charles said. "They just point."

"You two had better point yourselves toward the henhouse," Rose said. "You can finish the geography lesson later, and from now on call them Chinese."

They disappeared through the door to the ell, and she went to the pantry to see what would make an easy but filling supper. She took the pan of leftover beef stew—"not bad," it was—and set it on the back of the stove, added wood to the fire, peeled three potatoes and dropped them into the stew, hoping that would stretch it far enough for four people. Then she stepped into the dining room, fixing to take care of it for Abby just this once. To her surprise, her father's soiled plate, fork and tumbler were still at his place. Then she noticed that a second used plate, fork and tumbler were at Sarah's place. She cleared away the things, wondering who on earth had come in to share Father's noon meal. Whoever it was, he had not cleaned his plate. She set it on the floor for Tom, even though the cat was nowhere in sight. But before she could even say, "Kitty, kitty," the big cat came out from behind the stove and started licking the scraps.

Rose frowned. It had been several days since she'd had time to hold the cat and stroke him. She would have to remind herself to do that on her next half day at school. He must miss Sarah as much as she did, at least in a cat way. Still, petting the cat was probably not what Miss Harty had in mind for her days off. Maybe tonight she would have a few minutes to sit in the rocking chair in front of the warm stove and hold the cat.

Before Charles and Abby came back, she heard her father's heavy footsteps coming along toward the kitchen. She heard him grunt as he pulled off his barn boots. Emily's father just walked right on in with his outdoor boots on, and she was so glad that her father didn't do that.

"Good afternoon, Father," Rose said as he came into the kitchen.

"Huh," he answered without really looking at her.

"Is your knee mending, Father? It didn't sound as if you were limping when you came through the ell."

"It's tolerable," he answered gruffly. "Tolerable."

Rose poured a little warm water from the teakettle into the stew, which was getting too thick, and stirred the pot. She heard her father open the pantry door and knew he must be reaching for the sugar bowl.

Oh, dear, she thought.

"Rose," he said, returning to the kitchen. "Rose?"

"Yes, Father?"

"Where's the money from the sugar bowl?"

"The last few coins went to the iceman this week, Father. I believe I mentioned it to you that day . . ."

"Thunderation!" he interrupted, looking down at the bowl in his hand. "You would think a man could keep a bit of money in his own house."

"I-I-I had to pay the iceman, Father," Rose said meekly.

"That infernal icebox. I told her and told her, it would send good money after something that melts into water in a few days."

Rose did not know whether to answer this or not. Or even what she could answer. So she went on stirring the stew in silence.

"Well, child?" he growled. "What do you have to say to that?"

Rose thought quickly. "The icebox does save food from spoiling," she said. "So even if the ice turns to water, it may not be a loss."

"Thunderation!" he said again. "That teacher of yours said you could figure. Maybe you will earn your keep at Mr. Goodnow's store yet."

He staggered a bit as he turned to put the sugar bowl away. She wondered if his knee were not quite as cured as he had said. At the same time, the other track in her head considered the remark about the store. Surely she was earning her keep by cooking, cleaning, washing and ironing. Surely she did not have to take a position at the store as well. That certainly would mean the end of school.

Rose's eyes burned as she went about the supper preparations. Keeping her head down, she took the weekly newspaper to the dining room and set it beside her father's place, where he was now waiting for his supper. As she bent over, he coughed and she caught a whiff of what she now knew was the drink. Before supper? That had never happened before.

She thought back to the soiled plates she had found in the dining room. Had he and some friend had a little hard cider with their noon meal? It did not seem possible, and yet, he had that strong smell on his breath.

"Did you find sufficient food for your dinner today, Father?" she asked as Abby and Charles came into the kitchen.

"What's that?"

"You had company for the noon meal," Rose said. "I was asking . . ."

"Your Uncle Jason and I took a bite together," Father said. "Plenty of food in that icebox of yours. And we finished the pie."

CHAPTER 19
Mystery Guest

The days flipped past faster than cards shuffled by Aunt Nell, and it was Saturday morning before Rose had time to sit down and hem her square dance skirt. She opened the oven door to let a little extra warmth into the kitchen, and sat by the window to get the best light for the small stitches she was making. She didn't want a single thread to show on the right side; and no puckers, either. The cat curled with his head on one of her feet, and she felt very content.

She had just reached the halfway point when she heard a buggy clatter into the yard, but she didn't get up to look. She had to finish the hemming, and interruptions were not part of her plan for the morning. But pretty soon she heard steps clumping along the passageway in the ell. She looked up when the knock came, but before she could say anything, the door opened a little and Uncle Jason stuck his head in.

"Receiving callers?" he asked.

"No, Uncle, but you may come in," Rose laughed. "Do you have your card with you?"

"I'll just get out of these boots first," he said and closed the door again. Rose bent to her sewing, determined not to lose any piece of a minute.

"Your Aunt Nell sent you some things," Jason said, as he reopened the door and sat down on the edge of the woodbox. "What's that you're making?"

"A skirt for the dance tonight, Uncle."

"Aha! Nell said you'd be after going to the dance, and one of the things in that basket is a new ribbon for your hair. Blue, it is. She was of a mind to send red, but she remembered you had new fabric that was mostly blue."

"She is too good to me," Rose said, putting down her skirt and beginning to poke through the basket he had brought. A pot of strawberry rhubarb jam, a few plump carrots, and a small bowl of floating island pudding.

"Much too good," she added, her mouth watering at the very thought of that smooth pudding with the cooked egg whites on top.

"Deserve every bit of it, you do," Jason said gruffly. "We should be getting over here more often, but I just can't seem to get away more than once in a fortnight. Next thing we have to get at is slaughtering one of the pigs, so ask your father if he's interested in some bacon or fresh pork. I'd trade for a couple of month's supply of eggs. Now, is there anything I can do for you, long as I'm here?"

"I am sorry, Uncle, that I missed you last time you

came, but if you come by only for a noon meal, I would be in school. I do hope you had enough to eat. Where was Aunt Nell that day? Did she go to town again?"

"Noon meal? Child, I have not been in this house for more than two weeks. And midday is hardly the time I'd be coming calling anyway. I take a dinner pail with me most days, and relish the times when I can get home to Nell's good cooking."

"But . . ." Rose began and then stopped. Her mind was teetering about, certain her father had said Jason shared his dinner, including pie. It was as plain as the knobs on the icebox door that two people had used plates and forks. If it wasn't Uncle Jason, who was it? And why had Father told her it was her uncle if it wasn't?

She knew her uncle was watching her, so she bent her head toward her sewing again. Not looking at him, she asked if he would mind getting some stove wood for her.

"Charles and Abby are on an errand to the store," she said, "and I am trying to finish my skirt before they get back. And I don't like going to the woodshed, Uncle Jason," she added, finally looking up.

"Of course you don't, child. I am on my way," he said and put out his big, callused hand to give her a pat so gentle she barely felt it.

She heard him pause to pull on his boots and then clump off through the ell. Pretty soon he was back with more wood in one trip than she and Charles could manage in three. He let the pieces roll into the woodbox with a crash, brushed his hands together and said he'd best be going. She heard him start along the ell and then stop. The door opened again.

"Was someone besides your father here for a noon meal, Rose?"

"I believe so," she said. She looked up from her sewing and saw a frown on his face. Hoping she was not turning pink, she said in a voice she tried to make very matter-of-fact, "We will see you this evening."

He hesitated, then nodded and was gone.

Rose took a dozen or so stitches, looked at them and pulled the thread through the needle, annoyed with herself. She had puckered the hem because her mind was on the noon meal and the unknown guest. She inserted her needle in each stitch, pulled it into a loop and removed it.

"Settle down," she scolded herself and went on stitching. But her mind split into two pieces, one focused nicely on the hemming, the other seeing the dining room table with two places, two soiled forks, two unfolded napkins, two used knives, two plates with orts of food on them.

Orts, she thought, plunging into another direction. Little word, little bits. She had liked its sound the first time she had heard it in school. "Nits and orts," Miss Harty had said. "Two tiny words for tiny bits of stuff—easy to remember and descriptive."

Rose flicked an ort of fabric fuzz off her skirt and wondered how you could tell a nit from an ort. She would like to ask Miss Harty that, but she did not want to sound impertinent. Then her left thumb felt the bump of a seam, and she realized she had finished the hem. Quickly she pulled out the straight pins and poked them back into Sarah's pincushion. She had left the flat-iron on the back of the stove so it would be hot enough to give the hem a pressing, but she didn't bother to set up the ironing board. Instead, she spread two tea towels over the end of the dining room table and ironed the skirt smooth.

There, she thought. With Aunt Nell's ribbon, I will be almost all new tonight. At the very thought of the dance, her stomach gave a little flop. Perhaps Newton would have a new shirt tonight. Flop, flop. You would think a freshly caught trout was trapped in there, she thought, and went upstairs to spread the skirt carefully on top of the bed she now shared with Abby.

"Father seems very cross," Abby whispered to Rose as they jounced up and down on the second seat of the buggy.

"What's that?" Rose said, pulled back from her day-dreaming to her little sister. Probably night-dreaming, she thought. Or dusk-dreaming. It was barely past dusk, and they were on their way to the dance. For the first time that day she had let her mind wander to Newton and this outing she had been so excited about all week. Everyone had managed to eat and bathe and get dressed, and she had on her new skirt and new ribbon.

"Father is grouchy," Abby said.

Rose looked at her father's stiff back on the buggy seat ahead. She noticed that he and Charles were both looking straight ahead, not talking. Perhaps he was out of sorts. She had been too busy to notice at suppertime.

"He is going to the square dance for us, Abby," she said gently. "He will be all alone there."

"I'll ask him to dance with me," Abby said, trying to make up for the fact that she had forgotten all about their mother's death at that moment. Rose smiled, hoping that her dances would all be taken.

"You will be doing every square with Newton Barnes," Abby said, as if she had just opened the door of Rose's mind and looked inside. "I heard a girl say Newton Barnes had taken a fancy to you. What's a fancy?"

"It means someone likes you specially," Rose said, feeling her belly do its Newton Barnes thing again. "Who said that, anyway?"

"It was in the cloakroom, and I couldn't see her," Abby said, pleased that she had finally gotten her sister's attention. "She did not see me, either."

Father pulled the buggy into a space near the Town Hall and waited for everyone to get down.

"Shall we wait here for you?" Rose asked. But he was already on his way to the livery stable to get the horse under cover for the evening.

"He's in a temper over something," Charles said. "I spoke with him on the way over, and he gave me those 'uh-uh' answers that make you know it's time to close your mouth."

"Well, we will just go on inside then," Rose said, refusing to let her father's mood cast any shadows on her evening. She opened the door and could see right off that nearly the whole town had turned out for the square dance. Dozens of people were talking in little groups all over the big room, and the fiddlers were tuning up on the stage. Rose's eyes flew around the room and then she felt the awful warmth growing over the high collar of her shirtwaist. He was in the far corner, his back to the door, talking with a group of the older boys from school and one of his brothers, who was a farmer on his own across the river.

"Shall we go to the cloakroom, Abby?" she asked, glad to hide her face by looking down at her sister.

"You are very pink, Rose," Abby said in her clear voice. "You should have put a scarf over your face. Are you cold?"

"I will be fine in a moment," Rose said, glad the little girl had misunderstood—and not sorry that her voice for once had been helpful, probably explaining Rose's color to everyone right around them. Who was the girl who said the "fancy" thing, she wondered, and then she stopped thinking about it when Alice and Emily came rushing toward her, skirts and ruffles flouncing.

"We have been waiting for you," Alice said. "We thought you would never get here."

"Your skirt looks extraordinary," Emily almost shrieked. "And the ribbon does match, it matches perfectly."

"Turn around," Alice ordered. Rose whirled obediently, feeling the loop of her braids swinging on her neck, half of the new blue ribbon on each loop.

"Oooh, your hair looks extraordinary, too," Emily

said. "How did you manage such smooth braids on your own head?"

"Practice, my dear, practice," Rose teased.

"It is time to dance, ladies," Alice said, linking arms with each of her friends. "You come along, too, Abby, and we'll find you a special beau for the evening."

"I do not want a beau," Abby said, but she laughed and took Emily's outstretched hand. The four of them squeezed through the doorway to the big room where the square dance caller was just taking his place on the stage with the fiddlers.

"Form a circle, folks, a gi–gantic circle around the hall, and make another one inside if you don't all fit. Should be lad, gal, lad, gal, if you please—and if you don't please, pretend to be one or t'other to make it come out right."

The crowd laughed happily, and his voice rode over their chuckles with, "Quite a crowd out here tonight, quite a crowd, and we will begin with a grand right and left. So let's get that circle going, everybody join in. Don't have to dance for this one. All join hands and get ready. Inside circle, circle to the right, outside circle to the left. Music!"

The fiddles began to sing; the caller to stomp his feet. Rose could not remember when she had been any happier than at this very moment, even though Mr. Hawks was on her left and one of the Granger boys on her right. She could see Abby in the inside circle between Charles and Father. She did not see Newton anywhere, but she didn't figure he'd gone home just yet.

Then the caller ordered ladies to face the gents, clasp right hands and start around the circle.

"When you get back home, clap to the music till both circles are done, then join hands and circle the opposite way," sang out the caller.

It seemed anyone new to this event would be hopelessly lost, Rose thought, but then she noticed people giving a little nudge here and there, setting folks right. She kept putting out first one hand, then the other, and suddenly it was Newton's hand, giving hers a hard squeeze as he went skipping past.

"Great ribbons," he muttered when his face was passing her ear.

She felt her face flush and her feet grow lighter still. They might be dreadfully long, she thought, but they danced as well as the little ones other girls had. She met Uncle Jason as she went around, and she saw Miss Harty in the smaller inner circle.

The caller announced a Virginia reel and everyone split into small groups, lines of men facing women, boys facing girls. Rose found herself across from Uncle Jason and grinned at him.

"Finished the sewing, I see," he said, as he swept her through the other pairs.

"Oh, yes," she said a little breathlessly. "And baths and supper and everything."

His thick brows pulled together a little, and his smile faded for a second. But then he twirled her back to her place in line and the set went on.

Minutes later she and Emily and Alice succeeded in

getting into the same square and waited for men and boys to join them. Rose was almost holding her breath with anticipation, but it was that same Granger boy who slipped up beside her, and Newton, arriving a few minutes later, quickly took the spot on her corner, next to Alice. Alice's eyebrows were disappearing into her hair as she tried not to laugh at Rose's disappointment. And then they were off, bowing to partners, bowing to corners, swinging partners and promenading around the set.

The Granger boy—this one was John, not Peter who had teased her in school—held her firmly as they promenaded, and she tried to move away a little. But then it was time to swing your corner lady, and Newton sent her feet flying, then promenaded her back to her new place, next to him.

"You probably thought I hadn't figured it out," he said very quietly as they bowed to each other. "At the end of the set, excuse yourself to get some refreshment, please. Next set, I want you as partner, not corner."

"I am a most competent corner," Rose teased, tilting her head, and then hearing herself, wondering where on earth that little business had come from. Well, she was happy and had no work to do at the moment, so she was going to just enjoy it. She wished her hands were more like Miss Harty's, though, and less like the brush she used to scrub the kitchen floor. At the refreshment table, joined by Alice and Emily, Rose took a cup of cider and drank it thirstily.

"He cannot take his eyes away from you," Emily said.

"My mother says we're too young to have beaus, but you have one without even trying."

Alice gave Rose a little curtsey and said, "I am pea green with envy."

"You actually look nicely pink," Rose said, laughing at her friend, "and it's a good thing. No one wants to dance with a green person."

"Hello, Newton," Emily said, seeing him over Rose's shoulder and giving the other two fair warning of his approach. "You have your dancing feet on tonight, don't you?"

"And we're about to join a new square, Rose, if you will," Newton said, nodding to Emily and Alice. "Will you both come, too? I think we need more girls who can really dance."

And so the evening went, with Newton managing to be Rose's partner nearly all the time, keeping her so busy that she barely noticed where Charles and Abby and her father were. She did see Father talking to Miss Graves near the refreshment table, and once she saw him coming back into the hall from outside. Miss Harty joined one of their sets, with a bachelor farmer from the next town as her partner, but Rose didn't see whether he stayed at her side for the whole evening.

"You look quite the young lady tonight, Rose," Miss Harty said as she and Rose did a do-si-do across the square. Wouldn't it be fine if Miss Harty had a beau, she thought. Do I have one, she asked herself, looking sideways at Newton. He certainly was being very attentive, and she had not been tongue-tied, which always worried her when it came to boys.

Be hard to tie up that thick, bumpy thing, she had decided by the time he swung her off the floor once more. She hated it when people stuck their tongues out, and she hated it when they slaughtered a cow or calf and brought the tongue into the kitchen, all talking about what a delicacy it was. Ugly, that's what it was. And never tied. Her mind fell right off that track as Newton put his arm around her waist and promenaded her tightly around the square. She felt a tingle all the way from her knees to the nape of her neck as his right side sealed itself to her left side, and while her face flamed, she knew it wouldn't matter. Everyone was red in the face from all the dancing, and the room was now quite hot as well.

Time flew as skirts swirled, petticoats peeked out, and the caller grew hoarse from singing out his commands. It seemed to Rose that they had only just arrived when Mr. Lang called for a grand march to end the evening.

"Couples only," Mr. Lang said. "Just the pairs, please."

Newton took Rose's hand, bowed and said with a grin, "Will you make me into a couple, pretty lady?"

"For five minutes, more or less," Rose teased, "certainly, sir."

And so they went round and round, one couple joining with another and another and another until they were sixteen people across, several rows deep, coming together in front of the fiddlers and the caller.

"A fine evening," the caller said. And the fiddlers struck up with "Good Night, Ladies," as everyone headed for the cloakrooms.

"Don't rush," Newton said. "They cannot all get their coats at the same time."

"Well, Father was not in good spirits tonight," Rose said. "So I must not keep him waiting."

"Spirits enough," Newton muttered, but he nodded and still holding her hand, threaded through the crowd with her in tow, heading for the cloakrooms, where they found Abby carrying Rose's wrap out to her.

"Well chaperoned, weren't we?" Newton said, his thumb stroking the back of her hand. And then he dropped her fingers and was gone.

CHAPTER 20
Not a Lady

Emily was waiting on the church steps when Rose stepped outside after Sunday services the next morning. She pulled Rose aside, and as if Abby weren't even there, said, "Well, well, well, Miss Rose, and what did our Newton say so softly as you were going to the cloakroom?"

"I hope," Rose said, rolling her eyes toward Abby and scowling a little, "that you had some time in church for your prayers and your soul, and were not just sitting there thinking about pouncing on me like a cat that's had no scraps for a week."

"Answer the question, please," Emily said. "And stop shushing me because of Abby. You don't tell people what we talk about, do you, Abby?"

"No, Ma'am," Abby said, her eyes wide. "I would never tell on Rose."

"So, answer," Emily persisted.

"He said we were well chaperoned."

"Wh-a-a-a-t?"

"He said we had been well chaperoned."

"Ah," said Emily. "The thing with his mother and not being alone with a lady."

"Are you a lady, Rose?" Abby interrupted.

"Hmmm. Not really, Abby. Ladies are grown-ups. But Newton was thinking of me as a lady in the future."

"In his future," Emily put in, "more than likely."

"Now, Em," Rose cautioned. "I am fourteen going on fifteen, and my future is making Sunday dinner within the hour."

"You make dinner like a grown-up," Abby said, skipping a little to keep up with the older girls.

Rose and Emily laughed but said no more. They had reached the buggy, and Charles and Father were already there. Emily spoke to them politely, then walked away to her own family, and Abby and Rose climbed in. As the horse trotted toward the farmhouse, Rose let her mind slip back to the night before, when she had ridden on this very seat after dancing so many squares with Newton that she could barely remember them all. She felt that tingle again, running up and down her spine and along her limbs. She had always loved square dancing, but she had never known it could be like that. It must have been the blue ribbons.

"This is your day to leave early, Rose, is it not?" Miss Harty asked the following Thursday as Rose came into the classroom.

"I had hoped to spend the afternoon at home, Miss Harty," Rose answered.

"And you certainly may do that," Miss Harty smiled. "But I would like to speak with you during the morning recess."

"Yes, Ma'am."

Rose kept her eyes on the oiled floorboards as she approached her desk, but at the last second she could not help looking up, even though she knew what she would see and knew she was going to be scarlet instantly. Newton was already at his desk, as he had been every day this week, and he was looking straight at her; not smiling, just looking. She knew, just knew, that Emily and Alice were watching, so she reached up a hand to brush her hair back and said a firm, "Good morning" to him.

"And good morning to you," he answered, his eyes dancing as she quickly turned and took her seat. "It appears to be a very good morning, now that you are here to shield me from the teacher's glare."

Rose almost giggled, she was so happy. She glanced toward Emily, who had her head nearly in the book that was open on her desk, then let her eyes slide the other way to see what Alice was doing. She wished she hadn't. Alice was staring, first at her and then at Newton. She hoped he hadn't noticed.

"Now it is time for arithmetic, so please turn to the proper page in your text and start the next problem. Anyone who needs help should raise his or her hand, and I will assist you. Emily, you may put your work on the blackboard, starting wherever you finished yesterday," Miss Harty said.

Rose let out a small breath. Another school day was under way. She was glad the arithmetic was first. Perhaps penmanship would come in the afternoon when she was home getting ready for Abby's birthday supper. She was so tired of forming row after row of Os and Ps and Ss. And she usually managed to drop a large black blot of ink somewhere on the paper. She hated refilling her inkwell, so she always left it too long, and then the ink was thick and likely to splatter.

Suddenly she heard an almost soundless whistling behind her. Newton was doing a few bars of one of the square dances. She looked for Miss Harty, but the teacher was working with Emma Goodnow at the front corner of the room, too far away to hear. Smiling as she worked, she went on with her problems, and the whistling soon stopped.

When the recess bell rang, she stayed in her seat. As Newton passed her desk, he asked if everything was all right.

"This is a half day for me," she said. "I have to talk to the teacher during this recess."

As soon as the room cleared, Miss Harty wanted to know if the half days were helping, and Rose nodded enthusiastically.

"I save that time for special things, Miss Harty," she said. "Today is Abby's birthday, and we will have a special supper, and I made a pudding she likes. And I need a little time to finish a square dance skirt I made for her doll."

"Your own skirt was beautiful at the dance, Rose," Miss Harty said. "Wherever did you get it?"

"I made that myself, with fabric Aunt Nell bought for me in town. And she sent me the ribbons for my hair."

"You had a fine time at the square dance, didn't you?"

"Oh, yes, Ma'am," Rose said, feeling her face get a little warm. "And did you enjoy it, Miss Harty?" she asked, suddenly remembering her manners.

"Indeed," Miss Harty said. "I noticed that you did nearly all the squares with Newton Barnes, and I hope that socializing will not interfere with your work in this room, since he sits right behind you. If he bothers you here, I will change your seats."

"He doesn't disturb me," Rose said, thinking that wasn't exactly true. Sometimes she found Newton Barnes very disturbing.

"Good. Now I want to go over the work you need to do to stay abreast of the class even though you will be gone for half the day. I expect you brought your noon meal, so you will be here until 12:30?"

"Yes, Ma'am."

Rose recited "The Children's Hour," wondering once more what the poet meant by "grave Alice." Surely she was very much alive in his tale of the girls she knew were his daughters. But a grave was where Sarah was, there in the cemetery. When she finished, without any mistakes, she asked Miss Harty.

"Oh, good heavens, Rose—words often have more

than one meaning. It is an adjective here, don't you see? And it means she is serious, solemn, not laughing like Allegra."

"Thank you, Miss Harty," Rose said, thinking her question must have seemed rather foolish.

"You should always ask, Rose, always. It is the best way to learn. And besides, your friend Alice is so far from grave that it must have been quite a mystery to you."

Rose laughed then, and Miss Harty reached for her hand. Holding it gently in both of hers, she said, "Now, please tell me how you are managing at home, Rose. Sometimes I worry about whether we are being neighborly enough to you these days."

"We are all right, Miss Harty," Rose answered, and in the aftermath of the square dance she really believed that everything in her life was all right. For the moment her fatigue was gone, she had forgotten about the missing coins in the sugar bowl, and she had heard nothing more about a need to leave school.

"We are really quite all right," she repeated.

"You must feel free to speak to me if things take a turn for the worse," Miss Harty said. "I do not gossip in the store or at the dinner table."

She squeezed the hand she held, thinking how rough and worn it was for a young girl, but then smiled as she remembered how happy Rose had been at the square dance.

"And," she added, "if you need any advice about young men who come calling, you may talk with me about that, too. You may think I am quite old and perhaps destined to be a spinster, but I will tell you, for your ears only, that I still have some chances of my own."

Rose could think of no answer to this, but she didn't have to. The Granger boy came in to ring the bell, and in a few minutes, everyone was trooping back into the room. The lessons resumed, continuing until it was time for the midday meal. Rose filled her cup with water from the pail at the front of the room, ate a thick slice of brown bread with butter on it and decided to save her apple, which was a bit wrinkled, for the walk home. When Miss Harty nodded to her, she started to get up and couldn't stand. Newton's foot was right on her skirt. She gave it a twitch, gave him a look and set off, knowing from his grin that he had done it on purpose.

"Beg your pardon, Miss Rose," she heard him say behind her.

"Pardon granted," she said over her shoulder. And then she hurried out.

Rose reached behind the icebox and retrieved the folded oilcloth where she had been hiding a doll's dress and petticoat she had made for Abby's birthday. Making a few stitches at a time, sometimes very late at night, she had listened with one ear for her father to come home, and with the other for any signs of Charles or Abby stirring upstairs. But the clothes were finished now, and she was certain Abby hadn't poked around behind the icebox. The old piece of tablecloth had been a sudden inspiration. It was waterproof enough to protect the clothes from any moisture behind the icebox.

The things really were pretty, Rose thought, and she was certain Abby would be pleased. She went to the dining room to put the gift on Abby's chair where she would not see it until it was time for the birthday supper. That's when she noticed the dishes, a noon meal for two people again and nothing cleaned up. Rose sighed. She would have a little less time this afternoon than she had planned. A bit angry, she gathered up all the dirty dishes at once and was just thinking how Sarah would have scolded her for carrying too much at once when she thought she heard someone laugh. She stopped so suddenly that the cups teetered atop the plates. She listened. Except for the ticking of the kitchen clock, the house was as quiet as church on a Tuesday.

"I must be losing my mind entirely," she muttered to herself, starting toward the kitchen again. Then she heard a deeper laugh and a sort of shriek, followed by another high-pitched laugh.

"Someone is here? In this house?" she said to herself. "Or is it ghosts?"

She gave a little shiver, put the dishes in the sink and decided the noises were real and were coming from above. It was necessary to be brave, she told herself, taking off her shoes and quickly tiptoeing up the stairs. Sure enough. The sounds were coming from Father's room, laughing and a kind of yelping. She stopped suddenly. That was Father's laugh. She had not heard that sound in weeks, but it was unmistakable. She moved toward the door of his room, almost afraid to breathe. The door was open about four inches, and her eyes widened. That was a petticoat and a shiny, dark green skirt in a heap on the floor, and surely Father's trousers were there on the braided rug as well. She raised her eyes from the floor and almost gasped out loud. She could see the foot of Father's bed, and a lady's bare feet and ankles were in full view on the bed. As she watched, one of Father's feet—also without stockings—poked at the lady's right foot. She heard a giggle, and a woman's voice said, "You are a devil, you are."

Father laughed, said something too low for Rose to hear, and she fled. At the bottom of the stairs she snatched up her shoes without pausing, then hurried through the kitchen, along the ell and out the door to the woodshed, where she collapsed on the dirt floor and for several minutes did not move at all. Then she began to shake and to sob. She did not know what was going on in there, but she knew it was wrong, she knew she hated it. She sat up, crying so loudly that she wondered if they could hear her as she had heard them. Still holding a shoe in each hand, she rocked back and forth, choking and gasping with fear and shock. Eventually, her sobs trailed into sniffles, and she realized her dress would be ruined if she did not get up. She made it to her knees on the dirt and wood chips and then collapsed again.

I am folding like a broken chair, she thought. And very slowly she pulled herself up to sit on a thick stump that Father and Charles used when they were splitting wood. She leaned back against the woodpile and wondered if it would fall on her, if she could give it a push and wait for the firewood to crush her. She wiggled a shoulder against the pile, but nothing happened. She took a deep breath and pushed back with her head and shoulders, but the stack held firm.

She let out a sigh so great that her head slumped forward. She let her head sink right down to her chest and realized she could no longer feel her heart pounding. As if the air of the sigh had carried her troubles away, she began to feel calm. She started to wonder about what she had seen. Was it Miss Graves, there on Father's bed? But people didn't lie down on beds in daylight, and certainly not on beds in other people's houses unless they were taken with an illness. There was no getting away from the fact that someone's limbs were on that bed, however, and someone's skirt was on the floor.

Then she remembered Emily snickering about her father and mother sending the children off to the store to buy penny candy. "They need a spell for themselves," Emily would say with a knowing look. But Miss Graves didn't live in this house. She must have all the time to herself she could want since she had no family to see after. Ah, Rose thought, but perhaps she was the guest at the noon meals, perhaps she was indeed spending time at this house. So, Rose thought with a flash of anger, why didn't she do the washing up?

She pushed against the woodpile again, harder than before, but it held like a mortared wall. Idiot, she said to herself. You can't get buried under a stack of wood and then get buried in the cemetery. Who would take care of Abby?

Oh, dear God, she thought. Abby's birthday supper. Abby's floating island pudding. Abby's gifts. She must pull herself together and get on with her tasks. Except she couldn't go in the house until she knew everyone was wearing clothes and sitting in the parlor, not laughing and yelping in an upstairs bedroom. Perhaps she had better go back to school and stay there until it was the proper time to go home. Then she would be expected, and everything would be in order.

She put on her shoes, crept into the house, took her coat and quietly left again. Hoping no one would look out a window, she set off for school once more. For a few minutes, she walked furiously, her mind as blank and dark as the school blackboard in the morning. Half crying, she had her head down and her mouth half open, trying to catch her breath in the cold air. She paused, pulled the sleeve of her coat across her eyes to get rid of the blur caused by her tears, and rummaged in her pocket for a handkerchief. She pulled out a white linen square with white tatting all around and wailed aloud. It was one her mother had made for her when she turned thirteen.

"Mother, Mother, Mother," she said half aloud. "Where are you when I need you so much?"

She glanced around to see if anyone was near, although she knew it was quite unlikely. People talk if they see someone walking along chattering to themselves, and she wanted nothing more than to go unnoticed. But at this time of day, most folks were in their houses or barns doing their work, and all the children were in school. As her brain began to come out of its brief hibernation, the silence seemed almost greater than in church, where at the very least you would hear the rustle of fabric and the scraping of boots as people fidgeted in the hard pews.

Then she heard a clear, two-note bird call, and she looked up toward the red pine trees near the roadside. She saw him almost immediately, a black-capped chickadee, one of her mother's favorites. "Phee-bee," the chickadee said, sounding the way the little children did when they sang their notes in school. She had always loved the fact that a chickadee said phoebe so clearly, while the real phoebe said its name as if it had laryngitis and needed a red flannel wrapping on its throat. The chickadee dropped to a branch nearer the ground, then dropped again and seemed to be looking right at her.

"Chicka-dee-dee-dee," he chattered, reverting to his name song.

Rose smiled, and then stopped smiling so fast that her mouth nearly froze in the grin. How could she possibly smile now? She must be losing whatever was left of her mind. But she kept walking, her eyes on the chickadee, and the bird kept hopping from branch to branch, closer and closer to her, chattering away as if he had advice to give.

She looked down at her dress and saw that shavings and tiny chips of wood from the shed were clinging to her skirt. Dirt was smeared across her apron, which she had forgotten to take off when she left the house. I can't go back to school like this, she told herself. So she turned back, and just before she reached her house, made another turn onto the old wood road that led to the river. The snow was over the tops of her shoes, and the hem of her skirt brushed a wide path as she walked quickly toward the river. She hoped she would hear the children as they came along from school. Then, surely, she would go home to an empty house and be able to go on with her work.

Reaching the river, Rose sat down on the large flat rock where she had rested so many times with her brother and sister and with her mother. She pulled her knees up toward her chin and locked her cold hands around her dress. She stared at the ice-covered river, considering whether it would hold her weight if she tried to cross. It was shallow here and might well be frozen almost down to the hundreds of pebbles that covered the riverbed. She wondered where all those stones came from, and why, with so many smooth rounded ones, your foot always managed to step on one with a sharp edge.

What am I going to do, she thought. I cannot get buried by a woodpile. I cannot disappear into the river. I probably won't freeze to death here before school gets out, although it is as cold as a witch's tit on this rock that is so warm in summer. Witch's tit? Where did that come from? She remembered suddenly and, despite her despair, nearly laughed out loud. It was when Great Uncle Samuel had come two summers ago, and they put salt in the big ice cream bucket, and cream, sugar and vanilla in the smaller pail and then took turns with the crank until the mixture was frozen. One taste, and Samuel had slapped his hand against his chest and roared, "Cold as a witch's tit!" Rose had almost jumped out of her shoes, and Sarah had shushed him, but she had heard her father chuckle, so she knew it was what adults called an expression, not swearing or taking the Lord's name in vain or anything like that.

The chickadee called again, from a branch right over her head.

"You followed me," she said, tilting her head back to look at him. He just cocked his black cap to one side, looking at her with one beady, black eye. "Dee-dee-dee," he chirped. "Dee-dee-dee."

She wished Sarah were there to hear the little bird. She would talk back and forth to him as if they were really telling each other things, and Rose would always ask if she was sure she was only saying nice things, since neither of them knew what "phee-bee" or "dee-dee" meant in bird talk.

Sarah. Sarah. Sarah. Never mind about her talking to birds. What about talking to Father? Would she say anything? Would it have happened if Sarah were still here? What exactly would Sarah do? That's the important thing. She made one hand into a fist and punched the palm of the other. Perhaps the house would burn down and they would all die, and then, if the Rev. Lockhead was right, she'd meet Sarah in heaven and be able to ask her. She punched her hand again. Ignorant girl, she told herself. Great lot of good it will do to ask a question after the need for an answer has gone up in smoke.

So, she would have to find the answer herself. She

couldn't ask Emily or Alice or Miss Harty or Aunt Nell. That would be mortifying, just in case this was something like when the cows tried to climb on each other's backs. Emily was always laughing about that and saying something about cows not being decent enough to wait until they were in the barn. But she couldn't pretend nothing had happened, that she knew.

She stood and shook out her dress, which was quite wet around the hem and up the back where she had been sitting on the damp rock. She started back to the house. Sarah always said when the problem was very big, you just started at the very beginning and went along a bit at a time, the way you read a new book.

"Read only the first line," she'd say, "and understand that. Don't go skimming through or try to see the end before you have absorbed all the lines between. Problems are like books. You work your way through them, and sometimes the ending is quite a surprise."

Rose tried to wipe her mind's slate clean and start at the beginning, but she wasn't quite certain just where the beginning was. As she made her way back to the house, she saw that the chickadee was flitting along near her, sometimes crossing the path, sometimes moving higher, but staying near.

He's a comfort, she thought. And he's just a little bird.

CHAPTER 21
Spilled Sugar

Rose had been in the house only a few minutes when Charles raced into the kitchen, hardly able to breathe. Rose was still wearing her wet, dirty dress, and she knew her hair was askew, but she tried to face him calmly.

"Whatever is the matter, Charles?"

"I forgot about Abby's birthday," he panted. "I want to get her some penny candy at the store. I sent her . . ." He gulped, took a deep breath and went on, "I sent her to the chicken coop and said I'd be along in a minute. Could I have some pennies from the sugar bowl?"

Rose, who had been on the verge of bursting into tears again, turned toward the pantry without a word. She fetched the sugar bowl from the high shelf where it was kept and peered in anxiously. Then, so suddenly that Charles cried out in alarm, she hurled the little blue and white bowl across the kitchen. It struck the wall above the woodbox and shattered. Several coins rolled across the floor.

Charles seemed frozen in place, but Rose wailed aloud and ran for the stairs, the sugar bowl cover still in her hand. As she blindly went down the hall, she heard Charles' footsteps on the stairs.

"Don't follow me," she screamed angrily. "Go away. Take one of those pennies and go to the store. Leave me alone!"

She flung herself across the bed she shared with Abby and sobbed. He took it all, she thought, all but a few pennies. She remembered the day Father put several dollars in there from the eggs and the hen he sold. He's not buying Abby any special treat for her birthday. It was the drink; it had to be the drink. She'll be fortunate if he even remembers to wish her "many happy returns." As if anyone could want this day to return, ever, ever, ever. She felt something touch her head and reached up to brush it away. She felt it again. She raised her face, her chin still on the coverlet, and discovered Charles' face right in front of hers, not five inches away. His hand reached out again, this time to touch her shoulder.

"I told you to go away," she said. "Why are you disobeying?"

"I don't want you to cry," Charles said. "And I want to know why you broke the sugar bowl. You must be really put out to break the sugar bowl."

Rose felt the tears coming again and nearly choked

trying to stop them. If she had collected all the tears she'd made over the past few months, she could make a waterfall.

"Take a couple of the pennies if you can find them, Charles. I broke the sugar bowl because it was nearly empty, and it should not have been. You run along now, do your errand, and I'll clean up the mess I made."

"But what are you going to do about the sugar bowl? Where will the money be kept? What will you tell Father?"

"I don't know, I don't know and I don't know," she answered.

"Pretty good arm for a girl," Charles said, suddenly recovering his usual mischievous outlook on things. And then he was gone, clattering down the stairs so fast that Rose was certain his feet hadn't even touched some of them.

For her part, Rose slid off the bed until she was sitting on the floor. She put her head against the quilt and sat for a while, sighing and snuffling and wishing she lived on the moon. Or at least in another town. A tear rolled down her right cheek and dropped on her hand. She lifted her head and felt the quilt. A lot of tears must have run out of her left eye—the bedding was quite damp in that one spot. She pulled herself to her feet, thinking she must look something like Sarah's aunt, who had to be hauled out of her chair into a standing position. The old lady occasionally came to visit and fussed and fumed all the while, making Rose and Charles and Abby run this way and that to do her errands. That,

Rose thought, almost brightening, was one good thing: great-aunt Rachel had not come to visit since Sarah had been killed.

"Killed," Rose said in a whisper. It was not just that she died. Lots of people died. She had been killed. He killed her. He would not buy an icebox; he would not pipe in the water; he stacked the wood badly. As surely as if he had chopped off her head like a chicken, he had killed her.

"I will not be killed," she said, startled at hearing her voice in the quiet room.

"Well, I won't," she said, planting her hands on her hips and stamping one foot. "I just won't."

Minutes later, her hair tidied and her apron in place, she was back in the kitchen, ready to make Abby's birthday supper and muttering to herself, over and over, "I just won't. I will not."

Dinnertime inevitably came, and Charles was concentrating on his food as if it were a math problem, although he occasionally glanced sideways at Rose. So far, he had said nothing. Father had both arms on the table, bending one to get his fork to his mouth, and silent except for the noises he always made when eating. Rose looked over the table, decided she had not forgotten anything and took her place.

Abby seemed not to notice that things were even quieter than usual. She was talking, talking, talking, chattering like a little bird, Rose thought.

"What time was I born, Father?" Abby suddenly asked.

"Eh? What's that you said?" Father asked, frowning at Abby across the table.

"What time was I born? Was it before suppertime or after?"

"Pfff—I don't know as I rightly remember. Rose here came along about four o'clock in the morning. I remember that well enough. It was nearly time for me to get to the barn and do the milking. The cows had to wait a bit that day."

He paused to take another bite of the chicken and dumplings and wiped a bit of chicken off his mustache with the side of his hand. Ort or nit, Rose asked herself. Oh, heavens, what a foolish mind I have. Boulders and mountains are what we're dealing with here, not nits and orts.

"But what about me, Father?" Abby asked, bouncing a bit on her chair.

"Don't interrupt, child," he growled. "I'm getting to that. Charles was delivered by Doc Burrows during the noon hour in haying season. The neighbors who were helping out were in the yard having their meal, and we gave Sarah a washrag to bite on because she didn't want anyone to hear her . . ." He stopped for a second and then went on, "But I don't exactly recall about you, Abby. It was before suppertime, though, I know that for certain because Charles and Rose and I sat down to a cold meal while you wailed upstairs as if someone had stuck pins into you."

"So I am already nine," Abby exulted. "I am nine right now, and I may have been nine for an hour or two."

"Next year," Charles said, "you'll be ten just about this same time. Fancy that."

Abby ignored him and turned to Rose.

"Do you remember when I came, Rose, do you?"

"Oh, yes," Rose said slowly. "Mother was in terrible pain that day, and the doctor didn't come until mid-afternoon, and you were born about ten minutes after he arrived. I remember his buggy coming into the yard so fast that it raised dust all around. And you were only about three minutes old when I first saw you—all pink and pretty and wrapped in a tiny blanket. You certainly are nine by suppertime, Abby."

Everyone talked then, and when Rose brought in the floating island pudding, Abby oohed and aahed. When she saw the new doll dresses Rose had made and the set of jacks Charles had bought her at the store, she oohed some more, apparently not even noticing that her father had not offered a gift of any sort. The problem, Rose thought, was that you never knew with Abby. She had been prattling away here at the beginning of the meal as if she had no cares at all, but Rose was pretty sure she had noticed how glum everyone was and had set out to do something about it. She really is so special, Rose said to herself. I won't let anything happen to her.

"I'll do your cleaning up, Abby," Charles offered. "You can try out the jacks or dress your doll."

Father pushed his chair back, the official signal that the meal was over, and the three children all picked up plates and headed for the kitchen.

"I'll be back by and by," Father said, taking his coat

from the hook by the woodbox. "Sleep tight, nine-year-old." And with that, he went out into the darkness.

"Well, at least he didn't go into the pantry," Charles said, not looking at Rose.

She felt herself flushing. She had cleaned up the sugar bowl fragments and retrieved five pennies that Charles hadn't found. She had put the pennies into a small glass dish that Sarah had used for pepper relish. She had no idea what she would tell Father when he could not find the sugar bowl.

For now, she would get Charles and Abby settled in their beds and then set about solving her various problems, which included getting her stomach to stay in one place.

Rose slid into bed beside Abby and listened to her sister's breathing. It was slow and even. Abby was sound asleep, sprawled on her stomach, one arm under her pillow and the other clutching her doll, which was wearing the dress Rose had made. The birthday, Rose thought, was not perfect, but Abby was perhaps the only one who really didn't know that, thank goodness. After a couple of minutes, Rose slid out of bed again. She had not undressed, except for her shoes, and now she picked them up and tiptoed down the hall. At the foot of the attic stairs, she paused and could hear Charles snoring very softly, so she knew he was asleep for the night.

Rose set her candle down in the kitchen while she put on her shoes and coat. Then she blew out the candle and let herself out through the kitchen door and the ell. As her eyes adjusted to the night, she realized she would be able to see quite nicely. The moon was small, but the snow made everything quite bright. She set off along the road, peering into the woods as she went, hoping she wouldn't run into any wild animals.

Mostly, she told herself, they wouldn't be ferocious, girl-eating creatures anyway. Just deer or foxes or—heavens to Betsy—a bear! Foolish girl, she chided herself. Bears and skunks and raccoons are taking a long winter's nap. She hurried on and turned the corner toward Emily's house. She hoped she could wake Emily without rousing the entire family, but she had to find out some things before she decided what to do. She could not go on trying to make everything seem fine all the time when it really wasn't fine at all. Sometimes she felt as if she were choking on all the things she kept inside.

At Emily's house, she went around to the north side, made a small snowball and tossed it at her friend's window, up under the eaves. Nothing happened. She tossed another, then a third. Then she saw the curtain move, and she could make out the outline of Emily's head. She waved, and Emily pushed up the window.

"Are you sleepwalking?" Emily demanded in a loud whisper. "Are you a ghost?"

"I need to talk to you," Rose answered, also in a whisper. "Come down."

The window shut, and Rose waited. After a few minutes she saw the light of a candle flicker on the kitchen ceiling. The door opened, and Rose went in. Without saying anything, Emily hugged her friend, and Rose suddenly felt the tears welling up. She didn't have time to go all weepy. She had to talk to Emily and get back to her bed before Father came home. But she cried anyway, assuring Emily through her sobs that she wasn't hurt, that no one was hurt or dead; that no, the house wasn't burning down. Then Emily pushed her toward the dining room and pulled out a chair for her.

"So, what is it?" she asked.

Rose had carefully worked out what she would say so that she wouldn't tell Emily too much, but she forgot all that when she looked at her friend's face. The story of the day spilled out, and even told in a whisper, the tale shocked Emily. She pulled her chair closer to Rose and reached for both her hands, holding them with whitened knuckles while she listened.

"You poor thing," she said when Rose had finished. "What a beast he is, a rat, a ferret, a weasel. A bull with a cow that springs all year."

"He killed her, Emily, he killed her," Rose said, not really taking in Emily's outburst.

Emily squeezed Rose's hands even tighter. She did not need to ask who had been killed. She had heard her parents talking one night about how Sarah Hibbard had died, and she knew that they blamed Rose's father. But she had never said a word to Rose because she couldn't bear to think about it and was sure Rose couldn't bear it either. And now she still didn't know what to say.

"I don't want him to kill me," Rose said softly. "Or Abby."

"How about Charles? Are we going to let him be

killed off?" Emily asked, her antic sense emerging just in time to take the edge off this conversation.

Rose almost smiled.

"He'll be all right," she said. "It's different with boys, and besides, Charles seems to know when to answer and when to disappear. But Abby's so little, and, and, and . . . oh, Emily, what if she had come home and found those clothes on the floor?"

What if, indeed, Emily thought.

"Fornication," Rose said. "It was fornication, wasn't it?"

"I told you, Rose, I already told you. Bulls jump on cows. Fornication, yes, that's what it was, all right."

"What on earth is going on here?" came a voice in the doorway.

The two girls jumped as if they had been struck, and turned to see Emily's mother standing there in her nightdress.

"What are you doing here, Rose? And what is this talk of fornication? The Rev. Lockhead talks of fornication, but the rest of us do not mention such things. Why are you not in bed in your own house? And you, Emily, what are you doing down here at this hour?"

Emily started to stammer an answer to the last question, not having any idea what to say to the rest of them, but her mother interrupted, and in a completely different voice, said, "Oh, dear, Rose. Oh, my dear. My dear child, what is it? What has happened?"

"Nothing, Ma'am," Rose answered, looking down.

"I could not sleep, and I came and threw snowballs at Emily's window, and she came down to talk to me."

Emily let out a long breath and wondered if Rose was really going to talk them out of this one. She could see Rose from the corner of her eye and was afraid her friend looked guilty of all sorts of things, way beyond being a bit wakeful. She glanced up at her mother, who was no longer paying any attention to her. Mrs. Stafford placed the candle on the table and dropped to her knees in front of Rose.

"You had better tell me," she said. "It will not get better in the hiding of it, whatever it is. What was it that kept you awake, Rose?"

"She cannot tell you, Mother," Emily put in. "She really cannot."

"I think she must," Emily's mother said, taking hold of Rose's hands. "I think, Rose, it is time you told me what is going on in your house that keeps you awake and paints those dark circles under your eyes and makes you nod off in school."

Rose looked up long enough to scowl at Emily, then turned back to her study of the floorboards. They were well polished, much more so than the floors at her house. She really wasn't doing a very good job there, she thought. Her boards weren't shiny, she could not sleep, and she had broken the sugar bowl. She sagged forward and Emily's mother put her arms around her. Rose began to cry again.

"Emily," her mother said sternly, rocking Rose back

and forth a little, "you are to relate what happened here tonight, starting with the snowballs."

So Emily, who would rather muck out the barn than answer that tone of voice, told Rose's story while her mother swayed back and forth with her arms around Rose, who went right on crying until Emily came to the part about fornication. Then she pulled away and said, "What if it had been Abby? What if it had been Abby?"

"Bad enough that it was you," Emily's mother said. "The question is, what do we do now? Are you strong enough to get back home and into bed before anyone knows you went out? Your father will be furious if he discovers that you've been wandering around in the night. And you cannot decide tonight what you will do next. You have to think about that and go right on making the oatmeal and getting your brother and sister off to school. What's it to be, Rose?"

"I can get home," Rose said. She stood up and went toward the door without looking at Emily.

"I had to say," Emily said. "Rose, I had to say. She won't tell anyone. She doesn't go to the store to trade tales with Mrs. Munson and the others. It will be all right."

"That's correct, Rose. I won't tell, at least not right now. So you get on home before someone finds your bed empty. Was your father asleep when you left?"

"He went out," Rose said. "He always goes out. I will go home now so I'll be in bed when he gets there. But he never looks into our room anyway."

She nodded to Emily and to her mother and went out the door.

"Fornication," Emily's mother said, almost to herself. "That sweet girl has to find the preacher's fire right in her very own house, right in Sarah's bed, no doubt."

"Rose thinks he killed her mother," Emily said, relieved that her mother's anger was gone.

"Killed Sarah?"

"He didn't stack the wood right. Rose overheard people talking about it."

"Oh, dear God, I should have put on my clothing and gone with her," Emily's mother said. She went to the door, looked out and could just see Rose making the turn from their road to the main street.

CHAPTER 22
A Near Miss

As Rose scurried along, she tried to figure out what she should do next. It was too bad Emily's mother knew the story, and she hoped she really wouldn't tell because it would bring disgrace on the whole family. Her father was still in mourning, and he was traipsing— she was sure that's what Aunt Nell would call it— around with another woman. She had to protect Abby if she could, but how?

It was so cold that her feet crunched on the snow, and pretty soon she came out of the woodsy section and into the open. Something moved right beside her, and she jumped before she realized that the moon was higher, and she had jumped at her own shadow. She stopped to look at the moon. She and Sarah used to go outside on a summer night to see a full moon or one of the slender little crescents that her mother said she liked even better. She wondered how far away the moon was, whether you could see the moon when you were in heaven, if you could see people you knew or if you were looking at the wrong side of the world. Perhaps Sarah could only see China or Australia, Rose thought. But would that be fair? Perhaps everyone stayed up all the time in heaven, never went to bed at all, just so they could watch the world turn until the part they wanted to see passed by again.

It came to Rose, as she stared at the moon, that Sarah was gone but she really wasn't. Why do I think these twisted-up things, she wondered. She is gone, dead. I can't talk to her. Still, every day she felt as if Sarah were there, sometimes in the kitchen, sometimes at the table, sometimes out of sight but near. Not in school, but then, Sarah had never been in school. Tears stung her eyes, but as she started walking again, she knew what she would do first. She would take Abby away from her father's house. Fornication, Emily had said. No one who was eight years old—nine, now—could live in a house where fornication was happening. She was not sure how she would do it, but she suddenly knew that she must. She could almost hear Sarah pushing her ahead, telling her to take care of her sister first. It was as if the moon had given her a message.

Rose shivered, and suddenly a little scared because of the hour, she glanced over her shoulder. Nothing moved anywhere. Except for the sound of her feet, it was so still that she was sure she would have heard a whisper from a mile away. She was almost home, but as she came near, she saw the gaslights on the hotel go out.

"Oh, dear," she said aloud. "Oh, dear."

She hurried up the steps and opened the door to the kitchen. The roar of her father's voice came before she had even stepped inside.

"And just where have you been, young lady? Or shall I not call you lady? This is no hour for you to be about!"

At the last second, Rose realized her father's hand was striking out toward her. She dodged, and the intended blow fell short. Her father almost lost his balance as his hand encountered only air. He's been at the drink, she thought, feeling a little shaky. But her strength returned quickly, and she stood quite straight, looking at a small crease in his forehead because she did not dare look him in the eye. This was no time to challenge him.

"I am a lady, Father," she said quite loudly, trying to override her father's voice. "And I shall go to bed now so I can be up in the morning to make your oatmeal."

"We'll have no traipsing around in the middle of the night from this house," her father bellowed, but he made no further move to hit her.

"Ah, yes," Rose said in a quieter voice, thinking she could count on her two hands the number of times her father had struck her in her whole life. "We certainly will have none of that in this house, will we?" And then she picked up one of the candles on the back of the stove, turned on her heel and disappeared from sight.

Rose heard her father's footsteps coming behind her,

then heard them going away again and decided he had gone to the outhouse. She was in her room by the time he came upstairs, and within a few minutes she heard him snoring. She tiptoed to his door to make sure his candle was out and then slipped in beside Abby, more wide-awake now than she had been out on the road.

Once under the covers, she started to tremble. Father had tried to strike her and missed only because she was quick and he had been at the hotel. She must take Abby to Aunt Nell's tomorrow and ask her aunt to keep her for a few days. That would give her time to work things out. She felt tears coming and clenched her fists. She must hold up. Right now, she must hold up. She forced her body to stop shaking and concentrated fiercely on blue sky. In a minute or two it came, the clear blue sky of summer. And then her breathing became as slow and even as Abby's.

Long before any roosters pulled their heads from under their wings, Rose was out of bed. She did not dare use the chamber pot for fear of waking Abby. Instead, she shook her pillow out of its case and stealthily opened a drawer in the chest between the windows. Quickly she pulled out two chemises and two pairs of drawers and added them to the pillowslip. She put in stockings, a waist, a petticoat and a skirt, and was about to put the bundle out of sight when her exploring fingers felt Abby's hair ribbons. Three of those, she thought. It will cheer her up.

With the pillowslip stuffed fatter than a Christmas goose, she dressed and tiptoed toward the stairs. The sky gave no hint of the sun, but it was halfway to gray. She knew it was early but thought Father must be in the barn. His bedroom door was closed, and she had left it ajar when she checked on the candle.

In the kitchen, she added kindling to the coals in the stove, and the fire flared. She put in a larger stick of wood, fetched the oats, poured some into a pan, added water and set it on the stove. Then she peeped into the ell. Her father's barn coat was not in its customary place, and the clock on the shelf over the sink read a quarter to five. He would be in soon, and she feared he would be in a terrible mood. Emily had said the drink made a person's head hurt, and Father was not one who bore a headache well. He must have had a lot to drink, she thought, or he would never have struck out at me like that.

She felt the tears coming again as a whole series of pictures flashed through her head: her father and mother laughing together when they all took a picnic supper down to the river; her father and mother sharing a hymn book in church and looking so handsome in what everyone called their best bib and tucker, whatever that meant. Father actually cooed at Abby when she was a baby, brought forget-me-nots to Sarah in the early spring, taught them all how to curry the horses and polish the metal on the harnesses. Certainly she had been punished on occasion, but she had never thought it unfair. Last night was unfair, she realized. He had no reason to hit her. She shivered.

Then his boots came along the ell. He was stopping

to take them off; now he was almost to the door. Rose turned her back and stirred the oatmeal vigorously. She had warmed a bowl so she could dish up his breakfast and then go back upstairs to wake the others.

"Good morning, Father," she said in an even tone as he came in and went to the sink to wash.

"Morning," he muttered.

She filled his cereal bowl and took it to the dining room. She fetched his mustache cup and slowly poured coffee from the saucepan on the stove, taking care to keep the grounds in the pan.

"Did you want toast today, sir?" she asked.

"Better get the children up," he answered without looking at her.

Better, indeed, she thought, and went off, grateful that she could just do his bidding for once. Now it would just be a matter of doing everything at the right time. She would have to leave the house after Father did or he would see the pillowslip and wonder what she was up to. And she would have to tell Abby something convincing. The truth, she thought, will be the easiest. She just would not tell her everything. She reached the top of the stairs and heard both Abby and Charles moving about.

"I'm going," Charles called from the attic. "I'm going in just a minute or two."

"Going where?"

"To the henhouse," he said. "And then, at best, my shoes will be dusty. At worst, I will have droppings stuck on the soles."

"And did you roll out of bed on the wrong side today, Charles?"

"Same side as always," he said. "The wrong side is too close to the wall."

"Father has plenty of space on the wrong side," Rose answered, "and he may have used it today."

"Fair warning," Charles said.

She went on to the room she now shared with Abby and quickly told her that she would be visiting Aunt Nell for a few days, and that she was not to mention the visit at table this morning. Abby looked surprised, then pleased.

"It's a secret?" she asked. "I love secrets."

"Your breakfast is waiting for you," Rose answered in her most grownup voice. "So get along with you."

Abby clattered down the stairs after Charles, and they put on their coats and went to the chicken house to do their morning chores. By the time they came back, Rose was ready for them, lunch pails packed. While everyone ate breakfast, Rose fetched the pillowslip containing Abby's clothes and put it just inside the parlor door where no one would notice it. To her dismay, Father lingered over his second cup of coffee and seemed in no hurry to go about whatever his business of the day might be. Finally, with Charles fidgeting near the door and Abby already in her coat, she told them to wait outside for her. Charles looked at her face and went without saying a word.

Rose put on her coat, picked up the bundle of clothes and almost ran out of the house. As she closed the door, she heard her father mutter something, but it didn't sound like a farewell, so she did not turn back.

"What on earth is all that?" Charles demanded. "Are you taking in washing?"

"Abby's going to Aunt Nell's for a few days," Rose said. "We'll see her to school, then you go on to Aunt's, please, and tell her I would take it as a great favor if Abby could stay through the week. You are so quick," she said, trying to smile, "that you'll be able to deliver the message and her things and still be on time for school."

"Where are you going?" Charles asked suspiciously.

"To school," Rose said, thinking that she almost never told a lie, but this was a lie.

"Does Father know Abby is going visiting?" Charles asked, seeming to sense something strange in the air.

Oh, why can't he just be as dumb as a Granger for now, Rose thought, knowing that color was flooding her face and would alert Charles that something was amiss. She did not want to explain or alarm Abby. She dropped back a step, and when Charles turned to look at her, she pointed at Abby and shook her head. He raised his eyebrows so high they nearly disappeared under his hair. He skipped a step as well, and moving close to her, whispered, "Is something wrong? You had better tell. I am the young man of the house."

"And you will have to take that part with great care," Rose said. "Starting right now."

She had no more time to deal with him. Abby had stopped walking and was waiting for them at the path to her school. Rose gave Abby a small hug and pushed the sack of clothes at Charles, telling him she would see him later. He took one more look at her and decided again that it was not a good time for questions. He threw the pillowslip over his shoulder as if he were a peddler, waved to Abby and turned off toward Aunt Nell's.

Rose stood looking at the empty road, then wondered for the eleventh time that morning if she were doing the right thing, or if she had lost her mind completely. We can't move out, she thought. No one does that. You can't stay, the other side of her head answered. No one could do that. She started walking again, very slowly. As each foot moved, it seemed to stick to the ground, and she began to mumble to herself.

"Now the left, now the right, now the left, now the right." Her feet must indeed be attached to her brain, she thought, because they were doing it. Left, then right, then left. At the next road that turned off, she abruptly altered course and went up the hill, away from home and away from school.

CHAPTER 23
The Search Begins

At ten o'clock, Miss Harty asked everyone in the room to put away what they were working on and get out their pens and their Palmer penmanship books. She gave the front row a small stack of lined paper, and each pupil immediately took one sheet and passed the pile along. While they were doing that, the teacher asked Newton Barnes to step up to her desk. She said she had to leave the room for five minutes and he was to take over the class.

"You will all start on page three," she said, "and I will be interested to see whether the older pupils form their letters any better than the younger ones. Mr. Barnes will be in charge while I am on an errand for five minutes."

She opened the door of the classroom and left, leaving it ajar.

One of the Granger boys snickered and muttered, "Door of the privy is about to slam. Some errand."

"Cold sitting there today," another of the older boys said.

"She might hear you if she's just outside the door," Newton cautioned from the front of the room. "We'll all be staying after school if those papers don't have any letters on them when she gets back."

As nearly all the children bent to their work, the older Granger, Peter, brushed his nose with his forefinger and gave a little hoot.

"Teacher's pet, teacher's pet," he started to chant, and then quickly picked up his pen as he heard footsteps and voices in the hall. But the sounds went past the classroom and on toward the front of the school. Newton frowned, wondering if Miss Harty's errand had anything to do with Rose's absence. But he could not ask Charles about her, of course—even if his friends didn't hear him, because the question would make Charles wonder why he cared. It was odd, though. She came in an hour late every morning, and took those half days off every week, but she never missed on the other days.

"Mr. Barnes," Peter Granger said, waving his hand. "Mr. Barnes, I am having a great deal of trouble here with my P."

Giggles broke out around the room, and Newton shushed them, then moved up the aisle to pretend he had taken Peter's question as a serious penmanship problem. He had just bent over the older boy's desk when he heard Miss Harty come back into the room. He glanced up without straightening and immediately saw that her face was flushed. Like Rose, he thought, a slight smile starting at the edge of his mouth. And then the smile stopped. Rose. She wasn't here. Miss Harty was upset. Something must be wrong.

"Newton, please take your seat," Miss Harty said. "You may all put your penmanship papers aside and return to the lessons we were working on before I left the room. Was there some problem with your handwriting, Peter?"

The Granger boy kept his eye fixed on the nib of his pen, which he was wiping with a small square of ink-stained cloth, and shook his head slowly. Newton could see that his ears were turning red. Quite a lot of color in here today, Newton thought as he took his seat behind Rose's empty one. She must be doing all those chores that seemed to stretch endlessly in front of her. He couldn't figure out how Abby and Charles and Rose always looked so clean and neat when they had to do all their own work, and their mother's, too. He had overheard his father commenting that Mr. Hibbard seemed to be at sixes and sevens ever since Sarah Hibbard's death. Was that the same as being at nines and tens? Better? Or worse? He did smile then, thinking that his brain was click-clacking along the way Rose's did, jumping from one thing to another and wondering about everything. She was what his aunt would call a piece of work. Or couldn't you call a girl that?

"Newton, can you hear me?" Miss Harty's voice demanded with more than a trace of impatience.

"Yes, Ma'am," he said, quickly throwing one leg and then the other over the bench and standing behind his desk.

"You did not answer," she said a little more evenly.

"Sorry, Ma'am, I was thinking about something else," Newton said, wondering if it was about to be his turn to have red ears.

"Step into the hall, please," Miss Harty said. "Peter Granger, you are in charge of the room for the next five minutes. Please take your place in front of the class and see to it that order is maintained."

An astonished Peter Granger stumbled to his feet and made his way to the front of the room, his heavy boots clumping as if they were too big for him. Newton headed for the door, following Miss Harty into the hall. As he pulled the classroom door to behind him, he noticed that Miss Alden, the teacher for Charles' class, was already there, and wondered why he had to talk to two teachers. He gave a little shiver, realizing immediately that it was only partly because it was as cold as a witch's tit out here. Now there was an expression he couldn't share with Rose, he thought, another small smile touching his mouth. Little did he know that she already knew the expression well, courtesy of her great-uncle Samuel.

Miss Harty turned to face him and said in a shaky voice, "We do not know why Rose Hibbard is not in school. Do you have any idea?"

"No, Ma'am," Newton answered instantly, wondering what had suddenly happened to his knees.

"No idea?"

"I have not seen her since yesterday in school, Miss Harty."

"Charles said they left Abby at school this morning, he went on to their Aunt Nell's, and Rose continued toward school alone."

"Then where is she?" Newton asked.

Miss Harty sighed. "That certainly is the question. Charles said he brought a pillowslip full of Abby's things to the aunt's house, and that Abby was to stay for several days, but Rose didn't tell him why."

"Perhaps you should ask Emily," Newton suggested, thinking that something very strange was happening. Children did not go visit their aunts unless someone was sick or had died. "Or Mr. Hibbard?"

Abruptly, Miss Harty told him to fetch Emily. Back in the classroom, he noticed Peter Granger was standing by the blackboard, his arms folded across his chest, and all the children were very busy with some kind of desk work. He could see out of the corner of his eye that Emily was one of the few who looked up when he came in, but she didn't meet his eyes when he stood in front of her and said she was wanted in the hall.

"I can't," she said. "I can't." But she rose and went out to see the teacher.

Something is terribly wrong, Newton thought, studying the teacher's face, but he could not figure out what it might be. If Charles saw Rose on her way to school, why wasn't she right here with the rest of them?

"Newton, I want you to walk down to the Hibbards' and see if Rose is at home," Miss Harty said. "If she is, tell her I sent you to make sure she had not been taken ill and ask if she needs the doctor. If she is not there, I expect you back here as fast as your long legs can carry you. Do you understand?"

"Yes, Ma'am," Newton said, starting for the door. He paused and turned to ask, "What about Mr. Hibbard, Ma'am? Am I to look for him, too?"

"No!" Emily said and then clapped her hand over her mouth.

Miss Harty and Newton both jumped, startled by the vehemence of her response.

"I think not," Miss Harty said, frowning at Emily. "Now, get your coat and be on your way."

Newton almost ran to the cloakroom and was halfway out the door before he had both arms inside his jacket. He pulled his knitted hat down over his ears and trotted down the road toward the Hibbard house. What would he do if Mr. Hibbard answered the door? He had always been a little afraid of Rose's father, who tended to greet people with a gruff voice and who rarely smiled. He would not borrow trouble, he decided, slipping a little on the hardened snow. He would wait and see.

"And what did that 'no' mean, precisely?" Miss Harty asked Emily, who was running the toe of her shoe along the crack between two floorboards. "Emily?" Miss Harty repeated when Rose's friend did not answer.

"Look at me, Emily," the teacher commanded.

Emily looked up, her eyes brimming with tears but her mouth closed so tightly that Miss Harty could not even see her lips. She knows something, and she doesn't want to tell, the teacher thought. Without moving toward the girl, she stretched out her arm and gently put her hand on Emily's shoulder. The tears spilled out then, and Emily drew in her breath with a sob that would have softened the core of an iceberg.

"Is it something you can't talk about?" the teacher asked.

Emily nodded and sniveled, then nodded again. Miss Harty reached in her pocket and pulled out a lacy handkerchief. She gave it to Emily, who wiped her nose and dabbed at her eyes.

"Is it a secret?" the teacher probed.

Emily nodded again.

"Is it something about Rose and her father?" Miss Harty persisted.

Emily nodded, her eyes still on the floor and her toe starting to trace the floor crack again.

"Did she tell you where she was going today?"

Emily looked up suddenly.

"Oh, no," she said, her voice suddenly strong again. "Oh, no. If she had told me, I would have said when Newton went off to the house. I haven't seen her since last . . ." Emily broke off, then finished, "since yesterday after school."

"I gather you saw her later on yesterday as well," Miss Harty said gently. "She's missing, Emily. We don't know where she is. We know she sent some of Abby's clothes to their aunt's this morning in a pillowslip; we know she started in the direction of school, but she did not get here. If she is not at home, we will have to look in other places. Is she at your house?"

Surprised, Emily quickly answered that she believed not. "Why would Rose go there?"

"I don't know," Miss Harty said. "But I need you to help me. Not cry, not set your mouth in a thin, closed line, not fiddle with that crack in the floor. I need you to think about anything Rose said that might have made her send Abby to her Aunt Nell's for a few days, and then disappear. Unless Newton finds her at home, of course. So look at me, now, and talk to me."

Emily looked up and realized that her face felt very hot. She must be getting all pink, just like Rose, she thought. What a horrid feeling.

"She sent Abby to Aunt Nell's," she said carefully, "because she didn't think a little sister should stay at that house right now. They have their troubles there, Ma'am."

"I am aware of that, Emily, but the troubles started months ago and nothing has changed much for better or for worse as far as I know. So, why now? It is not like Rose to do things without explaining them and then just go off somewhere."

"She has her reasons," Emily said, still stubbornly holding on to what she knew.

"I am certain she has," Miss Harty began and then turned to see Newton coming in the door.

"She's not there," he said. "Her father came to the

door and asked why in thunderation, begging your pardon, Ma'am, I would think she was there when she was supposed to be in school, that she didn't get every day off from her studies."

"Did you say she was not in school?" Miss Harty asked, suddenly anxious.

"No, I figured to leave that to someone else," Newton said. "I just said I'd look for her here, that I was running a little behind myself today."

Miss Harty gave a small smile, thinking that when you expected children to do the right thing, they often did. At this very moment, for instance, that fresh-mouthed Peter Granger was probably keeping perfect order in her classroom. But the smile didn't last long. If not at home, then where could she be? It was so cold outside, and Rose never wore quite enough warm clothing.

"Perhaps she's at her Aunt Nell's," the teacher said, thinking aloud.

"I checked there on the way back," Newton said, standing very straight. "Mrs. Harris said she had not seen Rose and wanted to know why I wasn't in school. I hope it's all right that I told her Rose wasn't in school today and you sent me to see if she was at home."

"Quite all right, Newton," Miss Harty said, "quite all right, except that nothing seems to be quite right at all."

"Excuse me," Miss Alden interrupted, "but did you tell Mrs. Harris that Rose wasn't at home either?"

"Well," Newton said hesitantly, "well, I really had to, Ma'am, because she asked why I hadn't gone to the

Hibbard house first, and I said I had, but she was not there."

"And what happened then?"

"Mrs. Harris frowned and said she would have to think on that. And then I left, Miss Harty."

"We are all thinking on it, Newton," Miss Harty said, with a frown of her own. "You had better take your seat again and see if Peter is managing that class."

Newton glanced at Emily, then turned away, pulling off his coat as he went. Miss Alden raised her eyebrows. Miss Harty nodded toward the other teacher's room, and Miss Alden returned to her class. Miss Harty turned her attention to Emily again.

"You must tell everything you know, Emily. I will not repeat anything unless I need to do so, but if Rose is somewhere out there in the cold, then we must find her as quickly as we can. There are times for secrets and times to break promises, and this may be a time to break a promise."

Emily looked up at her, her face quite damp from tears, and stammered that Rose didn't want Abby to get killed, but that Charles was perfectly safe because boys were different, and girls couldn't be where fornication was going on, and that Rose knew about fornication from the Reverend Lockhead preaching about it, but she didn't know what it was until Emily had explained about cows jumping each other and Rose had seen Miss Graves' clothes.

The words tumbled out in such a rush that Miss Harty could barely sort them out. Abby not killed,

Charles safe, fornication, Miss Graves. Miss Graves? The Graves woman was rarely called Miss by anyone in the village. She was more commonly called "that woman." What did the Graves woman have to do with Rose? Ah, perhaps she did not want to pursue that thought at all.

"Emily," she said, taking the girl's hand and leading her to the bench just down the hall, "you must slow down. Let's take these things one at a time. Who was going to kill Abby? Sit down here, look at me, and tell me."

"Mr. Hibbard."

"That's good. Now, who was fornicating?"

Emily's face turned red, and she started to look away again, but Miss Harty put one finger under her chin and turned her head back again.

"Who, Emily?" she asked again, so softly this time that her voice was barely audible.

"Rose's father and Miss Graves."

"And who told you Abby was going to be killed, and Rose's father was fornicating?"

"Rose."

"When?"

"Last night at my house."

"What time?"

"After I was asleep. Oh, Miss Harty, I should not have told you any of these things. Rose came in the middle of the night and threw snowballs at my window, and I let her in, and she said she thought her father had killed her mother, and I promised I wouldn't tell, and my mother already made me," Emily said, starting to sob again.

Miss Harty put her hand on Emily's shoulder. "You are doing nicely, Emily, but I need the rest of the story. You said she was worried about someone killing Abby."

"She said Abby couldn't stay there because the wood wasn't stacked right, and her mother was killed by the wood, and Miss Graves' taffeta skirt was on the floor, and her bare legs were on the bed . . . "

Emily's voice trailed off. She couldn't go on. It wasn't fair to Rose. A friend had to keep secrets. Rose had said so. Perhaps she was just a weak person, one of those shilly-shallying people the Reverend Lockhead was always talking about; someone not strong enough to be a real friend. The tears were rolling down her cheeks now, and she wiped her face with the sleeve of her shirtwaist.

"What floor was Miss Graves' skirt on?" Miss Harty persisted, handing her the handkerchief again.

"The floor of Rose's father's bedroom," Emily said, sobbing. "I should not be telling you any of this. Rose is never going to speak to me again."

"Right now, Emily," Miss Harty said as gently as she could, "the only important thing is to give her a chance to speak to anyone again."

"She wouldn't stay outside in this cold, Miss Harty. She wouldn't. Would she?"

"It depends on what she is thinking," Miss Harty told her. "Where would she go if she wanted to think . . ."

The sound of footsteps coming quickly up the steps outside the school interrupted her, and she and Emily both stood up to see if Rose was coming back to school.

But the steps were too heavy to be Rose's, and it was Jason Harris who came through the door, blowing on his hands and stamping snow off his feet.

"Found her yet?" he demanded.

"No," Miss Harty said. "She has not been in school today."

"I should have been after Silas a little harder," he said, "after she mentioned to me that someone had been there for the noon meal, and she thought it was me. Er, I mean I, Ma'am. And when Charles brought Abby's things today, we had a second chance, and we missed that, too. Mrs. Harris is nigh onto beside herself, and I am almost there with her. Where do you think she went?"

"I don't know, but we must start looking right away," Miss Harty said, the worry on her face quite apparent now. "It is so cold, and it will be dark in just a few hours. Perhaps we should send the children home and start a search."

"Or let the older boys help with the looking," Jason said. "If you could go to the hotel and post office and let folks know Rose may be hiding in a house or barn somewhere nearby. Then you should get on home, I think, so we will have a central person to report to. I will look along the roads in the middle of town after I inform Silas that we don't know where Rose is. She can't have gone far," he finished, sounding as if he didn't believe it himself. She had been gone for at least three hours already, he thought to himself. And it was close to zero out there, colder yet if you were out in the wind.

Miss Harty returned to her class, told the younger

ones and the girls to get their things gathered together; school would be let out for the rest of the day. She told the older boys Rose seemed to be missing and asked if they would help with the search. She told them they must go in pairs or threes so no one else would be lost. Newton Barnes, she said, should take Charles with him because he knew Rose's favorite spots—except, as she already knew, those places were spring and summer and fall places where Rose went to find wildflowers, mosses, wintergreen, chickadees and woodpeckers.

"What about Abby, Ma'am?" Charles wanted to know. "I usually see her home."

"Emily will take care of that," Miss Harty said, thinking that Emily needed something to do, something uncomplicated. "She will take her to your aunt's house."

"I think we should divide up the town so we don't keep crisscrossing," Newton said.

"Right," Miss Harty said. She separated the boys into four groups and together they split the town into four sections, marking the areas on a sheet of paper and labeling farms and roads to go by. The boys were pushing toward the door, and Miss Harty thought how odd it was that people could get so excited about looking for a missing person, forgetting as they searched that the end might prove very hard. Ah, but they are just boys. She stopped them again.

"When you hear the church clock strike four, make your way to my house," she said. "In case she hasn't turned up before that," she added quickly, as a look of consternation crossed Newton Barnes' face. Now that one, she thought, had too much reality in his face. She felt he had reason to worry. The boys nodded and charged toward the door with so much energy that Miss Harty wondered if they would open it or plunge right through it. She can't be far away, she thought. Rose wouldn't leave Abby, no matter how upset she was. No other fourteen-year-old she had ever known had a conscience like Rose's. But where was she, and was she keeping warm? Had she crossed over the edge into that strange land where common sense no longer had a grip on the mind?

From behind her, she heard a voice asking about helping out. It was Alice, who had put on her coat with the others but was lingering. The girl's face was unsmiling, her dark eyebrows pulled so tight they almost touched each other above her nose.

"I can search, too," Alice said. "I want to, Miss Harty."

"The girls," Miss Harty began and heard her mind shift gears. "The girls," she began again, "have all gone home except for Emily, who is taking Abby to the Harris house. But you may help with the search. Tell me, if you can, where Rose likes to go to if she wants to be all by herself."

"She goes to a big rock near the river in the woods by her house," Alice said, her face clearing with the same excitement Miss Harty had seen in the boys. "Should I look there?"

"We will both go," Miss Harty said firmly. "You will

show me. And then we will stop at your house to tell your mother that I need your help. You and I are not going to do much searching, but we are going to get ready for Rose. We must build up my fires, warm blankets, make some soup . . . "

"I will leave my books here, Ma'am?" Alice said in a questioning tone.

"That will be quite all right," Miss Harty said, turning toward the stove. She checked the fire, then closed the dampers part way, and went to get her coat. Minutes later, she and Alice were outside the school and on their way to Rose's rock by the river.

Walking behind Miss Harty, Alice noticed that the teacher's skirts made their own path through the snow, which made the going that much easier for her. She must have a small hoop under there, Alice thought, or the snow would push the skirt instead of the skirt pushing the snow.

You are thinking just like Rose, she thought to herself and almost smiled. She knew that was exactly what she needed to do. Think like Rose. Emily had told her about the midnight visit. It was a secret, of course, but that's what friends did. They told their secrets to each other. So Rose was worried about Abby and took care of that. And then what? Would she come down here to think what to do next?

"Are you all right back there?" Miss Harty inquired, half looking over her shoulder but still walking.

"Fine, Ma'am," Alice answered. "We are almost there."

And then they were there, where the big flat rock provided seating for three or more. But it was quite empty.

"Something brushed snow off the rock," Alice observed. "She might have been here."

"And has gone," the teacher answered, lifting her chin and calling, "Rose? Rose?" into the quiet woods. "Rose?" she called, a little more shrilly.

"Dee-dee-dee" came the answer from a chickadee who soon landed just above their heads on a pine branch.

"She talks to those birds," Alice said. "And sometimes I think they know what she's talking about." She turned a little red. "Ma'am, begging your pardon," she added.

"Do not concern yourself with the Ma'ams, Alice. We have more important matters on our minds right now. We will go on to speak with your mother, and then to my house to get ready for Rose."

"They will find her, won't they, Miss Harty," Alice said, tears suddenly appearing in her eyes.

"I have great faith in those boys, Alice," Miss Harty said, turning away so Alice would not see how dewy her own eyes were. She wished she felt as confident inside as she tried to appear. Where could that girl be? And was she all right? Or had she just given up, once she knew Abby was safe. Miss Harty wished she knew. And she had seen the same rush of fear on Newton Barnes' face as he reported that Rose was not at home, nor at the Harris house.

They made their way to the road, then to Alice's, where her mother said she would bring soup and fresh bread to Miss Harty's in just a few minutes. At the teacher's house, Alice barely had time to wonder at the many books on the shelves before she was set to work filling bed-warming pans with coals from the dying fire.

"Take those right into the first bedroom on the left upstairs and slide them in. No doubt you know exactly how to do that?" Miss Harty said.

"Oh, yes, Ma'am," Alice said, determined not to forget her manners again.

"And then build up this fire out here so we can boil water or heat soup or whatever we have to do," Miss Harty said. "I am going to get some dry clothing for myself."

She left the room but came back almost immediately to ask if Alice's clothes were wet as well. But Alice assured her that she was all right and that probably her mother would think to bring along some dry things. Miss Harty nodded and went out again. Alice finished filling the bed warmers, then added three sticks to the fire and went into the room Miss Harty had indicated would be used for Rose.

She has to come, Alice told herself as she lifted the quilt and homespun sheet and slid the two pans into the bed. She has to. She could not run away, not after putting up with all these things for so long. Or is that when you do run away? When you can't do it any more? Alice did not know the answers. She lived in a house where she was expected to do her share of housework and chores, but her mother carried the main burden for the house; her father for the barn. The whole family pitched in when it came to the vegetable garden, from planting to harvest. And my mother, Alice considered, always knows what we have to do next, all year round. At Rose's house, she is the one who has to know that. That list in her head must look like a diary— hours, days, tasks, on and on and on. Perhaps she has gone off. But where? And without saying goodbye?

While all these things went through her mind, Alice was tidying up in the kitchen a little, getting a pot of leftover soup out of the icebox and putting it on the back of the stove—not enough there for more than one person, she thought, hoping her mother would be along soon. She placed the extra blanket from the guest room on the top shelf at the back of the stove. It won't burn there, but it will get very warm, she thought, giving the blanket a little pat.

She was so busy and so wrapped up in her thoughts that a knock on the door made her jump right off the floor. Before she could get there, the door burst open, and Charles rushed in, red-faced and out of breath.

"We found her, we found her!" he shouted. "Newton is bringing her. I came ahead to say." He stopped, choking a little, and added, "She's very still. But Newton says she will be all right. Do you think she will be all right, Alice?"

Alice hugged him, started to sob, and ran to the stairs where she nearly bumped into Miss Harty who was coming down at a near run. The two went back to the kitchen, where Charles stammered out his news again and then dropped into the rocking chair by the stove, unable to say any more.

"Give him a sip of that soup," Miss Harty commanded, bending to remove his boots and put his feet on the ledge of the stove. "Just a swallow. He can barely breathe."

She pulled Charles' coat open and removed his mittens while Alice moved the soup toward the front of the stove and brought a tablespoon to the boy. He swallowed it without any problem, and she went for another. When he swallowed that, she brought the pan over and gave him more.

"You may answer my questions by either nodding or shaking your head, Charles," the teacher said. "Do you understand?"

He nodded.

"Were her eyes open?"

He shook his head.

"Was she moving, and did she move after you found her?"

He shook his head.

"Did Newton tell you she would be all right?"

He nodded.

"Could you tell if she was breathing?"

He nodded.

"She was breathing?"

He gulped and nodded again.

"Is Newton almost here?"

He nodded once more.

Miss Harty let out a long sigh. She glanced toward the stove and nodded with approval when she saw the blanket on the stove shelf. She took it down and covered Charles from his chin to the bottom of his socks.

"Please get another blanket for the stove, Alice," she said and turned toward the window.

"You may speak, Charles, whenever you feel you are ready," she said in a voice that sounded as if she were not ready to speak herself.

"At the cemetery, she was at the cemetery," Charles said in a croaking voice. He was still gasping. The teacher turned back to him, putting her finger to her lips.

"You will have to wait a bit, Charles, before you speak again," she said. "Just nod or shake your head to answer me. Was she at your mother's grave?"

The boy's head bobbed up and down. Miss Harty went back to the window, and Charles saw her pull a lacy handkerchief out of her pocket. She blew her nose very hard, and Charles, who was starting to warm up, wondered how the teacher had been taken with such a terrible cold in the short time since they had all left the school.

"Here they come," Miss Harty said suddenly. She moved quickly to the door and was out on the path to the driveway so fast that Charles barely had time to get up from his chair. But he could not make it to the doorway. The room spun around him, and he folded up in the chair again, hugging the blanket to his chin.

Seconds later Miss Harty returned with Newton Barnes right behind her; Rose in his arms.

"This way," Miss Harty said shakily, starting toward the stairs.

"I think," he said in a firm voice, "we had better put her down right here by the stove and warm her as quickly as we can. I saw a calf like this once . . ." His voice trailed off, and Charles heard an odd choking sound. Then Newton went on, "Warm blankets, cloths of cool water, cloths with warm water . . ."

Alice pulled the warm blanket off the stove shelf and spread it out on the floor. Newton laid Rose on the blanket, and they quickly wrapped her up. Miss Harty was already there with a cool cloth and a bowl of warm water with another cloth in it. Newton put the cool cloth right over Rose's face, which was pink, patched with white.

"You lie right down there next to her, Alice," Miss Harty commanded. "Close as you can get. The warmest things in this house are the people. Get that cold coat off, Newton, you are giving off cold air."

The boy scrambled out of his coat and took the warm cloth. He pulled off Rose's mittens and wrapped her right hand in the cloth. Miss Harty quickly fetched another cloth and did the same for the other hand. Alice hugged her friend.

"You are right about transferring our warmth," Newton said. "Perhaps you could lie down on the other side, Miss Harty? I hugged that calf all night, and in the morning he was on his feet again."

She dropped to the floor instantly and covered half of Rose's body with her own. Newton started removing Rose's shoes and gently began squeezing her feet with his big hands. None of them looked up when the door opened and Alice's mother came in with a large pot of soup. She put it on the stove, bent down to open the oven door to let out more heat and then asked what needed doing.

"See about Charles," Miss Harty answered right away. "He should be coming around—should be able to talk by now. And are those boys still outside?"

"The ones who were with me are there," Newton said. "They agreed to wait in case we needed anything. I forgot about them. I wasn't thinking."

"You are thinking quite enough, young man," Miss Harty said. "One of them can go for the doctor, and the other one should get the minister to ring the church bell. Perhaps everyone will realize that means we've found her."

"What about Mr. Hibbard?" Alice's mother asked.

"And tell him, too," Miss Harty said, so harshly that Newton stopped what he was doing to look at her.

Alice's mother sent the messengers on their way and knelt in front of Charles, whose eyes were now wide open, fixed on the strange sight before him. Newton was rubbing his sister's feet, and Alice and Miss Harty seemed to be lying almost on top of her.

"I didn't fill the woodbox," said a very small voice from the floor.

"Rose?" Newton said, straightening up. "Was that you, Rose?"

"I didn't fill the woodbox," the voice said again.

"She's coming to," Miss Harty said, sitting up. She

took the cloth off Rose's face and saw that the girl's eyes were still shut. "Or maybe she's not, quite."

"Try one of the warm cloths on her face now," Newton said. "It doesn't look quite so patchy anymore. Maybe she doesn't have real frostbite. Ma'am. Please."

Miss Harty almost smiled at Newton's return to his usual good manners. He must be thinking she's going to make it, she thought. A calf, indeed. But at least he seemed to know what to do, and so far no one else had come to give better advice.

She started to rub Rose's hand with the cloth.

"No rubbing," Newton said. "Just place it there, then reheat it when it cools off. You can rub the skin right off if there's frostbite. Ma'am."

There it was again. Were all these children so terrified of her that they remembered their "yes Ma'ams" and "no Ma'ams" and "if you pleases" even during a dire emergency? She dipped the cloth in the bowl of warm water and wrung it out, then wrapped Rose's hand again.

Alice gave her the other cloth, and she repeated the process.

"I didn't fill the woodbox," came the words again, barely a whisper this time.

Miss Harty and Newton looked at each other.

"I took care of it for you," Charles croaked from his chair. "It's as full as it can be, Rose."

CHAPTER 24
The Warm-up

The little group in Miss Harty's kitchen heard the church bells start to toll. Between the clangs, the weak voice from the floor said, "I broke the sugar bowl."

"We can get another one," Charles croaked as quickly as he could, and relaxed a little when Newton threw him a grateful look. "If Mr. Goodnow doesn't have them, I'll take the train to town and get one."

"Shhh," Alice's mother said. "You need to rest."

"Rose needs me more," Charles said, sitting up a little bit more. "She always takes care of us, and now we have to take care of her because, because, because . . . " His voice rose into a wail. "Because I'm afraid she's going to die, too, and then we won't have anybody . . . oh, no, oh, no," he ended, as the door opened and his father stormed in.

"What in tarnation is going on here?" Mr. Hibbard shouted, banging his snowy boots on the rag rug by the door. "Why is Rose on the floor? Why are you lying all over her? Is this where she's been while half the town is combing the woods for her?"

"Because she nearly froze to death in the cemetery, Mr. Hibbard," Newton said in a very quiet voice, "we are trying to get her warm again, and this is the warmest place in the house, and the people are the warmest things in the house. She has been here for about ten minutes or so—would you think that is about right, Ma'am?"

"Perhaps ten minutes," Miss Harty agreed, deciding that she needed to say no more. Newton had taken care of the questions for the moment. She hoped Mr. Hibbard was absorbing the information and was going to calm down—a little of his ranting and raving went a long way with her anytime, and she had even less patience for it now. She changed the cloths on Rose's hand again and told herself that the girl's fingers were getting warmer. She saw Alice do the same for Rose's other hand and gave her a small smile of encouragement.

"You are doing fine," Miss Harty said.

Alice nodded but did not smile. She pushed her body a little closer to Rose and hoped she wasn't just imagining that her friend felt warmer.

The door opened again, and Emily came in.

"I heard the church bells," she said. "I came as fast as I could." Then she saw Rose lying on the floor and clapped her hand over her mouth so only a tiny squeak of her scream came out.

"Is she all right?" she stammered as soon as she was in control again.

"She spoke, Emily," Miss Harty said without looking up. "Perhaps you could refill the bed warmer."

Emily slipped off her wrap and edged around Mr. Hibbard as if he were a spider. She fetched the warming pan and emptied it into the stove. She replaced the lid, lifted another, and with the tongs by the stove picked out glowing coals and put them in the pan. She took one more look at Rose and left the room silently, but the little group could hear her start to sob as she went up the stairs.

"You will tell me what's going on here," Mr. Hibbard began again, his voice a deep rumble in the quiet room. "This is my girl, and by God I have a right to know what you are up to and why there's no doctor here. Move over, boy, and let me have a look at her."

Newton moved about an inch, and Rose's father stepped closer and stared down at her white face.

"You should take your coat off, sir," Newton said in a voice so steady that Miss Harty marveled once again at how composed he was. "It's giving off a considerable amount of cold."

"By thunder, I am not about to take orders from a young whippersnapper like you," Mr. Hibbard said.

He took another step forward just as the door opened once more and Dr. Potter came in, his black bag in his hand, and his coat off almost before he was over the threshold.

"Excuse me, Silas," he said. "I believe I am needed right where you are."

Rose's father whirled, ready to argue again, but immediately moved off when he saw the physician.

"What have we here?" Dr. Potter said to Newton, quickly taking in the fact that the boy seemed to be in charge.

"She was nearly frozen, Doctor," Newton said. "And we just did what I had done for a calf that was born outdoors when it was below zero last winter. Her hands seem better. She spoke a minute or so ago, but just to herself, not to us, something she was worried about. I don't know if she's in her right mind . . . I know she's not a calf . . ." His voice trailed off, and he looked anxiously at the doctor.

"We kept her here because it was the warmest," he added, thinking the doctor would wonder why they had put Rose in such an uncomfortable place.

"Good as a stable," the doctor said, kneeling beside the still form. He took her pulse, felt her hands and face, nodded at Miss Harty and Alice to continue what they were doing. "The boy knows what he's at," he said. "We'll get her into a bed soon, though."

"It's warm and ready, Doctor," Miss Harty said.

"Heard she'd gone missing," Dr. Potter said as he continued to examine Rose. "Where'd you find her?"

Newton explained briefly and then said he thought Rose's brother might need the doctor, too.

"Take her up to a bed," Dr. Potter said, "while I take a look at Charles. Did you run off, too?"

"No, sir. I was in the search party, and it was very cold and then I ran here fast as a rabbit to let them know Newton was coming with Rose. He carried her all the way, sir," Charles said, his voice sounding a little better.

"What's all this about running away?" boomed Mr. Hibbard. "You young ones went off to school as usual this morning, did you not?"

Charles suddenly turned very red and did not answer. The doctor immediately told him to open his mouth and say a-a-a-h, then repeated the command when he sensed the boy's father moving closer.

"Did you not?" Mr. Hibbard said, pushing his face toward Charles. "Answer me."

"I think, Silas, I will have to ask you to either step aside or step outside," Dr. Potter said. "We have much to do here, and frankly you are pretty much in the way. And from the smell and sound of you, I think you may not be quite sober."

Alice's mother, still tending the soup, gasped, and Mr. Hibbard began to sputter. But Dr. Potter brushed him away and went on examining Charles, at the same time telling Newton to get a move on and carry Rose upstairs.

"You go along with him, Ruthann," the doctor said gruffly. "Keep things in order. I'll see to her again in a minute."

"Ruthann," Alice muttered, unthinking. "My name is Alice." But she saw Miss Harty get up, and suddenly realized the teacher had a first name, too. And the doctor had just used it. She sat down on the floor again, waiting to see what would happen next. She did think Rose was coming to, at least a little. Perhaps she should say some kind of prayer, but the only ones she knew were full of words she had never understood, so she had no way of knowing whether they would get a person well or not. And "Now I lay me down to sleep, I pray the Lord my soul to keep" wasn't exactly what she wanted. The "If I should die before I wake" part might be asking to put Rose in the ground next to her mother.

Alice looked around for her own mother and saw that she was busy getting more soup for Charles. She sneaked a sideways look at Mr. Hibbard, who was near the door, shifting from one foot to another as if he had ants in his pants. She wasn't supposed to use that expression, but it was only passing through her head, so no one would know. She gave a small giggle, thinking he really did look as if something was keeping him on the move.

"Shhh," her mother scolded, and Alice smothered her laugh. "You'd better see if the bed-warmer needs new coals again. That child is about as cold as a human can be and still be breathing."

Newton was up on his knees, lifting Rose off the floor as if she were a fluff of milkweed rather than a tall, not so small girl. Alice scuttled to one side to give him room, and he went through the door to the hallway with Miss Harty whispering directions to him.

"And where in tarnation has she been when she was supposed to be in school?" Rose's father suddenly burst out.

"In the cemetery," the doctor said calmly. "Sitting on your wife's grave. Several hours, I would reckon, she was just sitting there on your wife's grave."

"Oh, dear God," Mr. Hibbard said, tears starting to

run down his cheeks. "What have I done?" He brushed his sleeve across his face, turned and went out the door.

"What indeed," the doctor said, putting his stethoscope away and buttoning Charles' shirt. "You will be fine, young man, as soon as you get a little more of that soup inside you. I think you can hold the spoon yourself at this point and stop acting like a hospital patient."

Charles grinned, sat up straighter and took the spoon from Alice's mother.

"Will she be all right?" he asked anxiously. "We need her to be all right. And someone has to go tell Abby we're all right, because even if she didn't know Rose was lost, she must know something is amiss."

"Have your brain back, too," the doctor said abruptly. "We'll see to Abby."

"You didn't answer about Rose," Charles persisted.

"And you must be as stubborn as your big sister," the doctor said. "With care, we shall hope Rose will recover. I am going to her now."

"Let's run," Rose said. And they lifted their skirts and set off in a mad gallop.

"This isn't ladylike," Alice panted just behind Rose's shoulder.

"Mrs. Munson can't see us, so it doesn't matter," Emily shouted from behind Alice.

One after the other, they raced between the gravestones, up one row and down the next, their feet sinking a little into the soft, grassy turf. Then Rose gave a whoop, leaped onto a stone and started hopping from one to the next.

"Have you lost what's left of your mind?" Alice shrieked, immediately negotiating the jump herself and following Rose.

"It's follow the leader," Rose said, starting to laugh.

Emily stumbled on her first try, and as Rose made the turn to start a second row, she saw her friend make the jump and hurry after them.

"That's it, Em. You have it now," Rose encouraged as she continued in the opposite direction. And why, she wondered to herself, her mind actually as intact as ever, were these pieces of marble and granite called gravestones? Grave enough, that was certain. Perhaps that was it. They could have called them serious-stones or solemnstones, she supposed. Or somberstones. Now that was really nice. She would call them somberstones from now on.

Some of these somberstones were pretty thin for hopping, but she kept turning her feet this way and that and somehow, almost magically, she stayed up there. Alice and Emily were following close behind, laughing and screeching comments at her back. Then, almost at the end of a row, she saw an open grave—a somber, that would be—ahead. But she saw it too late. She went off the last stone, landed in a pile of newly dug earth and slid right into the cavernous hole in the ground. She closed her eyes as she fell, and landed with a loud cracking sound. She forced herself to look and saw to her horror that she was standing on a pine box in a hole so deep that she could see nothing but dirt walls around her.

Then she felt the lid of the box rising beneath her feet and heard her mother's voice saying, "Don't worry about the sugar bowl. Don't worry about the woodbox. Take care of yourself."

She started to scream, just as Alice and Emily reached their hands down for her. As she clung to their wrists, still screaming, they pulled her back onto the grass, and all three fell in a heap beside the open grave.

"It's a somber," she shrieked. "It's a somber, and the sugar bowl does not matter."

She squeezed Alice and Emily's hands as hard as she could. She was breaking into a drenching sweat that was both hot and cold. She heard a voice saying, "It's all right, Rose. Everything is all right. The sugar bowl does not matter. You are safe. You are all right."

It was soft here on the grass, she thought. Quite soft. And the voice said she was safe. So she held onto those two hands as hard as she could, and she opened her eyes. She saw that it was Miss Harty holding one of her hands. That was Emily on the other side, holding the other one. What were they doing in the cemetery? And there was Charles who was supposed to be in school. This wasn't the cemetery. This was a room she had never seen before. But it was her quilt. She wiggled her toes and saw the familiar squares stretching out before her. Leftovers from Aunt Minnie's housedress; a bit of one of

Abby's dresses; that blue and white print that Mother had used for a Sunday dress. She moved her feet apart to make a valley. It was her quilt, but it wasn't her bed. She let her eyes wander around the strange room, feeling as if they were just barely part of her body. People were watching her. The familiar red flush started under her chin and began to flow up over her face. She hated people looking at her like that.

"Welcome back, Rose," Miss Harty said in her calm, teacher voice, and Emily started to cry.

"Fetch the doctor, Charles," Miss Harty said. "I think her fever has finally broken."

"Don't let me go back there," Rose said, and she felt her body start to shake. The quilt blocks seemed to be trembling, too. She struggled to sit up.

"You are in the guest room of Miss Harty's house," Emily said, "and you can't sit up yet."

"Why not?"

"Because you are ill, and you'll have to wait until the doctor comes. And your voice is croaking, so maybe you shouldn't even talk, except we all want to know what you were doing in the cemetery."

"Hush," Miss Harty said, taking the tumbler from the bureau and holding it to Rose's cracked lips. "Try a little water, Rose."

Rose drank greedily and lifted her head to follow the rim of the glass as Miss Harty pulled it away.

"A small amount at a time, young lady," the teacher said. "You may have another sip in a minute or so. But you can have another pillow, I think." And she lifted Rose just enough to tuck a second pillow behind her shoulders.

"The room is going around," Rose said weakly. "Can you make it stop?"

Aunt Nell put her knitting aside and stood up from her rocking chair by the door.

"Close your eyes, child," she said, "and things will stop moving. You have had little enough to eat for the past several days, and your head is spinning. The room, in fact, is standing still, however it might look to you."

Rose obediently closed her eyes again, but popped them open almost immediately.

"I'm afraid to shut my eyes," she said. "I don't want to have the dream again. I don't want to fall into the grave again."

"Then keep them open, Rose, until the dream goes away," Miss Harty said in the voice Rose remembered from first grade. It was the way the teacher had talked when you fell on the gravel and took all the skin off your knee and had little stones inside the cuts. She clung to the teacher's hand, and Aunt Nell brought a cool cloth and told her to keep her eyes open under the cloth. Sure enough, the room stopped whirling about.

A few minutes later the little group heard the door open downstairs, then close again with a bang. Feet raced up the stairs, and Charles burst into the room, stopping short when he realized this was still a sick-room and he was being very noisy.

"Doc's on his way," he said. "And Father, too. And Uncle Jason was with Father, so he's coming along, too. And I stopped at the church, and Mr. Crafts was there, so I told him Rose was awake, and he said he had a mind to ring the bell."

Charles grinned at the thought of all these accomplishments, and crossed the room to peer at Rose. Gingerly, he picked up her free hand and gave it a squeeze. She opened her eyes and tried to smile.

"Gave us a scare, Rose," he said. "You really tossed a sugar bowl this time."

"What happened, Charles?" Rose asked. "Why am I here? And why are you all looking at me?"

Charles looked at Miss Harty and at Aunt Nell, and both of them nodded, so he sat on the edge of the bed and told Rose what had happened, and how he and Newton had found her and brought her here and how she had not spoken to any of them for three days.

"Three days?" Rose was incredulous. "I've been just sleeping away for three days?"

"You had a high fever, and you said things sometimes, but we couldn't figure anything out except that you were worried about the sugar bowl," Charles said.

The door downstairs opened again and was shut quietly. The little group in the bedroom heard the murmur of men's voices, growing louder as they climbed the stairs. Then, before they reached the top, the door opened once more and this time, it slammed shut. A third man's voice could be heard, and Miss Harty saw

Rose flinch, close her eyes and wriggle down in the bed.

"Nothing to fret about, Rose," she said, squeezing her hand. "We are all right here, taking care of you." But she saw the apprehensive look on Charles' face and felt a flash of anger at this man who had caused his children so much fear and distress that he had nearly lost one of them. The room was suddenly very still, and everyone heard Dr. Potter's quiet voice say, "I will be going in to the sickroom now, and you will wait here— both of you, Silas, both of you."

"That's my girl in there, Doc," Mr. Hibbard protested.

"Something you might have considered a little earlier on," the doctor replied calmly, opening the door just wide enough to slip through with his black bag in his hand. He pushed the door shut and motioned to Nell, who was back in her chair in the corner.

"Just set your chair here," he said, indicating the door. "In case anyone fails to follow the doctor's orders."

Then he turned to Rose, whose eyes were still shut.

"I thought you had come to," he said quietly. "Have you gone back into hiding again?"

Rose opened her eyes and looked past the doctor's shoulder at the door. No one was there except Aunt Nell, who was moving her chair and then sitting down against the closed door. She felt Miss Harty squeeze her fingers again.

"I am here," Rose said.

"So I see," Dr. Potter said. He took away the washcloth that was across her forehead and laid his hand there.

"Can't tell much after a cool cloth has been in place," he muttered.

"The room was going around," Miss Harty offered.

"Small wonder when you open your eyes after this many days," he said. He pulled a gold watch out of his vest pocket and stared at it while his fingers found Rose's pulse in her wrist.

"Days?" Rose's voice had a funny little squeak in it.

"Three nights, close to four days, child. We were beginning to think you didn't like any of us. But you have survived, and so have we," the doctor said. "And that heartbeat of yours is running along almost as it should now."

"Three nights? Four days? Is that true? I thought they were funning me." Rose was beginning to feel like a fool. She felt her face getting red again. "Where am I?" she asked, struggling to sit up a little more.

"Take it easy, child. You are probably weaker than a kitten whose eyes aren't open yet. We could try a little soup here, Ruthann."

Who on earth is Ruthann, Rose thought. And where am I? Why won't anyone tell me where I am? She felt Miss Harty let go of her hand and realized, as Alice had earlier, that the teacher must be Ruthann.

"This is Miss Harty's house," Dr. Potter said, answering that question at least. "You have been very ill, sometimes as out of your mind as a hound dog at full moon, but you will be all right now . . ."

"Really?" Emily cried out. "Really all right?" And to Rose's amazement, her friend burst into tears and buried her face in the quilt.

" . . . once you've had a week or so of quiet," the doctor went on, ignoring Emily's interruption. "You gave us a turn, but now you've taken a turn for the better. No, Silas, not yet," he said, seeing that Miss Harty was trying to balance a mug of soup and hold off Rose's father at the same time.

"She's my daughter," Mr. Hibbard said, but he backed off, and Aunt Nell was able to close the door again.

"She is, in fact," Aunt Nell muttered almost to herself, "Sarah's daughter. Without a doubt."

Rose knit a stitch, slipped the next one, knit another and then passed the slipped stitch over. She continued across the needle to the last three stitches where she slipped one, knit one, passed the slipped stitch over and knit one more. She loved seeing the toe of a sock begin to narrow. It meant the end was in sight. Besides, knitting and slipping was much more interesting than just going around and around and around.

She quickly did the decreases on the next two needles, which had fewer stitches, and was back at the beginning. Then she put the sock down and stretched her legs in front of her. She wondered if the doctor would let her go outside after today. She knew now why the chickens rushed her when she opened the door to their coop. They wanted to get out. They were trapped in that small space, and they were sick of it. If she squawked, would someone take pity on her? Squeaky wheels get attention, why not squawky hens?

A strange shiver ran from the middle of her shoulders right down her back. Someone walking on my grave, she thought dolefully, thinking about how she had walked on it herself that cold day when she didn't know where to go or what to do next. Hadn't her father said she was too tall to get married? So she would be one of those spinsters who patted the heads of their nieces and nephews, and became very old and crabby and eventually was buried next to the parents. She and Emily and Alice had read lots of those gravestones at the cemetery—baby names, parents' names, unmarried daughters' names, all in one place.

She had tried talking to Sarah at the cemetery, but no answers had come. She was sure the Rev. Lockhead had said people in heaven watched over those left on earth. But if her mother had been watching, she would have answered. Still, Rose knew her mother had to be in heaven. Even if God were having a crotchety day, he could not refuse admission to Sarah.

She had made a fool of herself that day, and she knew everyone thought so because no one was talking to her about what she had done. Even her father, once Dr. Potter had let him see her, had just looked at her, patted her hand once or twice and said he hoped she'd be herself soon.

Being herself wasn't the best thing she could think of. Herself was always tired, cooking or cleaning or ironing or studying, or getting Charles and Abby off to school or piecing together a supper from leftovers in the icebox. She thought perhaps she liked what she was now, which was not herself at all. She had spent three days now in Miss Harty's parlor, knitting these socks and poking the fire in the stove and having a visitor or two each afternoon. She still could not quite absorb the fact that she had spent three other nights in this same house without remembering a bit of it—except what was apparently a dream, the dreadful dream about falling into an open grave.

She shivered again, this time because that dream still drifted through her eyes sometimes, still clear as a bell: she and Emily and Alice leaping along the top of the gravestones and somehow never losing their balance until the very end. She kept trying to shut out the dream, but it went through her mind like the wind before a storm, rattling her brain like so many leaves.

The clock on the shelf bonged four, and she cocked her head toward the door. Abby would be coming soon, and maybe Alice or Emily. She heard footsteps, then the kitchen door scraped open and a boy's voice called, "Hello, hello! Anybody home?"

Rose's stomach gave a familiar flop, but she answered quickly. It was Newton Barnes. She knew she had him to thank for rescuing her, and she had a vague memory of seeing his face right above hers when she was lying on a floor somewhere, so cold. Or was that a wandering dream as well?

Newton poked his head around the door of the parlor and grinned at her. He gave her a small wave, then retreated. She heard him add a stick to the wood stove in the kitchen, and he brought another in for the parlor stove.

"What, no chaperones? I shall have to hide in the closet if anyone comes," he said solemnly. "Especially if it's Mrs. Munson or Miss Harty-har-har. I will stand way over here with my coat on and hope no one notices my tracks outside."

Rose began to laugh and then to cough. She coughed so hard she thought her stomach might jump right out into her lap, but Newton brought her a tumbler of water and the cough calmed down.

"You are much better, I see," he said.

"And I have you to thank, they tell me."

"It was nothing," he said. "Just listening to Charles, then throwing you over my shoulder and carrying you here to get warm. Nothing a-tall. Course, you are alive because of us, I reckon, so that's something, isn't it?"

He reached for the water glass in her hand, took it from her and set it on the lace-edged doily on the small table beside her. Then he leaned down, took her face in his hands and tilted it up. He kissed her gently and quickly on the mouth.

"You did want to be alive, didn't you?" he said, straightening and snatching up the half-full tumbler. He strode off to the kitchen, and she heard him mutter what sounded like, "I wanted you to be, that's certain." Rose did not move. Suddenly she felt weaker than she had in days.

Then, before she could even start to think, the door

banged twice, and Abby pelted into the room, pink-cheeked and out of breath, with Emily right behind her. And then, with a frown on her face, Miss Harty, who saw Rose's face and shooed everyone out like so many chickens, then asked her patient if she were overtired.

"I need to see them, Miss Harty, I really do," Rose begged.

So the teacher let everyone come back and made them promise to be serious so Rose wouldn't cough.

"Perhaps," she said, "you could tell Rose about today's schoolwork so she can begin to get caught up."

Rose looked up quickly. She didn't think she would be going back to school. As soon as she was herself, as Father put it, he would expect her to take up her household duties again, and she did not think she could do all those things again. She had learned that, at least, at the cemetery, before she became too cold to think.

"You will be doing schoolwork, Rose," Miss Harty said with a small smile. "It's arranged. You will be working at Mr. Goodnow's as soon as you are yourself, and you will continue your studies."

"So you can be a teacher," Emily chimed in.

"They had a meeting," Abby said, "and I'm to stay at Aunt Nell's for the time being, whatever that means. And Charles will stay at home. And you will . . . I don't know where you will be."

"How did you learn all that?" Miss Harty asked. "Were you the mouse outside the parlor door when we talked it all over? Were you eavesdropping?"

"She's always eavesdropping," Rose said. "It's what

makes her very understanding about things, even though she's little."

Everyone except Abby laughed then, including Newton, who had come to stand in the parlor door.

"They're not laughing at you," he said, noticing that Abby was trying to look even smaller than she really was. "They sort of like the idea of your ear being at the keyhole."

Both Abby and Rose gave Newton grateful smiles, and Miss Harty, who had noticed that bit of extra color in her patient's face when she came in, wondered what had passed between Rose and Newton prior to her arrival. He should not have been here, she thought. Then she scolded herself. Who had a better right than Newton? If it weren't for him and that sick calf theory of his, she might not even have a patient.

"I brought you some schoolwork today, Rose," she said aloud. "If you can turn the heel on a sock, you can start doing some reading. Dr. Potter is also anxious to get you on your feet a little more. He has this outlandish idea that patients just keep on being poorly if they don't get up and move about."

"I think I would need some help with a hike," Rose said, but she grinned as she said it, and Emily realized it had been a long time since Rose had smiled like that.

"How about starting with a walk to my dining room, then back here, upstairs and down again?" Miss Harty asked.

"Oh, yes, Rose, come on. Let's make your feet dance a little," Charles said. "Saturday is the square dance."

Rose put down the sock and reached out her hands. Emily and Charles each took one, tugging gently as she eased herself up from the low, comfortable Morris chair. The room moved around a couple of times and then steadied itself. She took a tentative step, still holding her brother's hand and her friend's.

Newton stepped aside, and the trio edged through the door sideways, crossed the kitchen to the dining room, turned and started back.

"My feet still feel like loaves of bread that haven't been taken out of the pan," Rose said.

"It's the frostbite," Newton said. "But it wasn't serious, and the doctor said you will keep all your toes."

"I should certainly hope so," Rose answered, alarmed to think it had even been a question. No one had really talked to her yet about her illness, but she knew from the looks on their faces that it must have been touch and go. Now that was another odd phrase. Touch? And go? The go part could mean dying, but what was touch? She stumbled and decided she'd better concentrate on putting one foot ahead of the other.

"I don't think I can make the stairs this trip," she said as they moved back into the living room.

"Then sit down," Miss Harty counseled. And with a sigh, Rose slowly sat, feeling three score and ten instead of her actual fourteen. Nearly fifteen now, she realized. The number of days to her birthday had shrunk considerably while she had her eyes shut and dreamed her dreams in Miss Harty's guest room.

CHAPTER 25
Dusting the Mind

Rose flicked the feather duster over the boxes on the shelves behind the cash box. If she stood on the footstool, she could reach the top shelf, but perhaps dust never went that high. She hummed as she moved along, wondering if she might be stirring up more dirt than she was removing. Funny that turkey feathers got turned into dusters. How many times had she watched a turkey hunker down in sandy earth and fluff dirt through its feathers to bathe. She reckoned that big tub in the kitchen was a better way, even when she had to share the water with Abby or Charles.

For a half second, she let herself wonder if she would ever share a tub with them again, and then she flicked the thought out of her head. No dust, she thought, no trail of dust. She finished the cartons and came to the items that were on display—a few pieces of ironstone set against a big platter that stood against the wall, a set of salt cellars, a speckled blue and white bowl that she thought would be wonderful for chicken fricassee, or even for what Sarah called "a mess of wax beans." She sighed a little, remembering summer suppers with just a big bowl of peas with butter and pepper, and some fresh white bread that they were allowed to dip into the butter-flavored broth.

"A mess of peas, a mess of beans." They weren't really a mess. Rather neat in fact. Perfectly round green peas floating in a pond of juice; yellow beans that were nearly all the same size, since Sarah always told them to cut the pieces just about one and a quarter inches long.

"A neat of peas, a neat of beans," she sang to herself, dusting carefully around what Abby used to call the breakafuls. She sighed again. She hoped Abby was all right at Aunt Nell's. She seemed as if she were. She was always smiling when Rose saw her on Sundays, and when she came into the store after school. Mr. Goodnow said Abby could have one piece of candy whenever she came in, but she hadn't passed that word on. She gave her one only some of the time, not wanting Abby to think she could plan on sweets every time.

She had no real idea how Charles and Father were getting on. She had heard Mrs. Goodnow tell Mrs. Munson she had seen "that woman" coming out of Silas Hibbard's house on more than one occasion, but it was not in the morning. Then she had rolled her eyes to add some meaning to her statement, but Rose could not imagine what difference the time of day made. Perhaps Miss Graves was dishing up some of the meals these days. She sighed again. Charles said when the rest of the family had Sunday dinner at Aunt Nell's he heard Father say Rose must come right back home when she was well enough to take her place in the house again. And then Uncle Jason said he thought they had all seen quite enough of that.

Charles wasn't sure what exactly they had seen, but he said Father was all red in the face—red as bee balm, Charles had said, which Rose thought was a remarkable image for a boy who usually spoke in one-syllable words, and puked when killing a chicken. Father could barely talk, Charles said, but finally sputtered something about Jason minding his own business and letting him take care of his flesh and blood.

That's when they had noticed Charles in the room and immediately sent him away. Charles told her he had shut the kitchen door with a bang and stomped through the porch and down the steps and out of sight. But he had dashed around the house and come up under the window, where he said he could hear just as well as if he had been sitting right there in the small Morris chair. He didn't think those windows were tight enough to keep out a winter wind by any means. Voices certainly went right through.

Rose didn't care about the state of winter drafts in Aunt Nell's parlor. She urged him to tell her more of what he heard, and Charles was more than willing. He said Uncle Jason must have said something he missed because the first thing he heard was Father's voice saying, "What in tarnation are you folks up to anyway? She's my daughter, and I'll have her under my roof as soon as she's well enough to get there!"

That's when Uncle Jason pounded his fist on the table, Charles had said, and Aunt Nell let out a shrill little "Oh!" and must have jumped. And then, Charles said, Uncle Jason told Father he would perhaps never be able to have his daughters under his roof again, that he had been at the drink like a man possessed and had taken up with a woman of the village and was not fit right now to raise children in the way they should be raised.

He said, Charles reported, "You will listen to me now, Silas, and then hold your peace on this matter. It would be proper for you to invite the Rev. Lockhead to your home, not Rose, and certainly not Abby, and to ask him to pray with you for the betterment of your life and yourself. Rose will stay where she is until your dear departed wife's sister says she may make a change. Abby will stay here."

Rose immediately wanted to know what Father had said, but Charles heard no response from him at all, and then he heard the dining room chairs scrape, so he skedaddled.

"I would have been whipped by each of them in turn,

Rose, if I'd stayed a minute longer," he said. "But when Father came home, he was making those grunting noises he makes when he's about to explode. Sounds just like a bear. And he was bearish, no doubt about that."

"He didn't strike you?" Rose asked anxiously.

"Didn't," Charles said. "Didn't go out after supper, neither."

Rose immediately asked what they ate for supper, and Charles reported that Aunt Nell had given them a basket. She would, Rose thought, feeling a little guilty about the meals. Her mind saw, all at once, little dishes of leftovers in the icebox, covered with that green fuzzy stuff that seemed to take over after a few days; the cake of ice down to nothing; the shelf in the pantry bare of pie. She shook her head, trying to clear those thoughts away, and went on to the next shelf. She paused at the china section where two identical blue and white sugar bowls and matching creamers sat side by side. They looked like fat little people, and she had named one set King Albert and Queen Victoria, the other Boaz and Ruth. Royalty and the Bible. That should suit chubby china people nicely. Rose knew she wasn't supposed to want what she could not afford—Sarah had always cautioned them not to covet things, and she certainly had listened to a great deal from the Rev. Lockhead about that kind of thing. But she had a great desire for one of those sugar bowls, if only to replace the one she had hurled across the kitchen.

It would take several pay envelopes before she would be able to save enough for the bowl. She wondered what

Father had thought when he found the few remaining coins in that dented old measure instead of in the sugar bowl.

She sighed again and moved on to the foodstuffs.

Several days later, Rose was cleaning Miss Harty's kitchen. She had her vocabulary list propped on the top shelf of the woodstove—she was into the Us now; working on unicorn, ubiquitous (her favorite, partly because she needed to be just that), urgent, ultimate, and unctuous (was that the reverend?)—when she heard wagon wheels. Miss Harty was upstairs changing the sheets on her bed, taking off the bottom sheet, moving the top one down and putting a fresh one on top. Rose couldn't believe how often the teacher did that—at her own house, sheets had been changed once a month at most, especially in the cold weather. Rose figured the teacher wouldn't hear the visitor so she went to the window. With dismay, she saw her father climbing down from the wagon seat. She started toward the door and then turned and ran for the stairs instead. Halfway up the flight she heard his knock, and she called out, "Someone has come calling, Miss Harty."

But Ruthann Harty had looked out also and was already on her way to the top of the stairs. "It is your father, Rose, and we will talk with him if he would like to talk. If he becomes abusive—you know what that means, I presume—we will ask him to leave at once. Do not be afraid. I will be right here."

Rose relaxed a bit, satisfied that Miss Harty would

take charge of her father the way she took charge of the Granger boys. What she could not know was that Ruthann Harty did not share her confidence. This man was so often angry. Miss Harty thought intense grief lay behind that anger, but when he flared up, her glimpse of Mr. Hibbard's real self was gone like lighted tinder. She could only hope he was in one of his gentler moods this day because she knew the matter of Rose would have to be settled soon. She glanced at the girl as she opened the door, and suddenly felt her spine stiffen. It was her signal to herself that she must face the moment, no matter what. This was a prize girl, a blue-ribbon-at-the-fair girl.

"Mornin', Miss Harty," Rose's father said as he scraped his boots and stepped into the kitchen. "Mornin', Rose."

The teacher and the girl each returned his greeting but said nothing more. Silas Hibbard looked from one to the other, waiting for them to speak, but the silence stretched like warm taffy—and about as sticky. He shrugged out of his coat and looked for a peg but found none, so he let it dangle from his left hand. He set his hat on the seat of the rocking chair.

"I came to see how you are and what you will be up to next," he said.

"I am feeling nearly myself again, sir," Rose said, not wanting Miss Harty to answer for her. "I am working three afternoons at Mr. Goodnow's, and I am working here for my board and room. I will be going back to school next week if Doctor Potter says I may."

"And when school is out?"

Rose looked at the floor, not knowing what to answer, and knowing he wanted her to say she would come home and bring Abby there, too.

"She will stay on with me," Miss Harty said firmly. "I need help with the house, the garden and the chickens. Rose needs help with her schoolwork . . ."

"She's not doing well with her books?" Mr. Hibbard interrupted.

"Rose is a superb pupil, Mr. Hibbard," Miss Harty went on. "But if she is to be a teacher, she will need to apply herself even more than she already has. Much can be done when the light is good on summer evenings."

"I am aware of her ability to do schoolwork, Miss Harty. We have had this conversation before. The question these days is why Rose took herself off to the cemetery on a day cold enough to freeze a cow's udder and then stayed there, sending the entire town into an uproar. Bells ringing, the doctor on the run, and I don't know what-all. Now she looks well, so now I ask, and I will be answered."

"She was upset . . ." Miss Harty began, but Rose touched the teacher's arm and took a half step forward.

"I will answer," she said. "You don't talk to us anymore, and you go out every night, and I heard someone say you were at the drink, so you stumble around when you get home and take coins from the sugar bowl that I broke, and I saw you and Miss Graves in the upstairs bedroom, and your legs were bare, and her skirt was on the floor, and I went to the woodshed and sat against those logs for a long time and prayed that the pile would fall on me, but it didn't."

Miss Harty and Rose's father gasped as if they were performing in unison, but Rose paid them no mind. She went right on, barely taking time to breathe, her eyes riveted on a space above her father's head.

"Even I could see that Abby could not keep on growing up in that house, so I made a plan to send her to Aunt Nell's and then, because the woodpile wouldn't fall on me, I went to the cemetery to talk with Sarah, but nothing happened there either. It was very cold, and I remembered someone saying that Mr. Chandler's brother had frozen to death a few winters back and that it was just like going to sleep, so I figured that would work better than the woodpile. And if I was gone . . ."

Tears spilled down Miss Harty's cheeks, and she put her hand on Rose's shoulder, but Rose shrugged it off.

" . . . If I was gone," she repeated, her voice steadying again, "Abby would have to stay with Aunt Nell, and I figured Charles would manage somehow. And then Newton came and rescued me, so that didn't work either."

Miss Harty seemed frozen in place, and Mr. Hibbard was staring at Rose as if he had never seen her before.

"You came home early that day? You saw . . ." Mr. Hibbard could not go on. He bowed his head and hid his face in his right hand. His voice muffled, he began to stammer.

"I never meant . . . I have tried to manage . . ."

He paused and looked up, scowling again.

"Thunderation, child, you must come home at once to take care of us."

He glared at Rose and saw that her face was scarlet and her hands, clasped in front of her as if she were praying, were shaking like aspen leaves before a storm. His coat fell to the floor as he reached his callused hands out to her, his face white around his dark beard. Then, as quickly as he had reached toward her, he dropped his hands, leaned down to get his coat and stomped toward the door. In a second, he was gone, but not before Rose had turned away and fled through the back door. Miss Harty heard the door to the privy slam and then heard the sound of retching.

"I must see to her," she muttered to herself. But instead, she sank into the rocking chair feeling as if she had been standing on a porcupine. She let out a long sigh and wondered if it was the first time she had taken a breath in the past five minutes.

"I wonder if he ever hit her," she said aloud. Then she stood, ran water over a tea towel at the kitchen sink and went through the back door to find Rose.

Rose wrote a careful note and left it on the kitchen table at Miss Harty's house, and then slipped quietly out the door, her books under her arm. It was dark but not really dark, and she wondered why anyone had ever said it was darkest before the dawn. She could see the road ahead until it turned, and the sky in the east was getting that pale washed-out look that meant the sun would soon color it pink or gold or purple. It had been weeks since she had been out this early, and she took a deep breath of the spring air.

As she hurried along, the sky went suddenly pink, the sun poked a round edge over the eastern hill, and she heard birds begin their chip, chip, chip. It's the warblers, she thought. It's the second week of May, and they're back, on schedule as if they had calendars in their heads. She tilted her head in hopes she would glimpse one of the tiny fellows, and then thought better of it. She had a mission and then school. It would be better not to trip over a rock and go kallarup into the road.

She reached her father's house and saw no lights in the windows. Softly she mounted the steps and tried the door. It wasn't latched, so she went in, moving as silently as a snake in the grass. Today, she thought, I will be ubiquitous. She could smell the wood fire in the kitchen stove, but she heard nothing. Quickly she went to the pantry and found the oatmeal bin, scooped out three cups and put them in a saucepan. She added water, stirred, and set the pan on the stove, where the fire was burning brightly.

He's in the barn, she told herself. He's already stoked the fire. She bustled around the kitchen, slicing bread and setting it on the toaster, then checking the dining room table. It still had crumbs from the day before, so she cleaned off the cloth and set places for Charles and her father. She put out the butter and the jam, and saw that the ice was low in the icebox. She set the sign in the window so the iceman would stop.

Everything was in place. She reached for her wrap and her books and suddenly heard her father's footsteps tramping through the ell. He would stop to take his boots off, so she would have time. She picked up her wrap and reached for her books, but she caught her toe on the rocker of the chair and the pile spilled onto the floor. As she stooped to gather them up, she saw her father's feet coming through the door.

"Well, look who's flown back into the nest," her father said as he came into the kitchen. He glanced at the stove. "And been putting on a bit of breakfast, I see. It's about time."

"I'm not back, Father. I just came to see to things before school and make sure you and Charles had a proper breakfast. I'll be going along now."

"What in tarnation is that supposed to mean?"

"It means," Rose said, "I don't live here anymore, but I still worry about you and Charles."

"If you were really worried, you'd pack your bags and get home where you belong," he started.

But Rose didn't wait. She could see that nothing had been achieved the other day at Miss Harty's when she had made herself sick spilling out her thoughts. She turned her back on him, her books now safely under her arm again, and lifted the latch on the door. He reached out to stop her, but she was too quick. In an instant, she was outside and almost running along the path to the road. She heard the door close, but she did not turn until she was a few rods away and could look over her shoulder. He wasn't coming. She turned off toward the river and reached her favorite rock. She had extra time before school started, so she sat down and listened to the rushing water and the warblers. Perhaps, if she was very still, they would come out of hiding.

She was so absorbed in her thoughts that she jumped when Newton said, "Hello, Miss Rose," almost at her elbow. "Didn't mean to startle you," he said. "I've been standing a little way up the path and decided it was sort of like eavesdropping to watch someone who didn't know you were there. So I spoke."

"Hello, yourself," she said. "How is it that every day you seem to happen along about the time I'm on my way to school, even if I am early or late, or take a different route as I did today?"

Why she should be surprised she could not imagine. He had been showing up just as she left for school for two weeks now, and she had begun to wonder about his sense of timing, since she almost never left Miss Harty's house at exactly the same time.

"I'll take your books," Newton said, dodging the question.

She handed them over and said, "That was the wrong answer, Mr. Barnes. You will have to do better."

"Well, it's the only time I see you without a chaperone," he said, starting to laugh.

That made Rose laugh, too, remembering the day in her father's house when he had insisted on leaving because she was alone. Good thing he hadn't waited for a chaperone to show up when she was freezing to death in the cemetery. Although she understood that Charles had been there, too, so maybe that counted.

"So are you loitering about, following me, or am I just fortunate to be the same late or the same early as you?"

"I am fortunate," Newton said. "Fortunate that you are alive, fortunate that you now live on my way to school, and fortunate that you will let me walk with you. How fortunate can one boy be?"

Rose felt her face getting hot, so she dropped her head and stood up. She started back toward the road, looking at her feet, not having any idea what to say. Emily would know, she thought. Emily always had clever things to toss back at people. Emily would say . . . what would she say? Rose couldn't imagine.

"I am the fortunate one," she said, putting her hand on his arm. "I have never properly thanked you for saving my life, and I will thank you right now."

"You already did."

"When was that?"

"You let yourself get well again instead of just trudging right on into that heaven the Reverend Lockhead is always blatting about. I don't think you had to let yourself get well. But you did."

"When I saw everyone there," Rose said, feeling very uncertain about letting out all these thoughts, "I didn't want to die anymore. Everyone looked so scared, and all the eyes in the room were pointing right at me as if they could look right inside my head. I couldn't go away then."

"And today you are going to win some of the prizes at school, I think, even though you spent all that time lolling about at Miss Harty's, knitting socks and sewing shirts."

"I was reading," Rose said, her voice rising. "I was reading and reading and reading and doing arithmetic until my head hurt. And now Miss Harty plans to make me go right on being in school this summer, even when I'm not and no one else is either."

"You're staying with her?"

She looked sideways at him. He was really smiling now, and he had shifted her books to his other hand so he could grab hers in his. A ribbon of warmth slid down her spine.

"At least for the summer," she said "But you haven't told me how you know where I am, and when."

"I have to confess. I am tired of walking to school alone, and I don't have enough books to carry, so I have been coming along about the right time most every day."

"And today?"

"Miss Harty saw me. She told me you had left a note. I waited for Charles to come out, and he said you made breakfast there, but he hadn't seen you. He told me to try the rock."

"Still finding me, isn't he?" Rose said, smiling.

"And still living at home," Newton said.

"Well, it's different for boys," she said, not wanting to talk about this anymore. She did worry about Charles. She pulled her hand away from his.

"Are you cooking the supper Saturday night?" he asked, quickly changing the subject.

"Why do you ask?"

"I'm invited."

"Well, I never," she said, wondering why Miss Harty hadn't told her company was coming for supper the day after tomorrow. They reached the school then, and Rose heard a chanting sound from the steps at the boys' entrance to the building. It took a minute for her to make it out, and then she wanted to hide in the lilac bushes by the door.

"Newton's gone a-courting, Newton's gone a-courting, Newton's gone a-courting," the boys were saying in unison.

"Pay them no mind," Newton said. "It doesn't bother me."

Rose didn't answer. She reached for her books and turned away from him, looking for Emily and Alice and a place to take her face, which had flamed up again. Twice in one morning, and the day barely begun, she said to herself. By then she had reached her friends, and seeing Emily's eager expression, glared at her and said, "Not a word, not one single word, thank you."

Ruthann Harty pulled her list out of her pocket, unfolded it and laid it on the counter in front of Mr. Goodnow, who squinted at it, then put on his spectacles to have a better look.

"Quite a long list here," he said. "But we would be glad to oblige you."

He reached behind him for two candles and put them beside the list. Then he set about fetching her other items, whistling softly as he worked. Six brown eggs from the basket on the shelf—he was pleased that the teacher always came here for the eggs from his wife's Rhode Island Reds—two yards of one-inch lace, two pencils and a writing tablet.

"Sorry, Ruthann," he said, looking up from the list once more. "We have no blue sugar bowls in stock just now."

Miss Harty moved along to the area where the china dishes were displayed and saw that indeed, Mr. Goodnow was all out of blue and white sugar bowls.

"I'll take four lengths of taffeta ribbon instead," she said quickly. "One plaid, one blue, one green and one yellow. Say twelve inches each."

"If it's for hair, it's safer to go half a yard," he said.

"Half a yard then—of each."

"Rose having a birthday or something?"

"Well, yes—but why do you ask?"

"She asked me for the afternoon off to do some fancy cooking at your house because company was coming for dinner. And I heard her pa tell her this morning that she was fifteen now and old enough to take hold of things better. She was only fourteen last week."

Frowning, Ruthann leaned forward quickly and said, "And just when, Henry Goodnow, did you hear Silas Hibbard talking to his daughter?"

"Why, this morning, right here in the store."

Henry Goodnow knew he had her attention now. He folded his arms across his chest, leaned back against the shelves behind the cash box and looked over his spectacles at her. He liked this teacher, and he would tell her what she wanted to know; had intended to from the moment she came through the door. But he wanted to be coaxed a bit. He did like a good story, and he knew this was a very good tale indeed.

"What did he say?" Ruthann asked. "And what did she say?"

"She was working over there by the front window, and he came in nice and quiet and walked right up to her. She nearly jumped out of her shirtwaist, but she stood her ground, I must say. I moved up a bit, real quiet so as not to disturb them but near enough so I could step in if for some reason it became necessary. I have heard . . ." He stopped and raised his eyebrows.

Ruthann nodded, and he went on.

" 'Rose,' Silas said, 'I have come here to see you so we can talk without getting excited. It would be unseemly for us to make a scene here in the store, so I trust you will not do so.' Cool as cream in the cooler, she looked at him and said, 'And you would be talking to me about what?'"

Mr. Goodnow paused, pulled out his handkerchief and wiped it across his forehead. Ruthann shifted from one foot to the other but waited without saying anything.

" 'I would like it a good deal if you could see your way clear to come home,' he said."

"Oh, no," Ruthann Harty whispered.

"Never fear, Ruthann," Mr. Goodnow said, relenting a little. "You can be mighty proud of that girl. She won't blow away in the wind. She has her feet on the ground and her head set on straight. Never fear. She looked right at him—and I reckon I'd have to think twice myself before I threw down the gauntlet to Silas Hibbard—straight in the eye . . ."

"For God's sake, Henry, get on with it. You have me on tenterhooks," Ruthann interrupted.

" . . . and said she wasn't going home, at least not now. "

"Good. Oh, good," Ruthann said, her eyes filling with tears.

Henry Goodnow realized he had spun out his tale beyond reason, so he spoke more quickly, telling the teacher that Silas Hibbard then talked about Rose coming around and making breakfast one day this past week, and how that made him and Charles want her back all the more. Then he said he hadn't done right by them or by Sarah and had not carried out his wife's wishes.

"Henry, exactly how did he word all that, if you can remember."

"Oh, it's engraved on my memory, Ruthann. He said, 'I have wronged you, I have not been faithful to Sarah's memory, nor to her intentions for our children.' "

"And Rose?" Ruthann asked.

"She might as well have been Ulysses S. Grant," Henry answered. "She gave not one inch of ground and showed no mercy. She said, again, that she was not coming back to his house, nor was Abigail. Then he asked her what she wanted; why she could not come home; what he could do to get her there. He was almost begging. She said he had to stop ordering them to come back, that he needed to take care of Charles the way Sarah—she did say 'Sarah,' Ruthann—would have, and he should stop drinking and stay home of an evening."

"And Silas?" Ruthann asked. "What did he say then?"

"At first he looked angry, but he could not stare her down. Those blue eyes of hers hardly blinked, and they never wavered from his face. So he told her he would try."

"His words, if you remember?"

"Oh, I recall quite well. He said, the words coming out slower than old molasses in February, 'You are a stubborn lass, Rose—take after your mother. She was a sweet woman, but if she made up her mind about something, moving her was tougher than getting an ox to pull that final sledge at the fair. I think I cannot ask you to come home, nor Abby, until I have turned the corner.' And then he started for the door. But he turned back, took off his glove, held out his hand and asked her to pray for him. 'I want you to know that I grieve for our loss as much as you do. And would sure look forward to a decent breakfast now and then,' he said. And then she smiled just the tiniest bit, shook his hand, and he was gone."

"She's going to be a teacher," Ruthann Harty said, snuffling as her tears spilled over the edge. "She has done this her way and all by herself."

"Well now, Ruthann, I think the girl and any number of town folk would be ready to testify that you had a hand in it, and did the girl a great deal of good over the past few years. Fortunate she had you."

"Did she leave?" Ruthann asked, still choked up.

"Went out back for a bit, and I heard her bawling a little, but she returned, eyes and face as red as gone-by zinnias, and finished up here. Said she would see me on Monday and went on her way."

CHAPTER 26
Sweet Birthday

Ruthann Harty was still smiling to herself when she pulled up her horse at the little house near the depot. She tossed the reins over the hitching post in front of the house and reached up to get her parcels.

"Just about anything can happen and sometimes does," she said, half aloud, as she started toward the door.

"Miss Harty, Ma'am," a voice said from behind her.

She turned, and her smile faded as if struck by lightning. Silas Hibbard was coming over from the depot, removing his hat as he approached. She didn't have time to get to the door, open it and slam it to before he could reach her. Besides, he must have known she had seen him.

"I would be obliged if you could give me a minute of your time, Miss Harty," he said, "though I am as certain as the sky is blue that you would rather not do so. I ask you for Rose's sake, since that's why I am here."

Rose faced him, Miss Harty told herself. She's but a girl, and she faced him. She put her parcels back on the buggy seat and stood as tall as she could. He moved closer to her.

"No point in half the town knowing what I need to say, although maybe I owe it to Rose to say it from the front of the church on Sunday, the way those witnesses do in the tent meetings." He looked at her, then looked off into the distance. She said nothing.

"I have been a poor excuse for a man since Sarah died," he went on, "but I told Rose this afternoon I would turn a corner. She still won't come home, and I don't know as I can blame her. But she has to be somewhere, and I was wondering . . ."

Rose's father stopped again. He looked down at his work boots, then glanced at Miss Harty's highly polished black boots. He cleared his throat and began again.

"What I am getting at is whether Rose could stay on with you until she's a mind to come home," he said very rapidly in a low voice that cracked a bit at the end. Miss Harty let out her breath and wondered if she had been holding it the whole time. She reached out one gray-gloved hand and touched the rough fabric of his coat.

"I would be proud to have her," she said, telling herself that she must be careful or this nervous bird would fly away before their business was done. For once, she was not afraid of this man.

"I haven't the means to pay you much, but we can bring by some eggs and . . ."

"Rose earns her keep at my house, Mr. Hibbard," Ruthann interrupted. "There's no need to worry yourself about that. She is a great help to me and good company as well." Her hand was still on his arm when they heard a buggy coming along the road, and turned to see Mrs. Munson coming by, dressed to the nines and with her whip held high. Ruthann dropped her hand to her side but was sure Mrs. Munson had already seen that. Then she heard Mr. Hibbard chuckle.

"Whatever are you laughing at?" she asked, a little put out.

"Like it or not, you will be talked about over the back fence and down at the store before the sun sets tomorrow," he said, chuckling again. "The Lord only knows what that woman will invent in her storytelling. Might as well finish our conversation. She'll be back along this way in a minute or two, if only to see if we are still here. As I was trying to say," he said, serious again, "I owe you a debt I cannot ever repay. We've been through a bad time, and without Rose we would not have made it as well as we did. I will pick up some of my share now."

Wondering how to end this encounter before the gossipy Mrs. Munson trotted by again, Ruthann said, "I will see to her properly." Then she turned her back, retrieved her parcels and went into the house, leaving him there beside her horse. From behind a curtain, she looked out and saw him pick up the horse's reins and lead the animal and buggy behind the house to the barn. She hurried to the kitchen and looked out that window. Sure enough, he was putting the horse in its stall for her.

"Whatever are you looking at, Miss Harty?" Rose said, coming up behind her. Ruthann felt the girl's body stiffen as she saw her father leading the horse into the barn.

"Why is Father here?" the girl demanded. "Why is he here?"

"He wanted to ask me if I would let you stay here," Miss Harty said gently. "It's all right. It's all right."

Rose's face instantly flamed, and she put her hands up to hide it.

"What did you tell him, Miss Harty?" she asked in a muffled voice.

"That you could stay."

"Oh, oh, oh . . ." Rose's voice broke off, and she started to cry. "You will have me here? You really will? For as long as I need to stay?"

"For as long as you need to stay."

Tears streaming down her face, Rose began to laugh. She wiped her face with her apron, then cried and laughed some more.

"That will be enough, I think," Miss Harty said in her teacher voice, thinking how exactly right it was to laugh and cry at this moment, but not wanting to do either. Then she noticed that Rose was trying to hide a bandaged finger. "Whatever did you do to your finger, Rose?"

"Thank you, Ma'am," Rose said, mopping her face some more, "for letting me stay. I cut it peeling the squash. It's all right. The potatoes are peeled, too, the chicken is in the oven, and Abby is bringing a pie."

"Did she make a whole pie, or are we eating just a crust?" Miss Harty wanted to know.

"A whole pie," Rose grinned. "But I think Aunt Nell mostly did the filling."

"We shall see. I have fresh-picked strawberries as well."

They worked together in the kitchen in silence for a while, Rose moving about with a step so light that Miss Harty realized how much this day had taken off the girl's mind. In her mind's ear, she could hear Rose moving with much heavier feet. Clumping, sometimes, to the blackboard and back to her desk. Or on the stairs in the little house. Not for the first time, she thought how often the body's movements reflected what was hiding in the brain.

"Mr. Goodnow told me about your father's visit today," she said at last. "You must have been quite frightened by that."

"He listened," Rose said, and Ruthann saw her mouth set in a thin line.

"Apparently," she said, and then they both went on with their work.

When everything was ready, Rose went upstairs to change her dress and fix her hair. Miss Harty put the two new candles on the table in her best pewter holders, and quickly rolled the four ribbons together and wrapped them in a small piece of leftover blue fabric, tying the parcel with a piece of yarn. She set it on the sideboard and put her calling card next to it.

Rose came back down just as Abby knocked on Miss Harty's door.

"Would you get that, Rose?" Miss Harty called from her tiny dining room.

Rose opened the door, and Charles jumped into view yelling, "Happy Birthday," and offering Rose a wrinkled brown paper bag.

"I'll take that," Miss Harty said, coming in just in time to intercept the present. Rose gave Charles a hug and told him he was the best present she could possibly get.

"I doubt that very much," Charles said, his eyes dancing. "The best present looks to me to be walking down the road in this direction at this very moment." Rose followed his look and felt the familiar flip-flop in her stomach. Newton was coming. He really had been invited; he was coming for her birthday supper.

"Move back," Charles said. "Move back, Rose. Your face is so hot it's going to set my Sunday shirt on fire, and it took me much of the afternoon to iron it into decent shape."

"Foolish boy," Rose said. But her eyes were on Newton, and she happily returned his wave. Newton, Charles and Abby followed Rose into the teacher's house, and Miss Harty invited them to sit in the parlor. Rose noticed that the dining room door was closed, which was unusual, so she wondered what the teacher was up to. In a few minutes, Miss Harty opened the door, and Rose's first thought was a worry. Had she made enough food? She saw seven places at the table and for one second had the sinking feeling that her father was joining them. Then Alice and Emily came bouncing out of the kitchen and took two of the places. The teacher told everyone else where to sit.

"You, too, Rose," she said. "I will bring the food."

By the time Miss Harty returned with the roasted chicken on a platter, surrounded by browned potatoes and chunks of squash, the guests were chattering away as if they had supper together every day.

"I'm to stay here," Rose whispered to Emily when she thought the rest of them were not listening.

"You're staying here?" Abby said. "Here? But what about me?"

"You are staying with Aunt Nell and Uncle Jason, and you will visit here for Sunday dinner," Rose said. "Well, that is . . ." She started to stammer and looked at Miss Harty. "I didn't mean . . ."

"But you did mean, Rose, and it's quite all right. We will have Abby as our Sunday dinner guest, except when you are invited to your Aunt Nell's," Miss Harty said. "And you will all be glad to know that Rose will work on her studies all summer, and by the end of next year, she will be ready for a small classroom of her own. Or she might go to normal school, if that's what she wants."

"Oh, oh, oh . . ." Rose said. Then she laughed. "That

seems to be all I can say today, Miss Harty."

"Quite all right, Rose. Now, suppose we eat this supper before it's cold and spoiled."

So they ate, and it wasn't long before the crisp, brown chicken had been reduced to a pile of bones. Then Miss Harty brought in a large glass bowl of the fresh strawberries and a pitcher of thick cream. She produced small glass dishes and asked Rose to spoon up the berries.

"We'll pass the cream," she said. "And save your beautiful pie for Sunday dinner tomorrow, Abby. It will be safe from mice here." Abby giggled and spooned up a large sugary berry. In a few minutes, Alice looked around at seven empty dishes and announced that she would clear the table.

"Then Rose can open her presents," Emily said.

For the first time, Rose noticed that the wrinkled little bag Charles had brought was in the midst of several little parcels on the sideboard. She did not remember ever having more than one birthday present in a year, and she looked around the table and smiled at everyone. So much had happened since the day when she had tried to make the woodpile fall on her head.

"I'm glad," Rose burst out and then stopped.

"Glad what?" Charles said.

"Well, glad the woodpile didn't crush me and glad I didn't freeze to death," Rose said, hoping she wasn't going to turn all red again.

"We're glad, too," Emily said.

"M-m-m," said Alice.

"We need you," Newton added.

"Do the presents, Rose," Abby cried. "Do mine last. It's the one wrapped in a linen napkin with string."

"I'll start with this one," Rose said, picking up the blue fabric tied with yarn. She untied the bow carefully and opened the fabric to find the new ribbons for her hair, and Miss Harty's card.

"Thank you," she said, thinking she could never, ever thank this teacher enough.

She turned to the next parcel, which felt hard to the touch.

"That's ours," Emily and Alice said together.

"It's a dictionary of my very own," Rose exclaimed. "So I can just look up those words that run around in my head."

"We wrote inside," Emily said.

"To our friend Rose, a friend forever, from Emily and Alice on her fifteenth birthday," Rose read. She felt her eyes start to swim and hoped the tears wouldn't start slopping out all over the place. She was beginning to think her eye pump never stopped working. She reached for Charles' wrinkled bag.

"Oh, Charles, you are a wonderful rascal," she said, as she held up a blue and white china sugar bowl. "But can I keep it here?"

"Keep it wherever you want," he answered. "I just thought you needed one. Never know when an angry moment might overtake you."

She scowled at him but didn't answer. Instead she picked up the next present, also in a brown bag but with a tiny bunch of mayflowers tucked under a blue ribbon. As she began to unwrap it, Newton started to speak and Miss Harty told him to be still.

Rose was a bit surprised that the teacher was being so abrupt with a guest, but she set aside the flowers with a small nod to Newton and then ripped the brown paper off another blue and white sugar bowl. She started to laugh.

"One to keep and one to throw," she said. But before she could go on, Abby thrust the napkin-wrapped parcel at her.

"Now mine, now mine," Abby said, seeming very pleased with herself.

Inside the cloth Rose found a creamer that exactly matched the sugar bowl. Both boys started to laugh, and without thinking, Charles said, "Did you think she needed a set?"

Abby's face clouded up just as Charles said, "Ouch," which told Rose that Newton had kicked him under the table. Miss Harty began to smile, and Alice and Emily didn't quite know where to look.

"I wanted to buy you a sugar bowl because Mother's broke," Abby said. "But when I went to Mr. Goodnow's all the sugar bowls were gone, and he told me someone bought one for you, and I loved the creamer and thought you should have both. Did I do the wrong thing?"

"You did precisely the right thing," Miss Harty said, her smile even wider.

"Oh, yes," Rose said. "At the store," she said, holding up Charles' present, "I call this one King Albert. And this one Boaz," indicating Newton's gift. "And the little creamer is Queen Victoria. I have been dusting them every day."

"So the one that still lives at the store must be Ruth," Abby said, nodding.

"Precisely right again, Abby," Rose said, thinking she had not felt this good since the last time she had walked in the woods with her mother. "And when I am a teacher, I will have you over for tea, and serve sugar lumps in two bowls and milk in the creamer."

"Unless you lose your temper before that," Charles said with a wicked grin. "We'd better go get that Ruth pitcher, too." But Emily wasn't interested in broken crockery. She knew she had just heard the best news in a long time, and she jumped up from her chair without even asking to be excused.

"You are going to be a teacher, you are!" she said excitedly, rushing over to Rose and putting her arms around her friend. "You finally sound as if you believe it, too!"

Rose looked down the table to where Miss Harty sat. "I believe it now," she said.

"And you should," Ruthann Harty said, starting to clap her hands as if a play had just ended. As her brother and sister and friends joined the teacher, Rose felt her face burning, but for the first time in her life, she didn't care.

"The party's over," Miss Harty said, "and I am afraid it is time for the aftermath."

"What's an aftermath?" Charles asked.

"Dirty dishes," Alice said, making a face.

Charles groaned, "But I do those all the time at home." He scowled at Rose and added, "I'd like you to come home, too. I didn't really mind doing dishes when we all did them."

"Charles," Miss Harty said in the voice she usually reserved for the Granger boys. "Rose is not coming home at this time, and you should not beg her to do so. I am certain you understand all about it."

"Yes, Ma'am. Sorry, Ma'am. Sorry, Rose. Not trying to spoil your birthday supper."

"Of course you aren't spoiling anything, Charles. And there's no need for you to do dishes here, either. Why don't you see Abby to Aunt Nell's and get on home yourself," Rose suggested.

"I want Newton to walk back with me," Abby said.

"I would be glad to walk with both of you," Newton said immediately. "And I will be back here before the eight o'clock train to help with the pots. Let's be on our way, you two."

Once they were out the door, Emily and Alice and Rose quickly cleared away the rest of the dishes, and Rose's friends insisted that she keep her cut finger out of the dishwater. The teacher agreed, so she and Rose put food away and dried the dishes, since they knew where everything went. They were nearly done with the china and the dessert dishes when Newton knocked at the front door and stuck his head inside.

"Anyone at home?"

They all laughed, and he immediately rolled up his sleeves and took over at the sink, going at the roasting pan and the other pots as if demons lived inside them. Rose was looking at his strong brown arms when she realized Emily was looking at her with a big smirk on her face, but she didn't say anything. In just a few minutes they were finished, and Miss Harty declared the kitchen in apple-pie order. Now that was a good one, Rose thought. An apple pie was very neat— crimped and with a pretty pattern of slits evenly spaced. Sarah's apple slices were all alike, too. Apple-pie order must be close to perfect, she decided.

"You are drifting away," Emily said, jabbing Rose in the ribs. "I am watching you go. That foolish head of yours is away somewhere, and it's not fair. It's like whispering a secret to Alice when I am standing right here."

"No, it's not," Rose said. "Besides, I was just thinking what it meant to have apple-pie order."

"I should have known," Emily said with a moan. "The next thing you will need is a dictionary of phrases and where they all come from."

"Is there one?"

They all looked at Miss Harty, who said she didn't know but would try to find out.

"I will see you two home now," Newton announced, "and I would like to ask Rose to walk with me, if that is acceptable to you, Miss Harty. We will be back within the hour."

Rose saw Emily poke Alice in the ribs and whisper something she didn't quite catch. Alice nodded, and then Miss Harty nodded, too.

"Take good care of her, Newton. It's not been easy

keeping her alive, and I want no harm to come to her now that things are better all around."

"You have no need to be concerned about me, Miss Harty."

So the four of them set off for Emily and Alice's houses, talking and laughing as they went. Rose changed places with Alice so she could ask Emily about her whisper to Alice.

"I just said," Emily said, tossing her head, "I just said he wants to kiss you. And now you are going to get all red, and everyone will ask what we are whispering about."

"Don't be silly," Rose said, striving to keep her face from changing color. She realized Emily would be fit to be tied if she knew Newton had already done that one time, especially if Rose told her she could still feel exactly what it was like. "Why would he want to do that?"

Emily giggled and said no more. A few minutes later, she waved to Newton and Rose as they headed back toward Miss Harty's house.

"Five chaperones, three chaperones, two chaperones, no chaperones," Newton said. "Are you shaking in your boots?"

"Of course not, you silly boy."

"Ah, but what if Mrs. Munson happens by?"

"She ought not to be out at this hour without a chaperone," Rose said, laughing.

"Let's go to your rock and see if the moon is coming up," Newton said.

"And hear the peepers," Rose said.

"Oh, we'll hear the peepers, wherever they are. They're the noisiest thing around here aside from Charles."

"They're the sound of spring, Newton," Rose said with a delighted sigh. "They're little frogs, and they're not actually singing. They rub their legs together and that's the sound it makes."

"Tell me another, Miss Rose," Newton said, taking her hand and turning off the road toward her rock and the river.

"What will Miss Harty say?" Rose asked.

"Within the hour I told her, within the hour. Did you not get all out of breath with the pace I set getting your friends to their doors? We have plenty of time for moon watching."

"And peeper hearing."

"And rubbing our legs together."

"Oh, no, young man, none of that unless we have a chaperone. Nice people don't do that."

"Just the frogs, Ma'am, just the frogs."

They reached the rock and sat down on its cool, flat surface; silent at last. The moon was still sleeping, but the peepers were starting to warm up for their long evening concert. Newton reached for Rose's hand and enclosed it in both of his, taking care not to hold the cut finger too tightly. She felt as if she might stop breathing entirely and hoped he couldn't hear her heart pounding and her stomach flopping. She looked down at the bandage on her finger. She didn't ever cut herself, but her mind had wandered and the knife had slipped off the smooth skin of the squash. What was it that Aunt Nell had said about her father? When he was courting Sarah he had been so "sappy,"—that was it—so sappy, that Uncle Jason wouldn't let him near a saw for fear he'd cut off his hand or leg. Was she getting "sappy?"

"Ah, there it is," Newton said, letting go of her hand and pointing. "Just a sliver there behind the big pine tree. It's that tiny little moon I like best of all.

"I love the full moon," Rose said. "I like to see its path across my floor in the middle of the night, and I like to see its face."

"Never saw it," Newton said. "Nights are for sleeping, not moon-gazing. You must be a very frivolous girl, gallivanting around in the middle of the night."

"I am," Rose said. "I am a flibbertigibbet."

"And I have only kissed a flibbertigibbet once in my life, so now I'm going to do it again," Newton said, suddenly pulling her close and tipping her face toward his. "Unless the flibber-whatever says no," he added.

"She won't say no," Rose said, wondering how Emily had known. "She remembers the other time." So he kissed her gently on the lips, and she thought she might faint right there on her rock. But the kiss lasted such a short time that it was as if she had been brushed by a butterfly. Almost before it had begun, it seemed, he had pulled away and looked at her.

"Sometimes I'm not flibbering," Rose said, speaking very softly so her voice wouldn't come out all funny.

"Sometimes I fall asleep right away and have a dream that scares me awake—or I wake myself so I can get away from it."

"What makes you dream bad dreams, Rose?"

"Sarah always said you had bad dreams when you were so tired you almost couldn't make it up the stairs, and when you were feeling guilty about something, and when you were afraid of someone or something."

"And which is it for you?"

"Oh, Newton, you know I am forever tired, falling asleep in school and yawning."

"But not any more," he said quietly. "Not since you moved to Miss Harty's. Didn't you leave the nightmares behind, too?"

"No."

"Guilty or afraid?"

"Both."

"Of what?"

"Worrying that I should be cooking and cleaning for Father, and terrified that someone will make me go back there."

Newton threw back his head and started to laugh.

"It's not funny," Rose said sharply, wishing she had not told him about her bad dreams.

"Of course it isn't funny, Rose. But if one of your things goes away, the others stay. If you get rid of them, you have the first one again. It's as if you were standing in a hot skillet, and the only way to escape was to jump into another one."

Rose sighed and stretched her arms out in front of her. "It feels just like that sometimes," she said.

"I only dream about you," Newton said, his voice serious again.

"That could be a nightmare," she answered laughing, "when you think about all the things I've put people through this year. Do you wake yourself up so I will get out of your sleep?"

"Oh, no. I just want those dreams to go on and on," he said, "even when you are running away from me."

"Do I always run away?"

"Nearly always," he said with a sigh.

"That's what flibbertigibbets do best," she said.

"And people who want to be teachers," he said with another sigh. "Which is why I try to catch you when I am awake. And then I have to wonder whether the dream is real, and whether you actually want to keep on running."

Rose did not answer; thought she could not possibly speak aloud this time. So she put one hand on his cheek, turned his head toward her, closed her eyes and tilted her face up. This time it was a long kiss, how long she did not know, but the music in her head drowned out the peepers, and she was certain no one else had ever had a birthday like this one.

The kiss ended, and Newton abruptly stood up. He pulled Rose to her feet and drew her toward him, a hand under each of her elbows. A picture of his strong, tanned arms flashed through her head, and her whole body felt as liquid as pancake batter. She wasn't sure her legs were worth anything at all.

"I want to see you every day," Newton said softly.

"I sit right in front of you," Rose answered, "at least for another week or two."

"Without chaperones," he said, and she could see his smile even in the near dark.

"But Mrs. Munson . . ." Rose began.

"Mrs. Munson be damned," Newton said, laughing. Then his arms went around her back, and without even knowing she was doing it, she linked her fingers behind his neck, and they held each other, rocking back and forth a little.

"I am so glad you are alive," he whispered in her ear.

"Me, too," she whispered back, certain her voice would crack if she spoke aloud. "And I want to stop running away in your dreams."

"Just don't run away when we are awake," he said. "I am beginning to think I will always need you to not run away."

"This," she whispered, "is the place I will run to."

"To me, Rose? Or to this cold rock?"

"You always make me laugh just when I'm close to speechless," she said with a giggle. "Which should I choose, you or the rock?"

"I hope you know," he said. "But we must go. It's about to be within the hour."

They reached the road and walked quickly toward Miss Harty's house, Rose grateful for once that she was tall and could pretty much keep up with his long legs.

As they neared the hotel, they heard loud talking and laughing, and suddenly Newton nudged Rose into the shadows at the edge of the road. She looked across and saw her father coming out, his arm around Miss Jenny Graves, who was holding up her skirt and laughing loudly. She stopped walking and watched as the pair moved away toward the Hibbard house, Miss Graves swaying slightly but her father seeming quite steady on his feet.

"Charles . . ." she started to say, and then she saw that the two people were not going toward the door of the house but down the path toward the pasture and the barn.

"They can't see the moon from there," she said. "It's the wrong side."

"Doubt they're much interested in the moon," Newton said with a frown.

She turned her back on the scene, reached for Newton's hand herself this time and started walking toward Miss Harty's again.

"The blood's stopped in two of my fingers," Newton said as they reached the teacher's porch, and Rose realized that in her effort not to cry, she was squeezing the very life out of his hand.

"Sorry," she said, and immediately wished she hadn't spoken. Just that one word opened the door for her tears, and they washed over her face in a silent torrent. Newton held her hand and waited, not knowing what to say but not wanting to leave her this way. "He said he would turn the corner," Rose sobbed, "and I wanted to believe him."

"Perhaps his road has more than one corner," Newton said quietly. "Most do."

That brought a tiny smile, and she remembered this was the second time within a few hours that she had laughed and cried at almost the same moment. They would be keeping her up in the attic one of these days if she didn't get straightened out.

"You are fine, Rose," Newton said, as if he could hear her thoughts. "I'm thinking of kissing you again, right here on the teacher's porch."

"You can't do that," Rose gasped.

But he did. And she kissed him back. Mother, she thought, would like Newton. His arms tightened around her and inside her head was the clearest blue sky she had ever seen there. I will stop running, she said to herself. I will be a teacher, but I will stop running.

Readers' Guide

1. Rose remembers her mother's mouth drawn into a thin line by the end of the day, yet her Aunt Nell tells her how much her father and mother were in love. Was Sarah unhappy in her marriage, or was her day typical of her time? Did the woodpile really fall accidentally, or did she pull out a log and make it tumble?

2. At times, Silas Hibbard seems cruel and unsympathetic, unable to comprehend his children's needs. Is alcohol his problem, or is it his solution? Is he evil? Is he overwhelmed with grief and therefore unable to cope?

3. Should Rose marry Newton in a year or so? She has two dreams; a future with Newton and a future as a teacher. Can they coexist? Should they coexist? How many dreams can a person have?

4. Discuss the work ethic of the New England farmers of the late 19th century. Was their dawn to dusk work habit a matter of survival, of upbringing, or of love for what they did?

5. Abby is only eight years old when the story begins. Still, she knows how to make a perfect piecrust; she sets and clears the table; she feeds the chickens and collects the eggs. She apparently does not get an allowance. How is she different from today's eight-year-olds, who would be in third grade at most schools?

6. Rose says she needs a primer for how to do various kinds of things for her family. She seems to know a great deal already, however, including ways to economize on food and still feed the group adequately. Discuss Rose's various skills in terms of today's fourteen-year-olds.

7. Going to church on Sunday morning was a regular practice for most of the people living in Rose's New England town. The min-

ister of the church preached the usual sermons about sin, heaven and hell, and transgressions like abuse of alcohol. Did Sunday morning carry over into the other six days of the week? Were the Hibbards deeply religious?

8. Rose felt very alone right after her mother was killed. She had relatives nearby and neighbors not very far away, but the person who paid the most attention to her was the teacher who had known her since she was three. Did the others not care? Or did they care and have serious difficulty fitting even one extra thing into their own daily lives?

9. The role of friendship in daily life is important in this book, including friendship among peers as well as between adults and children. Silas Hibbard seems to have few friends while Rose has several good ones. Why?

10. Consider the difference between Silas Hibbard's approach to children and that of Miss Harty.

11. Compare the 1880s to today in terms of the problems faced by teenagers. While people in the 1880s were much more silent about problems like adultery, excessive drinking and lack of communication, the issues existed then, as now. How does the book show that times basically don't change? What are the differences in the ways Rose coped and the ways troubled teens today would?

12. When the book ends, some of the story lines are left dangling. What are they? How might they be resolved if the book had several additional chapters?